ETERNAL SEA

ALICE ALFONSI

JOVE BOOKS, NEW YORK

HAUNTING HEARTS is a registered trademark of Berkley Publishing Corporation.

ETERNAL SEA

A Jove Book / published by arrangement with the author

PRINTING HISTORY
Jove edition / January 1999

The Penguin Putnam Inc. World Wide Web site address is http://www.penguinputnam.com

ISBN: 0-515-12434-6

A JOVE BOOK®
Jove Books are published by The Berkley Publishing Group, a member of Penguin Putnam Inc., 375 Hudson Street, New York, New York 10014. JOVE and the "J" design are trademarks belonging to Jove Publications, Inc.

PRINTED IN THE UNITED STATES OF AMERICA

10 9 8 7 6 5 4 3 2 1

To Gail Fortune,
an editor's editor.
You're the best.

On still blue nights of darkness and high stars,
Soft comes a sound as gentle as June rain:
The song of roving wind on bending spars,
The laugh of risen ships bound out again.
With creamy tops'ls whispering to clean skies,
And sweet hulls treading old blue water down—
Hulls that have lain where winding seaweed lies
Deep down, deep down, by many an ancient town.

Ah! they return, those foundered gypsy ships.
Hearing the drum of screws they cannot rest;
Old ports call out and quiet quays and slips,
There are fair isles to sight, new seas to crest;
And when a night comes stiller than the dawn
They rise again—and sail forever on.

—GORDON SEAGROVE,
Ghost Ships

Prologue

BLUE NIGHTS COTTAGE
NEW YEAR'S EVE, 1849

Sounds of panic filled the air. Shouts and cries and running feet. Wolfe staggered off the porch, stumbling like a blind man into the ethereal veil of wintry mist and irrevocable dark.

Blood gushed from his wound, staining the icy slope that led down to the frozen murk of shoreline. He fumbled for his pocket watch, but his eyes were losing focus, so he brought the timepiece close to his face to discern the position of the hands.

"Hang those devils," he whispered raggedly into the wind. "Fifteen minutes to midnight . . . I must hold on . . . for Jenny . . ."

Droplets of icy spray pelted his cheek—a familiar sensation from windward watches—agony now amid a torturous storm of throbbing pain. The shore rocks swam before his eyes as small pinpoints of light began to flash into his vision.

Still clutching the empty cat-shaped urn to his chest, Wolfe stumbled blindly down the shoreline, away from Muldavey and his gang of murdering thugs. He meant to hide in the mist until the scurvy lot cleared his home. Then he would creep back to his cottage, to Blue Nights.

But within minutes his legs gave out and he sunk to his knees in the sand, his cheek smacking hard against the slick surface of a sea-smoothed stone even as his lips formed breathless words. "I cannot die yet . . . I cannot die yet . . . I cannot . . ."

But Wolfe knew that he was dying.

And he also knew, as a superstitious sailing man, that unless last rites were said over his body, his soul might be lost forever.

"Forgive me, Jenny," he whispered. "For failing you in so much . . ."

His hazy eyes focused on the brass container in his hand. He clung to it now like the memory of his betrothed's last wish.

Reaching into his pocket, Wolfe grasped the lock of her hair, then placed it inside the urn as her letter to him had instructed. Next he plucked a lock of his own and did the same, joining his with hers.

Finally, he looked toward the rough dark waters. With each new wave, the sea rushed closer, as if eager to embrace him. Wolfe tried to recall the words by which he'd committed his own sailors' bodies to watery graves.

" . . . Deliver me, dear Lord, not into the bitter sorrow of eternal death, but commit my body to the deep, and grant me"—Wolfe's breath caught as vicious pain stabbed through him—"grant me resurrection of the body when the sea shall give up her dead . . ."

Wolfe was too near delirium to notice the warm trembling of the cat-shaped urn in his hand even as his body grew colder. He was too blind to see how the eyes of the cat glowed more golden even as the light in his own eyes dimmed.

But before his eyes closed, the sea captain swore he saw a light in the distance. Closer and closer it came, floating above the waves like a luminescent sailing ship come to press him into service.

"Commit my body to the deep . . ." he managed to rasp once more just as the stroke of midnight came. Then Eric Wolfe's eyes finally closed, and, like a possessive lover, the salty black sea reached out her watery arms to claim him.

Just as he had asked.

Part One

It is found again.
What? Eternity.
It is the sea

—ARTHUR RIMBAND,
L'Éternité

Chapter One

In the lonely darkness, twenty-year-old Miranda Burke rose from a strange dream and crossed the cold, bare guest bedroom floor of her uncle's drafty seaside mansion.

Stopping at the tall windows, she stood barefoot in her thin white nightgown, her wild auburn curls falling freely down her back. The moon was high and its celestial light rolled upon the lapping black waves like pearls on velvet.

Miranda reached to unlatch the window, but it was tightly locked. Her fingers struggled with the polished steel, applying her usual brand of stubborn force until it finally gave. When the two heavy glass panes swung open, and the salt breeze touched her face, she sighed with deep relief.

Since she'd been a small child, the sea had been a comfort to her, like the familiar voice of a special friend. Even

7

now, after her strange dream, she'd come to the sea for reassurance.

Fog-shrouded dream images still haunted her: an old, odd-looking house by the sea, and the figure of a man standing tall at its windows. Miranda felt as though she should feel something for this house and this man, but her waking self had no idea why. She'd never seen either before.

Suddenly, far off in the distance, something caught her eye. A glowing light was moving swiftly closer to shore. Miranda watched it curiously as it neared, and blinked at the trick being played on her vision.

She moved to the bedroom's dresser and pulled at the top drawer to remove her late father's antique retractable telescope. Hurrying back to the window, she snapped open the instrument and focused on the glowing light that seemed to be flying above the black water.

Miranda's breath caught in her throat. Years of summers by the sea with her dad had made her an expert on the look of sailing vessels at night, but none had ever looked like this.

The ship resembled one of those nineteenth-century Yankee clippers from her father's reference texts. But its hull was covered with barnacles, and planks were actually missing. Its sails were tattered, too, as if it had been through a terrible storm. And, though it sailed under a brilliant moon, it seemed to be glowing with its own powerful light.

It was a vessel straight out of sailors' legends and seafaring lore.

To Miranda's stunned mind, it was an incarnation she'd never imagined could be real, until now . . .

"*Ghost ships—*" Miranda murmured aloud the next morning at the kitchen table of Crystal Breakers' spare and spotless kitchen.

The two words sat alone on the title page of the battered leather-bound notebook before her—one of ten volumes that Professor Milton Burke had kept on folklore of sailors and the sea. Her late father had hoped to publish it all one day, but his heart had failed him before he'd been able to make that wish—like so many others—come true.

Miranda quickly turned to the title page, eager to find some answers to last night's mysterious sight. Her eyes swiftly scanned her father's bold, masculine scrawl.

Over the centuries, sailors have attributed many common characteristics to ghost ships. They are most often seen as luminescent flying ships soaring above the waves or even over the land . . .

Many cultures believe in these specter ships. They are thought to be manned by spirits who have met with tragic ends and are impressed by the sea herself for service. These ghost sailors are believed to collect the souls of the drowned or aid living seaman in acute peril. . . .

A shiver crawled through Miranda's body. It was an even creepier feeling than she usually got sitting in the stark, chilly rooms of her uncle's mansion—a glass box of slick surfaces, sharp angles, and deceptive mirrors. The kind of place that made you feel empty inside.

These ships usually have some purpose. They carry a message, warning those who see them of changing weather and coming storms—

Miranda glanced outside. It didn't *look* like rain.

With a sigh, Miranda took a dejected bite of her breakfast. If only her father were there. He'd be able to help her puzzle out the significance of what she'd witnessed the night before.

Miranda finished her hasty breakfast. The Pop-Tart was clearly outclassed by her Aunt Joan's obscenely expensive Takashi dessert dish. But Miranda didn't really care.

The mansion's snobby chef had turned up his nose at her breakfast choice, offering to whip up an egg-white omelet instead—a specialty of the house at his bankrupt New York City bistro.

But she and her late father had always shared Pop-Tarts for breakfast on Saturday mornings before they went sailing, and she wasn't about to change that habit now.

"Miranda! Where a-r-e you?"

The sound of that voice set Miranda in immediate motion. In three seconds flat she'd stuffed the last little piece of Pop-Tart into her mouth, grabbed her notebook and backpack, and streaked out of the kitchen.

"Miranda, *answer* me!" The sharp voice of Joan Cunning Burke burst Miranda's bubble of belief that she'd make it out of the house for once without being grilled. The bellow carried down the gleaming white staircase with undisguised reproof. It was a tone of voice Miranda had learned to expect in the last year since she'd come to live with her relatives.

She's perfectly annoyed, thought Miranda. *And perfectly annoying.*

"I'm going out, Aunt Joan!" called Miranda, moving closer to freedom—*just a few more yards.*

"What? Where?"

"Don't worry. I'll be back soon!" Miranda made it into the foyer, where a geometric-patterned chandelier hung above a pair of faceted glass double doors. To Miranda, the passage stood like the last checkpoint between war zone and sanctuary. *Almost there—*

"Miranda, stop right now!"

Miranda's hand was poised on the knob. *So close.* But she'd been cut short by Joan Cunning Burke's serene arrival. The tall, slender, fortysomething woman floated down the gleaming white marble staircase, her tennis skirt perfectly pleated, her long legs perfectly tanned. Her bobbed blond hair was cut in perfect angles against her jaw, which matched the perfect angles of her coldly modern home.

"Where are you going? You're *not* going to start taking that dreadful little sailboat out this summer, are you?"

Miranda bit her lower lip, trying to come up with a fib.

It was a hesitation long enough for her aunt Joan to assume she'd guessed correctly.

"I *thought* we discussed this last night at dinner," she chided in her usual I'm-being-perfectly-reasonable tone. "Taking out that leaky sailboat of your late father's is much too ridiculous an endeavor for a lone young lady. I'd much rather you come with me now and take some tennis lessons at the club. Sandra Holt-Asten's daughter is looking for a doubles partner, and I told them—"

"It's not leaky!" Miranda blurted out, facing her aunt's eyes, the pale color of a cold winter sky. "And I have no interest in batting air-filled balls across a net at an airheaded opponent."

"*Tone,* Miranda. *Watch* that tone. And haven't I *advised* you to tie back that unruly hair of yours?"

Miranda defiantly looped a few of her wild auburn locks around an ear. Why was it her aunt always made her feel like a bug under a microscope—an unkempt, unworthy, and unattractive bug at that?

"I like my hair loose. And my father taught me to sail that boat himself. He said I was a natural sailor, and I am. I can handle her as good as—"

"As *well* as, dear."

Miranda took in a furious breath, her hand tightly gripping the polished crystal doorknob behind her. "As *well* as any of the weekend sailors at your Sandbridge Yacht and Beach Club."

"You're being ridiculous, not to mention impertinent. I think it's time we *sold* that infernal boat."

Miranda was ready for another retort, but her tongue suddenly stilled. She couldn't stand to lose her dad's boat.

A year and a half had passed since his final heart attack, though it seemed like only yesterday he was lying pale against the bedsheets of the cardiac ward, eating Hartford Hospital's lame version of a Thanksgiving dinner and promising how they'd be taking the *Sea Sprite* out the following summer.

But he would never again be taking the *Sea Sprite* out with her. He could be with her only in spirit. And Miranda's financial future was now in the hands of her father's half brother Theodore, the workaholic owner of the Pita Pockets fast food chain.

Miranda's uncle spent most of his time away on business trips, leaving his sole niece in the company of his critical third wife, a woman he'd married just eight months before. A woman whom Miranda's father had never even met.

"Ah, Miranda, those old ships of wood made men of iron!"

Miranda could still hear her father's words. The man's love of sailing was surpassed only by his penchant for quoting old romantic sayings about the history of it. But it was Milton Burke's words of praise to his daughter that still buoyed her spirits—how he'd called her a "natural sailor," and marveled at her ability to judge wind and weather from some deep instinct.

At times, Miranda felt as though those memories were her last anchor. Sailing had become more than a hobby she'd shared with him, it had become a part of her identity.

I'm cornered, thought Miranda in despair. She had no more than forty dollars in her pocket, and her small monthly allowance did little more than pay for the boat's upkeep and docking privileges at Runyon's Boatyard.

Milton Burke had left no money to Miranda. And, as an incentive that his adventure-loving daughter complete her higher education, he'd arranged that his savings and life insurance money be held in trust by Miranda's uncle until she turned thirty.

"Please, Aunt Joan . . ." Miranda managed to bank the fire in her eyes and force her voice into a tone about ten notches less defiant than it had been a moment before. "Please don't sell the boat."

"Well . . ." With a rather obvious show of feigned indifference, Joan ran two fingertips up and down the polished banister of the staircase, then frowned at imagined grains of dust. "I suppose we can put off the sale if you can manage a few *favors* for me this summer."

Miranda took a deep breath to steady herself. "What favors?"

"You can stop arguing with me, for one."

Muscles knotted in Miranda's neck. She grit her teeth. "Yes. Okay. I'll try."

Joan's pale eyes narrowed. "And you can get that ridiculous hair cut."

"What!" Miranda's hand automatically went up to protect her chaotic russet curls. In her estimation, they were her only truly unique feature, a genetic gift from a mother she barely knew. "But I've been growing it since I was a little girl—"

"Precisely. It's time you stopped growing *it* and started growing *up*. I want you to come to the club parties this year—"

"But my father never belonged to that club. I won't feel comfortable—"

"Nonsense. All you need are some new clothes," continued Joan, undaunted. "And a more sophisticated hairstyle. I'll take you to New York next week—"

"But I don't think—"

"*Unless* you'd rather have me call down to whatever boatyard you've got that *leaky* old thing," Joan ho-hummed as she examined her latest French manicure. "And have them put it up for sale . . ."

Miranda watched her new aunt. The woman peeked up from her seeming indifference with steely manipulation in her chilly blue gaze. Miranda knew she was waiting for her to crumble. *Well,* thought Miranda, *I'm not giving her the satisfaction.* After all, her hair would grow back, wouldn't it?

"All right, I agree."

"To the boat's sale?"

"No," said Miranda. "I'll have my hair cut. I'll do as you ask."

Joan's blond eyebrow arched slightly. "I see."

"It's getting late, you know," said Miranda quickly, deciding to try a little manipulation of her own. She looked at her watch. "Aren't you on your way to your morning tennis lesson? With *Rolf*?"

Miranda used every ounce of willpower not to roll her eyes. It was disgustingly obvious her aunt Joan had a crush on the Austrian émigré. The muscle-bound athlete had come to their home for drinks or dinner at least ten times since they'd arrived ten days before.

"Oh, my, is it that late?" At Miranda's reminder, her aunt's forehead knit in annoyance, then, as if she remembered that this would cause wrinkles, she quickly forced the muscles to smooth. She glanced at her own watch, the diamond tennis bracelet sparkling as she slightly twisted her wrist. "Yes, I'd better get to the car . . ."

Miranda couldn't have bolted fast enough. She turned quickly and pulled the door open.

"One more thing, Miranda!" called Joan. "Josh is coming home from Yale for the summer. He'll arrive for dinner tonight. I expect you to be there and to dress. He'll want to see you."

"Your son doesn't care about seeing—"

"I *thought* you said you'd start listening to me, dear," sang Joan over her shoulder as she turned on her heel and headed for the carport door. "Be there. And be dressed appropriately. Or it's bye-bye boat."

Miranda exhaled pure venom as she slammed the front door and strode to the drive, where her bike was parked. She strapped on her backpack, mounted her ten-speed, and pedaled hard, letting the sea air flow through her long, wild curls—at least she'd have them for a little while longer.

"If only I could get away," she muttered as she pumped her legs. "If only I could find a place where I could just be left alone."

Miranda's bicycle flew along the wealthy homes of Sandbridge, past the yacht club and down the quaint, expensively laid cobblestone streets. When the surfaces changed to cracked concrete and the strolling villagers traded J. Crew khakis for old T-shirts and ripped jeans, she knew she'd reached the old familiar side of the village.

This was the area where the "rounders," or year-round residents, lived. It was the older, working-class, seafaring section where she and her father, who lived the rest of the year in Hartford, had happily rented their modest summer bungalow year after year.

Miranda pedaled to the worn dock of the old boatyard, more than ready for a day's sail. She knew any frustrations with her controlling aunt would float away once she was out on the sea again.

She waved hello to her best friend, Tina's, grandfather, Ron, found *Sea Sprite* bobbing happily in the water, and stepped onto her polished mahogany deck. After zipping up her hooded red windbreaker, she donned her father's big blue sailing cap—stuffing her hair up under it to secure it firmly—and prepared to cast off. In no time she was flying swiftly over the bright blue waves of Long Island Sound and smiling into the wind.

She'd been away too long—first at an exclusive all-girls college she could barely tolerate—and now with relatives who could barely tolerate her. It was a relief to find peace on the water.

"Hello waves! I'm back!"

Miranda adored the blue-green spray, the fresh salt smell, but what she especially loved was the feeling of being completely and utterly free. On her own and ready for anything!

For a long time she headed nowhere special, toying with the idea of finding her ghost ship. And then, strangely, the wind shifted.

Miranda tacked skillfully, ready to counter and stay on her southern course, when she felt a sudden, odd fluttering in herself as an overpowering need swelled within her.

Run with the wind, the sea seemed to whisper. *Let go . . . fly . . .*

She did, allowing the sail to fill and the boat to run briskly north-northeastward—the same direction as the ghost ship, she suddenly realized.

With uncanny speed, the boat flew, and she let it, traveling a long time, until the wind finally began to slacken. She saw that she'd come to a less-populated area of the Connecticut shoreline, close to the Rhode Island border, where older houses stood alone on rugged, rocky beach fronts, clear of the quiet Sound and facing the rougher view of the open ocean.

That's when she spotted the mouth of a little cove.

Without hesitation, Miranda pointed the *Sea Sprite* toward the little half-moon-shaped inlet cut ruggedly into the Atlantic shoreline. She pulled out her father's navigational chart but saw no name attached to the cove.

"How odd . . ." she whispered, working the tiller to steer her sailboat fully into and around the small bay. The rocky shoreline appeared very wild and overgrown for the area, and her spirit began to despair. There were no homes or other buildings that she could see.

"No place to hide," she muttered, toying with the idea of finding a place to run away.

As the sailboat moved farther in, she began to feel an eerie calm descend over the water, making it smooth as glass. The strange calm, along with the dark and stark isolation, unsettled her.

For a moment, she thought she should turn back. But in the short span of Miranda's life, her curiosity and her stubborn will had never before failed to overcome her fears.

Miranda forced her gaze, along with her boat, to continue around the cove. Then her vision came to a halt. There *was* a building there.

A *house*.

It had been hard to recognize at first because of the tall trees and overgrown greenery surrounding it. But she could see it now. It sat large and solemn on a rise above the rocky beach. The pale blue octagonal structure looked at least a century old. And it also appeared abandoned.

Perfect, thought Miranda.

Then she looked a little more closely, and her limbs

stilled. The place was somehow familiar to her, like something she'd seen before.

"My dream," she murmured. "You're the house in my dream."

Suddenly, Miranda got the oddest feeling of possessiveness about the house—as if she had a right to occupy the place. "Now, where did that come from?"

Miranda studied the cottage and found her heart going out to it. The place seemed so sad sitting there. So isolated and neglected. So alone.

Immediately, she felt a kinship. And she knew it was calling out to her—that it somehow *needed* her to save it from being so pitifully abandoned.

That something, *anything,* would need her, or want her, just the way she was . . . well . . . that alone was enough to dispel any final doubts in Miranda.

With resolution, she tacked the boat around a little rocky island off its beach and swung in to get a closer look.

Chapter Two

Blue Nights Cottage

Who the devil was this?

Vessels *never* dared venture into Crescent Cove, not during June and December—the two months of the year the Sea Wolf haunted here. From behind his second floor master bedroom window, the captain's ghostly form quaked with mounting anger.

Seafaring men were about the most superstitious lot on the globe, and Eric Wolfe knew that a slight, priggish wave of dread was all he needed to send out over the bay waters. That alone would make every last one of those infernally curious weekend swabbies fly right back down the shoreline from whence they'd come.

But *this* sloop's swabby patently *ignored* his warnings!

"How dare this man disturb my peace! And my first dawn back on land in five full months!"

With grim fury, Wolfe tracked the intruder's sail, trying to recall if he'd ever seen this particular craft before.

Single-masted. Sail billowing with the salt wind. *Sea Spirit* scripted on her stern—

"*No. It's* Sea Sprite. *Not* Spirit," Wolfe whispered, realizing he'd misread the name. He cringed with the irony. *He* was that now, was he not? Nothing more than a sea spirit. An invisible puff of air.

Barely substantial.

Hardly alive.

And doomed to serving the sea on her ghost ships for ten months of the blasted calendar. "*And now, my first day on leave, and I must contend with this intrusion!*"

Wolfe glared at the sloop, watching the craft's captain deftly tack around a tiny isle that sat two hundred yards beyond the pebbly shoreline at the base of his seaside cottage.

"Not bad," he grudgingly admitted. At least the captain was competent at working the wind and tiller.

With unhappy interest, Wolfe watched the sloop sweep closer. When he finally got an eyeful of her eighteen-foot frame, he let out a long, low whistle.

She was a beauty. Sleek. With graceful lines and perfect ballast—nothing that would give unwanted bulk or heaviness. She moved easily and effortlessly, her sails crisp and white.

For a moment the pretty little hull tilted in the wind, as if she were showing off for him, and Wolfe nodded in appreciation of the gleaming mahogany, its rich reddish-brown color winking flirtatiously in the morning sun.

With growing curiosity Wolfe watched as the sloop was guided inward. He tried to make out the face of her captain. In billowing red windbreaker and battered blue captain's cap, the scrawny young man was still diligently working the tiller and sail, but the boat was too far away for Wolfe to see the captain's face clearly.

The sloop finally neared the shallows at the base of the hill that ran to his back porch. Its captain dropped anchor right next to his run-down dock.

Wolfe had been a masterful captain in his day. He knew a skilled captain when he saw one. And despite his annoyance at being disturbed, he had to admit he saw one now.

Stowing his impatience, Wolfe observed the lithe mariner as he industriously furled his sail, coiled lines, and double-checked the craft's anchorage. Wolfe was eager now to gaze upon the face of this visitor, this goodly master of the *Sea Sprite*.

But when the sloop's captain finally removed his cap, Wolfe's jaw slackened a quarter-inch. A tumble of wavy auburn hair fell down the captain's back, and then, in a flash of quick motion, the boxy red windbreaker was unzipped. The sloop's captain turned, and with a lazy, catlike stretch revealed a pair of breasts, small but perfectly round and straining beneath a thin white shirt.

Wolfe's jaw dropped another quarter-inch.

He wanted her.

The thought disgusted him. Just as the sheer impotency of his existence disgusted him. And yet the corporal notion whipped savagely through him nonetheless. Like the memory of a limb severed, such glimmering feelings often tricked him into believing he had blood and bone and muscle—a form.

A life.

But the truth was a mere reflection of that. Insubstantial and elusive, his form was no more solid than sunlight upon the crest of a wave. On the water, as part of his service to the sea, his form could materialize, but on land he was nothing more than an invisible puff of air, a trick of light.

Eric Wolfe's ghostly image folded the semblance of muscular arms across a broad chest. Over a century ago, the New England sea captain had thoroughly enjoyed the power and strength of his mortal body—handed down to him through a mix of Viking and Celtic lineage, peoples who'd thrived upon the seas.

Over those mortal years, Eric had been acutely aware of the vital effect his powerful body had had on women. In his callous, shortsighted youth, he'd used that effect well, easily bedding and pleasuring many women over the years of his life. It wasn't the only reason he'd been known as the Sea Wolf, but it certainly had been one.

Ah, but he was not the man he was.

Not in any sense.

The events of the past had battered him and then receded like tidewater from beach sand. And through the many decades since his death, Wolfe had come to accept his present existence, and lack of corporal privilege—except, of course, in such instances as this.

It was galling, *most pointedly galling*, to have no substantial form when he was around a mortal woman to whom he was attracted.

And she was attractive.

Like her little sloop, she was graceful and sleek. Russet curls, the rich color of the mahogany hull, spilled long and wild along her slender neck and shoulders and down the back of her lithe torso. He liked that she kept it loose, free to fly about on the sea wind like a colorful, billowing spinnaker. Her face, too, seemed agreeable, though it was too far away to discern particulars.

Wolfe wanted a closer look, but he dismissed the notion at once. He dared not try to take in more of her. Better to keep her at a distance—as he preferred to do with all mortals, *especially* mortal women.

Better for his peace.

Still, Wolfe could not turn away. So, instead, he simply dissolved through his bedroom's French doors and stepped onto the planked balcony. There he stood, like a captain at his ship's prow, and, for a long time, simply watched her—and she in turn watched him . . . or, rather, the house.

Wolfe knew the girl could not see him; no mortal had ever been able to see him, that is, not on *land*. The sea, of course, was another matter. There he could achieve a substantial materialization.

When the girl stood up, wiped her hands on her jeans, and moved to climb upon his decaying wooden dock, Wolfe's ghostly form stilled. *What in hell is she doing?*

A bolt of fear streaked through him as he watched her

step carefully along the rotting boards. *She's going to break her neck!*

Wolfe tensely watched the girl feel her way along the old boards, testing each step before allowing her full weight to move forward. Grudgingly, he admired the patience and care it took her to traverse the thirty feet of planking—the same she'd displayed as captain of her little sloop.

Still, he disliked her obvious intention to venture closer.

"Go back, girl," he whispered, rippling the air around him as she planted both sneakered feet solidly onto his pebbly shore.

But she did not heed his warning. She came toward him instead, the crests of sun-dappled blue at her back. For a moment, against his better judgment, Wolfe actually enjoyed the sight. He even fancied her a mermaid come to shore.

She looked younger than he'd thought at first. Nineteen or twenty perhaps. Young by the standards of these present times, though not by his own—he'd formally proposed marriage to Jenny at such an age, and on a bright June day like this as he recalled. Nevertheless, even if she weren't too young for the thirty years he'd lived as a man, she was certainly no match for the hundred and forty years he'd spent as a ghost.

Still, he wanted her.

"Don't torment yourself, Wolfe," he told himself. *"Go back to the sea."*

But he could not. Not yet. The sea had granted him leave from his duties for one month. And his ghost ship would not return again for him for another thirty days. So, instead, Wolfe decided he had only one recourse as she timidly ventured closer. The only way to secure his precious peace in his own home—

Scare the living daylights out of her.

"Awesome . . ."

Miranda's eyes widened at the sight of the abandoned old cottage. She'd never seen anything quite like it, nor had she *ever* been so instantly enchanted by the mere sight of a house.

It was remarkably built, with an octagon-shaped front wing jutting forward, like a ship's bow. The foundation was made from local stone—mostly gray and brownish rounds—the upper three floors were sturdy-looking wood, though the pale blue paint was cracked and peeling.

The best feature of all, in Miranda's view, was the wide wraparound planking that served as a porch on the first floor and a balcony on the second. Both came to a subtle point at the front of the house, which further emphasized the feeling of a ship's prow.

"You look as though you could slip down the hill and float right out on the water," whispered Miranda to the house.

Her gaze next rose to the attic story, which consisted of a single small octagon-shaped room with wide windows all around. It was an odd room, like the top of a lighthouse. She could see it would make a wonderful sort of crow's nest, a lookout perch for the open ocean. She wondered if the former owner had used it that way.

No matter, though, the entire place was in sad shape now. The windows were filthy, the porch railings splintered, and, like the rest of the cottage, in bad need of painting, and, all around the place, weeds and vines had grown unchecked.

"But you're not beyond saving." She knew it in her heart just as she knew at once that *she* wanted to be the one to save it.

Venturing around the house, she could see that trees and brush were thick. They partially blocked the dirt drive. No roadway was visible beyond, and she knew at once why the place sat unmolested.

No one knew it was there.

It could not be seen from any road. And, tucked away in the isolated, unmarked cove, it could barely be seen from the water.

"What a fine hiding place this would make," whispered Miranda, her mind working on this new idea. "Especially for someone who wanted to run away. And not be found.''

A secret smile curved Miranda's lips. She had found the place she'd been looking for, the place where she could slip away and hide from her problems. The place where she would finally be left alone. Be left in peace.

But, as she ventured closer, deciding to explore the inside, something strange happened. The moment she stepped into the shadow created by the house, a strange chill began to overtake her—strange because it was otherwise a very warm day. Miranda noticed something else odd too. The birds. The moment she'd stepped into the house's cold shadow, their chirping had suddenly ceased. The world around her had instantly become very quiet.

And very still.

Miranda swallowed, and she gazed into the darkness of the house. The fine hair on her skin prickled, and she got the distinct and unsettling impression that she wasn't alone.

She looked harder at the house, squinting into the first floor windows. But there was no one. At least, no one whom she could see. She turned her gaze upward and gasped for a moment at a trick of light on the balcony.

Was it a shadow? Or the shape of a man?

She thought she'd seen something from the sloop but was certain it had been a deception of the shade. Now she wasn't so sure, and the feeling made her more than a little uneasy.

"Hello!" she called out loudly, a slight trembling evident in her voice.

She waited for a reply. Watched for some sort of movement. "See, Miranda, there's nothing. No one," she told herself firmly. "So get a grip."

With resolute movements, she zipped up her red windbreaker against the sudden chill of the shade. For good measure she even drew up the hood.

An unexplainable chill wasn't going to dissuade her from checking out the hideaway she'd been searching for, she decided. Then she began to move forward again, farther into the house's chilling shadow.

When Eric Wolfe saw this trespasser flip up the hood of her windbreaker, he realized just how ridiculously *vulnerable* she looked. At first Wolfe felt hesitant to frighten her *too* terribly. After all his years of haunting Blue Nights, he'd never had the stomach for giving females nightmares.

Wolfe had always thought that females were *supposed* to fear ominous-looking abandoned houses like this one. They were *supposed* to assume such places were haunted. And they were *supposed* to, at first sign of threat, run in fear back home to the safety of their warm little beds!

Wolfe exhaled in frustration as he watched the girl move forward toward his home. *So much for "supposed-tos" with this one.* She wasn't frightening like a typical female, was she?

No, she displayed the confidence of a seasoned sailor facing a gale.

She bounded up the steps, and the movements thoroughly annoyed him. It was the lively, fearless bounce, he decided. It made him feel as though she were mocking his efforts. *Fine, Red Riding Hood. Go on and play. Just beware of the Sea Wolf.*

The ghost dissolved with fluid ease, moving from the balcony back into his cobwebbed home. He floated down the staircase, stopping when he saw the carved oak of the front door being pushed open on its creaking hinges.

The girl timidly stepped forward into the musty darkness of the old seaside cottage. Wolfe remained on the staircase, confident that she would never see him. He was a transparent spirit, after all, a mere specter who turned at times into a troublesome poltergeist.

On land Wolfe was completely insubstantial. Always had been. And usually he was accepting of this existence. But there were times, over the past 140 years, when Eric Wolfe had wanted to be more in his own home, to make himself *heard* or even *felt* by the mortals who'd dared to inhabit it.

At the moment, however, those levels of existence were beyond him, so, with begrudging fascination Eric Wolfe simply watched the girl as she entered his house and began to explore it. He was resigned to the fact that he would not be able to converse with her—not even to tell her that she'd handled her little sloop rather well.

Wolfe knew that even contemplating such communication was ridiculous. He was *haunting* this house, making certain people steered good and clear of it.

He knew that he should be getting down to the business of driving her out. He should be moving the covered furniture, or knocking down dusty paintings, jostling the ragged rug or rapping on stained walls—all of the usual poltergeisty endeavors that had scared off previous inhabitors of his home over the last century.

But he didn't do any of these things. Instead, he gave in to the need to simply move closer to the girl.

And was instantly sorry he had.

Rosy cheeks on ivory skin with bright aquamarine eyes. It was a face with distinct features. That odd mix of typical American mutt: high aristocratic cheekbones crashing against a snubbed peasant nose. She was by no means a stunning beauty, but she was quite comely, and her bright eyes and vibrant expression made her even more so to him.

Wolfe hated to admit it, but he found himself entranced as she traversed the first floor of his old home. He was secretly pleased by her obvious admiration for his cottage. The curious pleasure in her wide eyes, the awestruck wonder on her pretty visage, the vexing half-smile that would wax and wane as she explored and examined his many personal belongings.

"*You like my house, don't you, Red Riding Hood?*" he found himself saying aloud. Then he stilled.

Because she had stilled.

"*You could not have heard me,*" whispered Wolfe.

But her head instantly turned in his direction. "Hell-hell-hello," she whispered, her voice rasping dryly at the back of her throat.

Shocked, Eric Wolfe remained completely still and completely silent. He had never before been *heard* by a mortal. Not even upon the sea—the only place where his ghostly form was permitted limited corporal materialization.

This had to be a fluke. A coincidence. She'd heard something else perhaps—a board creak or an animal squeal.

But not his words.

"Hello," repeated the girl, more firmly this time. "Who's there? Who spoke?" She turned her head this way and that, then step by step moved back the way she'd come.

Eric Wolfe felt too stunned to move. To speak.

She'd *heard* him.

But how could this be?

Before he could answer himself, he realized that she was leaving.

"Wait!" he called out to her before he could stop himself.

But she was fleeing full speed now, racing down the grassy hill toward her little craft.

Wolfe followed only to the edge of the porch. He watched as she skipped quickly over the decrepit dock, pulled anchor, and paddled away from his shore. In no time, the little sloop's white sail was raised, the wind was harnessed, and the girl captain was guiding her way out of his cove.

For some reason, her departure left him regretful.

Ah, Wolfe, you insubstantial fool, don't start getting soft on mortals now, he told himself.

This was what he'd wanted, wasn't it? To drive all mortals away from his seaside cottage. To be left in peace.

But despite Wolfe's own counsel, he could not keep an odd disappointment from taking root in his spirit.

"Keep your weather eye open, girl," he grudgingly murmured, unable to look away until her snowy sail carried her gently off, like a white-winged gull on a merciful breeze.

Chapter Three

"Psssst. Miranda!"

Late that night, Miranda peered down from her second-floor bedroom window. In the dark garden below, the tip of a Virginia Slim burned red. Its filter end was attached to the mouth of a young woman in flannel shirt and jeans, her short cap of black hair shimmering in the moonlight as she turned her round face upward.

"Hang on, Tina," Miranda quietly called to her friend. "I'll be right down."

Miranda drew back into her sparsely furnished bedroom and quickly stripped off the mint-green cocktail dress her aunt had forced her to wear for dinner. She pulled on jeans, a plain white T-shirt, and her red windbreaker. Then she checked the lock on her bedroom door and went to her backpack, where she'd stuffed clothes, a flashlight, and a long coil of good strong rope.

She pulled out the rope, secured one end firmly inside the room, and threw the other out the window.

Everything's ready, thought Miranda, glancing back a

moment, not one ounce of regret inside her. *Everything's in place.*

On the garden walkway below, the dark-haired girl carefully preserved her lit cigarette, placing it on the pavement. Then she grabbed at the dangling end of rope until she'd caught it. "Okay, Red," she called. "Hand over hand, and shimmy."

Miranda began her climb down. She'd already placed thick thumb knots into the rope so it would be easy. She could hear the disco music coming from the first floor and was glad it masked any noises from outside.

"Thanks," said Miranda when her rubber-soled Docksides finally touched the ground.

"No prob. Want a smoke?" asked twenty-year-old Tina Runyon, her nail-bitten hands reaching for the pack in the pocket of her oversized flannel shirt. Garbed in her usual ripped jeans and sporting three earrings through each of her earlobes, Santina Runyon was a Sandbridge "rounder." Her grandfather owned Runyon's Boatyard, and, like most of the people who lived in this small Connecticut seaside town year-round, Tina tended to steer clear of the upper-class summer residents—unless they were serving them drinks or cleaning their homes.

Since Miranda and her father had always taken their summer rentals in the "rounder" part of Sandbridge, Tina and Miranda had fallen into a natural girlhood friendship, spending almost every summer hanging out together.

"No thanks on the smokes," said Miranda. "I'm trying to give it up. Too expensive."

Tina shrugged, then bent down to retrieve her lit cigarette. She brushed off the end, took a drag, then thought better of it, throwing it back down and crushing it with the heel of her black sneaker. "So, what's with the Bee Gees? Somebody taking a trip down memory lane?"

"Aunt Joan's reliving her New York clubbing days and teaching Rolf to disco."

"Rolf? Who's—"

"Her Austrian tennis pro."

"Oh, wow. *This* I gotta see."

"No, Tina—"

"Aw, c'mon," urged Tina, grabbing Miranda's sleeve. Miranda reluctantly followed Tina around the side of the mansion, where the music grew louder. Tina recklessly popped her head in front of the first floor window, and Miranda instantly grabbed her friend's shoulders and yanked her backward.

"Be careful!" Miranda whispered in alarm.

"Okay, okay," said Tina, then both girls moved carefully closer, letting their heads inch around the edge of the windowpane until they could make out the scene inside.

The disco beat of "Staying Alive" was pounding against the modern furnishings, abstract sculptures, bare floor, and stark walls. Miranda's aunt was showing a large, muscle-bound man a dance move. To the girls, it looked like Martha Stewart showing Arnold Schwarzenegger how to bump.

Tina nearly burst out laughing and Miranda smacked a hand over her mouth. "You've got to admit," mumbled Tina into Miranda's hand. "John Travolta, this guy is *not.*"

"Don't make me laugh," warned Miranda, taking her hand away. "If they hear us, I'll get busted, and my aunt's already threatening to wire my window with an alarm."

Tina nodded. "I'll be good," she whispered, then pointed to a third body in the room. The blond young man in a navy blazer and khaki pants was sitting in a black lacquered ladder-back chair. His expression seemed to find as much discomfort in the situation as the seating. "Who's the stiff in the corner?"

"That's Josh Cunning. Joan's only son."

"Gee, Red, he's not bad looking. What's his story?"

"He's a graduate student at Yale. Psychology." Miranda regarded the lanky young man. He'd been polite at dinner but pretty cool toward her, not saying more than two words directly to her during the whole evening.

"I think my aunt is trying to push us together," said Miranda. "I overheard her say he'd be a 'good influence'

on me. But I'm the last thing he's interest in — and I can't
say he's my type at all. He's like most of the guys I've
met lately, above it all, you know? He'd rather sit there
and assume he's got you all figured out rather than actually talk to you.''

"Of course, Red, don't you know the technical term
for that?''

"What?''

"*Snob.*''

Miranda laughed softly as Tina smirked, yet the girl's
dark eyes turned quickly back to Josh, remaining transfixed for a few seconds more.

"You think he's cute, don't you?'' asked Miranda.

Tina shrugged. "I suppose he's not so bad on the eyes.
But guys like that never go for girls like me. Too bad they
don't know what they're missing.''

Miranda sighed as she realized that what she was doing
now with Tina—standing on the outside looking in—
mirrored her exact existence at Crystal Breakers. The truth
was, Miranda didn't fit in there, and the even bigger truth
was, she didn't *want* to.

This wasn't the life her father or mother wanted for
their daughter. Miranda knew it, and the pressure from
her aunt to change was much more than an irritation. It
was a betrayal. An assault on her very identity.

Tugging her friend's elbow, Miranda firmly whispered,
"C'mon, let's get out of here.''

They walked down the drive and onto the street, and
Tina looked over at Miranda. "You really hate it here that
much?''

"The Spanish Inquisition would be more fun.''

"Jeez, Red, that's hard to believe,'' she said, then
turned back to take in the full view of Crystal Breakers.
"I mean, *look* at the place. It's, like, a *mansion.* I mean,
I thought your uncle was loaded and your new title would
be 'princess.' ''

"Take a closer look, Tina. Glass and steel and concrete.
Hard lines and ground lights. The only thing missing is
the bars on the windows.''

"Meaning what?"

"Meaning one girl's palace is another girl's prison."

"But—"

"I'm an inmate, Tina. Sentenced to live with them. They don't want me here. My uncle's the one who's my blood relation, but he's never around, and when he is, he just pats me on the head like I'm some stray puppy and tells me to mind my aunt, who can't stand the way I am."

"Yeah, I suppose that pretty much sucks."

"I want to be left *alone*. I don't want to be nagged at every day, pushed around, manipulated, and told to change. I want *peace*."

"No offense, Red, but, like, join the club."

"No. I'm not putting up with it any more."

"What do you mean?"

"I'm leaving."

"Yeah, that's good. Keep sneaking out to keep your sanity. Like tonight. So, c'mon, let's—"

"No, not just tonight. For good."

Tina stopped and stared at Miranda. "What do you mean *for good*?" she asked, her eyes narrowing. "You're not, like, thinking of running away or something?"

Miranda nodded. "I've got clothes in this backpack and I've already stocked the *Sea Sprite* with food and supplies."

"But that's stupid!" Tina blurted out. "You'll be giving up a posh pad—and what about your education and your trust fund?"

"I don't want to wait a decade to be free. And I won't have to because—" Miranda stopped short, wondering if she could trust her friend.

"Because *what*?"

"Because I've found a good place to run away to. A rent-free place where I know I'll be happy. I've got it all figured out."

Admittedly, Miranda had been momentarily spooked by the voice in the blue cottage, but on her way back to Sandbridge she'd calmed down and convinced herself that it was nothing she should be afraid of. The blue cottage was the perfect hideaway, at least for the summer, and she was convinced it—whatever "it" was—wanted her there.

The cottage certainly seemed to be calling out to her and—haunted or not—Miranda was resolved in her escape plan, and spent the rest of the day preparing for it.

"Miranda, don't do anything crazy. Please."

Miranda glared at her friend. "What's with you, Tina? I thought *you* were the rebel. Now you want me to stay in this postmodern prison?"

"What I want is for you to stay safe. Running away with no money or means of support doesn't solve anything. It only makes life rougher. Ask my older sister. She was actually happy to get caught shoplifting and have the police drag her butt back to clean sheets and hot meals."

"See, that's just it. I won't be going to the streets. And I care more about keeping my father's sailboat and my sanity than I do about clean sheets. Besides, I'm twenty now, an adult, and it's time I strike out on my own. Even if it does seem reckless."

Tina threw up her hands. "It is *reckless!* You'll be screwing up your future. Sheesh, Red, it can't be *that* bad," she challenged, her gaze straying back to the magnificent structure, its walls of glass, steel, and stone making it appear a crystal palace. "Just swallow their crap and get through it!"

Miranda bit her lip in annoyance. She'd expected support from her friend. Not this. "Fine. Whatever," she managed tightly. "I suppose I'll think about it," she lied.

"Good. You do that."

An uncomfortable silence fell between the young women as they walked down the shadowy street. Finally Tina broke the ice. "So . . . like, what do you wanna do tonight? Go to the Crow's Nest? I think Live Wire is playing."

"Actually, I was hoping we could go to your grandfather's boatyard."

"The *boatyard*? Why? To see the crappy paint job I did this afternoon?"

"No, I'd just like to go there."

Tina's eyes narrowed as if she knew Miranda had an ulterior motive. *"Why?"*

"Just . . . *please.*"

Tina's brow knit, but she didn't argue any further. "Oh, all right. C'mon."

The two friends cut through the yard of a large seaside home and made their way to the beach, where they began their usual game of walking the line between the dry and wet sand, flirting with the rhythmic lapping shadows that marked the end of land's certainty.

"Black water's pretty excellent," said Miranda absently, looking into the waves. "Don't you think?"

"Nope. I prefer blue, and things that I can *see*, thank you very much."

"But doesn't it remind you of those wonderful ghost stories your grandfather used to tell us?"

"Wonderful?" Tina shivered. "Those stories gave me the creeps."

"Not me. I liked them." Miranda was silent for a moment. "Do you think those stories were true?"

Tina laughed. "You're kidding, right? There are no such things as *ghosts.* Be real."

Miranda's stomach knotted at Tina's words, and she said nothing more until they reached the beach near Runyon's Boatyard. There they found a flickering campfire on the sand.

Ronald Bartholomew Wolfe Runyon, a former mackerel schooner captain with a face that had more lines than a navigational chart, lit up his pipe as he sat on an old wooden chair by the fire.

The seventy-year-old seaman had once lived upon the water, but his arthritis was slowly crippling him and his ability to sail had been taken from him forever. Now he was limited to boats with engines, like his old rusting trawler. But most of his time was now simply spent reminiscing about the best of his days spent on the ocean.

Miranda and Tina had barely greeted him, when Miranda began asking Old Ron whether his stories about ghosts had been true.

"For me, they are, girl."

"For *you*." Tina flopped down on the sand and crossed her legs. "Granddad, like, what does that mean, exactly? It's a little obscure, you know?"

Miranda leaned toward Old Ron. "What about ghost ships," she prompted. "Have you ever seen one of those?"

Old Ron scratched his trimmed silver beard for a long time. "Why are you askin'?"

Miranda wanted to tell him she saw one last night, but after Tina's ridicule on the beach, she hesitated, then shrugged. "Just wondering."

Ron Runyon tugged on his pipe and blew a fine smoke ring. "Did see one once," he began slowly. "There was this stormy dark night in thirty-eight, and I was at the helm on the poop, coming in toward Blackrock Shoal near Georges Bank, off the cape, when the waves began tossin' us and the fog got so thick, I couldn't see beyond the rail."

"It's a schooner story," whispered Tina.

Miranda elbowed her friend. "Shhhhh."

"Well, I was sure we were done for. The waves were awashing over the rail and much of the crew was trembling below deck. I knew Blackrock had taken down more ships than were docked in Boston harbor, and I was saying my prayers, when I suddenly saw a glowing light comin' toward us. I thought it might be a lighthouse, but it was movin' like a ship, a ship soaring above the waves. And then I saw 'em."

"Saw who?" asked Tina.

"The ghosts. Ghosts o' dead sailors climbin' over the rail. Boardin' my schooner."

Tina giggled and elbowed Miranda, but Miranda ignored her skeptical friend.

"Not one word was spoken," continued Old Ron, "when that hardy ghost captain came and his strong hands took the helm from me, I stared at him. His eyes were blue as the sea, his hair black as the storm, and a white glow surrounded his whole form. Then I passed out cold.

"When I came to, the sun was shining and we were beyond the shoal, safe and sound, and floatin' free. There was no sign of that ghost captain or crew, but I say they plain saved my schooner from disaster that night. Saved my life and my crew."

Tina rolled her eyes and Ron chuckled. "I know, my young darlin's, I know," said Ron. "The tale of a ghost is dearly hard to believe unless you yourself have had the contact."

"But I have," Miranda blurted out. "Or . . . I think I might have . . . I don't know how to tell."

One of Ron's bushy silver eyebrows arched, and Tina stared dumbfounded at her friend.

"Red," said Tina, "what are you talking about? You're kidding, right?"

Miranda shifted uncomfortably. "I saw this house today," she told Old Ron. "Near Stonington—"

"Stonington?!" Tina exclaimed, more than a note of parental reproof in her voice, "What the heck were you doing so far up the shoreline?!"

"Knock it off, already, Tina. You're not my aunt, you know."

The rebuke was sharp and stung Miranda's longtime friend into silence.

Miranda was sorry she'd snapped like that at Tina, but she was getting sick and tired of being treated like a child. Old Ron, at least, might believe her, and Miranda looked to him now for some kind of support.

The old seaman seemed to be deciding whether Miranda was telling him the truth or acting out a prank. He tugged coolly on his pipe, then sent a fragrant white plume toward the crackling red-orange campfire flames before speaking.

"Was the house near the shore?" he finally asked. "If it was, it's liable to be a sailing man's ghost."

"A sailor?" Miranda asked, her curiosity piqued. She hadn't considered that possibility before. *"Ah, Miranda,"* her father's voice reminded from her memories, *"those old ships of wood made men of iron!"*

With growing excitement, Miranda pulled her father's old navigational chart from her jeans back pocket and unfolded it. "It's in a cove. Near Stonington. See, right here. I marked it. Do you recognize—"

"That there's Crescent Cove."

"It is?" asked Miranda, slightly surprised. "Why doesn't the map say so?"

"Only the locals call it that. Never been officially named. Land's private property. Been that way since I was a child."

"But *who* owns it?" asked Miranda. "And the house that's on it?"

"Mmmm." Old Ron thought it over a minute. "I think they're kin of mine—branch of the family tree. Wolfe's the surname. Is that the house you're speakin' of, girl? Blue Nights Cottage? You're not tellin' me you were actually *in* that ol' place?"

Miranda hesitated a moment, but finally admitted. "Yeah, I was. I came across it on a sail today."

"Steer clear of that old cottage," warned Ron. "Young girl like you shouldn't want any part of that place. Bad history."

"But . . . why?" asked Miranda, feeling her spirits deflate. "What happened there? And why doesn't anybody live there now?"

"Ye've got to understand, girl, when a salt from New England has a grudge, he's liable to take it right to his grave. Or well beyond."

"But what *happened* there?" insisted Miranda.

"From what I recollect, Blue Nights was the scene of tragedy. Double murder, I believe. Yah, there's a curse hanging over the place as well. No one who's moved in over the years has ever stayed more than six months."

"So Blue Nights Cottage *is* haunted," whispered Miranda. Her eyes widened. "Wild. Do you know anything else?"

Ron Runyon studied the girl before him. "You're not

going to listen to an old man's advice, are ya, girl? I can see it in your eyes, you're going back to Blue Nights.''

Miranda bit her lip and stared at the sea's black water in thought. "I think the ghost wants to talk to me. I think he . . . or the house—I know this will sound crazy—but I think they're both . . . lonely.''

Ron puffed his pipe, his eyebrow arching. "I see.''

"Knock it off, Miranda,'' Tina nudged her friend. "Stop kidding around, okay? I'm not trying to boss you or anything, but you're, like, freaking me out.''

Miranda looked directly at her friend. "Don't you get it, Tina? I'm not kidding.''

Tina's eyes met Miranda's, first in confusion, then hurt, and finally in disbelieving anger. She turned to her grand-father. "Miranda's had a bad time, Granddad. She lost her father, was forced to leave her home, and now her aunt must have her on Valium or something. She doesn't really believe in this stuff—''

"Stop it, Tina. You don't know what I believe.''

"Miranda, it's one thing for my grandfather to tell these stories. He's told them since forever. But it's another for you to pretend you've seen a ghost—''

"Okay, fine, *don't* believe me. Go on and get the men in white coats, then. And make sure they bring the strait-jacket too.'' Miranda angrily folded her arms across her chest. "Go on. I'll wait.''

"Granddad, tell her she's nuts, will you? Tell her not to be stupid and that there are not such things as ghosts. That your stories are just *stories*.''

"Ah, ladies, ladies . . .'' Old Ron regarded his grand-daughter, then Miranda, and finally he let his gaze move out over the water. "Do you know what the Vikings be-lieved about the sea?''

"Granddad, like, this is not the time to get obscure again.''

"They believed it was a symbol o' death—and do you know what else they believed?''

"Uh, no,'' said Tina flatly.

"They believed it was a place of rebirth. Of new life.''

Tina sighed. "How could they believe it was *both* things? That's stupid."

"No, my darlin', both are true. And that's what I'm sayin' 'bout your friend here. Perhaps, for some, Blue Nights is a bad place; but for your friend here, maybe it's calling her to something. Perhaps it's something you and I can't understand, but something she needs. Something unfathomable yet eternal. Like the sea herself."

"Sorry, Granddad, but all I don't understand is what you just said."

Miranda said nothing, her gaze moving from Ron's brown eyes to the crackling fire, and then on out to the vast dark unknown that lay beyond the shadowy shoreline.

Something *was* calling to her as surely as the lapping sound of salty waves. She could *feel* it—deep inside herself.

Tina touched her friend's arm. "Miranda, don't go back there. Do you hear me?"

Miranda's eyes turned to her friend. "Tina, I know you mean well," she said softly, "but when I get into my sailboat again, where I end up won't be up to me anyway."

"Then who in the heck will it be up to?"

"The sea, of course," said Miranda, briefly glancing at Old Ron before her eyes turned back toward the dark waters beyond.

"The eternal sea."

Chapter Four

The dawn brought danger.

Eric Wolfe knew the signs. Clouds, fat and dark, hung low, like weighted tent canvas brushing the watery gray horizon.

Although his mortal sense of smell had long before left him, Wolfe now carried another kind of awareness, and he was able to recognize the damp molecules of heavy air that swept in on every fresh gust.

Wolfe sighed. He'd known the sea in all her moods. Lavender joy and blackened rage, fetching blue and gray foreboding. Like a long-loved mistress, her intimate acquaintance had been enduring but bittersweet. In his mortal days she'd held him captivated. But over these decades it had become more and more apparent to Wolfe that she had simply held him captive.

The first slash of bone-white lightning ripped across the misty sky, illuminating the dark waves miles away. Wolfe paced the rickety porch floorboards of Blue Nights, hands clasped behind him, each step driving him deeper into restless fury.

He cursed this dreary mood along with the dreary dawn.

"What's the matter with you, Wolfe?"

The day before he'd been content enough.

"Must be that blasted mortal," Wolfe decided. *"The female sailor with the red hair and jacket."*

Heaven only knew why she'd sent him down this spiral of tension and unrest.

A silly young woman was all she'd been, he assured himself. Yet, she'd *heard* him speak. He was sure of it.

How, he asked himself for the thousandth time. How, after 140 years of *not* being able to communicate one word to any blasted earth-bound mortal had this girl alone been able to hear his ghostly musings? What in hell did it mean?

The question intrigued him.

And then disturbed him.

"Perhaps she's a trick," Wolfe suspected. *"Sent my way by the damned spirit of Leach Muldavey."*

That thought solidified Wolfe's tumultuous feelings, hardening any residual yearnings for the girl's return. He found himself kicking out at a stone. Without bothering to focus his ghostly energy, Wolfe's foot sailed right through it.

The surprise of it made him laugh, but only for a moment. As the first roll of thunder came across the bay, Wolfe's dark mood returned, a vexing ire echoed in the very sky. He peered toward the water again and was suddenly overwhelmed with the feeling that something more than a storm was coming in on the waves.

Somehow Wolfe felt that something was coming especially for him.

"Shut up, you stupid thunder!"

Miranda would have shaken her fist at the sky if her hands weren't busy trying to keep the *Sea Sprite* close to shore. The wind was blowing hard, its air heavy with the threat of rain, and she struggled to keep her little sailboat on course.

Because her craft had no running lights, she'd spent a quiet night in Runyon's Boatyard, zipped up in a weatherproof sleeping bag at the bottom of the *Sea Sprite*'s mahogany hull.

"I should have taken my stupid chances with the stupid dark!" she railed against the wind. "It would have been better than this!"

When the dawn broke with foul foreboding, Miranda had cursed her luck, but had refused to turn back to Crystal Breakers and the life she'd come to despise. Casting off from the boatyard this morning was the only way, she'd decided. Her one chance.

Don't look back, now, Miranda, she'd told herself.
You can't look back.

For the last hour she rode the wind toward Crescent Cove. Now she was almost there, and she looked toward the ominous clouds with a combination of fear and rage.

Hold your water! she commanded the clouds.
Hold your height, she ordered the waves.

But the sea defied Miranda, turning on her like a jealous schoolgirl.

The wind went wild and sheets of cold rain pelted down. Unable to control the sail, she furled it, then grabbed for the boat's long oar. The waves had kicked up, and she fought them hard, struggling to guide the boat toward shore under her own power.

But with every stroke, Miranda realized she could not beat the strength of the sea. It was carrying her farther and farther from Blue Nights, not closer.

"Damn you, stupid, stupid!"

She didn't know whether she was cursing herself or the sea, or both. After all, the sea was beginning to act like a living thing toward her. It seemed to be *fighting* her will, even mocking her puny little attempts to thwart its own awesome power.

Gritting her teeth, Miranda refused to give in. She paddled harder, jittery panic seeping into her veins like the chill from the stinging sheets of water now pouring down from the sky.

Suddenly lightning ripped through clouds, striking a metal buoy only one hundred yards away. The thunder followed so closely and so loudly, Miranda thought her eardrums would burst. But they didn't, and she resumed paddling.

She didn't know if minutes went by or hours. But with every ounce of strength left in her, she kept the strokes going until finally her arms became two iron anchors, barely able to move without agonizing pain. As a fog surrounded her, she realized her bearings were blown. She wondered if she'd gotten turned around somehow. Was she still heading toward shore? Or was she going out to sea?

She tried to find the boat's compass, but the waves were rougher than ever now, and she could barely keep her balance. Peering into the foggy gray outline that may have been the shore, Miranda finally prayed to heaven for help.

That prayer, and the faint scent of burning electricity, were the last things she recalled before the blinding flash bit her sailboat's mast in two and the wildly flying boom struck the back of her head, sending her into black oblivion.

"Oh, for God's sake. Not her. Not again."
When Wolfe saw the flash of lightning strike an object on the foggy edge of his cove, he quickly moved to the small attic that served as his crow's nest. The octagon-shaped room was surrounded by tall panes of glass, two now broken. Nevertheless, inside, a ship's telescope was mounted, giving Wolfe a bird's-eye view of Crescent Cove and the waters beyond it.

Through the eyepiece he spied the little mahogany sailboat he'd seen the day before. The *Sea Sprite* was bobbing perilously in the high surf, in danger of capsizing any second. Wolfe concentrated his energy and adjusted the telescope's focus. It was then he saw the young woman's determined face, and a moment later disaster struck. The ship was dismasted and its pretty captain rendered unconscious.

"Blast!" he cursed. "Blast and damn, you silly, silly girl!"

Wolfe raced quickly from the attic and toward the beach, stopping just short of the waves. He paced the sand in fury, knowing he could not travel over the water.

Not without a ghost ship.

Like a beacon, Wolfe sent his energy on the wind across the water. It was a phantom distress call that would travel to any ghost ships in the vicinity. Then he sent his awareness to the bottom of the cove, feeling around for a sunken craft—any sort of craft.

The jackpot came in the form of a leaky old rubber raft sunk by a family who'd come and gone from Blue Nights fifteen summers earlier. Wolfe's energies raised the yellow raft, now muddied and strewn with seaweed.

As a mortal craft it was far from seaworthy. But it was no longer a craft for mortals; now it was transformed into a ghost craft, perfectly fit for the use of spirits and wraiths. The rubber raft glowed white as it levitated above the waves, shining through the mist as Wolfe's energies pulled it toward him. When it reached him, he climbed inside.

Wolfe felt the familiar solidity coming to his form, the materialization that came only over water. He quickly grabbed one of the two oars and began to push. The ghost raft floated over the waves much faster than any mortal craft could move, and Wolfe was upon the *Sea Sprite* in only a few minutes.

In no time he was climbing on board, searching for the *Sea Sprite*'s own oar. But before he took it up, he could not stop himself from turning to the unconscious girl.

With his materialized hand he brushed her wild auburn curls from her young face and neck and felt for her pulse. It was strong, uncommonly so, throbbing against his fingers with defiant life.

For a moment Wolfe was overcome by a flash of memory. Jenny Smithton had been about this girl's age when he started courting her. Wolfe could see himself, a young buck in the Smithtons' genteel parlor, stroking Jenny's fragile wrist, observing its pale skin and weak pulse. In the years that came after his initial advance, Wolfe would come to think of Jenny as a delicate heirloom, a china doll with yellow curls and crystal blue eyes. Beautiful, but, like a china doll, too fragile and weak for the man he'd become. In his mind he'd dismissed her as a swoony and lethargic girl living a sheltered existence of ridiculously romantic ideas.

It was not until she fell seriously ill that Wolfe learned of Jenny's weak heart—an ailment her family had kept secret for most of her life. An ailment, he had realized too late, that had kept her a prisoner in that confined, sheltered life.

An angry clap of thunder brought Wolfe back to the present and his vision back to the unconscious girl before him. With sudden force, a high wave slammed against the hull, and Wolfe was thrown backward. His fury rushed back to him like surf to sand, and he quickly snatched up the boat's oar.

With the strength he'd once possessed as a mortal man, Wolfe shoved the wood to the water and dragged the oar through again and again. It was heavy, hard work to move a mortal vessel, one hundred times the effort of a ghost craft, but Eric Wolfe would not allow failure.

He defied the unrelenting wind and rain, defied even his mistress, the sea. Inside, he felt a driving force he could not define. But it would not rest until it had brought this girl back to Blue Nights Cottage.

Wolfe paddled the *Sea Sprite* until he'd reached the shoreline at the base of his property. When he felt the sloop's hull hit the shallows, he gathered the unconscious girl in his arms, then leaped out of the boat and waded, thigh-deep, in the seawater.

Wolfe cursed in frustration as he felt his grasp on her slipping away. But there was nothing he could do. The closer he came to land, the less solid he became. He barely managed to get her upon the wet sand of the beach before his form faded back into a translucent spirit. Dropping quickly to his knees, he laid the girl down as gently as he could upon the wet sand.

Thunder boomed nearby as the steady rainstorm continued and Wolfe contemplated the problem of moving the girl into the house. He could achieve a state of solid form on the water. It was the sea's way of making sure he could aid mortal ships in peril. But on land he was nothing but spirit. While he was able to move small inanimate objects by concentrating energy, he could not possibly move the girl that way.

Still, Wolfe knelt in the sand, slipped his ghostly arms beneath her knees and torso, and concentrated. He rose, trying with his last remaining strength to lift her, but his arms merely passed through her mortal body as he moved to his feet.

"Damn my ghostly impotence!" Wolfe cursed, then dropped to his knees, determined to try once more. But again he failed.

A third, fourth, and fifth time he attempted to lift the unconscious girl. It was on the sixth try, after using his last ounce of determined fury, that he fell, completely exhausted, next to her.

"She'll catch her death," he rasped in wretched anguish. His face lay mere inches from her own as he gazed into her youthful features and a part of him despaired. She was soaked to the bone now, her auburn hair plastered against her cheek, her ivory skin pale from the chill as the high winds continued to lash sheets of rain against her and the surf lapped at her lower legs. She would die if he did not get her warm and dry.

"I cannot let her perish . . ."

Wolfe rasped the words to the unrelenting sky, knowing this was much more than a reactive wish to protect any human life. For Wolfe, it was somehow much deeper. He felt it was dire that he save this girl, though he could not yet fathom why.

A strike of lightning ripped through the slate-gray clouds, and Wolfe's head suddenly rose with hope. As the brief jagged flash faded from the sky, he saw another, steadier light far off on the horizon.

The dull glow swiftly moved toward him, growing brighter by the second. Wolfe closed his eyes in thanks as he recognized the familiar lines of his old clipper ship flying over the waves as if her hull possessed wings.

"Windward," he rasped to the girl, though she remained unconscious. *"Thank heaven, it's my* Windward.*"*

She'd been the fastest, sleekest ship he'd ever handled as a living captain—and, as it turned out, a dead one.

Struggling to sit up, Wolfe watched her enter Crescent Cove and quickly approach the shore of Blue Nights.

"Ahoy, there, Cap'n!" came the call from the bow.

"Mr. Riley!" Wolfe cried to his first mate through the rain and mist. *"Come closer, man. Close as you can to shore! Then come down and help me here!"*

"Aye, sir!"

With instinctive trepidation, Wolfe watched the huge, glowing vessel approach land. Even after all these years as a spirit, Wolfe still felt twinges of dread at seeing a sailing vessel as large as the *Windward* come so close to shore. For a moment Wolfe flashed on that terrible vision of the *Lizzie* being pounded to pieces when she'd run aground in fog south of Boston harbor in 1848.

Wolfe had been a mortal captain then, but he felt just as impotent then as he did now, helpless to do anything more than listen to the sounds of destruction through the fog; and, finally, in the morning, witness for himself the wretched wreckage that the sea's fickleness could visit upon man.

Back then Wolfe had called it bad sailing. But now he knew better. Now he knew such disasters could sometimes be the capricious will of the sea.

"Steady as she goes!" called the first mate.

The glowing lines of the *Windward* loomed large as it neared, skimming over the tops of the tumultuous waves. In 1847, she'd been one of the largest American ships built, and, in her glory days, she'd spread nearly ten thousand yards of canvas.

But these were not her glory days. She was a ghost ship now, pulled at the end of her life from the barnacled floor of the ocean with a ruptured hull, broken spars, and ravaged sails.

As the storm continued around him, Wolfe watched the *Windward* coast quietly in, hesitating just a few feet beyond the line where sand met wave. He glanced down at the unconscious girl, then back up to find three ghostly forms of his crew descending a rope ladder thrown over the side.

"Hurry it up!" commanded Wolfe impatiently as, still exhausted, he drew himself to his knees.

The glowing spirits of each seaman dropped to the shallows and waded ashore, their forms becoming more and more translucent as they neared dry land.

Patrick Riley was the first to meet the Sea Wolf. Next came the ship's carpenter, Angus Bonner, then China Jack—an ordinary seaman—and finally Tommy Noll, who served as ship's boy.

"Here we are, Cap'n," announced China Jack, a thick-waisted, thick-armed sailor who'd spent a good part of his mortal life in the Eastern tea trade, collecting sharp knives and tattoos.

"Yes, that's apparent enough," snapped Wolfe. *"Now—"*

"Hey! Look at the mortal girl!" cried Tommy Noll, the wiry youth who'd come aboard as ship's boy at thirteen.

"She's a fetchin' lass," commented Angus Bonner.

"Awful wet though," China Jack pointed out. *"Cap'n, hadn't we better do somethin' 'bout helpin' her?"*

"Yes!" Wolfe barked, *"If you can stow the chattering! Now, let's get on with it!"*

"Get on with what?" asked Tommy Noll.

"It's all right, Captain, we'll help," said Patrick Riley quickly, seeing Wolfe was ready to keelhaul the lot of them.

Wolfe sighed and met the eyes of his lanky, bearded first mate. Riley had a much calmer way about him than

Wolfe at times that calm could lose control of the crew, but at other times it could serve to settle Wolfe's dangerous temper.

Wolfe allowed Riley to help him to his feet, then the captain stared at the ghostly crew before him. Though they appeared a motley bunch, he knew their strength together could be formidable. And, yet, a living being was the weightiest force on earth, concentrating overwhelming energy, and will into a shell of skin and bones. The *Windward*'s skeleton crew might not be enough to lift the imposing burden of a mortal.

"Listen, Mr. Riley," Wolfe began firmly. *"And all you men . . . we have to get the girl inside Blue Nights."*

The ghosts all glanced uneasily at one another.

"But she's on land! *How're we gonna lift—"* began Tommy Noll, who stopped cold when he saw the glare in store for him from the Sea Wolf. *"Ah, I'll stop the chatter, sir."*

"You do that," snapped Wolfe, then he explained his idea, and the men nodded.

"All right, men," called Mr. Riley as Wolfe got into position. *"Heave to!"*

The four ghosts together concentrated their energy on the young woman's inert form. Slowly, Wolfe attempted to lift her from the sand, adding as much of his own remaining strength to their energies as he could manage.

It's working, he realized with relief as he finally felt her body rising. Wolfe carried her with steady steps toward Blue Nights, his men following a few paces behind. He climbed the porch steps and kicked at the back door. That extra bit of expended energy was almost his undoing. Wolfe stumbled forward into the musty air of his home's run-down parlor.

He tipped his eyes to the staircase but he knew he'd never make it up there with her, so he staggered to the long sofa, covered by a dusty sheet, and dropped her on its ripped cushions.

"There, girl, you've made it to Blue Nights," Wolfe managed to say before collapsing to his knees. Then,

though he didn't know what on earth possessed him, Captain Eric Wolfe uttered four words he'd never before spoken to any female, living or dead.

"Welcome," his lips whispered in her ear. *"Welcome to my home."*

Chapter Five

Fifteen minutes later, when Miranda's eyes finally fluttered open, the rain was still battering the coast. Sheets of water lashed the octagonal walls of Blue Nights Cottage, and the wind howled through its eaves.

Miranda's vision was foggy at first. She peered into the dimness of the room, trying to make out shapes. For a moment, she thought she heard voices, but she couldn't be sure. Her head was pounding, her clothing soaked, and her arms felt as if fifty-pound weights had been strapped at her elbows.

When her vision finally cleared, she blinked, not believing what floated before her eyes. Was she dreaming? She wasn't sure. Looming before her were three faintly glowing male faces that certainly *seemed* real enough. Miranda stared in confusion as her eyes widened with growing trepidation.

"Somethin's spookin' her," remarked the youngest-looking face of the three.

"Yep," agreed a big, rough-looking one.

"Must be the wind," suggested the somber-looking third.

Miranda's dumbfounded shock turned swiftly to panic. She swallowed and closed her eyes, hoping the three-headed vision was a delusion. But when she opened them again, the faces were still there, and this time with bodies attached!

The first glowing form looked like a blond-haired kid about thirteen or fourteen. The second image was a man with lean cheeks and a receding hairline. And the third was big, beefy, and more than a little intimidating in appearance. He wore a red kerchief tied over the top of his sandy-colored head, a ponytail fell past his shoulders, and tattoos covered both of his thick bare arms.

The young one leaned closer. *"Now she* really *looks spooked,"* he said. *"Think she sees us, China Jack?"*

"Naw, Tommy," said the rough-looking one with the ponytail as he unfolded one of his crossed arms to playfully slap the back Tommy's head. *"Mortals can't see nor hear us on land."*

"I dunno," said Tommy. *"What d'you think, Angus?"*

"Can't yet say," said the lean, quieter man as he stroked his long chin.

"All right, Tommy, I'll prove it," said China Jack, waving his hands in front of Miranda's face. *"Look girl! Can you see this?"*

"I don't think you should—" began Angus, but Tommy cut him off.

"That's a hoot!" Tommy roared. Then he put his fingers in his mouth and made a funny face. *"How 'bout thisth? Can ya sthee thisth, girl?"*

"Y-y-yes," stammered Miranda at last, doing her best to swallow down her rising panic.

Now it was the crew's turn to look spooked.

Tommy Noll stood frozen, his fingers still in his mouth. *"Shthe didn't shthay what I thought shthe sthaid, did shthe?"*

Angus pulled Tommy away. Frantically, he looked into

Miranda's face. *"Girl, ya can't see nor hear me, can ya?"*

Miranda stared up at the lean man they called Angus, her fear giving way to frustration. What did they think anyway, that she was blind and deaf?

"Of course I can see and hear you," she stated flatly. "My eyes are open, aren't they? And I'm answering your questions. I can see and hear all three of you!"

Angus, Jack, and Tommy glanced at one another, then all three recoiled in horror and ran, screaming, out of the room.

Miranda stared after them, perplexed.

Then she abruptly sat up. Unfortunately, the sudden movement made her sickeningly dizzy, sending her right back down again. With a shaky hand she felt behind her throbbing head. Her fingers traced the outline of an egg-shaped bump rising beneath her scalp.

"Oh, no . . ." she murmured, and then felt darkness overtake her once more.

"Cap'n Wolfe! Mr. Riley!"

Wolfe turned from his conversation with Patrick Riley to see Tommy, Angus, and China Jack flying from Blue Nights like sqanking gulls from a collapsing spar.

"Now what," muttered Wolfe.

"Don't know," said Mr. Riley. *"But they sure are acting like they've seen a—"*

"No," warned Wolfe. *"Don't say it."*

"What?" teased Riley. *"Ghost?"*

Wolfe cast an unhappy glance at his first mate, then turned his attention to the three crewmen rushing toward them.

"Cap'n, she can see *us!"* Tommy Noll blurted out.

Angus Bonner and China Jack nodded frantically in complete agreement.

Wolfe waved a hand at the panicked seaman. *"You're all three daft,"* he said dismissively, then turned back to Riley.

"Dammit, Cap'n! It's true, I say!" shrieked Angus. *"That girl can see us!"*

Wolfe stopped cold. Quiet Angus Bonner had done a lot of things in his life—and in his afterlife—but one thing he did *not* do was shriek. The British-born seaman was about the most solemn, somber man Wolfe had ever sailed with.

Wolfe rubbed the back of his neck as he slowly turned to study Angus. Obviously, *something* had spooked him, along with Tommy and China Jack.

"Angus," Wolfe began in an even tone, the kind that Mr. Riley usually used. *"Now, why don't you just think about what you're saying here? Mortals cannot see us on land. It's not possible. Must've been a mistake. Or mis-understanding."*

"Captain's right," said Riley.

"Sure, I am," affirmed Wolfe as his piercing blue gaze swept the faces of the three ghosts before him. But not one of them seemed slightly persuaded by Wolfe's calmly presented logic.

"But, Cap'n," murmured China Jack timidly. *"She really did seem to see us."*

Wolfe's lips tightened, then he threw up his hands. *"All right, then, if you're all so damned sure. Show me."*

China Jack glanced at Angus, who nodded back. *"Aye, sir,"* said Jack, and all five seamen started toward the house.

With agitated strides, Wolfe quickly moved into the lead, surmounting the gentle slope from the beach to his back porch in only a few seconds. He swiftly entered Blue Nights and moved directly to the girl's side.

She was still unconscious, and that bothered Wolfe. He would have liked to have seen her awake and moving around by then. The worry seemed to overwhelm him as he gazed into her lovely young face, and Wolfe was suddenly self-conscious about his feelings with his men so close.

"Well," said Wolfe, forcing any emotion from his

words. *"She appears to me just as I left her a few minutes ago."*

"But Angus was right, Cap'n," Tommy Noll piped up. *"I made a face like thiths and shthe told us shthe could sthee it."*

Behind Tommy, Mr. Riley's brow furrowed in dark disapproval. *"Tommy, such pranks may be amusing in dry weather, but not during a squall."*

"Aye," said Wolfe. *"This is no time for foolery! You men get the* Windward *back under sail at once. The storm's worsening and there are mortal ships out there in need of aid."*

"Aye, sir, Cap'n," said Jack and Angus quickly.

Tommy shrugged and nodded.

"All right, you heard your captain. Back to the ship," ordered Mr. Riley. Then, as the men did as ordered, he turned to Wolfe.

"You'll be all right with the mortal girl?"

Wolfe glanced back, the evidence of his deep concern etched on his ghostly features. *"Aye."* He looked back to his first mate. *"I'll be fine."*

"But, Wolfe . . . you can't abide having mortals *at Blue Nights."*

"I know" was all Wolfe managed to say. *"Come, Mr. Riley, I'll walk you out."*

Wolfe met his crew at the shoreline. *"Thanks for your aid, Mr. Riley, and all you men. Shove off, and take care. I'll see you in a little less than a month."*

"But, Cap'n," China Jack spoke up, *"the girl. She—"*

"Don't you worry now, Jack," said Wolfe, placing a hand on the big man's shoulder. *"I think I can well handle a puny little mortal. Just as long as I don't have to hoist her."*

"Aye, sir," said Jack with a shrug, then turned and headed for the ship.

With hands on hips, Wolfe restlessly watched from the rocky beach as each of his men grasped the rope ladder and ascended the side of the *Windward*. Wolfe had already advised Mr. Riley to patrol the more treacherous passages in the area, especially Blackrock Shoal near Georges Bank, and the dangerous currents south of Boston harbor.

A part of him considered taking command now, but he needed the time off. Thirty days was all he'd have before his ship would return for him. So he simply watched the departing form of his luminous *Windward*, a diminishing beacon of pale white light on a blanket of stormy gray.

When the last bit of gossamer glow faded, Wolfe turned toward his old home, ready to ascend the gentle slope that led to his back porch. But for a moment he found himself distracted, overcome by an indefinable mixture of unsettling notions.

Standing in the rain and wind, Wolfe stared at his old cottage. *Something is different,* he realized. *But what?*

Then it struck him: There was a *living* being inside his home. Energy radiated from within the cottage, filling the emptiness with a pulsing wellspring that warmed the walls and poured out of the windows. It had been years since he'd come home to find a mortal inside his home, and he'd almost forgotten how very different it felt.

Yet, something about *this* particular life energy struck Wolfe as unique. He squinted at the cottage, not understanding why *this* mortal was different from the others.

There had been many over the past 140 years—families, couples, and historians; workmen, architects, and Realtors. Wolfe had come back from the sea countless times to find such mortals daring to inhabit his Blue Nights, that is, until his terrifying hauntings had driven them off.

But why is it I'm in no hurry to drive this *one off?*

It was then the emotions slowly came over him, like waves of seawater. They were strong impressions, rooted deeply in his spirit, residuals of mortal feeling that Wolfe had not experienced in some time.

First came a sudden sense of affection for Blue Nights, how he'd designed and built it to his own specifications, how he'd expected to live out a long, full life there. Then came a more powerful memory—a sturdy belief that visited him at the end of every long sea voyage. Wolfe had always told himself that he'd someday be sharing this home with his wife and children: Jenny and a small, noisy brood of Wolfes.

The captain had seldom bothered to reassure his betrothed of his cozy expectations. He had always taken their future for granted. Unfortunately, the *someday* of their future had never come.

The loud rumble of thunder through the cove shook Wolfe from his moody musings. He turned his head to the tempestuous clouds, disgusted with himself.

"To hell with my memories," he spat out, squinting at the sky. The rain came down in sheets, though he could not feel it. Nor could he smell the sea, feel the wind, or—

"Ah, to hell with my regrets as well!"

What were such regrets anyway but sad, unredeemable remnants of a half-lived life? Such sorry laments disgusted him. He refused to tolerate such ridiculous self-pitying in other spirits—so how could he excuse his own indulgence?

Breaking away from the beach, Wolfe swiftly climbed the hill to the house. *It's time I saw how Little Red Riding Hood is doing,* thought Wolfe. *I hope to heaven she's well enough to send directly on her way.*

But she wasn't. When Wolfe entered the house and moved to the old, ripped sofa, he saw that the girl's eyes were still closed. He observed her with concern, recalling the sight of that collapsing mast. He wondered how badly the blow to her head had been.

In that moment, Wolfe had never wished for mortality so strongly—or at least the ability to materialize on land. If he could just *feel* the back of her head, or gently stroke her cheek to see if she was suffering a fever.

For nearly an hour, rain continued to lash the cottage walls, wind continued to rattle its windows, and Wolfe stayed dutifully at the girl's side, mostly pacing the rotting wooden floor and glancing out at the restless cove waters.

The girl simply refused to stir. Her breathing remained

strong through the steady pelting and angry howling, but her eyes remained closed.

Finally, Wolfe's own energy began to lag. He moved to the porch, focused his energy, and carried his favorite rocking chair into the parlor. He set it in a dark corner of the room and sat, his gaze settling on the girl's face.

She's attractive, thought Wolfe dispassionately, though she was not as pretty as Jenny Smithton. Jenny had been conventionally lovely, with cornsilk hair, round apple cheeks, and pale, ivory skin.

This girl's young face carried a light smattering of freckles across the bridge of her snub nose and a mottled redness to her thin cheeks, a likely result of too much sun.

Yet, he liked her face. Very much. It had more character than Jenny's, and more strength. He recalled its expression just before the boom struck the back of her head—the rage at the sea's cruel power, the grit and determination to fight it to the last.

She reminded Wolfe of someone.

For a moment, he thought it over, then chuckled softly in the shadows. *"I'll be hanged,"* he murmured, realizing exactly of whom it was the girl reminded him. *It's me. It's my own damned self.*

"Ah, Red, if only you weren't so young," he whispered with a weak smile, *"and I weren't so dead."*

Chapter
Six

When Miranda finally opened her eyes, a part of her thought maybe she was back in her father's beloved old clapboard summer cottage—the one on the "rounder" part of Sandbridge. The one she'd happily lived in every summer of her life.

She looked for the little yellow roses on the wallpaper, the ones her mother had picked out for her bedroom when she'd been six years old.

But there were no yellow roses.

Then she thought she might be in her uncle's Sandbridge mansion. But the familiar, musty old-house smell that touched her nose put that idea to rest inside of a split second. Everything at Crystal Breakers was perfectly spotless and ultra new. Mustiness was an artifact that implied history, and if the Burkes' summer home was anything, it was a temple to the modern age.

Miranda yawned and rubbed her eyes. She felt weak and woozy as she propped herself on her elbows and slowly sat up.

"Ouch," she complained as she touched the back of her head. The bump was still there, and quite tender.

Outside, a lazy patter of rain sounded against a nearby window. The sun had sunk low on the horizon. Suddenly she remembered the storm, the sickening sound of the *Sea Sprite*'s mast breaking, and then the blackness.

But what had happened next? Had someone pulled her out of the bay? Whose house was she in, anyway? A fisherman's?

Miranda peered into the dim room, trying to make out shapes among the shadows. "Wait a second," she whispered. "This looks awfully familiar . . ."

And then she remembered.

"Oh, my God! I'm here!" she cried as her gaze took in the run-down parlor and antique furnishings. "But how did I get *inside* Blue Nights Cottage?"

A sudden burst of male laughter rolled like thunder from the darkest corner of the room. It was a deep, rich sound that sent pricking needles through Miranda's entire being.

Instantly, she jerked her gaze to the nook from where it had come. A curtain of darkness met her eyes.

"Who's there?" she demanded in a voice much weaker than she would have liked.

For a long while, Miranda didn't move, didn't breathe. A trickle of sweat slipped from her neck to the crevice between her breasts, making her want to squirm. But she remained frozen, sitting up on the ripped, mildewed cushions of the sheet covered parlor sofa, listening for another sound.

"I *said* who's there!" she tried again, doing her best to inject power into her voice. The loud beating of her terrified heart was the only answer she got.

"Okay!" she called into the dark. "Then I'm coming over there!"

Though her limbs felt sore and weak, Miranda forced her legs to swing down off the sofa and her feet to hold her weight. Standing actually felt fine, but the first step forward sent a dizzy spell through her, and she found herself stumbling instead of walking.

"Blast it, Red!" boomed the deep voice from the corner. *"What in hell are you doing?!"*

Miranda's eyes widened as she fell forward. A tall, broad-shouldered form stepped toward her from the shadows. It was a man, and his arms were outstretched.

For a split second, Miranda thought he was going to break her fall, but as gravity claimed her body, she saw herself passing right through his widespread arms. Miranda reached out instinctively, trying to grasp a handful of his black cable-knit sweater. She *thought* she'd reached the man's chest, but her hands ended up clawing at nothing but air.

With a cry, Miranda landed on her hands and knees. An instant later, she was turning around, planting her rear on the bare planks of the parlor floor. More stunned than hurt, she looked up to find the man crouching next to her.

"Who . . . who are you?" Miranda demanded.

But the man said nothing, and she found herself staring into the bluest eyes she'd ever seen. They were a cobalt color, so deep and dark that they almost appeared black. Long, raven lashes matched his short-cropped hair, which capped a face the likes of which she'd never before seen in all her life.

The features themselves were regular enough; in fact, they were quite handsome: a straight nose, ruddy cheeks, and a square jaw with a cleft in the center of a strong chin. But it wasn't the features that held her captivated as much as the expression on them.

She'd never before come face-to-face with a man who held such unyielding force in his looks. The expression alone was intimidating—as if he'd been to hell and back, as if he'd seen and done things she could not even imagine. At once, Miranda compared him to those portraits she'd seen in her father's old books on seafarers.

. . . those ships of wood made men of iron!

Now, why was her father's favorite old saying coming

back to haunt her now? wondered Miranda. And then she stopped.

Haunt her, she repeated to herself.

Miranda suddenly got a very bizarre notion. And only one thing would rid her of it. Swallowing her anxiety, Miranda slowly reached out her hand toward the man.

Instantly, he pulled away.

"Please," whispered Miranda. "I—I just want to . . . I just need to . . . please?"

The man gave no indication that he'd heard her. His dark blue eyes simply continued to stare straight at her, his expression rigid.

A tremor of dread shook Miranda, but she refused to let it stop her. This time, as her hand reached out, the man did not pull away. Her fingers moved straight toward the man's broad chest, and then straight *through* it.

Miranda's eyes widened as she realized the only thing she could feel was a slight tingling on the very surface of her knuckles.

There's nothing solid to this image, she realized. *No substance at all!*

With a jerk, she pulled her hand back.

"Oh, my God," Miranda rasped on the tiniest breath. "Y-y-you really are a gh-gh-gh—"

Miranda flashed back on old Ron Runyon and his ghost stories. He'd warned her about this, but she hadn't *really* comprehended. Certainly, she'd never thought it would be like this!

"This *can't* be happening," rambled Miranda aloud, closing her eyes and rubbing her forehead. "I mean, the entire idea of visiting a house that *might* be haunted is one thing. But actually putting a hand through the chest of a seaman . . . well, that's just . . . *insanity!*"

"Good God, girl. Can you . . . can you actually see *me?"* asked the ghostly man.

Miranda opened her eyes. The man seemed to be in as much a state of shock as Miranda herself. "Of course I can *see* you! I'm staring right at you!"

"You can see me. And you can hear me as well?"
asked the man.

"Yes, I can hear you—" Miranda began, then stopped
suddenly, a feeling of terror crossing her features as she
finally recalled the three floating faces and realized at once
that it hadn't been a nightmare.

"Oh, my God! Where are they? Where are they!" cried
Miranda, frantically looking to her left and right.

The ghostly man's gaze didn't leave Miranda's face.
He squinted with a combination of confusion and impatience. *"Where are who?"*

"The faces! The three faces!" cried Miranda. "When
I was on the sofa earlier, I opened my eyes, and I saw
three faces floating over me, and—"

"Describe them."

The ghost's tone was so sharp and commanding that
Miranda was actually speechless a moment.

"Describe *them*," he repeated, and Miranda realized
the ghost's tone was at least twice as intimidating as his
glare.

"W-well, one w-was . . ." she began, then cleared her
throat and clenched her fists, trying with every particle of
her being *not* to act like a ninny. Or, at the very least,
stop her stammering. "One was scary-looking, with a ponytail and tattoos and—"

"China Jack," said the ghost flatly.

"And the other was kind of serious-looking with a receding hairline and—"

"Angus Bonner."

"And the third was much younger, a boy of thirteen or
so—"

*"Tommy Noll. Aye, I know all three. They're members
of my crew."*

"Your *what*?"

The ghost didn't answer. All of a sudden, he seemed
distracted, and more than a little annoyed. He rose to his
feet and began to pace.

"I can't believe it," he muttered. *"They were telling*

the truth. She can *see us, and* hear *us, and on* land . . . *I can't believe it. I simply can't . . ."*

The ghostly man stopped and stared down at Miranda, his hands on his hips. *"Can you see me now?"*

Miranda looked up. He seemed very tall. Skyscraper tall. Towering and dominant. She swallowed and nodded. "Yes."

"How about now."

"Oh . . ." Miranda saw the ghostly man's image actually flicker for a moment. But she could still see him plain as day. "You . . . you sort of got paler . . . but I can still see you all right."

The ghostly man squinted down at her in annoyance. *"You claim you can* still *see me?"*

Miranda's brow furrowed. "What do you mean *claim?* I said I can see you. And I can."

The ghostly man rubbed his square jaw. Then he paced for a few moments, stopped, and stared intently. *"How about* now.*"*

Miranda shrugged. "Still there. Slightly paler, but really not that much of a change."

"You cannot *see me now. I have* willed *that you cannot see me."*

"You've *willed* it? Right. Whatever. But, as I said, I can still see you."

The ghostly man looked even more annoyed now, possibly borderline angry. *"Prove it, then."*

"How?"

"Find me . . . if you can."

Miranda watched as the ghostly man moved away from her. He made absolutely no sound as he floated across the room. It was creepy to watch, yet Miranda's curiosity was more powerful than her fears.

Slowly, Miranda rose to her feet. Her head ached and she still felt woozy, but she managed to follow the ghost's path across the musty room, through the sheet-covered mounds of furniture, until she came to a stop right next to him, at the large stone fireplace.

Before he could stop her, she reached out to put her

hand through his broad chest again. "Tag, you're it."

"Blast it, girl! Don't do that!"

"Do what? Find you? It was your idea."

"No. Don't put your hand through me."

"Why? Does it hurt?"

The ghostly man's blue eyes glared down at her. *"No."*

Miranda waited for more of an explanation, but one wasn't forthcoming. The no was said so curtly and with such finality that Miranda didn't dare ask him to expound on it.

And, yet, she *was* curious.

"Does it tickle?" she asked. "That's how it feels when I—"

"Stow your female chattering," barked the ghost.

Miranda tried not to quake under the imperious tone and the glare of the twin blue beacons. Still, a part of her bristled at his insult. "So, do you believe me now? I mean, it's pretty obvious I can see you. And hear your—"

"Aye, we've established it. Now I suggest you be on your way."

Miranda stared up at the ghost. Her aquamarine eyes widened in surprise, then blinked in dismay. "I'm not leaving."

The ghostly man placed his hands on his hips. *"You're going, girl. Don't dare cross my will."*

Miranda's eyes narrowed. "I would have thought you'd like some company, living here all alone. Or, is *living* not the right word? I mean, you're . . . you're sort of *dead*, aren't you?"

The ghost continued to glare.

"What's your name?" asked Miranda. "Is this your house? When did you die? Have you been here long—"

"Belay the chattering!" boomed the ghost, his hands flying into the air. In a sudden swift blur he moved from Miranda. She was stunned by the silent speed at which he could cross the musty old room.

"I swear to heaven, I must be daft for pulling you out of my cove. I should have let you go down with your ship! I'll not get a moment's peace with a mortal female *in my*

house! Be gone, girl! Be gone, I say! And don't dare come back!''

And then he was gone.

Miranda stared dumbfounded at the empty space that a moment before had held the striking image of the handsome, broad-shouldered man. She crossed the room and looked about, but there was no sign of him.

She peered into the next room, an ancient dining room with stained wallpaper and broken chair legs, but he was not in there. She searched the rest of the first floor and even walked out to the porch, but the ghost was nowhere to be seen.

Had he been able to find a way to disappear after all?

Miranda didn't know. But she did know one piece of his diatribe had answered an earlier question: Now she knew exactly how she'd ended up on the sofa of Blue Nights Cottage.

The *ghost* had been the one to pull her from the cove.

The dead man had saved her life.

Miranda swallowed uneasily as she looked around. Any ghost who'd saved her life wouldn't then decide to harm her. Would he? No, she was sure—or at least *pretty* sure—she'd be safe there.

"Sorry, Mr. Ghost," she whispered to the evening air. "But after all I've been through, I'm not leaving now. Nope, not a chance."

Maybe no one would understand, least of all the ghost, but deep down Miranda felt like a part of her actually belonged in this place; even had a right to be there, and it was going to take more than a little yelling to drive her away.

With that thought Miranda turned on her heel and walked right back inside.

Chapter
Seven

The next morning dawned bright and clear.

Wolfe had spent the night in his favorite room—the small octagonal attic that sat atop Blue Nights like the crowning tier of a wedding cake.

Wolfe knew this was the best spot to observe the girl's departure. Now that the light of day had come, the captain was certain he'd be seeing Red's little windbreaker moving off the back porch and down the gentle slope that led to the decrepit dock. Any moment now, he would chart her path away from Blue Nights, hopefully for good.

Wolfe waited impatiently for the sun to rise, his gaze fixed on the grounds below.

But there was no red windbreaker.

No girl.

Wolfe waited another hour. The sun climbed higher into the bright blue sky.

"Where the devil is she?" he muttered, pacing the old, rotting floorboards of the small attic.

Had she fallen unconscious again? he wondered, concern for her beginning to seep annoyingly into his spirit. He was just about to give in and descend through the house to find her, when he saw a flash of red moving away from the back porch of Blue Nights.

"*Aye! 'Tis about time!*"

Wolfe watched the girl exit Blue Nights and approach her sailboat. The mast was useless, of course, cracked in the center and bowing down like a puppet at the end of a performance. But Wolfe knew she could jury-rig the sail to the standing half-mast or even paddle it well enough into the bay, where another boat could tow her.

As he expected, Wolfe watched her step into the mahogany hull. It tipped to and fro in the blue bay, its high polish winking in the sunlight. But the sloop did not move beyond the decrepit dock. The girl was too occupied with rummaging around it. Wolfe watched curiously, waiting for her to cast off.

But she did not. Instead, she turned and stepped *out* of the boat.

"*What in heaven . . .*"

Wolfe crossed his arms, perplexed, as the girl strode back up the gentle slope that led away from the cove and toward Blue Nights. Her arms were loaded down with big zippered bags she'd pulled from the craft's hull.

"*Ah . . . I see,*" whispered Wolfe. "*She must be leaving on foot.*"

Wolfe was certain she'd begin walking down the dirt drive. It was overgrown, but she could hike the quarter-mile to the main road and hitch a ride into Stonington. He was certain that was her intent—until she strode right back into his home!

Wolfe's jaw dropped.

The girl had, quite confidently, returned to Blue Nights. The slam of the door told him very clearly that she did not mean to leave at all. She meant to *stay*.

Rage tore through Wolfe.

"*I've made a grave mistake,*" he told himself. "*I've been much too agreeable. But I shall correct that error. Now!*"

He swiftly descended the steep, narrow staircase to the second and then the first floor, where he found the girl unpacking her things. He fumed in the shadows, trying to decide exactly how to route her.

For a moment, her lithe movements across his parlor distracted him. In no time, she'd removed white sheets from the old furniture and rolled up the raggedy rug from the floor. With an old broom she'd found in the kitchen closet, she set to sweeping an inch of dust from the worn floorboards.

Amid her flurry of activity, she seemed to Wolfe as industrious and efficient as any member of his crew. It crossed his mind that she might have made a first-rate seaman—except, of course, for her obvious inability to follow orders.

That thought, and the scratching straws of her broom nearing his dark corner, prompted Wolfe to begin the task he'd vowed to perform.

"Do you not understand the English language?" he pronounced in a contemptuous tone, a voice he usually reserved for the most thick-skulled of his crew.

The girl shrieked at his sudden outburst. Jumping back three feet, she clutched her broom to her chest, but it seemed a pathetic shield to Wolfe. With boldness, he stepped from the shroud of shadows, ready to frighten her senseless.

"Oh, it's just you," said the girl, calming. "Don't sneak up on me like that again, okay? You nearly frightened the living daylights out of me!"

A cheerful light had entered the girl's fetching blue-green eyes upon seeing him, and Wolfe had to resist the urge to respond in kind.

"You forget, girl. Fear is now my stock-in-trade," he returned sharply. *"So be gone with you—and any attempts you have to make this place more than what it is. A tomb!"*

With his last words, Wolfe used his energy to pull the broom from her hands and fling it across the room. A small peep came from the girl as her eyes tracked the broom's flight. With a crack, it hit the wall and fell to the floor.

"Have I made myself clear? Get out of my house at once!"

Wolfe watched the girl carefully, expecting her to turn tail and flee. The cheer left her eyes and her bottom lip trembled slightly, but the rest of her remained rock steady. Then, with stiff movements, she folded her arms across her chest, propped her hip in defiance, and glared.

"I'm not leaving."

Stubborn female.

The words echoed in Wolfe's memory, suddenly seeming perfectly appropriate. He recalled thinking them a few months ago when the *Windward* had guided a pleasure yacht out of a fog bank, and a young man had the devil of a time getting his lazy girlfriend to help trim sail.

"What's your age?"

"T-t-twenty."

The answer struck Wolfe. It was the exact age Jenny Smithton had been when he'd proposed marriage to her. But she'd never been like this—so full of contrary fire and reckless boldness. Wolfe tried not to admire it, or become attracted by it. He stood his ground and glared back at the intruding young mortal.

"What the devil is it that prompts you to defy me?"

"Defy you? But—I'm not trying to defy you."

"Blast it all, of course you are. Why, if you were a member of my crew, I'd have you thrown in the brig for directly disobeying my order."

"But my staying has nothing to do with obeying or disobeying you! It has nothing to do with you at all!"

"Nothing to do with me! It's my house, you silly girl!"

"Your house? Since when can a dead man own property?"

"I am not dead, exactly."

"You're a ghost!"

"I'm a living spirit—a distinction you would not understand until you've crossed over."

"Try me."

Wolfe began to pace. What in blazes was going on
here? He had presumed only to scare her off, and now
she was drawing him into conversation.

"This chattering must stop now."

"But—"

"There is one *God in heaven. And* one *captain of this
ship! I* command *you to leave. Now."*

"We're not on a ship. Besides, I wasn't brought up to
take commands. My father raised me to be a free and
independent thinker—"

"Then your father is an idiot—" The words had barely
left Wolfe, when the girl launched herself at him.

"Take it back! Take it back!" she cried in a furious
whirl of pounding fists.

Wolfe stepped away as the girl's arms flailed uselessly
against him, passing through his form like twigs through
a cloud. Despite the angry power behind her blows, a
ticklish tingling was all he could feel—that and a small
amount of regret at his rather heartless words.

"Stop it, girl!" he finally shouted, slipping around her
in the blink of an eye and appearing at her back. *"You're
being ridiculous."*

"Take it back!" she insisted. "Say you're sorry!"

"I'll not. *A girl child is best raised to learn obedience
to the male will. It is her lot. To give one such as you
airs of independence merely ruins your chances at making
a good match."*

"I don't need a good match. Or any kind of match. I
can make my own way. This is the modern world. Women
can be whatever they want to be. Do whatever they want
to do. Your time is over. Dead and gone. Like your sorry
self!"

Wolfe arched an eyebrow, stung by the girl's words, yet
undeniably attracted by her mettle. And, in truth, it was the
attraction that truly disturbed him. The memory of a wildly
beating heart and sweetly tightening loins washed over him
now like a South Pacific breeze. Aye, the pleasurable feeling of having a warm female in his bed was not something
he'd forgotten—even after 140 years.

Ah, girl, if I were a mortal man . . . what I'd do to you now . . .

Wolfe observed the vivacious glow of her skin, the ringlets of auburn framing her face, the slender, delicate figure. His palms and fingers twitched at the sense memory of touching such a lovely young woman. How he burned to sweep the long curtain of curls from her curving neck, to brush a feathery kiss against the cream he'd expose there.

Wolfe could almost feel her slight shudder beneath him, the shallow breaths, the soft whimper of need for more of his touches, more of his kisses—

This is torture.

Wolfe moved across the room, away from her. Not a moment longer could he have this girl in his home. No, not girl, but woman—for no mere girl could boldly fight and flirtatiously reason as she had.

He had to secure her departure as soon as possible.

But how?

His old mode of haunting had not worked.

His old mode of reasoning had not worked.

Well, thought Wolfe, if the threat of a *dead* man could not scare her, perhaps the threat of the *living* part of him would.

Aye, she was bold and strong, but young. Likely inexperienced with men. And a vigorous display of Wolfe's manhood would surely put Little Red Riding Hood on that path toward home, where she belonged. All the captain had to do was play that role he knew so well: the part of the Big Bad Wolf.

A mischievous smile touched the captain's lips as he closed the distance between them. Then he spoke in a low, beguiling voice, his lips close to her ear.

"You say I am 'dead and gone,' but I am not dead," he growled. *"You see me. You hear me. I exist. I am not gone."*

The girl remained silent. Wolfe could hear her heart beating loudly as he began to circle her. He enjoyed her flushed face, her rapid breathing.

Aye, she's frightened now.

"And so, woman, if you are not gone from my home by sunset, all the better. For, come nightfall, I promise that I will not be the one who is sorry."

Wolfe's proximity became more ominous even as his voice became more seductive.

"Then stay, if that is your will. But be forewarned, there will be consequences. And know this, when I was a man, they called me Sea Wolf—for, as the ladies of my time well knew, my prowling spirit rose with the moon."

And with that, Wolfe was gone.

For minutes Miranda stood speechless in the center of the musty parlor.

She was stunned by the ghost's beguiling threat—and her own reaction to it. The truth was, Miranda had been expecting your average, standard haunting. Any expected frights the ghost might have thrown her way, she surely could have handled—flying vases, stomping feet, plaintive howling.

What Miranda had *not* been prepared for was a seduction.

"I've never heard of a sexy ghost," she whispered.

Miranda's first instinct, once her initial shock was gone, was to grab her things and flee. The town of Stonington was probably no more than a few miles from Blue Nights, and she could easily call Tina from there.

"And then what?" muttered Miranda.

Then she'd probably have to return to Crystal Breakers, her tail between her legs. Once her aunt Joan found out about the *Sea Sprite*'s part in her near-fatal escape, the woman would certainly sell it and Miranda would finally lose the most important tangible link to her late father.

Miranda shuddered at the thought of returning. The idea of facing humiliation, of having to live in a home where she didn't belong, to act as if she were part of a family who wanted her to change into someone she wasn't—it was all unthinkable.

No, thought Miranda. *The Sea Wolf is just trying to scare me. And I won't let him.*

"He's not even a man," Miranda reassured herself. "He's just a filmy puff of air in the shape of a man, that's all."

But, then, why was it this ghost man could send tremors of heat through her entire being?

When it came to the opposite sex, Miranda had to admit she was pretty much a complete novice. While some of the girls she'd known had weekly experiences with the hot and heavy stuff in the front seats of secondhand junkers, Miranda had never experienced more than friendly dates to the movies. A little kissing was about the extent of her real experience—although she'd often fantasized about much more.

Still, none of the innocent fumbling she'd ever experienced with young men her age had come even remotely close to setting off within her body the kind of explosive chain reaction the Sea Wolf had—and with nothing more than the use of his voice.

Then again, thought Miranda, his *voice* was the only thing that could invade her. The phrase "howling at the moon" came instantly to mind as she recalled the way her fists sailed right through his form.

"He can't even touch me! What the heck am I scared of anyway?" With a sigh, Miranda turned back to the musty parlor, determined to sweep it clean and air it out. It would be the first of these many rooms she'd make inhabitable.

"Fine, Sea Wolf, you go ahead and keep up your little act," murmured Miranda with a defiant smile. "I'll show you who's scared."

"Aye, now *she'll run back to her safe little bed,"* murmured Wolfe as he ascended the staircase.

By the time he'd reached his favorite lookout spot, Eric Wolfe expected to see the back of his guest's little red windbreaker as it flew away from his home.

Once he'd reached the attic, Wolfe crossed the small

room's floor to the antique telescope. Immediately, he
zoomed in on the bobbing sailboat. He adjusted the focus.

"*Where is she?*" he muttered.

Wolfe scanned the entire beach area. Then he gave up
and quickly circled around, peering into the loose forest
that had grown close to the front of his home. Sunlight
streamed down to the forest floor, but there was no sign
of a little red windbreaker moving through those trees.

In confusion, Wolfe drew his eye from the glass. He
rubbed his chin, perplexed. *Why has she not yet left?* he
wondered.

Descending the staircase, Wolfe wondered if she'd perhaps stumbled as she raced out the door. Perhaps she'd
twisted an ankle.

But when he reached the first floor, he found her—
exactly where he'd left her—in the parlor, back to her
industrious cleaning. She'd found a bucket, had torn the
furniture coverings into rags, and was now wiping down
the dusty parlor, including its grimy windows.

"*I'll be damned,*" whispered Wolfe, a mix of fury and
anticipation raging through his spirit.

There was only one thing to do now, thought Wolfe as
he watched the girl work. As promised, with the moon's
rising, the captain would have to make good on his threat.

Aye, time for the Sea Wolf to prowl once more.

Chapter Eight

CRYSTAL BREAKERS MANSION
SANDBRIDGE VILLAGE, CONNECTICUT

It was close to sunset when Tina Runyon's black sneakers squeaked through the freshly watered garden grass of Miranda's hated home. Quietly, she crept toward the open window.

Peeking her head above the bottom frame, Tina nearly gasped when she saw who was standing there. It was Emmitt Muldavey, one of the county's deputy sheriffs.

Tina was surprised that the law—if that's what you called Emmitt Muldavey—was involved already. She thought it would take more than *one* day before a person would be considered missing. At least, that's what the county sheriff's office had told her parents when her older sister had gone AWOL.

Of course, Miranda Burke wasn't Patty Runyon, some wild daughter of a "rounder" family. Miranda was the niece of an upstanding summer resident: Theodore Burke,

king of Pita Pockets fast food chain and major payer of
Sandbridge property taxes. When someone like that disappeared, the law would take notice a lot quicker.

Tina still couldn't believe Miranda had actually done
it. After all, Crystal Breakers was one of the most magnificent seaside homes in the village. Miranda's bedroom
alone was twice the size of the Runyons' shabby living
room.

Sure, Miranda claimed she was unhappy. But, sheesh!
Tina never would have let a little nagging from an over-
tanned country club queen drive her from the lap of this
kind of luxury.

"Mmmmmm." The overweight deputy sheriff mumbled as Joan Burke informed him of her niece's disappearance. The rope that was found and the clothes
missing. With one hand, he pulled up his ill-fitting tan
pants by the belt buckle, then scratched the back of his
thinning sand-colored hair, and finally spoke. "Well, now,
looks like you've got a runaway on your hands."

Tina rolled her eyes. *Another brilliant conclusion from
the town guard dog.* Everyone knew that Emmitt Muldavey had been little better than a big bully in high school
and he'd taken the sort of job that gave him a license to
continue his favorite pastime.

The law was never fairly applied in and around Sandbridge. If you were wealthy, or one of the rotten Muldavey tribe, the laws suddenly became as flexible as a
Ukrainian gymnast.

"We *know* we have a runaway on our hands," sniffed
Joan Cunning Burke. "What we *want* to know is what
you will be doing about it?"

"Well, you see, Mrs. Burke, the girl is twenty. She's
not a minor, so there's not much the law can do—"

"I don't care about the law. She's a missing person,
and we want her found. What if she didn't leave on her
own? What if she were abducted, kidnapped? I'm telling
you I'll make it worth your while if you find Miranda."

"But if she's left the area, my jurisdiction doesn't allow
for—"

"*You* take care of looking in this county, and *we'll* take care of looking beyond."

Tina noticed a look exchanged between Mrs. Burke and her preppy son, Josh Cunning. That morning Tina had seen Josh zooming around the village in his little red sports car. He'd put the top down and his golden hair was flying about in the wind. Tina sighed. The boy really was beautiful.

Sitting in the corner, talking on a cell phone, was a tall, distinguished-looking middle-aged man with neatly combed silver hair and a trimmed silver mustache. Tina recognized him as Theodore Burke, Miranda's uncle. He looked to his wife as he hung up the phone.

"Are we through here now?" asked Mr. Burke in a clipped, businesslike tone.

"Oh, yes, sir," Deputy Muldavey blurted out. "All through. I'll do my best to find your niece, sir, you can be sure of that. No problem. No problem."

"You do that," said Mr. Burke, and, after Muldavey had left, Theodore Burke turned to his wife. "I've hired the investigation agency my law firm recommended. And now that we've done all we can, I suggest we dress quickly. We're due at the yacht club for dinner."

"Yes, dear."

Joan Cunning Burke watched her husband leave, then turned to her son. "Josh, I'd like you to make some inquiries around the town."

"But why?"

"I hate to admit this to you, but Emmitt Muldavey is first cousin to your no-good father. And while he may be the law around here, and one of your relatives, he's clearly quite far from your equal in intellect. So I'd like you to help."

Josh nodded. "All right. I'll try."

"Good, now I'm off—"

"Wait a minute, Mother. I need more to go on here. Did Miranda show any signs of being unstable before this?"

Joan frowned. "Unstable? You're beginning to sound like a psychiatrist."

"I should hope so, Mother, I'm about to finish my graduate degree."

"Oh, yes, of course."

"A young woman doesn't run away from her family unless there are underlying psychological issues."

Joan nodded. "I suppose you're right. When we find her, do you think she should see a therapist?"

"At the very least," said Josh. "Perhaps even a stay at the hospital."

"Really? Do you think so?"

"Of course. She lost her father relatively recently. Perhaps she's having an episode. Can you tell me if she's been acting strangely."

"Well," said Joan after a moment, "she has been unnaturally difficult about a few things—that leaky boat of hers, for instance."

"A boat. Hmmmm." Josh paced a bit. "Would you say she was *fixated* on this boat. Obsessive about it?"

"Why . . . now that you put it that way, yes, I'd say so. I don't know why I didn't see it."

"Where did she keep it? At the yacht club?"

"No, Miranda hated the club. I think she kept it on the shabby side of town, a little grubby boatyard. Yet another reason I'd wanted it sold." Joan sighed. "You'll find it. Now, I'm sorry, but I must get ready for dinner—"

"Mother, please. I need more information. Did she have any friends?"

Joan shrugged. "I don't think so."

"Where did she generally hang out around town?"

Joan shrugged a second time. "I don't think she did."

"Mother, can't you give me more to go on?"

"More to go on?" Joan sighed. "Just this: If Miranda Burke gets herself knocked up by some piece of trailer trash, our best chance to keep her trust fund in the family is over. And that fund, Teddy tells me, is close to two million dollars. So I suggest you find her as soon as possible."

"Mother, are you once again implying what I think you're implying?"

"Oh, now, Josh, don't get defensive. My Teddy has me under a strict prenuptial agreement, so I can't very well help you financially, and your own father is in debt up to his Armani racing glasses. If you don't find a way to pay off that expensive education, and those other exorbitant debts of yours, you'll be living a rather lowly life in the next twenty years, even with a psychiatrist's salary. That's not what I ever wanted for my son. So, please take Mother's advice, find Miranda, sweep in like a knight in shining armor, and keep her money in the family—"

"But I don't even know if I like the girl!"

"Like? What's not to like, Josh? She's smart, she's young, she's . . . somewhat attractive—"

"Mother, please stop."

"Fine. But it's just as easy to make a bad marriage with a poor girl as a rich one. And Miranda, unlike every other wealthy girl you'll meet, no longer has a living parent who might object to a son-in-law with debts as vast as the Grand Canyon. So think about it, that's all I ask."

Josh sighed as his mother left, and from outside the window, Tina's eyes widened. The young man looked distraught by the conversation that had just taken place. He began to pace the room, then he rubbed his neck, and finally collapsed into a chair and buried his face in his hands.

Tina decided that she hadn't given Miranda nearly enough credit. Joan Cunning Burke wasn't just some nag. She was a monster. How dare she try to push her son into a marriage he obviously didn't want.

Tina's heart went out to Josh. He seemed so vulnerable sitting there with his head in his hands. All she wanted to do was climb in the window and hug him close.

A sharp noise sounded nearby—the sheriff's car door closing—and Tina nearly jumped out of her black sneakers. With care she withdrew from Crystal Breakers, an idea forming in her head.

Chapter
Nine

BLUE NIGHTS COTTAGE

From an old rocking chair on the rickety wooden porch, Miranda finished her dinner and decided that her simple peanut butter sandwich tasted better than any of the gourmet meals Chef Raymond had prepared back at Crystal Breakers.

It was the freedom that made it taste so wonderful, she decided, and the feeling of being in a place she was making her own. Yes, her hands were dishpanned, and her limbs sore, but her fatigue was oddly satisfying—in fact, it reminded her of something her dad used to say after late nights working on his seafarer's notebooks. *Miranda, there's nothing like the kind of tired that comes when you're working toward something that matters to you.*

She never understood her father's words more than at this moment, watching the vibrant colors of sunset unfold over a place like Blue Nights—a house full of history and character . . . not to mention an especially intriguing spirit.

The idea that she was sharing her new home with a ghost was privately thrilling to Miranda, and, despite his obvious ill humor that morning, she was looking forward to their next encounter.

She'd tried to discover more about the ghost by going through the things on the first floor. But most of the items were not original to the house—not surprising with a home this old. Yet, Miranda gathered from her encounters thus far that the ghost had been a seaman, and from his bossy nature, clearly a *captain*.

She would try to find out more at his next appearance. She sighed with fluttery anticipation, wondering when that would be. She hated to admit it, but deep down she was actually a little infatuated with the handsome spirit.

The day had been a little lonely after the captain had gone, but she'd kept herself busy enough, managing to wipe down, de-mustify, and air out the parlor of Blue Nights quite efficiently.

So, shelter is taken care of, thought Miranda as she washed down her sticky sandwich with the thermos cup of milk in her hands. Tomorrow she'd work on cleaning up the kitchen and then she'd begin to think about the remaining basics—like food and money.

For the moment, food was taken care of. Tonight's dinner had come compliments of the Burkes' pantry and her own bit of shopping at a convenience store back in Sandbridge. The food, however, wouldn't last her much more than two weeks. By then she'd have to figure out how to find more. She had every confidence she would.

She rose and stepped across the rickety porch floorboards, then hugged one of the vertical posts. Surveying the blue rippling of Crescent Cove, she smiled, closed her eyes, and inhaled the fresh sea air. It smelled different at Blue Nights. All the lush greenery seemed to make the air sweeter than anywhere on earth she'd been before.

"This is so peaceful, so beautiful, I never want to leave. . . ."

For the first time since her father died, Miranda's spirit felt unfettered. No more nagging voices belittling her. No more lawyers dictating where and how she had to live. No more threats and manipulations to change who and what she was to please someone else.

"I've just got to make better friends with the ghost who lives here," she whispered.

Miranda just wished she could get the threatening words of the ghost out of her head—and most especially, the seductive way he'd said them. The fact was, she was there now. To stay. At least for the summer anyway— and he'd just have to get used to the idea.

The sun was setting quickly into gathering clouds, and Miranda headed toward the lapping waves of the cove. A slight nervous thrill was making her feel restless. After all, the ghost did claim he would return when the moon rose.

The anxiety alone prompted her into pacing along the beach. Stretching her legs was exactly what she needed, though she didn't have much time to do so. As a gust of damp wind touched her cheek, Miranda realized twilight was swiftly sailing into Blue Nights and—from the smell of things—a storm was coming.

"Blast . . ." whispered Wolfe from his perch atop the house. He could not tear his gaze from the long-limbed silhouette of the girl as she strode along his rocky shoreline.

When he'd first caught sight of her, walking away from Blue Nights, Wolfe had held out one last hope that she was heading for her boat before night fell. But he quickly saw that she was simply taking in the last breath of day, enjoying a sunset walk along his beach the way he had as a living man.

Watching her, Wolfe could almost recall the smells in the air at this time of year—the pine, honeysuckle, and wild mint in the nearby forest, all mingling with the salty freshness of the sea air. He closed his eyes and found himself attempting to inhale.

But it was no use, he no longer had lungs. Even on the sea his sense of smell had never returned to him.

The thought angered him. *"Mortals are a curse to me,"* he muttered. Their presence only reminded Wolfe of what he was not. He had forgotten how much unhappy regret and resentment they stirred in his spirit.

Wolfe gazed again at the girl while the sun slowly set. As twilight slipped over the beach, she turned and headed back toward his home with an annoyingly determined stride.

I don't understand it. I warned the girl, thought Wolfe as he spied the rising moon. *Perhaps she thinks I'm bluffing.*

Regardless of what she thought of Wolfe, however, the girl claimed she was a free and independent thinker—and her choice was clear enough: She meant to stay this night.

Thus, Wolfe was left with no choice.

He'd simply have to prove that his threat was real. The Sea Wolf *would* come prowling. And by morning he should certainly be rid of her.

As the evening light darkened, so did Miranda's worries. In the bright hours of sunshine, courage had been easy to maintain. By the limited glow of her camper's lantern, however, she discovered it was a fleeting commodity.

After changing into her nightclothes—an oversized white T-shirt and a loose pair of old gray gym shorts—she tried to distract herself by settling in on the parlor's old sofa and reading one of her father's notebooks.

This one was a book of old sea chanteys. Sadly, her father had barely begun collecting these—for there were only about fifteen, and it had been his dream to collect a whole book of them. Nevertheless, Miranda began to read. She'd barely begun, when a sharp creaking board on the staircase made her nearly jump out of her skin.

"Hello there?" she called weakly.

The darkness loomed around her. She peered into its silent stillness, trying to make out something other than the dim lumps she knew to be deteriorating pieces of once-fine furniture. Beyond the faint glow of her camper's

lantern, however, she saw nothing—certainly no shape
that even vaguely resembled the handsome ghost captain
who had called himself a sea wolf—and yet she felt
strongly that something was there.

Watching her.

Miranda swallowed nervously and tried to turn her attention back to her father's notebook. After she read the
same sentence five times, she shut the book.

"I've got to distract myself," she whispered softly, deciding the best course of action was to find a way to relax
and fall asleep.

Leaning forward, she placed the notebook on the floor
and fished a hand in her backpack for something to distract her. When her fingers closed around a slim, hard
handle, she pulled. It was her hairbrush, the perfect way
to relax, she decided.

Slowly, by the light of the camper's lantern, she began
to brush her long curls, counting softly to herself with
each stroke. At stroke number fifty-six, she yawned,
happy that her idea was working its magic. Soon she'd
be tired enough to lie down on the sofa and fall asleep.

Suddenly, a sharp rapping sound came from inside the
room. Miranda stilled, the brush in mid-stroke. *It's the
ghost, it has to be,* she thought as an ice-cold shiver
skimmed over her bare legs like a chilly evening breeze.

"A little cool tonight, don't you think?" she called out
nervously, hoping she could strike up a congenial conversation with the ghost, the kind they'd had the first time
they'd met.

Silence met her ears.

"Fine," she snapped. "Don't answer. Be rude—"

Out of the darkness, a thin, musty blanket was thrown
over her bare feet. Miranda gasped. Her brush slipped
from her fingers and clattered to the floor.

"Thanks," she squeaked, desperately trying to hold off
her swelling panic. "A little musty though. Guess you
don't have Maytag washers in the afterlife, huh?"

That's when she felt the blanket begin to move. She bit
her cheek to keep from crying out. She could see no

hands, no arms, and yet the blanket was moving slowly—
so very slowly—up her bare legs.

Show no fear, she commanded herself. *If he sees he
can't scare you, then he'll stop.*

Swallowing uneasily, Miranda watched the blanket's
ascent from her ankles to her shins, then from her shins
to her knees. Finally, it inched slowly up her thighs.

Frozen still, Miranda couldn't help but feel the ticklish
intimacy of the act. The very idea made her heart race
once more, but this time in a different way.

This ghost had just that morning called himself a wolf.
He was watching her like one now, realized Miranda,
stalking her like prey—and he was making the blanket
move in a ticklish way that reminded her of a feathery
touch.

In an instant, Miranda realized she'd made a terrible
error in judgment. While she'd assumed the ghost himself
could not touch her with his own hands, he could obviously touch her in *other* ways.

In one frantic movement, Miranda tore the blanket from
her legs and threw it to the floor.

"Stop it," she commanded. "Right now!"

A low, deep rumbling sounded. The timbre and power
of it reminded Miranda of distant thunder, and yet it
seemed to be more than that.

She glanced out the window to find the night had become misty, the air heavy and damp. Gusts of wind were
coming in off the ocean, and Miranda remembered what
she'd guessed at sunset, that another storm was heading
her way.

I'm trapped, she realized. Fleeing into the night now
meant fleeing into a storm—insanity on the water, stupid-
ity on the land.

A second deep rumbling rolled through the room, and,
despite the signs of coming rain, Miranda knew the sound
was not thunder. It was *laughter.* An otherworldly laughter, something that did not come from a mortal, but came
as a force of nature.

"Where are you?" she demanded. "Show yourself! Or are you afraid?"

"Not as afraid as you," murmured the Sea Wolf in a deep voice that seemed to resonate all around her. If it had come from one corner or another, she might have kept her head. But it seemed to come from nowhere and everywhere at once—the eerie nature of it stripped her nerves raw.

"You're not scaring me!" she shrieked to the blackest shadows in the room.

Laughter came again. *"You're a pitiful liar, girl."*

Miranda's face flushed red with anger. "Stop laughing!" she shouted, but he did not, so Miranda leaped to her feet and grabbed the lantern.

"Where are you, ghost?" she demanded again. "Show yourself!"

The laughter died off as Miranda began to move through the room, thrusting the light before her like a medieval sword. This way and that she cast the lantern, first toward the staircase, then toward the back door, then near the passage to the kitchen.

As she rounded the room, her skin prickled. She knew he was there, she knew it! She just had to locate his arrogant, laughing image, then she'd chew his ear off—or whatever he had instead of an ear—and demand that he leave her alone!

Miranda thrust the lantern into the last dark corner, but it was empty, then she turned, stepped forward, and stopped dead.

The edge of the light illuminated a pair of strong arms folded across a broad chest. Gathering her courage, she took a step closer and raised the lantern.

There, next to the fireplace, the Sea Wolf's form stood. His image was magnificent, powerful, and as stunningly imperious as ever. A black cable-knit sweater covered a broad chest; black slacks covered his long legs, and, his face was just as strong and handsome as she remembered—and just as hard and fierce.

The ghost's expression was menacing; his blue eyes

shimmered through the dark and his posture was rigid as iron, as if he were about to brace himself against the sea's deadliest gales.

In the face of such a presence, Miranda suddenly lost her tongue. Yet, she still had her wits. She began to talk to herself, trying to calm down and think logically, as her father had taught her during her many sailing lessons. *Miranda, in the face of fear, don't panic. Find a solution.*

A solution . . . a solution, thought Miranda. She needed to make friends with him. But how?

Talk, she quickly decided. She needed to get this former sea captain to converse with her as he had last night and again this morning.

Miranda's first words were raspy, but she did her best to sound unafraid. "S-so, you s-said you were called Sea Wolf? Why is that exactly?"

The ghost did not answer her. Instead, he slowly moved forward. Miranda automatically stepped back. The ghost arched an eyebrow and moved forward again. Once more, Miranda stepped back.

"What is the matter, Red?" the ghost finally murmured, stepping forward yet again. *"Did you not say you were unafraid?"*

"My name's not Red," challenged Miranda, moving back.

"Ah, but it is."

"Why, because of my hair?"

"No, because, wearing your red hooded jacket, you've dared to come with your little basket to a place in the woods where you don't belong."

Miranda's eyes narrowed. "That's not funny."

In the distance came another rumble. For a moment she thought the ghost was laughing at her again, but as the sound grew, she realized it truly was nature—the distant thunder as the sea's storm swept closer.

Then, like the storm, the ghost moved closer too.

Miranda stepped away.

"Why run from me?" taunted the ghost. *"If you're not*

Little Red Riding Hood, then you shouldn't be afraid of a wolf.''

"J-just keep your distance, okay—"

But the ghost wasn't taking any orders from her—not to mention a stammered suggestion. The ghost moved closer still, and this time Miranda found herself bumping back against a flat, hard surface.

"Oh," she murmured.

Without hesitation, the ghost moved to block her, and Miranda instantly saw she'd been trapped into a corner of the room.

He was tall, she realized, a good ten inches above her five-foot-four-inch height. She tilted her head back to look into his face. The deep blue eyes were staring straight at her with an intensity that made her legs feel weak.

"I'm not leaving here," Miranda said defensively. "I told you this morning, I'm staying and—"

"And I told you this morning," interrupted the ghost, *"that if I found you in my house tonight, there would be consequences.''*

Miranda licked her lips. Her breathing had long ago become rapid, and a dampness now slickened her palms. Thunder rumbled and she felt her heart race. "What kind of . . . consequences?"

The ghost's lips curled slightly, seemingly happy she'd asked, which made her instantly sorry she had. All of a sudden, Miranda felt the need to flee.

"Please move back," she rasped.

"Why?''

"B-because I feel trapped here."

"On land, I've no substance," whispered the ghost. *"If you think yourself trapped, then simply walk through me.''*

Miranda stared at the ghost. She believed what he was saying, yet a part of her was suspicious. "What will happen if I walk through you?"

The ghost smirked. *"Find out. Or are you—''*

"I told you! I'm not afraid!"

"Then prove it.''

Miranda took a deep breath and inched forward. Only to quickly jerk back. "Please, just move."

This time the ghost did laugh. *"You* are *afraid, girl. Admit it, and be gone with you from my home."*

Miranda felt her lower lip tremble. She was instantly angry at herself for showing him any weakness, but the ghost's challenge left her with a difficult decision. She stared at the broad chest in front of her, recalling how she'd put her fingers through it the night before.

Just step forward, Miranda. Close your eyes and do it!

Walking through him should have been easy as pie. But she simply could not do it. The Sea Wolf's chest looked so solid—and the ghost's nearness felt so menacing. All Miranda could do was stand paralyzed before him, her aqua eyes wide.

Thunder rumbled again, and Miranda looked up to meet the ghost's hard blue gaze. As she did, she was surprised to see his expression slowly change.

His cold eyes warmed in the lantern's low light. And then his rugged, handsome face began to bend toward her. *"Hang me,"* whispered the Sea Wolf.

Miranda's jaw slackened. A part of her was alarmed, knowing it was madness for a ghost to kiss her; yet another part saw this magnificent, fearless sea captain bending forward and reacted with sheer girlish infatuation. It was that part of her that allowed her head to tilt toward his, her lips to gently open.

The sea captain's ghostly lips appeared full and soft and Miranda wondered how they'd feel, how they'd taste. They came closer and closer and then they were touching her own—but there was no sense of a touch. All she could feel was an eerie ticklish tingling against her mouth.

The shock of feeling no substance to his kiss sent a quiver of panic through Miranda's heart. Before she could think what she was doing she launched herself forward, right through his body. In the next moment she was stumbling, stunned and shaken, out the other side.

Chapter Ten

What in the name of heaven just happened? thought Wolfe in shock as he turned to see the girl tumbling to the sofa. He himself felt just as surprised as she looked, just as unsteady and weakened.

The kiss had not been planned. Wolfe's only aim tonight had been to intimidate and frighten the girl out of his home for good. And it seemed as though it had been working too—until he'd looked down into her lovely face.

She'd appeared to be so vulnerable and so sweet, like a blasted sea nymph. And, like a mysterious sea creature, she'd bewitched him, mesmerized him into thinking for an *insane* moment that he was still flesh and blood.

This sort of thing had never happened to him before. On occasion he had felt the memory of his mortality rise within him, but he had never completely forgotten what he was.

She'd done that to him, tricked his spirit's mortal memory into taking command, and in the next instant Wolfe had found his hard intent softening, his stiff posture bending. All of a sudden he'd yearned simply to taste her.

I must have gone daft, thought Wolfe. *I no longer have the ability to taste, or touch, or kiss!*

It had not been his plan, but he had done it anyway, in a moment of madness. And then it seemed she had launched herself through him.

"Wh-what happened?" the girl suddenly stammered from the sofa.

Wolfe turned. The girl still looked shaken. About as shaken as he felt.

"*You passed through me,*" Wolfe snapped angrily. "*Was that not apparent enough?*"

Wolfe could see that his tone had disturbed the girl, but the experience had unnerved him; and, as the captain had learned long ago at sea, feelings of fright were best met with a good dose of fury.

"But . . ."

"*Belay further questions,*" pronounced Wolfe. The girl stared up at him soberly, as if hurt by his harshness. Wolfe immediately felt guilty and begrudgingly added in a slightly softer voice: "*For the moment, if you please.*"

Then he looked away, into the cold, barren hearth. He needed time to think. After all, he was still recovering himself.

Mortals have passed through me before, reasoned Wolfe, *many times. But never have I experienced more than a slight ticklish tingling.*

With this girl, he'd felt much more than a mere mortal passing through him. It was the difference between a candle flame and a raging inferno, a heat that seemed powerful enough to burn down a house.

Such a life energy was something Wolfe had never before encountered. And it stunned him. The act had granted an intimate connection, like an embrace of many dimensions.

He could not recall feeling anything quite like it before—in his life or his afterlife. And it made him feel strongly that she was more than just another mortal and her life energy was somehow very special to him.

Wolfe turned to study the girl on the sofa, now staring in thought at the glowing lantern she'd placed on the floor.

"Did you feel what I felt?" whispered the girl, looking abruptly up, straight into his eyes.

Wolfe weighed his answer. *First she hears me as a living man; then she sees me as a living man; and now she makes me feel as if I am alive.*

A part of Wolfe was deeply touched—while another part of him was reeling at the entire idea. His afterlife was set and settled—just as his own seafarer's life had been before it had ended.

Wolfe did not want change.

And he would not welcome it.

"I felt . . . nothing," lied Wolfe in answer.

The girl blinked and looked away. "Oh," she said softly. "Excuse me, then, if I . . . offended you . . . or anything, you know, by walking through you."

Wolfe cursed himself. *"You did not offend me, girl."*

"Good. I mean, you did *dare* me to walk through you, you know?"

"Aye, girl, I did."

"It's *Miranda.*"

"What's that?"

"My name. It isn't *girl,* and it isn't *Red.* It's *Miranda.*"

Wolfe's expression softened. He liked discovering her name.

"Miranda," he whispered in a low, musical voice that seemed to please her. *"Admired Miranda,"* he murmured from memory, *"the top of admiration's worth. What's dearest to the world."*

"You know *The Tempest!*"

Wolfe's eyebrow arched. *"You needn't sound so amazed. Reading's a common enough pastime during off watches, and Shakespeare's been around since the sixteenth century. I have not been dead as long as that."*

"Yes," said Miranda, "sorry." Then she laughed. It was a light, fluttering sound that reminded Wolfe of wind through his topsails.

"I take it you were named for the character in the play?"

Miranda nodded. "It was my father's favorite."

"Was?"

"He's dead." There was a long pause as Miranda considered her next words. "I was wondering. Would you know how to—to—"

"Contact him?" guessed Wolfe. Why was it all mortals thought being dead was like joining a damned gaming club?

"Yes," said Miranda.

"Miss, it does not follow that because he is no longer living, and I am no longer living, that I should therefore know of his whereabouts."

Miranda's brow furrowed. "Why not?"

"Because being dead does not win one some sort of membership entry on a society roster. I assure you there is no afterlife registry."

"Well, can't you give me a general idea?"

Wolfe tried to keep his temper. *"My good woman, as near as I can tell, spirits of the living, such as your father, pass on directly to heaven."*

"But . . . how do you know? I mean, look at you. Why are you—"

"I was a rare case. Near my death, my spirit was committed to the sea. And so I serve her."

"Serve her how? I don't understand."

"Nor should you. Such matters are not for the living, which is why I want you to leave my place of rest."

Miranda was silent a long time. Wolfe could see the sadness on her face, the painful signs of loss and rejection. He did not enjoy the sight.

"Girl—" he started crisply, then something inside him stopped his next words. He moved closer, hunched down to her level on the sofa, and began again.

"Miranda . . ." he whispered, and when he spoke this time, his voice was soft, his compassion apparent. *"Why is it one so young and alive should wish to stay in a place for the dead?"*

"I don't think of this place like that," she said. "From the first time I saw Blue Nights, I wanted to live here. I felt that it wanted me here, needed me here. You see, outside of Blue Nights, I don't belong anywhere. Nobody needs me or wants me," Miranda finished with a shrug. "Not anymore."

Wolfe's spirit felt heavy at Miranda's sad confession—at the unflinching way she'd accepted her fate. Not for the first time, she reminded him of himself.

"An orphan, are you?" he asked softly.

Miranda nodded.

"Like I was as a boy."

Miranda's eyes widened with hope. "Then you understand?"

"I suppose I do," said Wolfe after a moment's contemplation. *"I had a ship once that made me feel as you do about Blue Nights."*

"A ship?"

" 'Twas long before the Windward. *I was first mate aboard a coastal schooner when I was given the chance to captain a brig. 'Twas my first chance to captain, and I took it. But she was barely seaworthy, having come from a punishing voyage at the lip of the Antarctica and back. Her spars were weakened, her helm a wreck, and the fo'c'sle was a blasted mess. But there was something about her that made me want her more than a spanking new vessel. Something that called out to me. That said she needed me to captain her.*

"I took on a crew, cleaned her up, and sailed her twice around the world. To this day I'm convinced she sailed agreeably for me because she knew how much faith I'd put in her."

Miranda's sad expression began to lift at his story, and Wolfe could not help but feel cheered at the sight.

"I knew you were a sea captain," said Miranda. "But I didn't know what you'd sailed. What's your name?"

Wolfe hesitated.

"Oh, c'mon. It can't hurt to tell me your name," coaxed Miranda. "Please?"

Wolfe sighed. *"Eric,"* he said softly. *"Eric Wolfe, late captain of the clipper* Windward.*"*

"A *clipper* captain," said Miranda with clear awe, "the fastest sailing vessels of their time. My father used to say that there isn't a sailor alive who knows a fraction of what clipper men knew about riding the wind and the waves."

Wolfe shifted under the blushing compliment. *"Well . . ."* he managed to say. *"I'm not one to disagree with a wise man like you father."*

Miranda smiled. "Thanks."

"You're quite welcome."

"And your name is *Eric*." She said his name slowly, as if trying a word in another language. "Eric Wolfe."

Wolfe liked the tender, careful way she'd said his name. He could not stop the small smile from brightening his face.

"So we can be friends now," said Miranda. "And I can stay here with you."

Wolfe's smile vanished. He rose to his full height, folded his arms, and stared down at her. *"I did not say you could stay."*

"But you understand me," pleaded Miranda as she rose to face him. "You just said you knew how I felt."

Wolfe turned from Miranda and began to pace in thought. *"Aye,"* he said. *"You seem harmless enough. But you are also disturbing my peace. And the idea that you can hear me, and see me, and—"*

Wolfe stopped and stared at the girl. He would not tell her how else she affected him—how she seemed to possess the power to make him forget he was a ghost; to make him feel alive. To make him feel things that he hadn't since he'd been a flesh-and-blood man.

That was what disturbed him most.

"What if I stay out of your way?" suggested Miranda, stepping up to him.

Wolfe swiftly moved back, determined *not* to become bewitched again. *"How will you do that?"*

"We'll make a deal. I'll stay on the first floor and you

stay on the upper floors. That way, you can have your privacy.''

Wolfe paced the room as he used to pace his decks, his hands clasped behind him, his brow knit, his jaw working.

"A bargain?" he asked, finally turning to face her. *"Is that what you propose?"*

"An arrangement. We'll be . . . house mates.''

"Like shipmates, but in a house?"

Miranda nodded.

Wolfe thought about this another moment. *"I suppose I can agree. But . . ."*

"But?"

"Every ship must have a captain."

Miranda stared at him. "This isn't a ship. It's a house."

"Every ship must have a captain," stated Wolfe again, ignoring Miranda's attempt at logic. *"And I am the captain of Blue Nights. You must agree to this. And, while you are here, you must therefore do what I command."*

Miranda sat back down on the sofa, looking a bit peeved. "But I just left a house where all they did was tell me what to do!" she exclaimed. She met his gaze. "I don't like being told what do to.''

"Then you're of no use to a well-run ship. And you've no business on one. So you'd better shove off."

"But—"

"You must do as I command," stated the ghost again, *"or else change your living arrangements."*

Miranda's blue-green eyes burned bright with contrary fire, and Wolfe could not help but be amused at her attractive vexation. But, he had to admit, he was also impressed by the bold strength of her will.

Wolfe himself had balked at orders in his foolish youthful days—he was only too happy that this lovely girl before him would never have to take the shipboard floggings he'd endured to bring him to maturity.

"I'll not argue further," said Wolfe crisply. *"You've heard my terms. Abide by them and stay, or shove off at day's light. 'Tis your decision."*

And, then, taking one last long look at her bright eyes

and furious expression, Eric Wolfe slipped back into the
shadows of the room.

Miranda wasn't ready for the ghost's abrupt vanishing
act. It was a tad disturbing, to say the least.

"Come back here!" she demanded. "I'm not through
arguing yet!"

She waited for the ghost's return, but he didn't. Silent
stillness was her only response, and then thunder rumbled
through the cove and the rain began to beat against the
walls of the house.

The chilly storm and lonely darkness sent a shiver
through her form. Goose bumps appeared on her bare
skin, and she wrapped her arms around herself.

"Captain Wolfe," she called, this time with more hope
than anger. But there was still no answer.

"Fine," she grumbled, refusing to plead with him. "Go
on and be a stubborn tyrant, see if I care!"

Miranda spied her hairbrush on the floor and picked it
up. Brushing her hair had dispelled her tension before the
ghost came, and she supposed it would do the trick again.

By the light of the lantern she began her agitated brushing, counting each stroke as she went. "One, two, three,
four . . ."

Miranda sighed. She knew she had no choice. She'd
have to accept the ghost's terms. She just didn't want him
to know that.

From cover of shadow Wolfe leaned against the staircase rail. He observed the girl brushing her hair, and became unwillingly entranced. It was hard not to be.

In the glow of the small lantern, her lovely mahogany
tresses shimmered with a vibrant fire. It reminded him
how they'd looked just a few hours before, in the last
crimson light of sunset, trailing down her back like a blazing colt's mane, alive with the same burning light that he
now knew lived in the girl's heart and soul.

For a moment Wolfe considered how pleasing and
beautiful it was to see something so very alive in his

home. And in that moment he forgot how tormenting such sights were to him, how they reminded him of his pathetic state.

Suddenly the bewitching urge came again, the strong desire to act as a man. How he wanted to reach out and touch those soft curls.

To touch. Ah, to touch . . .

How he missed the tactile sensitivity of a living man's fingertips. Though the sea granted him materialization on the water, his sense of touch was severely muted compared to a mortal's.

Wolfe bent his head to consider his ghostly hands. They appeared as they had in life, large and strong and callused. He wondered, in retrospect, how sensitive his hands actually had been. For as long as he could remember, he'd had those calluses—ever since he'd come aboard his first sailing vessel as a young mate.

He still remembered the cutting pain of hauling rope, the punishing burn of wind and salt as he swabbed the decks, the streaks of rawness, the blood mingling with sweat. Soon enough, though, his tender skin had thickened.

Along with his emotional hide.

He'd grown a callous over his soul, and over his heart, he realized now. It had been necessary to live with the sea, to survive under her harsh tyrannies, her fickle cruelties. But it had robbed him of home and family, of marriage and love.

In this moment, however, watching the girl's lovely hair cascade in the low light, Wolfe found his spirit yearning not for hardness, but for softness. For a way to reach out and touch the girl who steadfastly refused to be driven from his home.

Perhaps there is a way to touch her after all, decided Wolfe. *Just one small way of saying good night.*

"Ninety-eight, ninety-nine, one hundred," Miranda murmured, then yawned and dropped her hairbrush back into her backpack.

As the rain continued to pour, and wind howled, she remembered the blanket. She wouldn't mind having it now, with the storm bringing a stiff chill to the air.

Leaning forward, she reached down to grab it out of the shadows, where she'd flung it before. But it was no longer there. She snatched up the lantern and cast light in the area around the sofa. But there was no blanket to be found.

Exhaling in frustration, Miranda finally gave up. After blowing out the lantern, she stretched out on the sofa, trying to ignore the chill on her bare legs by watching the lantern's pearl-gray thread of smoke dissipate on its way toward the ceiling.

Drawing her knees up and yawning, she let her eyes fall closed, and had nearly drifted to sleep, when she felt a feathery touch on her legs.

It's him, she thought as streaks of panic and excitement twined together and raced through her bloodstream. Miranda lay still, squeezing her eyes shut, bracing herself for whatever would happen next.

As it had before, the touch moved from her ankles to her shins, to her knees. Then it moved higher still, over her thighs, then over her hips and torso and shoulders.

Suddenly, she realized, the chill was gone, and Miranda opened her eyes to find herself snugly covered with a soft, thick blanket. It was much warmer than the musty, threadbare one she'd been searching for earlier.

Miranda waited for him to speak or show himself, but there was only silence. She peered into the looming dark, but saw nothing more than lumpy shadows.

"Thanks, Captain Wolfe," she whispered into the murky room.

She was nearly asleep again when she thought she heard a low deep voice murmur, *"Good night, Miranda."*

The words floated upward and, like the thin stream of smoke from the extinguished lantern, seemed to eerily dissolve, particle by particle, into the night.

Chapter Eleven

"Hang me!" cursed Eric Wolfe the following morning.

When he'd made the deal with the little wench the night before, he'd never imagined she'd be capable of making such a racket.

"How can one silly girl make more noise than a crew full of swabbies!"

Peace in his own home was all he wanted, but from the crack of that morning's sunny dawn, he'd been plagued by the sounds of the girl's industrious cleaning.

It vexed him in the extreme.

For hours he'd paced the second floor, moving from bedroom to bedroom, refusing to descend to the first floor and appear to her. He didn't want to face the tumult of emotions she was capable of creating in him, at least not this early in the day.

So, he moved up to his small, glass-walled attic, where he'd been surveying the cove's waters ever since. At least up there he didn't have to put up with all the damned banging and rattling down below—though he could still hear faint echoes of it, even from his high perch.

Gazing out at sea, a dark speck suddenly caught Wolfe's eye. The black form on the blue sea sent an icy chill through the ghostly captain. It was a chill he had not felt around these waters in a decade.

Moving to the glass, he focused the lens, trying better to make out the sighting, but the tiny black dot moved away before he could gain a better view of it.

Wolfe pulled his gaze away, feeling disturbed.

Could he have glimpsed one of the devil's dark ships? He hoped not.

A devil's ship could wreak havoc in any waters it plied. A ghost ship like the *Windward* would be the only hope for poor mortal sailors if a devil's ship chose to cause its brand of deadly maritime mischief.

Just to be sure his crew was warned, Wolfe closed his eyes and reached out with his power, sending out a ghostly message to his *Windward*.

Wolfe was about to return to his glass, when he became aware of Miranda's voice two floors below, floating up the staircase as clearly as a ship's bell. Was she calling him? he wondered, and cocked an ear.

" 'Farewell and adieu to you fair Spanish ladies/Farewell and adieu to you ladies of Spain . . .' "

"What in blazes?" muttered Wolfe.

" 'For we've receiv'd orders to sail back to England/But hope in a short time to see you again.' "

Good God, thought Wolfe, she wasn't calling him. She was *singing*. And singing a sea chantey at that! Well, this was the last straw!

Wolfe turned from his telescope and launched himself at the staircase. In no time he'd descended to the first floor, flew across the parlor, and burst into the kitchen.

" 'Oh, we'll rant and we'll rove all o'er the wild ocean—' "

"What in the devil do you think you're doing?" boomed Wolfe.

Miranda barely glanced up from her work swabbing the countertops. " 'Oh, we'll rant and we'll rove o'er all the wild seas—' '' she continued without missing a beat.

"Did you not hear me, girl?"

" 'Until we strike soundings in the channel o' England/ From the U-shant to Scilly is thirty-four leagues.' "

Miranda grinned. "What's the matter? Am I off key?"

"You're off your nut."

"I'm just singing a chantey. Heavens, you act as though you'd never heard one before."

"Not from the mouth of a female."

"Don't be a chauvinist."

"A what?"

Miranda's brow furrowed. "You don't know what a chauvinist is?"

"I know what a silly wench is, for I'm spying one now."

He was also spying a terribly adorable one. In ragged shorts and a dirty, oversized shirt, Miranda looked like a bonny pixie pirate, with her auburn hair pinned up and a red kerchief tied jauntily over it.

Her sea-colored eyes were bright, her cheeks flushed, and her voice as spirited as wind and wave. She reminded Wolfe of a sunny day's sail, and his blue eyes glittered in appreciation.

"A chauvinist *thinks* himself superior to the opposite sex," Miranda informed him.

Wolfe folded his arms across his chest. *"Then he's a sound-minded male, to be sure."*

"A pigheaded male, you mean. A woman can do as good a job as a man."

Wolfe saw this argument as pointless—besides which, he wasn't about to admit to her that the first day he'd seen her he'd assumed that her excellent sailing ability was that of a man's. So, he simply changed the subject.

"Regardless, I'll not have sea chanteys sung at Blue Nights—period. Why in blazes do you think I come to land? For peace and quiet!"

"I'll sing more quietly, how about that?"

"Not if it's sea chanteys, you won't."

"But I like them. My father collected at least a dozen,

and I've learned them all," said Miranda with clear self-satisfaction in her voice.

Wolfe raised an eyebrow at the obvious pride the girl put into her little achievement. He had to force himself to keep from laughing.

"What?" asked Miranda, seeing she'd said something that was obviously amusing.

Wolfe shook his head and waved her off. *"Ah, never you mind."*

"No, I want to know what's so funny. Tell me!"

"So be it. You act as though learning a dozen chanteys is some kind of feat. But there are hundreds *of chanteys, girl. My men knew at least as many among them."*

Miranda's eyes widened. "Hundreds?" She nearly choked on the word. "I knew there were a lot . . . my father said so . . . he was collecting them when he died. But *hundreds*?"

"Aye."

"Imagine how many were lost to the maritime historians," murmured Miranda.

"No matter," said Wolfe. *"They were useful to the men when they needed them. Time keeps what it needs and discards what it has no further use of."*

"I don't believe that at all. What's lost to the world is the world's loss—that's what my father used to say."

"Ah," said Wolfe, considering the philosophy. *"I like that. Your father was a very wise man."*

Miranda smiled slyly. "He was quoting my mother."

"Your mother?"

"She was a better historian than my father. He said so all the time."

Wolfe's eyes narrowed. *"You're a clever one."*

"Yes," said Miranda, "and probably no less clever than you."

Wolfe chuckled softly. He refused to agree with her, but he wasn't about to disagree either. Instead, he turned his attention to the room where he now stood. The Blue Nights kitchen had been a dirty mess of cobwebs the last time he'd passed through it.

As he surveyed the run-down kitchen, all cleaned and mopped and polished, he had to admit the girl was a hard worker.

"Everything shipshape and Bristol fashion, Captain?" asked Miranda, observing where his attention had strayed. "As good a job as one of your crew*men* would do?"

"Aye," said Wolfe. *"But don't let it go to your head."*

Then he gave her a wink and exited the kitchen. He was almost to the cottage's back door when he heard her voice again.

" 'Many thousand miles behind us/Many thousand miles before,' " sang Miranda. " 'Ancient ocean heaves to waft us/To the well-remembered shore.' "

Wolfe stopped cold and turned in fury, unable to believe she would so boldly defy his direct order. He burst through the kitchen doorway, ready to cut loose a string of curses, when she met the fire in his blue gaze head on.

" 'Cheer up, Jack, bright smiles await you,' " she sang merrily. " 'From the fairest of the fair/And her loving eyes will greet you/With kind welcomes everywhere.' "

The choice of verse was meaningful—Wolfe could see it in her affectionate gaze and her sweet smile. Suddenly the knife left his tongue and the storm left his eyes as he saw the warmth and joy in her lovely young face.

Wolfe decided at that moment that he could live with Miranda's singing after all. So, without another word, he simply turned in silence and departed.

"Thanks for the visit, Captain!" called Miranda.

Wolfe wanted to bite out a sharp reply; but, for some incomprehensible reason, he found himself chuckling instead. And all of a sudden he felt very good about Little Red Riding Hood living under the Sea Wolf's roof.

Very good indeed.

Chapter
Twelve

RUNYON'S BOATYARD
SANDBRIDGE, CONNECTICUT

It was early that afternoon when Tina Runyon spotted golden-haired, J. Crew–attired Josh Cunning approaching her grandfather's boatyard.

Good, thought Tina. Since her eavesdropping at Crystal Breakers the night before, she'd been expecting him. So she was more than prepared for the encounter.

Hurrying inside the main building, Tina quickly changed into the clothes she'd brought that morning in a brown grocery sack. When she emerged from her grandfather's office, her baggy jeans, oversized T-shirt, and grubby sneakers were gone. In their place were her sister's short, tight jean skirt, heeled sandals, and a white tank top that clung to her high, small breasts.

Tina's eyes were now as seductively black-lined as any good Egyptian's, her lips were nicely glossed, and blush now accented her cheekbones.

All set for battle, thought Tina excitedly. After all, she hadn't been watching her older sister all these years without figuring out a few things when it came to manipulating the opposite sex.

"Hi, there, can I help you?" she called as Josh Cunning neared the boatyard in navy blazer and khaki slacks. Tina ignored the wolf whistle from a few townie punks on their way up the beach and walked right up to the handsome preppy.

Josh's pale blue eyes surveyed Tina as she moved closer. Tina knew she'd scored a point when his admiring gaze lingered a moment too long on her breasts. *Gee, Yalie, guess I finally got your attention.*

"Why, yes," answered Josh in round, cultured tones. "I wonder if you wouldn't point me to the proprietor."

"Uh, I'm it."

"You?"

"I mean, well, my grandfather actually owns the boatyard, but I take care of things when he's out. I actually know more than he does about this place—he's advanced in years, you know." Tina lowered her voice with theatrical melodrama. "On medications."

"Ah, I see. Well, here's why I've come. I'm looking for a boat that's docked here called the *Sea Sprite.* Do you know it?"

"*Sea Sprite . . . Sea Sprite . . .* you know, we *did* dock a sailboat by that name once. But I believe the owner moved it some time ago, could have been last summer."

"Oh, really? Well, just the same, I think I'd like to speak with your grandfather." Josh shaded his eyes and began to look around the boatyard. It was late and most of the boats had been out for their morning fishing and come back already. Tina's grandfather had gone into town, and Tina knew this was her last best chance to get Josh Cunning off the scent of Miranda's *Sea Sprite,* and maybe interested in something better—like herself.

"Tell you what, come on inside the office for some lemonade and we'll wait till he gets back from lunch."

"Why don't you just tell me where he went, and—"

"Oh, Granddad could be any number of places—over a dozen in this area alone. He likes variety," lied Tina. She knew very well, like clockwork, Old Ron went to Barney's Fish and Such on Mondays and Wednesdays and Sarah's Diner on Tuesdays and Thursdays. And on Fridays he went straight to Ryan's Pub at exactly noon and stayed there swapping old sailing stories until well into the evening.

Since today was Friday, Tina knew she was safe. The office was hers alone for the entire afternoon.

"Come in—" Tina stopped herself before she'd said *Josh*. She wasn't supposed to know who he was—certainly she couldn't tell him she'd been listening at the window of Crystal Breakers for days now. "Um ... what's your name anyway?"

"It's ... uh ... Jeremy."

Tina nearly stumbled over her heeled sandals. *Boy, we're really doing up the secret agent thing, aren't we?* She escorted "Jeremy" into the cluttered office, which was actually quite cozy, shutting the door behind them. The old leather sofa had seen better days, but the weathered wood of the walls was the kind wealthy summer residents paid top dollar for. Nets and tackle hung from the ceiling, and game fish and two shark jaws were mounted on the walls. The café-curtained windows were open, and a nice sea breeze kept the air fresh despite the mustiness apparent with the building's age.

"Sit down," said Tina.

She moved to the small refrigerator in the corner. Inside was the pitcher of lemonade, and Tina was careful to bend just the way she'd seen her sister do in this same short skirt.

Certain she'd caught Josh's attention, Tina turned abruptly after grabbing the lemonade pitcher. With satisfaction she noted the intense expression still lingering on his face, the angle of his attention was clear.

It's working, thought Tina with glee, certain "Jeremy" would now be putty in her hands. Maybe she'd send him down the coast to Millstone in search of the *Sea Sprite,* or maybe to Newgate Beach.

"And what's *your* name?" asked Josh, not appearing in the least embarrassed at being caught staring at a girl's rear.

"Tina," she said simply as she filled two glasses with lemonade and handed one to Josh, who was sitting on the low leather couch. Then she sat on the scarred oak desktop and made a show of crossing her bare legs—just the way her older sister would.

Josh's brown gaze traveled slowly up Tina's legs. She liked the feeling of that, her own attention on his long, golden lashes as they swept up. He really was quite handsome, thought Tina as she admired his golden hair, bronzed skin, and white-toothed smile.

As she surveyed him, he surveyed her. Then he took a sip of the lemonade and pronounced one word while staring directly into her black eyes.

"Tart."

Tina's dark eyebrows rose, unsure if this was an accusation or a come-on. One thing she was sure of—he wasn't referring to the lemonade.

Hmmm. thought Tina, *now what would Sis say? Probably something about having sugar just for him. But I can't pull off a line like that without bursting out laughing. I guess I'll just stare. And wait.*

Tina brought her glass to her lips and sipped. It sounded loud in the quiet room. Except for the ancient fan revolving in the corner to keep the air circulating, the only other noises were distant—the lapping of salty waves, a buoy's bell, a far-off shout from a boatman. All the café curtains were shut, so she couldn't distract herself with the view of the bay, and then Josh stood up.

Tina panicked a moment, afraid he was leaving. She wasn't done convincing him yet that Miranda's boat was docked somewhere else. She put the glass of lemonade on the desk behind her, ready to jump up to block his exit.

But Josh wasn't leaving, he simply stood up to remove

his blue blazer. "Cold in here," he said, tossing the coat over the back of the sofa. "But I'm sick of the coat."

Tina felt the sudden chill too. In fact, the sudden ice-cold breeze seemed to pass through the room like a living thing. It seemed out of place and, for some reason, filled her with an odd kind of unease.

Maybe he'll be more comfortable without his coat, decided Tina hopefully, and then she watched Josh turn.

Instead of sitting back down on the sofa, his lanky form stepped close to her. With a casual ease he placed a palm down on the desk on either side of her, trapping her between his arms. He leaned in, so close she could feel his warm breath on her cheek. He smelled of expensive aftershave and of beer—something imported, no doubt, thought Tina. No cheap suds for this dude, that was certain.

"What game are we playing here?" he asked, his voice velvety smooth.

Tina licked her lips to stall. "No game. Aren't we waiting for my grandfather?"

"I am. But it's pretty clear you're waiting for something else. And that you want it pretty badly."

"Oh, really," Tina said in a breath, her voice growing shaky at Josh's nearness. Suddenly, Tina wasn't sure what her motives were. She'd begun the charade by telling herself she was helping out her friend. But now Tina knew it was more than that.

This little act was more for herself than for Miranda, Tina admitted to herself. In fact, it suddenly felt like the near-perfect playing out of her fantasies—that a boy from the rich part of town would actually give her some real attention.

"Yes," said Josh, studying her carefully, "I think you're waiting for this—"

And then his lips were on hers so quickly that Tina hadn't even been able to draw in a breath. His lips were thin but strong, and his kiss was hungry and raw and wonderful. It wasn't Tina's first kiss by any means, but it was the first one she'd ever had from someone like Josh—

a grown man, not a boy. The thought of that sent her heart racing more than the kiss itself.

"I was right, wasn't I?" he murmured against her mouth.

"Mmm. Yes." she answered.

Her arms automatically moved to embrace him, and the kiss deepened. Josh's mouth was opening and his tongue was urging her own lips to part for him. This was heaven, thought Tina, letting her eyes close. She could feel the passion in his kiss, and she realized in delight that it was a passion for *her*.

She had incited this.

The knowledge brought a heady feeling of power, and knowing she had the power made her feel invincible. It made her feel worth something. In fact, it made her feel worth more than she had ever felt in her life—

Suddenly, that icy feeling of unease again crept over her skin, and a moment later she felt a clumsy fumbling below her. Josh's hands were moving downward and doing something as he kissed her. In the next few seconds, she felt his hands on her bare legs.

Tina was so surprised by the touch of his cool, smooth hands on her warm, bare legs that she jerked slightly away. But his kiss continued in earnest, and she didn't resist when he moved to stroke the sensitive skin behind her knees.

Tina tried to relax as her mind flashed on the possibilities of a romance with Josh. She could just see her friends and her sister Patty as she sped by them with Josh in his little red sports car, the top down, the two of them laughing and holding hands as the sea air rippled through their hair.

She could see them dining together at the yacht club restaurant, and dancing at the Wayfarer's Nightclub. And then, after a year or so, he'd ask her to marry him, and they'd find one of the mansions here in the village, or build one of their own—after they honeymooned in Paris or Venice, or some other far-off romantic spot.

Tina smiled as he continued to kiss her. She could feel his hands stroking higher and higher on her legs. When her skirt seemed to get in his way, she felt him inching it up higher on her thighs. Then, slowly, he moved his body closer and his hands began to nudge her legs apart.

Why was he doing that? All of a sudden, Tina felt a little uneasy. She resisted a bit, pushing to move her legs back together, but Josh's smooth, silky, soft hands were stronger than they looked.

She decided to pull away a little. Tina was sure Josh didn't understand. She needed to tell him to slow down, that she liked kisses all right, but he was going too fast.

Her mouth withdrew, but as her lips began to form the word "wait," one of Josh's hands flew up behind her head, pushing her back to his own. His tongue was no longer gentle now; he was shoving it into her mouth with uncomfortable force, preventing her from speaking, from protesting.

With movements that were now a little frantic, Tina pulled her arms from around him and shoved at his chest. *That* message had to be clear enough, decided Tina, thinking he'd slow down now.

But Josh didn't slow down. A low kind of laughter bubbled from his throat. That's when Tina really began to struggle, her body writhing to pull away, to make him understand that she wanted him to stop, but Josh was much stronger than she had considered—the fact was, she never thought she'd have to consider it. Maybe a rounder punk would try to force himself on her, but not a boy from the rich part of town. At least, that's what Tina had always thought—she thought that Josh was different, a gentleman—

Before she knew it, he was pushing his body farther between her bare legs, and Tina realized in horror that the fumbling that had gone on a few minutes before had been Josh's freeing himself from his pants.

In the next instant, both of Josh's hands were under her thighs, and he was jerking her forward on the high desk so that her tight skirt hiked up high enough to uncover her underwear. Then he forced her legs even wider and reached under her skirt to tear away the crotch of her pink cotton panties. In shock, Tina finally awakened to the realization of what was happening to her.

"Let me go!" she cried, pulling her mouth from his. "Stop this!"

But Josh kept moving forward, one hand guiding himself between her thighs. He wasn't even looking at her now; his face was beaded with sweat and partially turned away. The smile was gone, replaced by a determined grimace. His voice whispered cruelly through ragged breaths.

"You wanted this, tart. Said so. Too late to stop what you started—"

Like hell, thought Tina, her gaze narrowing with her own determination. In a flash of rage she groped for whatever she could find on the desk. Her hand connected with the glass of lemonade she'd set down behind her, and in one swift motion she threw the liquid into his open eyes, then struck the empty glass to the side of his head.

Josh shrieked as the stinging lemonade hit his eyes, then the blow came and he reeled back. It was enough of an opening for Tina to tear herself away. She lunged for the door, nearly falling off her sandals as she moved. But she managed to pull it open and stumble into the open air. She didn't stop there though. She moved as fast as she could, pulling down her skirt as she ran.

Fifty yards from the office, she ducked into a toolshed at the edge of her grandfather's property. Panting with anxiety, she waited, watching the office. It took a few minutes before Josh finally emerged, his blazer on, his pants zipped and his golden hair combed back into place.

His face carried the same cool and haughty expression it always did. *Bastard,* thought Tina, her whole body trembling at the sight of him. How could he look as if nothing had happened at all?!

Her legs hurt, she realized. They felt bruised where he'd dug his fingers into them. Her thighs could feel the ripped shreds that had been her panties.

She wanted nothing more than to fling herself at him and beat him with her fists. But she knew it would be useless—just as useless as reporting the incident to the sheriff's office, where Emmitt Muldavey would likely take her complaint. Tina well knew the law in this town leaned one way—toward the wealthy summer residents.

It would be her word against his, and she knew who would be believed.

When the jerk had finally moved out of sight, Tina felt her whole body folding. She didn't try to fight it. She let herself crumble to the floor of the shed.

Well, thought Tina, at least she'd helped Miranda. Josh Cunning wasn't likely to be tracking down her grandfather about one *Sea Sprite* now.

And in the next moment, she began to cry.

In the shadows of the shed where Tina sat, the invisible ghost of Leach Muldavey moved to survey what he'd wrought. When he saw the little Runyon girl in tears, he laughed with pure unbounded glee.

Nothing gave the dead, scar-faced pirate more pleasure than taking hold of the devil inside one of his own descendants and fanning the flames to the nastiest end imaginable. Especially when it involved revenge on the bloodline of Eric Wolfe.

Lucky for Leach, his Muldavey family had been fruitful and multiplied over the last century and a half. He needed those descendants to perform his little cruelties.

Josh Cunning was well removed in the Muldavey bloodline—but he was connected nonetheless, and Leach had had no problem turning the boy's spark of lust into a predatory assault.

From the ease at which he'd turned the boy, Leach knew Josh had done the same thing many times before— perhaps not as quickly, but just as cruelly.

This little Runyon brat had managed to escape before the real fun began, but Leach was still entertained. He should have anticipated that she'd be a tricky one—not unlike her bastard of great-great-great-great-great-uncle,

Eric Wolfe, whose own tricky blow with that damned cat vase had exacted Leach's untimely death on the porch of Blue Nights Cottage.

Leach still burned with hate for Wolfe because of that, never mind that Wolfe had been reacting to Leach's gun pointed at him. Leach wasn't about to temper his century and a half of hatred with such distracting details.

The sea had made Captain Wolfe pay with his service, but Leach planned on exacting his own justice for the rest of eternity. Wolfe's descendants—no matter how far removed—would all bleed just a little for his crime.

Leach laughed again at the sight of the Runyon brat's tears. It was good to be back in this part of the world—it had been ten years since the devil's ship had swung back this way.

It was hard work, manning the black ship, wreaking havoc upon ships at sea and collecting the souls of the damned for passage to hell. But for Leach it had been worth the effort.

Now that he'd been granted a brief respite on land, Leach was ready to make a little more mischief before he paid a visit to Wolfe himself.

Departing the little shed, Leach moved to follow Josh Cunning into town. There had to be more of his relatives about, and aye, what fun he'd be having now!

Why, Leach almost felt sorry for anyone even remotely connected to Captain Eric Wolfe.

Chapter Thirteen

Since her arrival at Blue Nights six days before, Miranda couldn't remember ever being happier. In fact, every day seemed more delightful than the last. She and the captain fell into a kind of routine that felt as natural as breathing.

She'd wake and eat a light breakfast from her provisions, then take a sponge bath with fresh water from the pump at the side of the house—now that the captain had used his power to get the rusty thing working again. Then she'd set to work cleaning some part of the house.

The captain, who seemed to prefer spending his mornings alone, would join her about lunchtime. She'd have a sandwich in his company, and then they'd relax together. Sometimes they would take afternoon walks in the woods or by the shoreline. It was during these walks that Eric Wolfe would share his mortal memories.

She'd learned of his youth, how he'd gone to sea at eleven as a ship's boy. How he'd served under two harsh captains in a row until "good" Captain McComb took him under his wing and brought Wolfe along from ordinary seaman to navigator and finally to captain by the age of twenty-two.

Tales of the sea filled Miranda's head now—endless thrilling adventures of a master clipper captain. Dangerous storms and mutinous crews, and elegant descriptions of deep-water sailing. By midweek she'd gotten the idea to begin writing these tales in the empty pages of her father's notebooks.

The evenings were lazy and enjoyable. Captain Wolfe had helped Miranda get the fireplace working again, and every night she would build a little blaze to dispel the seaside's night chills. Then they'd sit by the hearth for hours, talking and laughing, and even singing sea chanteys.

Miranda was singing one such chantey now as she finished wiping down the filthy steps of Blue Nights. When she had more dirt on her than the staircase itself, she figured it was time to call it a morning. Grabbing a bar of soap, a towel, and a fresh T-shirt and pair of shorts, she walked around the house to the pump, then thought better of it.

She was way too dirty for just a washcloth treatment. She turned toward the bay and surveyed the beach. As usual, she hadn't seen or heard the ghost, as it was morning, and Miranda assumed he was either resting or was busy elsewhere in the house. Either way, she figured she had the cove waters to herself.

That solves it, decided Miranda. *A bathing swim will do the trick.*

The air was still and the sun quite warm as she kicked off her sneakers, pulled off her dirty clothes, and waded into the cove, the bar of soap gripped in her fingers.

The cool water felt good against her sweaty skin, and she quickly soaped up, scrubbing the grime off every inch of her body and head. Then she tossed the cake of soap back to the sand and dove under the cove's shimmering waves, swimming back and forth to rinse herself clean.

The wash felt wonderful, and she popped to the surface laughing with satisfaction. Tilting her head to the sun, she let its bright yellow warmth shine down on her face.

"This is paradise!" she shouted to the crystal cove and the towering trees that ringed its banks. Kicking out, she swam naked up and down the shoreline of Blue Nights until she grew tired.

Then she turned on her back, closed her eyes, and floated happily in the warmth of the afternoon sun. Listening to the lapping waves and flapping sea gulls, she couldn't help but imagine a daydream that would make her paradise complete.

She was standing on a ship's deck with handsome Captain Eric Wolfe, his strong arms firmly around her, his lips moving sweetly against her own.

"Where the devil are they?"

For yet another morning Wolfe was fruitlessly searching the horizon. From his attic he peered through his telescope, hoping for a second glimpse of that devil's ship or some sign of his own *Windward.*

It wasn't long before he became aware of a much more pleasing sight—and right in his own cove.

"Ah, innocence and joy . . ." he whispered when he caught sight of the beautiful young form, *"what blessed winds have brought you to me?"*

There she was, Miranda, more alive than ever, bathing and romping naked in the bright blue waters. A part of Wolfe felt guilty at invading her privacy, but he was the ghost of a *man,* after all. And his natural male inclination was to appreciate the charms of femininity.

So he stepped up to the front window, his arms crossed, a smile on his face. With rapt attention he quietly watched as she turned on her back to float serenely in the calm water.

Her auburn hair, which she usually kept tied up on her head or covered with a kerchief, was now streaming around her like the fiery crown of a sea princess. And her lovely young form, which she usually kept draped beneath baggy clothes, was now sweetly revealed, bared to the sea and the sunlight. Her shoulders, torso, and belly were as

white as a gull's, her young breasts firm and round with
pretty pink tips that puckered in the cool water.

"Again, Miranda, I feel you bewitching me," he murmured, amazed at her vivid transformation from pixie pirate to seductive angel.

The sight of her sent waves of feeling through his form,
calling up memories of his mortal manhood, of racing
blood and pounding heart, and tightening loins.

It was a sight that invited recklessness.

A sight too tempting to resist.

So, when she swam back toward the shore, Wolfe
turned from the attic window and descended the staircase,
a glimmer of mischief in his eye.

After wading back to land and slipping on a fresh T-
shirt and jeans, Miranda decided to take a closer look at
the *Sea Sprite*.

Before the accident in the storm, the little sailboat had
been her planned mode of transportation to the nearest
port towns for food and supplies. Now that its mast was
broken, however, she'd have to travel on foot, or by hitch-
ing.

Stonington would be close to an hour's walk, but it
seemed she had no other choice unless she found a way
to repair her boat. With care, she walked along the decrepit dock until she reached the end, where her little sailboat bobbed on the sun-dappled waves.

She stepped onto its deck to get a closer look at the
broken mast, when she noticed the object of her day-
dreams appearing as handsome as ever on the back porch
of Blue Nights.

With a bright smile Miranda waved happily to Eric
Wolfe, hoping he would join her.

She didn't have to hope for long.

"Ahoy, Captain Wolfe," she called as he walked
across the sand toward the old rotting dock. "Did you
miss my sea chanteys?"

"No." Wolfe laughed. *"I simply missed you."*

Miranda's eyebrows rose in surprise. The captain had

been friendly to her this past week, but he'd never led her to believe she was more than a temporary guest in his home. Certainly, he'd never said anything remotely resembling his feelings toward her.

"You're kidding, aren't you?" she asked as he stepped to the end of the dock. "There's a punch line to come, right?"

"Punch line?" Wolfe asked, standing over her, his brow furrowing.

"You know, the end part of a joke."

Wolfe smiled. *"I'm not joking, little mermaid."*

"Little *mermaid*?" Miranda's eyes widened. From the hull of the boat she shaded her eyes better to view his face. "You were . . . watching me?" she whispered.

"I was admiring *you,"* said Wolfe softly.

Miranda was speechless. She supposed she should have felt embarrassed or angry at his admission. But she didn't. After all, Blue Nights was his home. It would have been foolish to assume he couldn't have glimpsed her bathing from any number of places on his property.

And so what if he did, thought Miranda. Wolfe was not a living man, he was nothing more than a ghost, a formless spirit, so what harm was there?

"Are you angry with me?" asked Wolfe.

"No," said Miranda honestly.

"I'm glad," said Wolfe, then he stepped down onto the hull of the boat. Miranda was so happy to be near Wolfe again that she did not fully register the boat's dipping movement—the kind of movement that would come from weight being added to the craft's hull.

Wolfe stepped up to her, and Miranda felt her heart beating faster as she gazed into the rugged planes of his face. For some reason, the captain seemed more substantial now that he'd stepped out over the water.

Maybe it was the boat's movements, thought Miranda. Maybe that was what was tricking her into feeling as if he were suddenly more solid.

Her eyes surveyed his chiseled jaw, dimpled chin, and the dark blue eyes, shimmering now with open affection.

And she realized that she could not help admiring him in return. In frustration, her fingers curled at her sides as she curbed the urge to reach out for him.

She forced herself to remember what had happened the week before—how she'd stepped right through him.

"You are very lovely," whispered Wolfe, *"in addition to being brave and clever. And I think I have never known any female who possessed as free and open a spirit as you."*

Miranda closed her eyes at those words, letting their sweetness resound in her ears again and again. For some reason, they touched her heart in a way deeper than any she had ever heard before in her life.

If only I could open my eyes and find you more than a wispy image, wished Miranda with all her heart. *If only you could reach out for me and pull me close.*

And then, in one glorious moment, Miranda felt a pair of strong, *solid* arms wind themselves tightly around her.

"Captain Wolfe," whispered Miranda as her eyes flew open in utter shock. "Eric . . ."

"Aye?"

"You're . . . you're . . ."

"Aye," whispered Wolfe as he touched a curled finger to Miranda's chin and coaxed her face to tilt toward his own.

"You're *touching* me," rasped Miranda with amazed joy.

She was speechless now, transfixed by the incomprehensible act taking place—and by the fathomless blue of Eric's eyes. With the longing already burning in her veins, she would not stop to consider what was happening or why. She simply yielded to his embrace as he pulled her closer.

Eager to taste him, Miranda stretched her body higher as he bent toward her, happy to offer up her lips as his mouth sailed downward.

The kiss was sweet and tender and full of feeling. She could sense it in his movements, in the way his large, strong hand caressed her back and stroked her hair. She'd never felt so cherished, so wanted, and the feeling danced over her like vibrant sunbeams over shimmering waves.

And then something clouded the sunlight.

Through Eric's long, dear, heartfelt kiss, Miranda began to feel that something was missing. . . .

Eric's lips were thick and soft, but they were strangely cool, almost cold. She reached a hand to his cheek as he continued the kiss, and it was cool to her touch as well.

Unnaturally cool.

Miranda's mind grew defiant at the evidence before her. She wanted Eric to be a fully mortal man. Alive and real—not just some kind of reflected image. She wanted him to hold her and kiss her like this for the rest of her life.

With a desperate urgency Miranda curled her arms around Eric's neck and clung to him as they kissed. His chest was as broad and strong beneath his black cable-knit sweater. It felt just as it looked, and she reveled in the rock-hard feel of it—but there was no heartbeat, she realized in dismay, and no sense of lungs moving in and out.

She tangled her fingers in his raven-black hair, but the strands had no life to them. They were like straw.

Cold, dead straw.

No, thought Miranda, refusing to give in to any doubts, any fears. He was a *man.* Every particle of her blossoming womanhood told her so! He was solid and strong, loving and tender, and she would not give him up!

Steadfastly, Miranda continued the kiss and embrace, desperate to keep her captain close, determined not to let him go.

Eventually, though, it was Eric Wolfe himself who broke off their contact. And Miranda was finally forced to release her stubborn hold.

Wolfe felt the desperation in Miranda's embrace long before he'd broken contact. The truth was there, between them.

She saw it in his face.

He saw it in the salty sheen that covered her eyes, and the single tear that slipped down her sun-kissed cheek. Wolfe reached out to catch the diamond droplet on the tip of his callused finger.

"*No taste,*" he whispered with a sad smile after bringing the teardrop to his lips. "*I remember there should be saltiness. But I no longer have taste.*"

"But . . . aren't you? You have to be—"

"*No,*" whispered Wolfe.

"But I can *feel* you . . . I can *touch* you . . ."

"*I am not alive, Miranda. I am only a materialization—and I can achieve that only over the water. 'Tis the sea's way of ensuring I have the ability to help ships in distress.*"

"I don't understand . . ."

"*I've been serving the sea for the last hundred and forty years. 'Tis my fate in the afterlife. To serve on her ghost ships.*"

"*Her?*"

"*The sea's.*"

"But I can touch you," argued Miranda, her voice betraying the growing panic within her. "I can hold you," she said, moving to him and wrapping her arms around him.

Wolfe closed his eyes, tormented beyond imagining by the feel of her slender arms clinging to his waist; her small, delicate head pressed desperately against his chest.

"*I've made a mistake,*" he rasped. "*I should not have given in to wanting to hold you.*"

"No," said Miranda, quickly looking up. "Don't say that. I'm glad you did."

Wolfe smiled weakly, touching her soft cheek. He could barely feel her skin—and yet the bit of feeling was worth the effort it took him to materialize.

"What do I feel like to you?" asked Miranda.

Wolfe hesitated.

"Tell me the truth," she insisted.

"*I cannot feel as a mortal man feels,*" he admitted, "*but the distant sensation is there.*"

Miranda reached up her hand to caress his jaw and touch his lips, and Wolfe kissed the tips of her fingers.

"And what of me, my girl?" he asked. *"I do not feel like a living man to you, do I?"*

Miranda's brow furrowed, making it clear enough to Wolfe that he was right and she did not wish to tell him so. Clearly, she did not wish to hurt him.

Her goodness moved him.

Still, he wanted an answer. *"Tell me,"* he insisted. *"How do I feel to you?"*

"You're very cool to my touch, but I can at least *touch* you, Eric. And that's good."

"Not good enough, Miranda," whispered Wolfe as he softly stroked her hair. *"Not for you."*

They clung to each other for a long time, and then Wolfe gently pulled at her arms, removing them from his waist. With one last caress of her cheek he turned from her and moved swiftly toward the dock.

"Eric, wait!" called Miranda, scrambling after him, but by the time she caught up to him, he was back on land, his form drained of its solidity.

He could almost feel her despair as she ran toward him, reached out, and watched her own living fingers pass straight through his shoulder.

"I am the ghost of a man, Miranda," he said softly as he turned toward her. Looking down into her sea-colored eyes, he felt the pain of regret slice through him. *"You deserve more. You deserve a real one. You should leave this place."*

"You *are* real to me, Eric," insisted Miranda. "More real than anyone I've ever known. I've never been happier in my life than here, with you. Please, Eric, please don't send me away. . . ."

Wolfe's heart nearly broke as he watched the tears slip down Miranda's cheeks. It was at that moment he suspected the feeling that tore through him was something more than simple affection.

What he felt toward this little mortal raged a thousand times stronger than affection. It was a blazing hot gale, and an icy cold blizzard, and the sweetest tender breezes all blowing through him at once.

His feelings were overwhelming. Consuming.

They stripped him raw—making him vulnerable to emotion in a way he had never known possible. Bliss and misery, agony and delight—all of it flowed through him, shaking his entire spirit. A dozen painful thoughts and a hundred blissful feelings twined like a coil of rope on a pitching deck. It was something he'd never experienced in his mortal life. And it touched him through the core of his being.

"You wish to stay?" he whispered, then watched her silently nod.

Wolfe knew the truth. Any amount of time Miranda had with him would be cut short when his month of liberty ended—and the call of the sea returned. Wolfe knew he could not deny his fated destiny, his impressed duty to the sea.

But how could he now deny anything Miranda asked of him?

"You may stay," Wolfe told her softly. *"But take heed, love, we cannot be together for long. Only for a few weeks more. It is my fate to return to the sea."*

Miranda searched Wolfe's face, then nodded, drying her eyes with the backs of her hands. How he longed to hold her close again, to comfort her, and dry her tears with his own hands.

"I understand," she whispered. "But, please, let me be with you until then."

A part of Wolfe felt it was cruel to let her become more attached—and yet a part of Wolfe needed to be as close to her for as long as he could manage it.

"Aye, Miranda," he agreed softly, moved by the joy he'd ignited in her shimmering blue-green gaze. *"How can I deny a mermaid princess with a will as steadfast as an anchor and eyes as grand as the sea?"*

Part Two

"There's a dimension that some
spirits have to wait in till
they realize and admit the
truth about themselves. . . ."

—R. A. DICK
(AKA JOSEPHINE
AIMEE CAMPBELL LESLIE),
The Ghost and Mrs. Muir

Chapter Fourteen

Two weeks passed with no sign of Miranda, and no word either. Tina Runyon was sure she should have had some kind of message from her friend by now.

"Granddad, I've been worrying about Miranda Burke," Tina confessed one morning. "What with all the boating accidents around the Sound lately."

"What's that?" asked Old Ron.

"My friend. Miranda. You remember, she was here a couple of weeks ago, talking about seeing a ghost in some house near Stonington, and you told her that story about a ghost ship saving your schooner crew."

"Oh, that girl. Your friend," said Ron, scratching his head. "Can't say as I know what happened to her. Couple of folks asked me about her a few times in town last week. Wanted to know 'bout her boat."

Tina's hands clenched into fists. "Was one of the folks

129

a well-dressed blond guy, by any chance?''

"Aye, that's right. I reckon that describes him."

"And was the other one maybe Sheriff Muldavey?"

"Mmm. Think so."

"And what did you tell them?"

Old Ron shrugged, then smiled. "Couldn't see that it was any of their business to go bothering her, so I told them the boat wasn't docked at my boatyard—which is the truth. Ya don't see it 'round here, do ya?''

"Nope," said Tina, smiling with relief and a bit of satisfaction. She hadn't told a soul what Josh had tried to do to her, and she doubted she ever would. Now her only shot at getting any justice was to insure that Josh didn't find what he was after—Miranda Burke.

"Like I said, though, Granddad, I'm getting kind of worried about her. And since I think she's up there near Stonington, would you mind taking me to find her?"

"Sure," said Old Ron, "but not today. Boatyard's too busy with charters. I'll take out the old trawler later in the week."

Tina chewed the inside of her cheek in frustration. But she had no choice. She wasn't much of a sailor herself, and with all the accidents lately, she wasn't taking any chances.

"You live 'round here, honey?" asked the gray-haired woman behind the counter of the small Stonington grocery store.

"No," said Miranda as she unloaded the items from her little shopping basket. "I'm just visiting for the summer."

"Visiting relatives?" pried the woman. "Who might they be?"

"Ah, they're not far from here," said Miranda, trying to sound casual.

"Whereabouts?"

"Not far."

"I didn't see you drive up. Did you walk, dear?"

Miranda didn't like the direction of this grilling. She

shoved up her sunglasses and adjusted her baseball cap, where she'd stuffed her hair.

"How much will that be, then?" asked Miranda with a smile, then glanced at her watch. "They're expecting me back. You know how it is, people get nervous these days letting a young woman out on her own."

The older woman said nothing more, but Miranda didn't like the suspicious way she kept staring at her as she checked out the groceries and bagged them into her backpack. And she also didn't like the creepy chill that had entered the air of the store. She wanted nothing more than to get out of there.

"Thanks," said Miranda as she picked up her pack. "Oh, I almost forgot. Do you have a mailbox around here?"

The older woman stalled a moment. Something funny seemed to enter her eyes as she said, "The outgoing box is in back. Give it to me, dear, and I'll see it gets put in with the rest of our mail."

Miranda hesitated a moment, but the woman seemed sincere enough, so she placed the letter to Tina Runyon into her hands. Then turned to leave the store.

The older woman carefully watched as Miranda headed out to the road. After noting which direction she was going, the woman stepped back behind the counter.

Pick up the phone, Esther, a voice seemed to tell her, and she quickly obeyed it. Within seconds she was dialing a number she hadn't called in months.

"Maggie, this is Cousin Esther," said the woman when the other party picked up. "I heard something 'bout your brother's son—no, the deputy sheriff. Wasn't he looking for some young heiress, disappeared out of Sandbridge?"

Holding the receiver between her chin and shoulder, Esther Muldavey held the letter up to the light to determine how much steam she'd need to open the envelope.

"Well, I'll tell you what, there's a suspicious-lookin' young woman just came by my store," said Esther, and in the shadows of the store, a dark figure quietly smiled.

Chapter Fifteen

"Eric!"

Miranda saw her handsome ghostly captain waiting for her on the farthermost edge of his property. She'd been walking over two hours now, yet her tired legs happily quickened their pace at the sight of him.

"Miranda, is everything all right?" he called.

"Of course—I'm just trying to get back to you as quickly as humanly possible!"

Miranda hurried toward Wolfe, wishing, for the ten-thousandth time in the last two weeks that she could throw her arms around him whenever she wanted—and not just when he was over water. Oh, what she wouldn't give to just once perform that simple little act spontaneously on land.

Other than that complaint, however, their time together had been sheer heaven. Eric had become the most attentive suitor a girl could have.

Since their first kiss a week earlier, he greeted her every morning with a cheerful chantey, while every night he tucked her into bed with a seaman's lullaby. And in between he shared his days with her. He'd even taken her to his sacred crow's nest in the attic and let her spy on ships through his cherished mounted telescope.

But the best part of all were the afternoons they spent swimming together in the cove. It was then, and only then, that she could feel his arms around her and press her lips to his own.

"Damn my cursed form," spat out Wolfe as he fell into step beside her. *"I wish I could have walked with you all the way into town."*

"It's all right, Eric. No big deal, it's just a long walk."

Eric had already explained that his liberty on land was limited to the original property lines around Blue Nights—which meant he could accompany her only about a mile of her five-mile trek to Stonington. Anything farther and he'd lose all strength.

It made Miranda sad to discover this, and she'd thought about it all the way into Stonington and back. "Eric?"

"Aye, love."

"Don't you ever feel like a prisoner here?"

"A prisoner?"

"Yes, I mean, you can't leave your property."

Eric laughed. *"Where would I go? Until I met you, I needed Blue Nights only for rest. I've no desire to roam about the countryside, if that's what you're getting at."*

"But just look around, it's so beautiful." Miranda gestured to the woods they were walking through—the towering pine trees, the white and yellow daisies, the elms and oaks and climbing vines.

"Aye, and I can see it just fine within my property lines."

"What about when you're at sea?"

"At sea the Windward *takes me 'round the world. That's enough roaming for any man, mortal or no."*

"And you've seen the *whole* world?"

"Aye, a good deal of it. As a mortal man I'd sailed as freighter and trader to China, Australia, Japan, England, Spain, North Africa, and the Spice Islands. And in my

afterlife, I've been to as many distant waters as cover our globe."

"Then what makes you come back to Blue Nights twice a year?"

Eric's brow furrowed in thought as they walked along, and Miranda found herself noticing how he moved like a hardened sailor. In a rolling gait his hands clasped behind him, the ghostly captain seemed to be constantly pacing his ship's deck, even in the midst of this New England forest. The realization touched Miranda, making her feel even closer to him.

"I come to Blue Nights because it is what the sea grants me," he confessed with care.

"What do you mean, *grants* you?"

"During the months I am on duty, I must stay aboard ship. If I come ashore for more than a few hours anywhere, even Blue Nights, all strength will gradually leave me."

"Then you *are* a prisoner," whispered Miranda, stopping to face him. "A prisoner of the sea."

"Aye," rasped Wolfe. *"You might say I'm her prisoner. 'Tis my fate."*

"But why?"

"When it comes to fate, my love, there is no why."

A tense silence fell between them as they walked the next quarter-mile. Miranda contemplated Eric's words, but deep inside of her, something refused to believe them. She felt that when it came to fate, there was always a why—a reason. Maybe Wolfe just didn't know that reason.

"Do not fret, Miranda," said Wolfe. *"My fate is not unpleasant, nor unwanted."*

"But how can you say that? You just admitted you're a prisoner—"

"All mankind is a prisoner—to some degree. Without a ship, my dear, you are a prisoner of this land, are you not?"

"Well, I suppose—"

"Without a coin in your pocket, or a scrap of food on

your plate, you are a prisoner of poverty and hunger.''

Miranda puzzled over this a moment. "But I would still have my freedom," she countered. "Freedom to choose. Freedom to seek out money or food. Or a ship."

"Freedom to choose is a man's greatest asset. And with it a man may finally choose duty. Does duty make man a prisoner, Miranda?''

Miranda's brow furrowed. "Duty is an honorable thing. My father taught me that. I never thought of it as making someone a prisoner."

"Yet, duty limits a man's choices, does it not? It restricts his path to that of honor, of fulfilling an obligation.''

"What are you getting at, Eric?"

"I may be a prisoner of the sea, but I also have a duty to her. Her arms took me in when I was near death, and she has granted me a useful afterlife—one that comes with restrictions. These limits I have long ago accepted. And I shall not question them now.''

"But . . . what if you wanted to *leave* the sea?"

Wolfe sighed and turned to Miranda. *"Have you ever heard of the Lizzie?''*

"A ship?"

"Aye.''

Miranda shook her head.

"She's in the record books, if you ever care to look her up.''

"Was she your ship?"

"No. I was captain of the Windward *when I came upon her outside Boston harbor. 'Twas back in 1848. A black gale raged that night as we approached land, and I saw the* Lizzie *southwest of us. Her crew had lost control of her. She was flung into the surf.*

"I was about to order lifeboats lowered, but fog swept in fast and the waves kicked up to thirty feet. Water washed our decks, and we could do little more than hold our positions, aware of distant screams of terror and agony as the Lizzie's *hull was pounded down.*

"That night, Miranda, when the sea's temper finally

calmed, we pulled no living body out of the water. I'll never forget the impotency I felt—the damned raging impotency of knowing men had died within fifty yards of me, drowning within a stone's throw of aid . . . it was awful. A nightmare.''

''But you must have done all you could . . .''

''I chose not to risk the life of my good crew by sending boats to help, but I've always wondered if I'd been too cautious. To this day, I do not know whether that choice led to saving the lives of good sailors—or losing them.''

Miranda felt overwhelmed by Eric's story. She had felt loss and pain, and she'd felt guilt and helplessness—but none of her young experiences could come remotely close to what this man had gone through. She wished she could think of something wise to say to him, but she couldn't.

''Miranda, I told you this to help you understand why I do not shrink from my present duties. On that night in '48, I was impotent. I could not aid drowning sailors like those on the Lizzie. *Now I can.''*

Miranda took a deep breath, trying to accept Eric's words. But it was hard not to be selfish. Despite his moving story, she didn't want the sea to have him, she wanted him for herself. Besides, she'd already lost so many important people in her life—wasn't it just *too* unfair to have to accept losing her captain too?

''Eric?''

''Aye?''

''How much longer do we have together?''

Eric waited a long time to answer her question, and when he finally did answer, the regret was more than evident in his subdued voice. *''We have two weeks or so, Miranda, little more than that.''*

''But do you *really* have to go?'' Miranda hated herself for sounding so weak, but she so wanted him to stay with her. ''I understand why you feel it's your duty to go back to the sea, but isn't there *some* way that you can stay behind—''

''Enough, Miranda. *You must try to understand that*

*our time is limited. Please, you must try to enjoy what
fate has let us share today, now."*

"I know," she said softly.

"I don't mean to be harsh," Wolfe told her after a
moment's unhappy silence.

"I understand," said Miranda. "But I suppose it's habit
now."

*"What? My tone of command? 'Tis ingrained in me by
now, my dear, 'tis as familiar as my name."*

"Not the tone, the good-byes. I mean, you must have
gone to sea plenty of times when you were mortal. You
must have had quite a bit of practice saying good-bye to
people who were close to you. Much more practice than
me."

Wolfe seemed to think through Miranda's words a moment. *"If by 'practice' you mean to convey that it was
easy for me to leave those I cared for, then your logic is
faulty. I assure you, Miranda, farewells are not easy. Then
again, to be fair with you, I did not have many people in
my mortal life to whom my good-byes meant very much."*

"But how could that be, Eric? You're so wonderful—"

Eric laughed. *"I fear every lady with whom I'd had . . .
ah, shall we say an* encounter . . . *would not agree."*

"And why is that?"

*"Because my life was not the sort where I'd be coiling
up my rope on land for long. And the female nature being
one that believes it can change a man left me at wit's end
with various women."*

"I take it they wanted you to stay, and you just said
'toodles' and shoved off."

"I would not be changed," stated Wolfe firmly.

"But why?"

*"I was not comfortable on land, Miranda—the customs
and ways gradually became more foreign to me than my
life at sea. I simply did not wish to stay earthbound for
long."*

"Earthbound? Right. Well, I guess you got what you
wanted."

"Aye." Eric laughed at Miranda's wit. *"I suppose*

that's so. Fate has now settled my options for eternity."

"But didn't you have a girl?"

"As I said, Miranda, I had many over the years. And I don't know why you insist on asking—"

"But didn't you ever have *one* special girl?" interrupted Miranda, ignoring his brushoff. "Didn't you have one girl you might have wanted to settle down with? One girl you could have married and brought to Blue Nights to start a family?"

Miranda watched Wolfe closely and tried to gauge the variety of emotions that swept across his face like storm clouds across a clear sky. Clearly, she'd hit a bull's-eye.

"Aye," Wolfe finally answered tonelessly. *"I was once betrothed."*

Miranda waited for more. "And? What was her name?"

Eric stopped walking abruptly, and Miranda stopped too. His eyes seemed to caress her face as he looked down at her.

" 'Tis not important now," he said firmly. *" 'Tis a past life. Done and over."*

"Look there," he said, almost forcing his tone to lighten, *"we're nearly home. I'll tell you what, let's sit on the grass while you have your lunch."*

"A picnic?"

"Yes, a picnic," said Eric with a wink. *"And a swim, if you like."*

"I like," said Miranda, deciding she could live with putting off her uncomfortable questions *and* her worrying about their limited time together—at least for the moment. "Let's have the swim first. Race you!"

Miranda ran with unbridled joy toward the cove waters. When she reached the pebbles and sand of the beach, she dropped her backpack and kicked off her hot sneakers and socks. Her two-piece suit was beneath her shorts and T-shirt, and she pulled off her clothes to reveal the bikini, then launched her sweaty form into the waves.

Refreshingly soaked from head to toe, Miranda popped to the surface and searched the shore for her captain. She smiled when she saw him and waved him in. As he always did, Wolfe waded into the waves with his clothes on. She marveled at the way his form became more and more solid as he moved into the water.

Laughing, she swam toward him, then, as the water became shallow, moved to her feet and waded up to him.

"Sailor, you're a disgrace!"

Wolfe's eyebrows arched. *"And why is that?"*

"You have too many clothes on!"

Wolfe looked down at her lovingly. *"Aye, sir."*

With glee, Miranda reached out and pulled at his cable-knit sweater. Wolfe happily yielded to her, bending to let her tug the sweater over his head. She balled it up and flung it to shore, where it transformed back to spirit matter as it fluttered down to the sand.

Beneath the black sweater was a black turtleneck. Miranda reached out for it, but Wolfe captured her hand and kissed it.

"I'll do the rest."

"Okay," said Miranda with a smile. She stood back and watched him pull off the turtleneck. Beneath it was a buttoned undergarment—a shirt attached to shorts. Miranda watched him undo the buttons, one at a time, then pull out of the shirt until his broad, strong chest was revealed.

Miranda tried not to stare too obviously at the rock-hard planes of muscle, but she was patently in love, and it was hard not to stare adoringly at a man as well put together as Eric Wolfe.

"Aren't you hot in those clothes during the summer?" she asked amid her secret, hopelessly adoring thoughts.

Wolfe's lips tilted in amusement. *"Spirits feel no heat nor cold, my dear. This clothing was merely the last of my mortal garb."*

"The last?" Miranda stared at Wolfe with a different expression. "You mean you *died* in those clothes?"

"Murdered," said Wolfe as he pulled off his shoes and socks and threw them, a little too violently, to shore. *"I was murdered."*

"Murdered!"

"Did I not mention that to you?"

"No!" exclaimed Miranda in shock. "Never. I had assumed you'd died at sea."

"I collapsed near the sea, as much as I can recall—and her waves swallowed me whole."

"Who killed you, Eric? Why? What happened?"

"Hush, little mermaid. Think of happier thoughts." Then Wolfe gave her reason to—he undid his trousers, then his long, muscular legs stepped out of them, leaving only the bottom half of his undergarment. The top half of his one-piece undergarment had fallen down, and he tied the arms around his waist. The lower part he kept on as swim trunks, out of deference to Miranda's modesty.

Miranda, however, was feeling less and less modest as they spent more and more time together. Faced with a solid, partially clothed male form—one she'd been yearning to touch all day—she did not wait for an invitation. She swiftly moved forward to put her hands on him.

"Ah, my Miranda," he whispered as she touched him.

Miranda's fingers felt giddily drunk as they danced wildly up the curves of his muscular arms, tracing the line to his wide shoulders, then his strong neck, jaw, and dimpled chin. Suddenly, she felt Wolfe's hands move to her bare waist and tug her possessively against his hard form, then his lips fastened on her own and Wolfe began kissing her with the sweetest affection.

Wolfe's skin was still unnaturally cold, but, in the cool water, Miranda found it less disturbing, and so she focused her mind merely on feeling the *physical* connection with the being that was Eric Wolfe. No matter how that physical connection was lacking, it was important that she feel this concrete proof of her connection to a spirit she'd come to love with all her heart.

And yet, even in this blissful moment, Miranda could not completely forget that this amazing joy was going to come to an end. Eric Wolfe would soon be leaving her—and, despite her efforts to focus on the here and now, the press of his lips, the strength of his body, Miranda found her thoughts returning to the idea of this veteran sailor's practiced good-byes.

All of a sudden, Miranda wanted—and, in a way, almost *needed*—to know more about Eric's mortal life. How was he murdered, and who was this girl he had never married? The poor creature must have been in Miranda's position dozens of times, saying good-bye to the man she loved, watching him set off for the sea. The questions bubbled up inside her from a source she could barely control.

"What was her name?" asked Miranda softly when their kiss finally ended.

"Whose name?"

"The girl. The girl you were going to marry?"

Wolfe stared down at Miranda in confusion. *"I . . . don't remember."*

Miranda frowned, unsure if he was being truthful. "But you never married her, right? You were murdered before you could?"

"Aye."

"She must have been special for you to become engaged to her. Did you love her?"

Wolfe's mouth slackened at Miranda's question. *"Why in heaven's name are you asking me about all this?"*

"I just . . . I just want to know." Miranda didn't know how else to explain it—the *need* to know sounded ridiculous, but that was truly how she felt.

"Our betrothal was arranged by our families when we were very young. And she was nothing like you."

"What does that mean?"

"It means I cared for her. But I did not love her. Not like you."

"You mean . . . that you love *me*?"

Wolfe appeared as if he'd been cornered into admitting something he did not wish to. Tension crossed his expression as he appeared to be struggling with himself.

"Wolfe? What's the matter?"

"Ah, my Miranda," Wolfe whispered, touching her cheek. *"How shall I answer you?"*

"The truth would be nice," said Miranda softly.

"The truth is not always easy."

Miranda's eyes shimmered as she gazed up at him. "Well, Eric, no matter what you feel for me, I know that I love you," she confessed boldly. "I feel as though I always have."

For a moment, Eric looked stunned by Miranda's words. He gazed at her with such intensity, she felt herself trembling inside. Then his eyes seemed to brighten, and she felt a kind of tingling through her entire being.

"Eric, what is it?" whispered Miranda. "Did I say something wrong?"

"Yes . . . no . . . I do not know," Eric murmured, still gazing at her. Then he shook his head. *" 'Twas a sense memory of mine, I think. A moment lost in time, come back to haunt again. Let it go, my dear, and let us enjoy this moment, and this day."*

"Aye, aye, sir," teased Miranda.

"Good," said Wolfe. *"Now, come, follow me."*

Taking her by the hand, Wolfe led her deeper into the cove waters. The sea swirled around Miranda's thighs, when Wolfe got the urge to turn and kiss her again.

This time, though, Miranda's eyes glimmered with mischief. "There's a price for that, you know," she teased.

"Aye, and what might that be?"

"You must follow the little mermaid!" she shouted, then released his hand and dove into the waves.

Behind her she heard Eric Wolfe's hearty laugh, just before his own powerful form splashed forward in joyful pursuit.

From some distance away, behind the shadowy trees that ringed Crescent Cove, the figure of a dark ghost trembled as he watched the cavorting lovers.

How dare my murderer romp happily here, thought Leach Muldavey. *How dare he laugh with a mortal girl near the very spot where he dealt me a deathblow!*

For days now he'd been spying on them, making his little plans in the shadows, and attempting to control his mounting rage at the audacity of what he saw. But vengeance would soon be his.

"*Damn you, cousin,*" murmured Leach with bitter venom. "*And damn the girl too. Soon enough, I'll see that you both stop your laughing.*"

Chapter Sixteen

"Eric?"

"Mmm?"

"Do you hear something?"

Miranda rose to her elbows on the grassy hill beyond the back porch of Blue Nights.

"Hear something?" echoed Wolfe sleepily.

"Yes," said Miranda. She glanced over at Eric and smiled. It was the afternoon after her trip into Stonington, and he had joined her on the grass after their daily swim. She was barefoot, dressed in shorts and a T-shirt, and after her lunch of cheese and fruit fell pleasantly asleep under the brilliant afternoon sun, Wolfe settled in next to her.

" 'It's ho! for I say on a worthy bark/ A brisk and a rattling breeze/ A gallant crew and a captain too/ To carry me o'er the seas . . .' "

"It sounds like singing," said Miranda, squinting under the bright afternoon sun. "Like a crew of men singing."

" 'To carry me o'er the seas, my boys/ where my own true love does stay/ For taking a trip in a merchantman's ship/ Ten thousand miles away'."

Next to Miranda, the sea captain rose from his reclining position to get a better view of the bright horizon.

"Well now," remarked Wolfe, *" 'tis about time."*

"What is?" asked Miranda.

"Ahoy, there, Cap'n!" called a rough voice from what sounded to Miranda like the middle of the sunlit cove. Miranda's skin prickled with alarm at the call, but when she squinted into the cove she saw nothing. Nothing at all.

"Ahoy!" shouted Wolfe with a wave.

"Eric?" she whispered, perplexed.

" 'Tis all right, my dear. Do not worry."

Miranda watched as her captain rose to his feet and stepped toward the edge of the cove. She fought the bright sunlight, rubbing her eyes. She lifted a hand to her brow to shade her vision and was finally able to make out a kind of shimmering light in the middle of the cove— almost invisible in the bright sunshine.

Once more Miranda rubbed her eyes. And this time when she looked into the cove, she gasped, finally making out the glowing outline of a huge Yankee clipper.

"Eric," she called uneasily. "Eric! There's a ship! A ship!"

"Aye, love, do not alarm yourself. 'Tis only my Windward.*"*

"Your . . . ?"

"My ghost ship, dearest."

Miranda's eyes widened as she took in the incredible dimensions of the craft that floated just above the waves. She rose to her feet and rushed down the hill to join Wolfe as he moved to the shoreline.

"I've never seen anything that big sail so close to shore!" said Miranda incredulously.

"Aye, 'tis a bit unnerving, even for me. But, as you see, she's not put down in water. She sails above it."

"Steady as she goes!" a tall, lanky man with a brown beard called from the deck.

"That's Mr. Riley," Wolfe informed her. *"Best first mate I ever sailed with."*

The glowing lines of the *Windward* loomed near the shoreline of Blue Nights. Within minutes, the huge ship had come to a stop just feet away from land.

"Yowza," whispered Miranda.

"Two hundred twenty-nine feet long, forty-one feet wide, and twenty-two feet deep," said Wolfe with unmasked pride. *"In my time she was one of the largest American ships sailing, spreading nearly ten thousand yards of canvas. Ah, my love, if only you could have seen her in her glory days . . ."*

"What happened to her?" Miranda took in the broken spars, ruptured, barnacled-covered hull, and torn sails.

Wolfe glanced down at her. *"Why don't I let my crew tell the tale. They went down with her."*

"The crew . . ." whispered Miranda nervously as she watched a small group of hard-looking cases preparing to disembark. "Is that such a good idea? Maybe I ought to wait in the house—"

"Nonsense—"

"Ahoy, Cap'n!" came the sudden call from a rough-looking sailor with a thick waist, tattooed arms, and a blond ponytail.

"Too late now," Wolfe teased Miranda as he pointed to the rope ladder dropping over the side. In the next minute his four crew members were swiftly descending to the shallows and splashing down one at a time.

"First one with the tattoos is China Jack," he told Miranda. *"Spent time in the eastern tea trade. Likes to collect knives."*

"Knives? How fascinating—uh, are you sure I shouldn't wait in the—"

"Jack's sharp on the sails and the helm. Next is Angus Bonner," continued Wolfe undeterred, *"British born and the best ship's carpenter I've ever seen. The little wiry one's Tommy Noll, ship's boy. Came aboard in Boston, a packet rat to the gold camps in California, but liked the sea life and stayed on. Last one's Mr. Riley, best first mate this side of the Atlantic. Level head. Keeps me sane when the crew's chatter drives me to the rail."*

"Bless my soul!" cried the ruddy-faced, balding ship's carpenter called Angus Bonner as he stepped up to Wolfe and Miranda. *"Looks like the cap'n's lost his distaste for havin' mortals in his home."*

"Aye, by heaven," agreed the burly China Jack. *"Why, the cap'n's even standin' right next to that mortal girl!"*

"What's the mystery?" cracked Tommy Noll. *"She's a lovely looker."*

"Aye," agreed Jack and Angus.

Miranda shrunk down a little as the ghost crew surrounded her, then boldly looked her up and down as if she were a used fishing boat just put up for auction.

"If I was the cap'n," cracked Tommy, *"I'd be thankin' my stars for the chance to live with a girl who can't see nor hear me. Why, if it was me, I'd be watchin' in the room every night when she takes off her—"*

"Belay your chattering, boy!" snapped Wolfe in an iron tone Miranda had never before heard from him.

"Sorry, Captain," Mr. Riley said as he approached Wolfe. *"We've had a rough few weeks. Storms blew in Halifax and then straight into Newfoundland."*

"Gulf of St. Lawrence, aye, boys?" asked Wolfe.

"Aye, sir," said China Jack. *"Half a gale just last night."*

Wolfe turned to his first mate. *"I take it you received my message about the devil's ship but could not respond until now?"*

"Aye, sir," said Mr. Riley. *"I offer my apologies."*

"Not necessary. The Windward's *duty is first to the seas she sails in."*

"Have ya seen anythin' more o' that bloody devil's ship, Cap'n?" asked China Jack.

"Not as yet," said Wolfe uneasily.

"That's a relief," said Angus Bonner.

"Aye," agreed Tommy Noll.

"Perhaps it's gone to other waters," offered Mr. Riley.

"What's a devil's *ship?"* Miranda finally piped up.

All of a sudden the ghosts around her froze so still, she thought they'd just been cast in white marble. Slowly, each and every face turned to stare dumbly at her.

"Eric?" whispered Miranda after the deathly stillness had gone on for ten creepy seconds. "What did I say?"

"Sh-she talked to the cap'n," whispered Tommy Noll. *"She talked right to him an' called him by name!"*

"Captain?" asked Mr. Riley. *"Can she—"*

"Aye," said Wolfe flatly. *"The boys were right the first time out. Their little discovery with her in Blue Nights two weeks ago was no game. She can see and hear all of us. So I'd mind my tongue and manners,"* threatened Wolfe with dangerous calm, *"else I'll be forced to flog the lot of you."*

"Aye, Cap'n, aye," murmured the group with eagerly nodding heads.

"And so, shipmates," said Wolfe. *"May I present Miss Miranda Burke."*

The four ghosts stared.

"Say hello," ordered Wolfe.

"Aye, sir," murmured the ghosts.

All four looked more than a little unnerved. It was Mr. Riley who obeyed the order first. *"Pleased to meet you, miss,"* he said slowly. *"Allow me to introduce myself. I'm—"*

"Mr. Riley," said Miranda.

The ghosts murmured among themselves in wonder, as if they'd just heard a trained parrot recite a Shakespearean soliloquy.

Miranda surveyed their uneasy faces. "Eric told me," she explained.

Riley glanced at Wolfe with an intrigued half-smile. *"Did he now?"*

Miranda noticed Wolfe shift uncomfortably.

"And what else did he tell you?" asked Mr. Riley with a raised eyebrow.

"He told me that you're the best first mate this side of the Atlantic," announced Miranda.

The men held their breath as they waited for Wolfe to react. But he merely nodded. *"Aye, that's true,"* he murmured.

"And you're China Jack," said Miranda, abruptly stepping up to Jack. The burly sailor jumped back so fast, she was beginning to think *she* was the ghost.

Undiscouraged, Miranda smiled up at him. "You're sharp at sails and the helm." Then she turned to the ruddy-faced, balding man. "And you're Angus Bonner. British-born ship's carpenter. Eric says you're the best carpenter he's ever worked with!"

"Thank you, miss," whispered Bonner, clearly stunned.

"And who am I! Who am I! Do ya know me too?" asked the thirteen-year-old ship's boy.

"Of course I do," said Miranda, "You're Tommy Noll, a pack rat who stayed on instead of going to the California gold rush."

"That beats all!" cried Tommy delighted. *"Don't it, Jack?"*

Jack nodded in agreement. *"She's a fine one."*

Angus murmured, *"Aye, she's got a good head."*

"And a brave manner to even be addressing us, I'd say," put in Mr. Riley.

Eric Wolfe beamed with pride as he looked at her.

"What's the big deal?" asked Miranda. "You're just part of the spirit world, right? Like Eric. And he's been wonderful."

The men all turned at once to stare at Wolfe, their eyes wide.

Mr. Riley's mouth quirked. "Wonderful, *eh?"*

"All right, that's enough idle chatter," commanded Wolfe. *"Why don't you men take a rest up in the shade of the cottage porch. I think my girl here's had enough sun for the day."*

"Aye, she's a bit pink, ain't she," remarked China Jack.

"But 'tis a pretty pink," offered Angus Bonner.

"Sure is," said Tommy.

"Mr. Riley, if you please," pressed Wolfe sternly.

"All right, men, to the porch! Look alive!"

Miranda glanced at Wolfe. "Look *alive?"* she whispered.

Wolfe shrugged. *"Figure of speech, my dear."*

Suddenly a thought occurred to Miranda. "Eric, the men know sea chanteys, don't they?"

Wolfe stared at Miranda as if she'd just asked to be assured that fish swam. *"Aye, Miranda, likely a hundred each."*

"Oh, great! I'm going to catch up with them, then," she cried, and trotted off. "Guys!" she called.

The men turned to find Miranda running toward them. Their faces reflected the oddest combination of unease and delight.

"Eric says you know chanteys!" exclaimed Miranda. "And I'm collecting them in a notebook, and it would be great if you could help me out!"

From the shoreline, Wolfe chuckled to himself as he watched the *Windward*'s ghostly crew admiring his little mermaid. She spoke animatedly, explaining all about her notebook and the sea songs she was learning from her "wonderful" captain.

Jack, Angus, and Tommy were as charmed as three uncomplicated males could be. They nodded and smiled and headed toward Blue Nights' porch with Miranda, each one stumbling into the others to get a bit closer to her.

Wolfe noticed Mr. Riley had already broken off from the group and was headed swiftly his way. Wolfe wasn't surprised. He waited patiently by the *Windward*, expecting the worst.

"So," began Riley, stepping up to Wolfe, *"you're captain* wonderful?"

Wolfe eyes rolled heavenward. *"She's young."*

"Very."

Wolfe frowned. *"She's the age Jenny was when I first began to court her,"* he pointed out defensively.

"You were twenty-three, then, Wolfe."

"I've the face and form of a thirty-year-old. You can't *be surprised by the age difference, Riley. 'Tis only ten years."*

"Wake your good sense, Wolfe! 'Tis not ten years be-

tween you and the girl, 'tis one hundred and forty!"

"But—"

"She's not of our time. And, unless it somehow slipped your notice, Captain, she's mortal."

"Easy, Riley, it has not 'slipped' my notice. But calm down now and consider this: She can see and hear us."

"Aye, 'tis strange indeed. But what of it?"

"I believe there is more here than a simple mortal with extraordinary sensory abilities."

Riley seemed to consider the captain's words. *"You're not suggesting she's part of that bastard Muldavey's schemes, or perhaps a devil's pawn?"*

Wolfe rolled his eyes a second time. *"Riley, for God's sake, can you not see her goodness? It shines through her like a lighthouse beacon. How can you think she was sent by a demon!"*

Riley glanced up to the girl, then back to Wolfe. *"A heaven-sent soul, then?"*

"Aye."

"I've never encountered one," he admitted. *"They're so rare."*

"But she has to be."

"For what purpose?" asked Riley, gazing back at Miranda.

"I have not yet determined it," admitted Wolfe. *"She's alone in the world now, says she's run away from an unhappy home."*

"Does she know anything of her past life?"

Wolfe shook his head. *"No. Not consciously. But I sometimes have strange sensations near her—feelings of vague recognition that I cannot fully reconcile. And she says she has strange, disturbing dreams, though she cannot recall the people or places in them when she awakens."*

"Might she be a soul you'd known before?" asked Riley. *"Might she be one of those . . . ah . . . soft admirers of yours who seemed to greet our ship at every new port of call?"*

"Might she be . . ." murmured Wolfe, his gaze again

returning. *"Might's a tricky word—part yes, part no."*

"Aye, but which part's likeliest?"

"She's nothing like any woman I've ever known. And yet, I feel as though I've known her."

Riley's gaze spent a long time studying Wolfe's face. *"And what of your present involvement with her?"*

"What of it?"

"Blast it, Wolfe, you know what I'm asking."

Wolfe sighed. He glanced at his first mate, then turned his eyes back to Miranda. She was charming his men with her bold remarks, intelligent wit, and strength of will. His feelings for her overwhelmed him.

"I do believe my heart is quite taken," Wolfe stated plainly.

"You have no heart. Not anymore."

"I do," asserted Wolfe. *"And it cares deeply for her."*

"You cannot be serious."

"I can, Mr. Riley. I assure you, I can."

Riley's eyes widened. *"Good God, Eric! Have you gone mad?"*

"I don't know," quipped Wolfe. *"Can a ghost go mad?"*

"You know very well we can. Have you lost your sense of who you are? What you are?"

"I doubt you'll understand this, Riley; but, in a way, that young woman is helping me find out."

"You're right, Wolfe, I don't understand."

"No matter," said Wolfe softly as his gaze looked up the hill again to find his Miranda's angel face. *"You do not have to understand. It's enough that I do."*

"Oh, yes! Sing me that one, then!" Miranda's words rolled down from the top of the hill in a breathless tumble of animated delight, falling right into the middle of Wolfe's conversation.

The captain didn't mind. He smiled as he glanced toward his porch, then back to his first mate.

"What say you, Mr. Riley," asked Wolfe. *"Shall we join our crew?"*

Riley frowned at his captain. *"Dammit, Captain, won't you listen to reason?"*

Wolfe met his first mate's eyes. *"No, Mr. Riley,"* he said firmly, then turned toward the porch. *"At the moment, I'd rather listen to a song."*

Chapter Seventeen

Miranda laughed with pure joy as the men sang her a short-haul chantey called "Haul the Bowline." She quickly scribbled the words down in her father's old notebook, next to the thirty chanteys Wolfe had already taught her.

"Great! Just great!" she exclaimed when they'd finished.

The three ghostly sailors all had differing reactions to Miranda's uninhibited enthusiasm. Angus Bonner blushed, Tommy Noll puffed out his chest proudly, and China Jack simply looked perplexed, as if he were being complimented for blinking or sneezing or crossing his arms.

"Now," continued Miranda, "how about singing me the one you sang coming into the cove. 'Miles and Miles Away' or something like that."

"*That's* 'Ten Thousand *Miles Away,*' " corrected Tommy.

"Aye, Miss Miranda," agreed Angus. " *'Tis used less for work hauls than for simple singin'.*"

"Can you sing it for me now?"

The three sailors glanced at one another and shrugged, then China Jack started with a rough, deep voice: " *'It's ho! for I say on a worthy bark/ A brisk and a rattling breeze—'* "

Then the other two joined in: " *'A gallant crew and a captain too/ To carry me o'er the seas . . . To carry me o'er the seas, my boys/ where my own true love does stay/ For taking a trip in a merchantman's ship/ Ten thousand miles away.'* "

The three were about to start the next verse, when Miranda held up her left hand. "Let me catch up," she commanded as her right hand hastily scribbled down the last words.

The sailors remained obediently silent for a few seconds until she firmly commanded, "Okay, gentlemen, next verse."

But the next voice Miranda heard didn't belong to China Jack or Tommy Noll or Angus Bonner. It did even belong to Mr. Riley.

" *'My true love she is beautiful/ My true love she is fair . . .'* "

Miranda's pen hung in the air as she listened to Eric Wolfe's voice. Instead of singing the words, he recited them so sweetly and so meaningfully that for a moment she stopped drawing breath.

" *'Her eyes are blue with a sea green hue/ And crimson is her hair . . . And crimson is her hair, my boys/ And while I sing and play/ She is pacing the sand in a distant land/ Ten thousand miles away.'* "

Miranda's head lifted to find Eric's piercing gaze on her. She swallowed silently for a moment, unsure whether she could completely trust her voice.

"That was very nice, Eric," she finally said softly, trying to control her urge to reach out for him, to step up to him and slip her arms about his neck and pull his lips onto her own.

The urge was echoed in Eric's own expression. It was a strange combination, realized Miranda, carnal desire on the face of a spirit, but there it was nonetheless. She saw him undressing her, perhaps picturing her the day she'd taken that naked swim in the cove.

Not for the first time, she felt the heat bloom inside her—a warmth that spread through her entire form. She felt the flush blaze on her cheeks and the familiar hot coiling in her lower belly.

She sighed quietly as she looked into Eric's burning eyes, and she knew at once that he wanted her—wanted her in a way a man naturally wanted a woman. And Miranda knew she wanted that too. For the first time, she wondered whether it would be possible between them.

The ghostly sailors sitting between Miranda and Eric clearly sensed the white-hot arc of mutual attraction crackling in the air. Among themselves the three said nothing, but their furtive glances and slackened jaws made clear their fascinated interest.

"*Miss, I see your boat's dismasted,*" Mr. Riley piped up from behind Eric, loudly breaking the tension.

Miranda shook herself clear of her captain's spellbinding blue gaze and dragged her attention to the lanky, brown-bearded first mate. "Uh . . ."

"*Aye,*" Wolfe answered for her, obviously seeing she could not quite find her full voice. "*'Twas struck down in the storm two weeks back. She's no longer seaworthy.*"

"*She would be,*" pointed out Mr. Riley, "*if we jury-rigged her, eh, Angus?*"

The ship's carpenter turned toward Blue Nights' decrepit dock to gaze at the *Sea Sprite*. "*Aye,*" he said. "*If we cut away at her mast and rig a short sail from the top o' her stump to the boom.*"

"*Aye,*" agreed China Jack. "*'Twould be less than an hour's work. Not like that time in 'forty-seven. Remember the wintertime passage 'round the Horn?*"

"*Aye, aye!*" exclaimed Tommy. "*'Twas somethin', miss,*" he said, turning to Miranda. "*A raging storm o' angry waves, clouds black like gunpowder—*"

"*Aye,*" agreed Angus, "*and ice glazed on the deck.*"

Miranda's eye found Wolfe's. "You were dismasted?"

Wolfe nodded silently.

"Any other captain would o' abandoned ship," said China Jack proudly, *"but Captain Wolfe started shoutin' orders at once."*

"Aye," agreed Tommy. *"He barked like the devil himself."*

"You jury-rigged in the middle of a storm around Cape Horn?" asked Miranda incredulous. "How?"

"Captain had us rig a trysail to the stump o' the main mast," explained Angus. *"Then we headed into the wind."*

Miranda gazed with awe at Wolfe, who merely shrugged. *"It cut down on the leeward drift. We were heading into the rocks."*

"Rocks?" Miranda's eyes widened.

"Aye, rocks, miss," said Tommy. *"Huge, jagged, mean-lookin' things like black sharks' teeth. We'd've been dashed for sure if it hadn't been for the captain."*

" 'Twas the crew," said Wolfe coolly.

"Captain's being modest," said Angus. *"The crew was in a blind panic when that two-hundred-foot mast crashed down on the deck. We never would o' pulled together without the captain."*

"Aye," said China Jack. *"And when we'd rigged her, the ship's officers wanted to just limp into the nearest port. But the Sea Wolf refused—instead, he drove us on, right into San Francisco, and right on schedule."*

"Them ship's owners were pretty pleased!" exclaimed Tommy.

" 'Twas a good day that day," said Wolfe, his eyes happily glazed over with the distant memory.

"Aye," agreed all of the men.

"So jury-riggin' that little boat's nothing to us," said Mr. Riley carefully.

Wolfe's eyes immediately cleared quickly. *" 'Tis not the same, Riley. You'd be wasting your time."*

"But it's our time to waste, Captain. Sea's calm as glass. Weather's clear as a bell." The first mate narrowed his eyes at Miranda as he added pointedly, *"And if it*

works, the girl can sail away and leave you some peace before you're due back aboard the Windward.''

Sail away and leave him some peace? thought Miranda unhappily. *Is that what Eric really wants?* She glanced at Wolfe for his reaction and nearly gasped. The iron-jawed captain was staring down his first mate with the fiercest expression she'd ever seen a man wear.

"You presume too much, Riley," bit out a fuming Wolfe. *"Miranda may stay as she pleases. I've given her leave."*

Riley remained cool under Wolfe's blazing gaze—as if he'd dealt with the captain's temper a thousand times before. His only reaction was to nod slightly and say, *"Aye, Captain."*

"Shall we fix the little one's boat, then?" asked Angus Bonner after a moment's tense silence. The seaman was clearly unaffected by the frightening undercurrent of tension between the two officers—as if it happened every day.

"Eric," Miranda said softly. "It *would* be good if they could jury-rig a half-masted sail. I'd feel better having the *Sea Sprite* seaworthy again."

"That's just it," said Wolfe, *"she* won't *be seaworthy. She'll simply be jury-rigged. 'Tis unsafe for a novice."*

"But I'm *not* a novice. I can handle her fine," stated Miranda firmly. "You know I'm a good sailor. You've seen me sail."

"I've seen you sail foolishly into a storm."

"That's not fair."

The other sailors glanced at one another nervously. While tension between Wolfe and Riley was commonplace, a face-off between their imperious captain and a stubborn young female he clearly fancied was a sight they'd *never* seen. Women had always been disconnected from Wolfe's sea life, like pretty birds fluttering along the shoreline—in sight at times but always remote.

Wolfe had never allowed a female to board his vessel, and he'd certainly never allowed one to challenge his authority in front of his crew.

"Sir," interrupted Mr. Riley, *"may we have your permission to get to work?"*

Wolfe's eyes narrowed a moment. He was about to answer when Miranda piped up. "You have *my* permission," she announced. "I'm the captain of the *Sea Sprite*, not Captain Wolfe."

With a triple gasp, Tommy, Jack, and Angus turned their shocked expressions to see Wolfe's reaction. Before the captain could speak, however, Mr. Riley turned to Miranda.

"The Sea Sprite *may be your vessel, miss, but we're the* Windward's *crew."*

Without missing a beat, Miranda stood up to Riley. "Yes, but aren't you supposed to help sailors in distress. Isn't that your duty to the sea?"

Mr. Riley's eyebrows rose. He stared at her silently, and Miranda knew she'd hit her target.

With trepidation, she glanced back at Wolfe's face, then exhaled with relief. Instead of anger, she found slight amusement in his expression—and even a begrudging sense of pride.

"You heard her, Riley," said Wolfe with a raised eyebrow and the quirk of his lips. *"Better get to it."*

Miranda offered to help with the rigging, but the sailors waved her off. As she followed their path to the shoreline, she watched Jack and Angus board her boat and Wolfe walk to the end of the decrepit dock to supervise his crewmen.

Mr. Riley and Tommy disappeared for a few minutes on the *Windward*. When they returned, they held a number of tools—old, rusted tools that looked like they'd been pulled from sea wrecks.

"Will those tools work?" asked Miranda as Mr. Riley passed her on the beach.

"Aye. Ghost tools work just fine provided they are used by ghost seamen," he told her, then he paused and turned to the ship's boy. *"Tommy, take these to your mates."*

After handing the tools to Tommy, the lanky first mate

stepped up beside Miranda and watched his crew set to working with Wolfe's keen eyes sharply on their every move.

"*Don't worry,*" Riley told Miranda. "*Captain will see they get it right.*"

Miranda observed Wolfe's close inspection of his crew's every move. "Was he like that as a mortal captain?"

Riley laughed.

"What's so funny?"

" *'Tis like asking if birds fly. Wolfe was as demanding a captain as I'd ever known. He had keen eyes. Predator's eyes. Always alert for weakness in the condition of his ship and his crew. His men feared his censure but trusted him with their lives. That tale the men told of Cape Horn was just one of many such tales. In his day, he'd made it around the Horn more times than any other clipper captain.*"

Miranda's heart warmed with admiration.

"*After his death, other captains vied for the* Windward, *thinking her record sailing was due to the ship itself. That was partly true, for she was one helluva fast ship, but those captains soon found it was the Sea Wolf himself who'd kept her sailing so sweetly. She went down only a few years after Wolfe's own death—on a voyage round the Horn with a captain of far less mettle and courage.*"

"Is that how you died, Mr. Riley?"

"*Aye,*" he said softly. "*Jack, Tommy, Angus, and me. We died under a poor captain. Wolfe had been a spirit then, of course, biding his time on some lumbering old ghost galleon. When he'd heard of the* Windward's *sinking, he traveled to the very spot.*"

"And you four were waiting?"

"*Aye. The other drowned crewmen passed to the other side without lingering. But we four had loved the sea so much that she claimed us for duty. We joined Wolfe, and together used our powers to raise the* Windward *from her watery grave. We've been sailing her ever since.*"

"I see," said Miranda. She studied Riley, aware of his

loyalty to his captain. "I want you to know, Mr. Riley, that despite my arguments with Eric, I *do* understand why he is the way he is."

"*Mmm. Do you?*"

"Any good sailor knows that the formula for disaster on the water is a ship with weak leadership. I know what's ingrained in Wolfe and I know why."

Riley nodded. "*'Tis life or death to be in control of a crew. And that controlling way is not lost easily when a man comes to shore.*"

"Yes," said Miranda. "Believe me, I noticed."

Riley glanced down at her. "*So you understand Captain Wolfe's abilities. And his importance to the* Windward?"

Miranda's brow furrowed. "I understand the captain's temperament. And I also understand he feels he has a duty to the sea."

"*Aye.*"

"But what if he changed his mind someday, Mr. Riley. Couldn't things change for him?"

"*We're bound to the sea, miss. Nothing will change.*"

"But how do you know that for sure? Eric and I . . . we . . ." Miranda wasn't sure how to put her feelings into words.

"*'Tis not good for you to think this way, miss,*" said Riley softly. "*Nor for him. What you two are playing at is dangerous. You are mortal. He is not.*"

Miranda knew the first mate's words were true, but she resisted nonetheless. Her gaze took in Wolfe's magnificent materialized form, now standing on the dock, the sea's blue-green waters behind him, the breeze ruffling his raven hair. When she saw Eric this way, it was hard to believe he was not mortal.

She glanced back to Riley, wondering what else he could tell her about Wolfe's life. Perhaps she could learn something—some key to helping her unlock the fate of his afterlife.

"He told me he was murdered," whispered Miranda. "Who killed him, do you know?"

"Leach Muldavey. A blackguard cousin."

"His own cousin?"

"By marriage, not blood."

"Why in heaven's name?"

"Muldavey had sailed with Wolfe on a voyage—his last as it turned out—to North Africa. Regular crew had been given leave for a month and most had left the area. He needed a crew fast, so he scrounged the docks for extra hands. Muldavey and his gang of thieving pirates volunteered—they also tried to wrest the ship from Wolfe on their journey back."

"A mutiny?"

"Aye. We put down the mutineers, chained them in the hold for the rest of the voyage, then dropped them in the drink when we pulled into Stonington harbor."

"They weren't put on trial?"

"No. Wolfe thought it would be wrong to convict his own blood, so, after we pulled them from the harbor, he warned the sopping lot of them to leave Stonington for good or else be held accountable."

"And they didn't leave?"

"No, miss. They left. But one night, weeks later, they came back. Muldavey found Wolfe alone at Blue Nights, and, at gunpoint, tried to steal some valuable items Wolfe had brought back from that voyage. When Wolfe resisted, they shot him."

Miranda's face paled at the tale. Though she consciously knew he had passed away, she could not bear hearing the details—bits and pieces that made his death all the more real.

"Stop, please," she whispered. "I don't want to hear anymore."

"Sorry, miss," said Riley with an uneasy sigh.

"Are you?"

"Aye," said Riley. *"I am sorry to cause you pain."*

Miranda glanced at Riley. She could see that he was a good man. She could also see his love for his captain.

"Mr. Riley," she began hesitantly. "What's the harm

in my being here? Just for a little while? Why are you so opposed?''

Riley's gaze drifted over her. *"Women are bad luck to him."*

"That's absurd."

" 'Twas a woman who entranced him in Rio—and afterward we suffered that disastrous dismasting around the Horn. And 'twas a woman who sent him on that fateful trip to North Africa—the voyage that led to his own death."

"But that's just superstitious, Riley. Wolfe doesn't think women are bad luck. He even told me he was engaged to be married."

Riley shook his head dubiously. *"Jenny Smithton."*

Jenny Smithton, Jenny Smithton . . . the name echoed through Miranda's skull with a strange familiarity, as if she'd heard it before. Had Wolfe mentioned the name? She was certain he hadn't.

"What about Jenny Smithton, then?" asked Miranda.

"Jenny was a lovely girl, but her genteel spirit could never have tamed the Sea Wolf. No one believed he would have gone through with that marriage."

"Surely he must have felt something for her."

"As a young pup, Wolfe had been charmed by her golden locks and sweet blue eyes, but a few years on the sea soon gave him an insatiable taste for salt. And the sea became a jealous mistress. That's why it's just plain bad luck to try staking any claim on the captain, miss."

"That's assuming an awful lot," snapped Miranda, suddenly angered by Riley's assumptions and insulting summary evaluation of this young woman named Jenny, who surely didn't deserve it.

"Don't you think Eric should be the judge of his own"—she was about to say *life* but caught herself—"destiny?"

"Let him go, miss" was all Riley said in response. *"He belongs to the sea—and always has. 'Tis a fixed fate."*

"You don't know that," Miranda said, refusing to accept Riley's view of it. "Eric might have married that girl—Jenny. He might have made a home for her here at Blue Nights, had a family.''

Riley sighed as he glanced toward the dock. The jury-rigging job was finished, and Wolfe was now heading toward them.

''Think what you will, miss,'' Riley said at last. *''But whatever his life once* could *have been was put to rest on this beach long ago.''*

Chapter Eighteen

The young woman on the beach of Blue Nights Cottage waved at the empty water.

"Farewell, Angus! Good-bye, Jack. So long, Tommy! Good sailing, Mr. Riley, see you tomorrow!"

From the shadows at the side of Blue Nights' northeast wall, Emmitt Muldavey shook his head sadly. "Talkin' to herself," he murmured. "Must be crackin' up all alone out here."

The overweight deputy sheriff wrote down his observations in a small black tablet, then scratched the back of his thinning, sand-colored hair and considered his options.

He *could* just grab the redheaded heiress now, but if she resisted, he'd have to cuff her and drag her nearly a quarter-mile to his car—that might lead to some nasty bruises, and Emmitt didn't want to do anything to jeopardize that fat bit of reward the Burkes were dangling in front of him for finding their little lost lamb.

No. Emmitt would not force her. It would be better if he drove back to Sandbridge, told the Burkes of her whereabouts, and suggested an ambulance—that way, the proper authorities could take her straight to the hospital.

That scenario would cause less injury, thought Emmitt, shaking his head in pity for the young woman. She sure was a pretty little thing too. If she weren't connected to such a wealthy and powerful family, he might have considered a bit of *recreation* with her.

Suddenly, the redhead turned back toward the house, and the deputy automatically shrank farther back into the afternoon's lengthening shadows.

He watched her attractive form stride up the gentle hill and head for the house's back porch. She did look awful fiery, thought Emmitt—the kind who'd do just about anything rather than be caught. Other young, pretty ones in trouble had been just like this Burke girl, and they'd swiftly agreed to a bit of fun in the back of his county sheriff's car to avoid jail time—it was Emmitt's own little plea-bargaining plan.

With a sigh, Emmitt pushed away from the house's wall and turned for the woods. All things being equal, Emmitt would have bet the ranch that Miranda Burke would have gone right along, no problem.

There'd been only one or two times when Emmitt's generous offer had been turned down, and he'd had to use a bit of forceful persuasion. But both times the young women had quickly ceased their struggling and given in to him.

That was no surprise to Emmitt. Seeing her predicament as inevitable always brought clarity to the female delinquent mind, and it would have been the same with this Miranda girl—if she'd been sane, or from a less prestigious household.

Pulling up his ill-fitting tan pants by the belt buckle, Emmitt finished clomping the quarter-mile through the Connecticut woods surrounding Blue Nights Cottage. When he got to his car he reached out for the silver handle, then froze.

An eerie chill ran over his hand and then, oddly, seemed to run up his arm and straight into his mind.

Where are you going, Emmitt? Don't leave now.

The voice that echoed through Emmitt's thoughts sounded like his own, but something about it made him feel as though it came from somewhere outside of him.

Uneasily, Emmitt looked around. But there was no one in the quiet forest, nothing but trees and moss and soft brown dirt.

C'mon, boy, why not have some fun with the girl? Nobody will find out. Just wait for dark, then slip into the house, coaxed the voice seductively. *She's gone raving crazy, hasn't she? Who would believe her anyway?*

Emmitt tried to shake off the notion. He had already decided not to do this. He wanted that reward. Resisting the impulse, he reached again for his door handle.

In the shadows of the woods, the damned spirit of Leach Muldavey focused a much stronger dose of his black power and arrowed it directly into his descendant's entire form.

Emmitt looked a lot more weak-minded than he actually was, which probably meant he was far more dangerous than dumb. Nevertheless, Leach had worked too hard to set this night up; he would not risk losing momentum now.

C'mon, Emmitt, feel the need inside you. The need and lust. You can get away with it, boy. You always have.

Leach did his best to conjure the image of Miranda swimming in the cove, of her attractive young form wearing nothing but two thin slashes of cloth. Why, the girl shamelessly bared her flesh to the sun like those slutty island women of Leach's time, whose every little hip swing just begged for a sailor's attention.

You're smarter than the rest of them rich people, whispered Leach. *You can take whatever you want.*

Hurt whatever you want.

You have the power.

The last words were what did it. Leach felt Emmitt giving in, felt his resistance weakening to the persuasive

words   the words he'd always lived by. The words that
stiffened his manhood.

"I have the power . . ." Emmitt finally whispered, and
then he turned away from his car and headed quietly back
to Blue Nights.

Chapter
Nineteen

"I'll try out the *Sea Sprite*'s new rigging tomorrow."

" 'Tis not new rigging, Miranda. 'Tis a patchwork job at best."

"But I want to sail her again. I love sailing her."

Wolfe sighed as he watched Miranda clear away the remains of her tuna salad dinner from the parlor side table. The *Windward* had sailed well away and the day's light was slowly waning. "*You'll do no such thing,*" he asserted.

"Why?" called Miranda from the kitchen.

"*Because I've hauled your mortal coil from the water once already,*" said Wolfe from the doorway. "*I shan't be happy performing an encore.*"

"That's a pretty drastic prediction, don't you think? I told you I can handle a sail."

Wolfe grunted.

"Go ahead and grunt! I'll show *you*, Eric Wolfe."

Not for the first time, Wolfe admired the sparks of defiance brightening Miranda's eyes. He watched her shoulders straighten and her posture stiffen as she strode past him, then back into the parlor.

With great difficulty Wolfe stifled a chuckle. He knew she'd have entirely too much power over him if he ever let on how much her stubbornness amused him, so he did his best to keep a stern face and strict voice.

"You'll not 'show' me a thing," he goaded as she followed her. "You'll obey my orders."

"Ha! And why is that?" asked Miranda, wheeling to face him with hands on hips.

"Because I'm giving you leave to stay in my home," said Wolfe with a raised eyebrow. "And you've as good as signed articles to my captaincy of Blue Nights."

"Yes, but not your captaincy of the Sea Sprite."

Ignoring her last point, Wolfe moved toward the large stone fireplace and began focusing his power to move sticks of driftwood from the pile in the corner to the center of the hearth. Seeing his actions, Miranda automatically retrieved a sheet of paper, crumpled it, then slipped it beneath some dry twigs.

The evening routine was well established now. Wolfe smiled at its comfortable familiarity. For a moment it reminded him of his satisfying days as an ordinary seaman on the good Captain McComb's tight ship. For a young orphan, belonging meant the world, and acting as part of a well-trained crew had made Eric feel a part of something—like a family member in a cared-for home, something he'd lost at a very young age.

Miranda turned suddenly and spied his smile. "What's so funny?"

Wolfe met Miranda's eyes. " 'Tis simple enough. I find it pleasing to be here with you, as if . . ."

Miranda waited a moment, then prompted, "As if what?"

Wolfe held her gaze a moment, then turned his eyes to the cold hearth. He focused his energy onto the paper. A spark created a tiny flame, which in turn ignited the dry twigs.

"Wolfe, answer me," commanded Miranda again. "As if what?"

Wolfe dragged his gaze from the newly lit fireplace. *"As if you were mistress of Blue Nights."*

Miranda blushed. "You mean, as if I were your wife or something?"

"Not 'or something,'" stated Wolfe plainly. *"Not for you."*

"You mean you would have married me?" she whispered.

"Aye."

Miranda stepped closer to him, eyes wide with unguarded emotion—the kind of vulnerability that the innocent so often portray, without regard to damage or danger or consequence. The kind that Jenny Smithton had so often bestowed upon him.

When he'd been mortal, Wolfe would have seen only the naïveté of such a display. Now, however, with the vision of a man who knew what he'd missed in life, he saw its rare and precious courage.

Deep affection shone clear as the sun on Miranda's face as her arms reached for him. Moved by that sight, Wolfe nearly responded, lifting his arms—then he caught himself. Abruptly the ghostly captain stepped out of Miranda's reach just before her fingers would have passed through his chest.

"Wolfe . . . ?"

"You forget too easily, little mermaid," he whispered.

Miranda's fingers hung in the air a moment, then curled into her palms like dying flower stems.

Wolfe studied her sad face. *"I'm sorry."*

The words were spoken awkwardly because they were strange to him. He could not recall having spoken them in a century—surely not since he'd become a captain.

"It's not your fault," said Miranda, clearly attempting to buoy the tone of her voice.

"'Tis my weakness, then, in wanting to keep you here."

"You are not *keeping* me here, Wolfe, don't be silly. I'm the one who forced myself on you."

Wolfe shook his head. " *'Tis a pointless course, this conversation.* "

"I agree," said Miranda. "Let's sit and watch the fire."

Wolfe moved close to the hearth, where two large chairs were ensconced, but Miranda called him back.

"It's a warm night, let's sit farther away. Here, on the sofa."

"Are you certain you want the blaze at all?" Wolfe kept forgetting that he could not feel heat nor cold. But, of course, Miranda could. *"I should have asked you—"*

"No, I want the fire. For light." Miranda glanced out the window. The twilight was turning quickly to evening, the stars peeking through the darkening curtain of purplish blue. She was quiet a moment, then spoke up: "Eric, about the *Sea Sprite*. What if you came too?"

"Came where?"

"Came aboard to try her rigging?"

"And what purpose would I serve, with your being so firmly established as the captain?" asked Wolfe.

"You'd be my . . . first mate."

"Ah, I see. A demotion?"

"It's only the two of us, Eric, after all. And it's just so you wouldn't have to worry about me or anything. You'd be right there."

"To drag your soggy self out of the drink when she capsizes, you mean."

"Try not to be so pessimistic."

"I'm being realistic, dearest. The sea is like a good captain, always searching for the slightest weakness in a ship or her crew."

"The sea's been like a friend to me. It's brought me to you, hasn't it?"

"A mixed blessing with your stubborn streak," teased Wolfe with a wink.

"Which is nothing compared to yours."

"I? Stubborn? Never!"

Miranda laughed in his face, which he knew he well deserved. So he laughed too. In a natural gesture she leaned toward him, and Wolfe felt the powerful urge to put his arm around her and pull her close. He knew he could not pull her to him, but he gave in to part of the urge, allowing at least the spiritual essences of his arm to slip across the tops of Miranda's shoulders. She smiled up at him, clearly feeling the slight tingling sensation that now shimmered through his limb.

"Let's take her out tonight," she suggested, her eyes a brightening reflection of the crackling fire.

"*Tonight?*" asked Wolfe in surprise.

"Yes."

"*And where would you have us take her?*"

"It doesn't matter. Just out on the water."

Wolfe studied Miranda, feeling that she had more on her mind than simply a ride in her little sailboat. "*What's your game, my dear?*"

The captain nearly laughed at Miranda's unblinking attempt at pure innocence. "No game."

"*You want something, Miranda. Admit it.*"

Miranda crossed her arms. "I just want a night sail."

"*Without running lights?*"

"Around the cove, that's all."

"*What do you want, Miranda?*"

"I . . ."

"*Tell me, little mermaid.*" Wolfe spoke softly in her ear. "*Say it.*"

"I want . . . that is, I want you and me to . . ."

Miranda's arms slackened as her face turned up toward Wolfe's with such longing, he could barely control the lightning response in his form. God in heaven, if he were mortal his lips would have fastened upon hers in an instant.

"*Tell me,*" urged Wolfe, suddenly needing to hear the path of her thoughts. "*You want me to be solid for you, do you not? You want to feel my arms about you.*"

"More than that," whispered Miranda.

Wolfe stared down at Miranda. Her face was flushed.

"I've never been with a man," she confessed. "But I'd like to be with you—that way. Can you . . . I mean, is it possible for you to . . ."

Wolfe never thought, after all he'd seen and done in his life and afterlife, that anything could shock him into silence, let alone a few softly uttered words from a slight young woman. But there it was nonetheless: He was speechless.

"Wolfe? Do you understand what I'm saying? I'd like you and me to—"

"*I understand, my girl,*" Wolfe broke in. "*I'm not so inexperienced in such matters as you are.*" The understatement of the millennium, Wolfe thought cynically. If only Riley could hear him now, he'd never let him live it down. *Live*, repeated Wolfe to himself. *Damn the word.*

"Oh," said Miranda. "How experienced are you exactly?"

Wolfe stared at Miranda, flummoxed once more.

"What's the matter? Don't you know?"

"*Confound it, girl, of course I know. I've just never been asked that particular question by a* female."

"That shouldn't matter. The truth is the truth, isn't it, no matter what sex the listener is. Can't you just tell me the truth?"

Wolfe stared at the girl with rising discomfort. Why did he suddenly feel as though she were a shipowner asking him for a catalogue of voyages successfully completed?

"*I am* highly *experienced! And, if the wenches were still alive, I should think I'd come highly recommended, to boot!*"

"Then it's something you remember how to do."

"*Upon my soul, you're not purchasing a sloop, here!*"

"It's just that I wanted to know if you'd ever . . . done it. I mean, in the state you're in now. Have you?"

A raw streak of something he could recall identifying as male sexual pride sent Wolfe to his feet, his hands in the air. "*This is an insane discussion. I am no longer a mortal man, Miranda. You are asking the impossible!*"

"But you seem so *earthly* for a spirit. You've kissed me, and touched me. Haven't you thought about—?"

"Of course I have. But it's madness."

"Then you've never done it before—I mean as a spirit."

"How could I? Upon the land, mortals cannot see or hear or feel me—and that includes mortal women. When in heaven's name would I have this chance to 'do it' with them!"

"But *I* can see you," exclaimed Miranda, her voice rising with her form to confront the Sea Wolf toe to toe. "And you're *solid* on the water!"

Wolfe's form stilled as he realized she did not understand her unique state—or vision. *"Miranda, sit down,"* he said evenly.

It took a moment, but she finally acquiesced, returning to the sofa. *"Miranda, listen carefully,"* said Wolfe, sitting beside her. *" 'Tis true that upon the water I am solid, but maritime ghosts like myself can be seen by mortals only on rare occasions, when the hand of death is near enough to lift their mortal veils."*

Wolfe watched Miranda take this in. "I don't understand. Then how is it that *I* can see and hear you just fine?"

"You are a special *soul, Miranda. That much is clear."*

"What do you mean by *special*?"

Wolfe regretted the anxious wrinkles settling on Miranda's brow; nevertheless, he felt it was better for her to know. *"It means that you have been given a gift,"* he said, choosing his words with care.

"What kind of a—"

"The gift of a second chance."

"Second chance? But I'm only twenty!"

"Your soul is much older, love."

Miranda's eyes widened with panic. "What do you mean, Eric, that I'm some kind of a, some kind of a—"

"We call mortals such as you heaven-sent souls," Wolfe explained gently. *"Mortals who have died, passed completely over, and gone to heaven, but who stubbornly*

cling to some sort of unfinished business upon the earth. So much so that heaven sends you back.''

"You're scaring me," whispered Miranda, shaking her head. "I'm nobody but Miranda Burke. That's all I remember ever being!"

"Calm yourself, love. Do not fear—"

Miranda rose from the sofa and paced to the fireplace and back. "I'm not afraid," she said. "I'm just . . . creeped out."

"What?''

"Upset. Unsettled. Like the deck of life just started pitching on me."

"Aye, I understand.'' Wolfe waited until Miranda slowed her frantic pacing. Then she looked to him again.

"So, I've been reincarnated. Is that what you're saying?"

Wolfe recalled hearing that word in the East. He knew its meaning. *"Aye,"* he said. *"That's what I believe.''*

"Then why did I come back? What's my unfinished business?"

Wolfe shook his head. *" 'Tis not a question I can answer. 'Tis something locked within your spirit.''*

Miranda paced again, then went to the sofa and sat down beside Wolfe. "Do you think it has something to do with you? And Blue Nights?"

Wolfe had a number of thoughts on this, and guesses, but he was reluctant to share them with her. The consequences of confusing her spirit with his own assumptions would be great. If he led her to believe the wrong thing, pointed her down the wrong path, she might waste her second chance on earth and never look inside herself for the answers.

No, Miranda, you must discover your destiny for yourself, thought Wolfe. *The answers are yours to find—when you're ready.*

"Eric?" prompted Miranda, breaking the long silence. "Did you hear me? What do you think?"

" 'Tis not important what I think,'' said Wolfe honestly. *"I do not know.''*

"But—"

"In this, love, you must be brave enough to think for yourself. Not exactly something you've been shy of doing since I met you."

Miranda smiled, her tense body relaxing slightly. A relief to Wolfe. But at the next moment she was frowning again, her gaze moving away from him and into the fire.

"Perhaps I should allow you some time alone?" Wolfe hated leaving her, but he sensed her need for privacy to think it all through.

Silently, Miranda nodded, and Wolfe rose from the sofa, heading for the back porch door.

"I shall walk upon the beach, love. But will return soon."

"Yes," said Miranda, suddenly looking up. "Come back soon."

'Tis not time yet, Emmitt. Keep still.

In the shadows of the woods the dark ghost of Leach Muldavey closely observed his distant relative. Like an annoying little gnat, Leach kept up a constant buzzing. Words to keep his thick-skulled, thick-waisted kin from changing his mind.

But time was running out.

"What the hell am I doin'?" murmured the deputy, pacing the soft soil beneath a tall oak. "I should just go back to town."

No, Emmitt, whispered Leach. *You want her. Remember the image I showed you of her ripe little form prancing about in the cove. Now, is that not worth the wait?*

Emmitt shook his head, clearly annoyed with the contrary voice in his head. "I'm tired of waiting," he murmured, glancing for the hundredth time at his wristwatch. "I'll just go in *now*, then."

You'll have your fun, but not until I say so, commanded Leach. *You must wait until then—until the time is right.*

From the trees Leach gazed at the empty beach and sighed. Where in hell's name was that ship?

Over an hour earlier Leach had sent out a call to his

devil's ship, but the damned vessel had yet to respond. Leach glanced back at Blue Nights and, for a moment, considered going forward with his plan without his backup gang. He *could* send Emmitt into the place alone, but he quickly rejected the notion.

Too clearly, Leach's memory recalled the last wretched moments of his own life—and the power of rage that the Sea Wolf was capable of unleashing. Leach had no intention of taking any chances this time. He would not face Wolfe alone. And neither would his hapless kin. The plan was simple enough. Once Emmitt started his round of fun with the redheaded harlot, Leach would make sure to have Wolfe pitifully immobilized.

Aye, thought Leach, *my gang of devil's deckhands will make sure old Wolfe has a front seat to watch Emmitt's fun with his little mortal slut.*

"Payback is so sweet," Leach murmured to himself with dark glee. *"But where is my ship?"*

Suddenly, Leach's gaze was distracted by movement near the house's porch. The silhouette of a tall, broad-shouldered man moved out of the shadows and swiftly toward the beach—too swiftly for any human.

"Well, well, Wolfe," whispered Leach in irritation. *"Where are you going, you damned restless spirit?"*

In the distance a low rumbling rolled across the water and Leach turned his head to the sky. Clouds were thickening, blotting out the face of the moon and glint of the stars. The night was turning blacker.

"Just as well," whispered Leach. But when he turned back to his relative, he found an empty patch of earth.

"Dammit, that's it," murmured Emmitt, who had begun striding for the house. "Thunder's startin' already. If I don't go now, I'll sure as hell get soaked to the bone."

No! cried Leach, racing to catch up to his dull relative. Wolfe wasn't even there to witness the attack! This wasn't part of the plan!

Wait, Emmitt, wait, stop!

But it was too late. The evil that Leach had set in motion had just slipped out of his control.

Chapter Twenty

With growing impatience, Eric Wolfe paced the beach. He felt uneasy and he wished he knew why.

Wolfe peered into the woods but saw only blackness. Then he turned his eyes to the sea. A jagged slash of light dropped down from the sky, and Wolfe counted out seconds until he heard the thunder boom softly in the distance. Fifty divided by five—the old mariner's trick came instinctively to him.

"Ten miles out," he murmured, standing erect, hands behind his back, as if on watch.

On watch.

With unease he glanced back to Blue Nights. The house was dark except for the parlor windows, which flickered with light from the room's fireplace. There seemed to be movement near the windows, and Wolfe had the vague feeling that something was not quite right.

Yet he did not know what it could be . . . and he did say he would give Miranda her privacy. So, Wolfe tore his gaze away from Blue Nights and turned it back upon the sea.

᛫   *   *

"Put the gun down," said Miranda calmly, though she felt anything but. For the last ten terrifying minutes she'd managed to stall this big, nasty county deputy with talk, slipping away from his continual grasp but as yet unable to make it to an exit.

"I told you, girl, and I'll tell you again. We can do it easy or we can do it rough."

"Easy, then," said Miranda, eyeing the gun barrel. "I'll agree, okay. I'd like to get off the hook here. I don't want to get dragged back to Sandbridge. So, I'll do what you want for a few hours—just like you explained."

"Yeah, okay. Let's get started, then," said Emmitt, a slow smile crawling across his wide face. "Time for some fun."

"Put down the gun first."

"No. You do as I say first. Come over here. To me."

Miranda felt sick to her stomach as she watched the overweight deputy move his free hand to the back of his belt and pull out a pair of silver handcuffs.

"Come *now,* girl."

Miranda's fists clenched as she forced her feet to move forward. One after the other. And then she gathered her courage and went for it, bolting for the back porch door.

The shot rang out but missed her by a mile—intentionally, she was sure—but she wouldn't let it scare her into stopping. Unfortunately, though, the deputy lunged for her, tackling her with ease.

In a flash Miranda felt the arm around her torso pulling her down, the swoosh of wind being knocked from her lungs and the painful impact of knees and elbows slaming down on the wood floor.

The hard fall sent tremors through her body, but Miranda refused to stop her fight. She began struggling like the devil within a split second.

"Stop your squirming, girl!"

"Help!" Miranda screamed at the top of her lungs. "Eric! Help me!"

"Go on, girl," the deputy said with a laugh. "Call on

your little invisible friend. But he ain't gonna be much of a match against a *real* man.''

Miranda felt a hard tug on her arm and yelped in pain. The next instant the same pain came to the other arm. The deputy was clearly a professional at this, realized Miranda. He'd cuffed her before she could even take a swing. Now she felt like a hooked fish, flopping around the floor with her hands cuffed behind her back and her legs pinned by the big deputy's bulk.

''Let's just calm down and take a nice little walk to the sofa, where we can get to know each other a little better.''

Miranda felt herself being dragged by her arms to her feet and pushed toward the sofa. Without ceremony the deputy shoved her face down on the musty cushions. Miranda turned her head, but was sorry she had. All she saw was the large man's thick fingers fumbling for his belt buckle.

''You're a son of a bitch,'' Miranda spat, her eyes shooting fire. No matter what, she vowed not to beg for mercy from this scumbag. She'd rather bite her own tongue first.

''Knew you'd be a fiery one,'' said the deputy, reaching into his pocket for a large bandanna. ''Which means I'd better plug that mouth of yours, else I'm bound to endure untold shrieking for help—not that anyone could hear your noise.''

Miranda saw the red bandanna coming toward her, and then, suddenly, it wasn't. She twisted to see what was going on and gasped.

The bandanna was floating through the air.

''What in hell . . .'' murmured the deputy.

Miranda blinked and looked again. ''Wolfe!'' she cried.

''*Aye*,'' he said, waving the bandanna around in front of the fat deputy's eyes. ''*It seems* someone *heard your* noise *after all*.''

''Dammit to hell!'' cried the deputy, reaching out to snatch the bandanna. ''What kind o' witchy trick are you playing?''

''Eric, he can't see you, can he?'' she asked.

"No, love. Nor can he hear me," he said, adding with a dangerous calmness, *"Shall I slit his throat for you?"*

"You crazy bitch," said the deputy. "You think you can play your crazy games with me. You got another thing comin'."

"Listen, you stupid deputy," warned Miranda, "The place is haunted. The ghost is here. With us now. And he's really pissed!"

"Fine," said the deputy. "Then I'll damned well give him something to be pissed about."

In shock, Miranda felt the deputy's thick fingers reach for the waistband of her jeans. But the rough tug lasted less than a second. She twisted farther around to see the bandanna was now tightening around the deputy's throat.

The deputy's eyes seemed to bulge out of their sockets as the material tightened. His hands flailed, his legs kicked, but Eric's powerful grip would not budge—inexorably, he used the bandanna to pull the deputy backward, away from the couch and Miranda.

"Get up quickly, Miranda—" commanded Eric.

She instantly obeyed, rolling off the sofa to the floor. She began to right herself when she saw the deputy had decided to fight back. Instead of struggling with the bandanna, he'd reached for his holstered gun and pointed it straight at Miranda's head.

"Run now—down to the beach!" Wolfe called to Miranda.

But Miranda sat frozen. "He's pulled his gun, Eric."

The deputy could say nothing. The bandanna was cutting off his air, so he pulled back on the trigger. The click sent Miranda's heart into her throat.

"Let him go," she rasped to Wolfe. "He'll kill me."

Wolfe's concentration on holding the deputy shifted enough to see the gun, but the ghost's change of focus allowed the bandanna to slacken and the deputy to break free. The big man suddenly stumbled forward, right into Miranda. Reaching down, he quickly grabbed a handful of her hair.

"That's it, witch. I'm tired of your voodoo games."

With the butt of the gun aimed at Miranda's temple, the deputy cocked his arm, ready to pistol-whip her into oblivion, when the gun suddenly plucked itself from his hand, turned around, and aimed itself at the deputy's nose.

"Devil's spawn!" cried the deputy in shock. "How did you do that!"

"Tell him to release you," said Wolfe calmly, *"or I'll blow what little brains he has out the back of his head."*

"You better let me go," said Miranda tightly, the pain shooting through her scalp. "Or my ghost will shoot you."

Instantly, Miranda felt the grip releasing.

"Run, Miranda!" Wolfe commanded. *"Down to the beach. Hide in the shallows. Go!"*

Miranda scrambled to her feet and for once did as Wolfe commanded without a moment's argument.

The deputy was in a blind rage now. Despite the gun's hovering threat, he lunged forward for it. The trigger released and the gun went off, the bullet missing the deputy and hitting the far wall instead.

Miranda tore from the house, stumbling into the heavy night air, her hands still cuffed behind her. Thunder rumbled as she ran down the back slope, through the grass and toward the shoreline. Behind her, she heard the porch door slam and the deputy shouting after her.

"Dammit," cursed Miranda as she turned to see the large man's form barreling down the slope, straight for her.

A warm gust blew off the ocean as her feet touched the sand. But she didn't stop there. As Eric had instructed, she waded into the shallow waves, stopping as the water hit her thigh.

"I see you, bitch!" screamed the enraged deputy. "I see you!"

A sickening chill crept through Miranda as she realized that with her hands cuffed, she would not have a chance swimming away. She trembled, knowing it would be terribly easy for the deputy to drown her, then remove the cuffs and claim he'd found her already dead.

The deputy pounded closer, reaching the shore. "Come out of the water. Now!" he demanded.

Miranda didn't move. Her throat tightened as she watched the man kick off his shoes and begin to wade into the water. What could she do? Where could she go?

Suddenly a tall, strong form was stepping between her and the deputy. *"Stay behind me, love."*

"Eric!"

The deputy kept coming, clearly unable to see that the Sea Wolf had stepped in as a ghostly shield.

"Here I come, bitch," he barked, barreling forward. "Ready or not."

"Not," said Wolfe, whose newly materialized fist clenched and cocked itself, then sprang forward with immortal power.

The blow struck the deputy's chin and yelped in pain and shock, stumbling backward. Another blow came, seemingly out of nowhere to him, and his arms pinwheeled. Losing his balance, he landed on the rocky bottom of the cove's shallows, a splash of saltwater hitting him in the face.

Miranda watched Wolfe circle the man in the shallows, then grasp him by the shirt. *"Ask him for the key to your bonds, Miranda."*

"The key," said Miranda. "Cough up the handcuff key."

Eyes wide, the deputy dug quickly in his pocket and held out the key. Eric lifted it, and Miranda knew it would look as though it were levitating itself in the air. The deputy's mouth gaped, then Wolfe pulled him to his feet and shoved him powerfully forward, tossing him toward the beach sands.

Wolfe quickly returned to Miranda's side with the key and released her. *"Tell him to get the hell out, or receive the worst beating of his life."*

Miranda was about to repeat Wolfe's words, when she saw a dark shape swooping down on them like a hellish black vulture. The blow came to Eric before she could blink an eye.

Then she felt her face shoved down into the water. Miranda struggled, but the ice-cold grip was stronger than any mortal's—and she was sure she was being drowned by the devil himself.

Chapter
Twenty-one

Stunned by the blow to his head, Eric Wolfe turned in the water to find a terrifying sight.

His Miranda was being drowned right before his eyes.

With a roar that rivaled the approaching thunder, Wolfe lunged for the black ghost, knocking it back twenty yards. Then Eric instantly pulled Miranda up and carried her toward the shore. He'd managed to get her a few feet from land, when he felt the black ghost's next attack.

The tackle came hard to Wolfe's torso and he fell with Miranda back into the shallows. He was glad to see her use her head. Quickly she scrambled forward, coughing up seawater as she moved toward land.

Wolfe turned to confront the villain, when a blow struck him on his solidified chin. Then another came from behind—*more than one,* he realized.

His own powerful fists began lashing out in all directions as he saw a small swarm of black ghosts now descend on him. Through the frenzy he recognized the devil's ship that had pulled into his cove, its black hull looming over them all like a deadly cloud of hell.

"*Hold him!*" came the sudden cry of a familiar voice.

Wolfe's spirit roiled with rage as he felt his arms and wrists immobilized, and then he heard the words that nearly sent him over the edge.

"*Hello, cousin. Long time no see.*"

"*Leach,*" rasped Wolfe. "*Leach Muldavey, you scurvy, worthless piece of filth.*"

"*Aye, that's me.*"

Wolfe heard the chuckling of the dark deckhands around him. His eyes narrowed with an old memory. "*I see you've got yet another gang of bully thugs to do your lowliest deeds for you.*"

"*They're me mates,*" snapped Leach. "*And they always enjoy a good bit o' mischief. Eh, boys?*"

The dark ghosts grunted and "ayed" their agreement.

"*So cast your gaze over yonder. For I see your pretty little mortal's about to have some fun at the hands of my descendant. Ain't that just too bad for you, Wolfe?*"

Wolfe shuddered as he saw the enraged deputy still standing on the beach, rubbing his jaw and watching Miranda struggle to shore.

"*Miranda!*" called Wolfe. "*Run, love! Run!*"

But she was too weak to get away. She was still on her knees when the cursed deputy grabbed her roughly by the wrist and pulled her through the wet sand.

"*Don't worry yerself, Sea Wolf. She's bound to enjoy him more than you. I mean, at least he's flesh and blood.*"

The dark figures around Wolfe laughed and his rage rose to new heights. He used every ounce of his might to break away—but it was impossible. He was their prisoner, and Miranda their innocent victim.

There was only one hope now. He closed his eyes and reached his awareness out over the sea. Then he smirked at Muldavey.

"*Too bad, Leach.*"

"*Too bad for you, ya mean.*"

"*No, you son of a bitch. For you.*"

A moment later, a thunderous boom echoed over the

water of Crescent Cove—and it had nothing to do with the storm.

"Ghost cannons!" shrieked the dark spirits holding Wolfe.

Wolfe turned his head to see the bright glow of his *Windward*, riding toward Blue Nights' shore like the galloping steed of a white knight. Clearly, they'd been on the devil ship's trail all along.

"Give it to 'em, Mr. Riley!" bellowed Wolfe over the water, and the cannon boomed once more.

In the next instant the dark ghosts fled. No surprise to Wolfe. Cowards at heart, such evil was always game for hurting the weak, but far less willing to fight a worthy opponent.

Now free, Wolfe wanted nothing more than to go for Leach Muldavey's throat. But Miranda was in danger, and he tore from the shallows in the blink of an eye.

Through the drizzling rain the deputy was dragging her up the hill toward the house. Wolfe was spirited matter again as he stepped upon the land, but he still had the ability to move objects. Spying a thick piece of driftwood, he focused his power and ran in swinging.

The blow to the deputy's legs cut him down at once.

"Miranda, roll away!" instructed Wolfe, seeing her exhausted state. With relief he watched her rally and put her form in motion down the hill.

The deputy tried to get to his feet again when the next blow came, this time to his stomach. The deputy doubled over, but this time he caught the edge of the wood and yanked hard, pulling it from Wolfe's grasp.

"Hold on, Wolfe!" shouted Mr. Riley as he and China Jack descended the rope ladder off the side of the *Windward*.

"Get after Leach Muldavey!" instructed Wolfe as he continued his tug-of-war with the wood. *"Keep him away from Miranda!"*

Riley and Jack quickly bounded to Miranda's side, where Leach was closing in. Their blows and kicks sent the pirate screaming and stumbling through the shallows.

Thunder rumbled as the rain picked up and another loud boom sang out in the cove as Tommy Noll and Angus Bonner fired another round from the *Windward*'s ghost cannon. The shot tore into the devil's ship at close range. Within seconds the black-hulled demon ship was setting sail out of the cove.

"*Wait!*" cried Leach Muldavey, bounding through the water after the trailing rope ladder. "*Wait for me!*"

"*Run, ya ugly slime-snake! Run for yer mother ship!*" cried the thick-armed China Jack, wielding one of his prize ghost knives as he chased after him. "*For if I catch ya, I'll cut out yer ghost tongue for sure!*"

Meanwhile, on the hill, the deputy was still struggling for control of the driftwood. "Let go of it!" he shouted to the air. "Or I swear I'll kill the girl."

Wolfe's rage gave him renewed power, and with one mighty effort he plucked the wood from the deputy's grasp, sending the man tumbling backward down the hill. Wolfe chased him with slight blows of the wood until he'd been driven to the shallows.

Mr. Riley's solid form immediately stepped up to the gasping man as Angus and Tommy descended the ship's rope and joined the group. China Jack was there an instant later, closing the solid ring.

The deputy attempted several times to rise and lunge again for Miranda, but the group's various blows and tugs soon kept him solidly in place, trembling and frantic and obviously perplexed as to what in hell was surrounding him.

Wolfe stepped into the shallows and beckoned Miranda to his side. With solid arms he pulled her against him. Looking down at her lovely face, he brushed her tangled red hair from her eyes. "*Are you all right?*" he whispered.

Coughing, Miranda rubbed her bruised arms and nodded. "A little banged up and tired, but okay, I think."

"*Thank heaven.*"

"Eric, am I crazy—or what were those shapeless black things I saw holding you?"

"The souls of damned sailors, Miranda. They are a blight on the seas—wretched, cold messengers of nothing remotely good. Drive them from your mind, for they are the stuff of nightmares."

"Captain Wolfe!" called Riley. *"What shall we do with the mortal?"*

Wolfe's eyes blazed with a dangerous venom. *"Yard-arm,"* he said crisply. *"Hang him."*

"No!" said Miranda. "You can't do that, Wolfe."

"I can."

"No. You're on the sea to save people's lives. Not end them."

" 'Tis justice."

Miranda looked at the deputy for a moment in thought. "There's another way," she said firmly. "Have Tommy bring down the deputy's gun from the house."

"Firing squad?"

"No. Just have him bring it."

Wolfe did as she asked, and within minutes the gun was in Miranda's hand. "Okay, crew, stand him up and hold him," ordered Miranda. The ghosts obeyed her.

Wolfe watched with curiosity as Miranda fearlessly approached her attacker. Thunder rang out over the sea as Miranda stepped up and looked him straight in the eye.

"Okay, jerk. You've got a gang of ghosts holding you. And they're going to be around you when you *least* expect it. So if you ever, *ever* think of attacking another woman, they'll have no choice but to shoot it off with your own gun."

Miranda took the gun and pointed it strategically. "Got it?"

The deputy sheriff's eyes widened in terror. From behind, China Jack nudged him roughly, and he blurted out, "Yeah, sure! I got it!"

"And one more thing. You're to resign your position with the sheriff's office immediately. Agreed?"

The deputy took a little longer to answer, so Miranda pulled back the gun's trigger.

"Agreed! Agreed!" he cried.

"Good. How did you get here?"

"Car. In the woods."

"Tommy, Angus, Jack, can you see that this jerk gets in his car and drives away?"

"Aye, aye, miss!" cried the three. Then they began to shove him forward. When they reached the dry sand and the spirits could no longer maintain their solid grip, the deputy bolted, running full speed toward the woods.

The three ghosts followed in hot pursuit, and Miranda's shoulders slumped.

"Well done, miss," said Mr. Riley.

Miranda nodded, particularly pleased to have earned such words from Wolfe's first mate.

"Let's get you out of the rain," said Eric on the other side of her.

Miranda nodded, and, as they ascended the hill, she glanced back at the *Windward,* a question boggling her mind.

"Wolfe?"

"Aye."

"Clippers don't have cannons."

"No. But Spanish galleons do, don't they, Riley," said Wolfe with an amused glance back at his first mate.

"Aye, sir."

"Such are the sea scavengers that we are," concluded Wolfe.

"Aye," repeated Riley. *"On the other hand, sir, we've always been prepared for the worst."*

"So I see," said Miranda with a smile. "And so I thank you, Mr. Riley—and the *Windward.*"

Riley failed in his effort to hide his pleasure at those words. So he simply let the broad smile take over his bearded face as he said, *"You're quite welcome, miss."*

Chapter
Twenty-two

"*Damn me,*" whispered Eric Wolfe.

The *Windward* had set sail over an hour before, back on the devil ship's trail again, and Wolfe had insisted that Miranda try to get some sleep. As if on deck during watch, the ghost captain began restlessly pacing the parlor of Blue Nights, throwing more wood into the hearth, and anxiously gazing at Miranda as she tossed and turned beneath the blanket on the sofa.

Outside, the brief shower had passed and the night sky was clearing again. Yet the storm within Wolfe was raging still.

How could he have not seen that harm could come to her out here all alone? He should have foreseen the threat of Muldavey, should have been able to shield her.

The familiar feeling of impotency streaked through the ghostly captain like an accusing bolt from the sky.

"*Damn me,*" he whispered again. "*And damn my soul.*"

"Don't say that," said Miranda softly from the sofa.

Wolfe turned, surprised to find her awake.

"What happened is not your fault," she insisted.

"It is."

Miranda rose to a sitting position, and the firelight cast flickering shadows on her young face and auburn hair. Wolfe thought it more beautiful than a sunset at sea.

"Don't get up," he urged her. *"You need to rest."*

"I *know* very well what I need, Captain," she insisted softly, kicking off the blanket. "And it's not rest."

"Then, what is it?"

"You."

He moved closer to her. *"I'm here, Miranda."*

"I know," she whispered. "But I need more than that tonight."

Wolfe thought in silence a moment and then nodded. *"Come,"* he said softly. *"And bring those along."*

Wolfe waited for Miranda to gather up her sleeping bag and blanket, and slip on her sneakers. Then he led her out into the warm night. When they reached the decrepit dock, he stepped over the water and felt the heaviness overtake his spiritual form. He reached out his hand, and Miranda took it, closing her eyes a moment in relief at the contact.

"Follow me," he whispered, guiding her carefully over the old boards. When they reached the *Sea Sprite,* he stepped down, then helped Miranda onto the deck.

Wolfe untied the long seat cushions and placed them at the bottom of the hull. Then he took the sleeping bag from her, unzipped it, and lay it flat.

"Your new berth, miss," he said with a wink.

Miranda's happy smile was all the thanks Wolfe needed. Together they stretched out and he pulled her against him. With a bliss-filled sigh she placed her head onto his sweater-covered chest and wrapped one slender leg around the thickness of his.

Together they looked at the night sky. The moon's face had returned now that the storm clouds had cleared and the stars were a spectacular twinkling canvas.

"The moon is so bright tonight," whispered Miranda lazily. "It's like a porthole to heaven."

Wolfe chuckled. *"Then, I suppose it would follow that heaven is looking down upon us."*

"Yes. And here we are, looking back."

After a few minutes, Wolfe heard Miranda's breathing become steady, and he thought she had fallen asleep. He lightly stroked her hair, then softly kissed it.

And, in the ensuing silence, he felt something move inside him—as if his soul had suddenly been filled with something. It was a feeling he did not recognize, and yet felt he should.

Love.

The word came to him like birdsong. Like a foamy wave on a polished hull. It came to him as a dream— naturally, in a way he could no more control than the sun or the gales, the stars or the rain.

He knew what affection was. And this was not affection. It was a thousandfold more powerful. Perhaps even, for the first time, more powerful than the idea of setting sail again.

"Is it wonderful sailing the deep water?" whispered Miranda between the sounds of a gentle lap of wave and creek of wood. She shifted against him and the combination of her sweet voice and innocently seductive cuddling conjured a near-mortal response in Wolfe's lower body.

"Wolfe?"

Wolfe tensed, fighting this new feeling pulsing through his materialized form. *"I . . . I did not know you were awake."*

"Yes. I'm too happy to fall asleep. So, talk to me about the wonderful world of sailing a clipper."

" 'Twas not always so wonderful, Miranda," said Wolfe softly. *" 'Twas a hard life. And a perilous one. Good men were lost to storms, accidents, snapped foot ropes. A hundred feet from yard to deck. Death and more death. I saw enough of it in my years at sea."*

"But you loved it, Captain."

Wolfe grunted. There was that word again: *love.* *"There were moments to love, I do admit."*

"Tell me one."

"*Let's see . . .*" Wolfe had told her of many things already. "*The Green Flash. Have I told you of that yet?*"

"The Green Flash? No. What's that?"

" *'Tis a sight witnessed rarely and only when the conditions are proper.*"

"What is it exactly? Have you ever seen it?"

"*Aye, but only twice. It comes when the earth is about to swallow the last light of the sun. The flash lasts no more than a moment. One burst of green that brightens the western horizon before the day dies. I used to tell my crew it was the sun's last gasp—a dying breath the color of renewed life.*"

"It must be beautiful to see."

"*Aye. 'Tis quite something.*"

Miranda curved her hand to Wolfe's cheek and rose on one elbow to look into his face. "I wish I could have seen it with you."

Wolfe touched her cheek and smiled. " *'Tis nothing compared with the flash of life I see in* these *eyes.*"

Wolfe saw the effect of his words in Miranda's sea-colored gaze. With deliberate slowness he reached both large hands to her head and pulled her lips to his.

She accepted him easily, moving her mouth against his with a hungry desire Wolfe had not felt in her before. He pushed his tongue forward, unable to taste, but willing at least to let her feel his own need for her.

Miranda moaned in delight at the invasion and moved her body closer to his own. Her delicate hand roamed his torso with comfortable familiarity, then moved lower, innocently stopping at the waistband of his pants. Immediately Wolfe stilled, feeling a response in his form that he had not felt since . . .

"*My God,*" he said on a breath.

"Wolfe? What is it?"

Wolfe closed his eyes, unable to understand. Not this mortal response, nor these carnal sensations pulsing through his materialized form.

"*We must stop this,*" rasped Wolfe.

Miranda's face fell. "Why? Is it me? Aren't you . . . attracted to —''

"Don't be daft, Miranda. I want nothing more than to make love to you. Here. Now. This instant."

Miranda took this in, then met his eyes. "Then why don't you?"

"You don't know what you're saying."

"I do. I want you to be the one."

"For heaven's sake, Miranda, I'm not mortal!" Wolfe pointed to the moon. *"Look to your celestial porthole, girl. Do you think heaven could ever look down on this without exacting a punishment. 'Tis not natural. Even the ancient myths of man have warned against such acts. 'Twould surely bring a perilous consequence."*

"But you love me."

Wolfe stared in amazement at Miranda. She'd said the words as if she had no doubt, and as if they were all the solution that the powers of heaven and earth required.

"How can you be so sure of this? That I love you?"

"Because I am! I love you. And you love me. If that's possible between a mortal and a ghost, then why not this next step?"

"Miranda—"

"No. I know what I want, Eric. And it's to give myself in love. And I love you."

"But, Miranda," rasped Wolfe, finding the next words about the hardest he'd ever said. *"I'm not a real man."*

It galled him to say it, but it was the truth, and he loved her too much to allow anything less than the truth between them now.

With care, Miranda moved her delicate hand down, tracing her fingers from his waistband to the area at the tops of his thighs. Gently, she caressed him. Wolfe gasped at the exquisite pleasure-pain she was unleashing within him, along with the streak of unbridled need.

"My God," he rasped.

"You *feel* real enough tonight," she whispered in his ear. "Real enough to fill me."

It was too much for Wolfe. He could no more control

the desire within him than the direction of the wind. With one swift motion he rolled her beneath him.

Miranda's eyes were wide with surprise as he gazed down at her in the pale moonlight. The silvery beams spilled on her face and neck, making her look almost ethereal. His eyebrow rose at the irony. Under the pure light of the orb above, he was moving closer to earth and she to heaven.

Wolfe dragged his deep blue gaze down her slender neck and drank in the outline of her pert young breasts, bare beneath the thin T-shirt. Instinctively he moved his hand to palm them. He felt each swell and change in his hand, and he reveled in the sensations coming through to him—his sense of touch was much more powerful than he could ever recall.

Her nipples were small and soft. With practiced ease he allowed his callused thumb to rub lightly over the first peak and then the second, glorying in their swift hardening at his touch.

"Mmm, yes . . ." she whispered, her eyes wide.

"Does that feel good, my love?"

"Yes . . . don't stop . . . please . . ."

The words lit a fire inside Wolfe and he suddenly needed to feel her bare breasts against him. With a bit of impatience he tugged at his clothing. She immediately helped him strip off his thick black sweater and turtleneck and toss them aside.

He was about to unbutton his undergarment, but she was there faster. Her slender fingers deftly released one button, then another, until finally she was spreading the thin cotton shirt wide.

He closed his eyes as she splayed her hands upon him.

"My God."

"Wolfe? What's wrong?"

"I can't believe it," he whispered with wonder, *"I can feel your small fingers upon me. I can feel their softest silky touch, their slightest ticklish movement."*

As a materialized ghost, Wolfe's sense of touch had been severely limited—as if a thick blanket were always

placed between him and the object touched. But the veil
had suddenly lifted, and he could now feel with a sense
of touch that was almost as good as a mortal's.

"Wolfe," whispered Miranda as the slow stroking
movements of her hands abruptly stilled.

Wolfe looked down. *"Miranda?"*

"You're warm," she said incredulously.

"What?"

"Your skin. It's—"

Wolfe's lips descended before she could finish. He
didn't know what miracle had come to them, but he would
not waste time questioning it. He needed to feel her, touch
her, taste her—yes, *taste* her!—before it all slipped away
again.

"Your lips are so sweet, and soft, and warm," murmured Wolfe. *"I must taste more . . ."*

Miranda gasped as, without warning, Wolfe jerked up
her thin T-shirt, exposing her breasts to the night air. He
paused a moment to gaze at their cream-white beauty in
the pale moonlight, then dipped his head to taste the pink
buds at their tips.

His tongue lathed first one nipple and then the next.
Yes, he remembered the sweet, sweet joy of making love
to a woman. Oh, how well he remembered!

Miranda was moving beneath him now, arcing herself
to offer more flesh to his hungry mouth. His lips drifted
farther down, to taste her soft belly. Then his hands
quickly worked to remove her jeans and sneakers and toss
them aside.

Miranda's hands were now curious, too, and she began
to explore his broad chest, swirling her fingers in the
coarse dark hair around his nipples. She leaned forward
to taste them, and Wolfe gasped at the cool, wet feel of
her lips upon each tip.

With as much patience as he could manage, Wolfe
pushed Miranda back against the deck cushions and sleeping bag. Desire burned in his blue eyes as he balanced his
upper body on his strong forearms. Holding her gaze, he
slowly lowered his upper torso closer. With deliberate

movements he rubbed against her, allowing his coarsely haired chest to graze over her erect nipples.

Miranda moaned beneath him as he stroked her. Then Wolfe let more of his body cover hers. With care he pressed down into her.

His rock-hard length was more than evident now beneath his clothing. He pressed it gently against her upper thighs, then between the sensitive apex of her legs, where a silky strip of cloth still covered her.

Miranda gasped at the feel of his length, and Wolfe met her gaze.

"Are you sure, love?"

Miranda nodded quickly. "Yes, of course."

Wolfe smiled, and he lowered his open mouth to hers, pushing his tongue between her lips and dipping in again to taste her.

He moaned her name and she answered him. Then he moved his hand down her body. With care he slid his callused fingers over her belly, then slipped them inside the waistband of the undergarment.

She bucked at this slightest touch and he murmured sweet, soothing words. He kissed her as he pushed her undergarment down her legs.

When he returned, he bestowed little kisses on her cheek and chin and lips. Then he moved his hand between her thighs and gently urged his finger upward, until he felt the soft nest of hair and the damp folds hidden inside.

Miranda let out a soft gasp of excitement.

"Easy," he whispered. *" 'Tis only the beginning, love."*

With practiced skill Wolfe explored her, then he explained softly, *"I must ease the way. Make you ready for me. Do you understand?"*

"Yes, Eric."

"Good, love. Now, just relax."

With a slow smile Eric pushed one finger into her. She was so hot and so wet that he would have questioned her inexperience—if it were not for her exquisite tightness.

Slow, he told himself again, feeling an almost painful

response in his lower body at this last discovery.

Miranda's blue-green eyes brightened as he moved within her, working to ease her tightness. She gasped softly as he pushed a second finger inside, working to widen her even more.

Finally, he positioned the tip of his thumb carefully forward to touch the place that would give her the most pleasure.

Miranda twisted and turned at the sensations Wolfe was creating within her. When she arched her back, Wolfe dipped his head, closing his lips about a nipple and sucking until she screamed out in delight.

"Yes, love, enjoy yourself..." he said with a laugh. He watched her rise to the sky and softly descend. Then he pulled away.

"Don't go," said Miranda.

"Just for a moment," he said, sitting up to quickly remove the remains of his clothing—thick woolen pants, shoes, and the lower half of his undergarment.

When he returned, spreading his naked, powerful length back beside her, Miranda rose.

"Now, where are you *going?"*

"To look at you," she whispered.

Wolfe propped his elbow and rested his head in his hand. *"Then look, my love,"* he said cockily. *"Be my guest."*

He smiled proudly at her open appreciation of his form, solid and strong and ready for her. With hesitation she reached out.

"Don't be shy," he whispered.

She nodded and let her fingers embrace him. Wolfe closed his eyes at the feel of her silky touch.

"I'm not sure what to do to give you pleasure," she admitted reluctantly.

"Anything *you do is fine*," gasped Wolfe as her inexperience served to create the most intense array of touches he'd ever known.

With the soft pads of her fingers she first traced a light path along his manhood, slowly circling the tip. Next she slipped her fingers around his thickness and began stroking from tip to shaft. Her innocent exploration was exquisite and, after a few minutes, unbearable.

"*Ah, God . . . Miranda . . . I can't . . . wait!*"

"Wolfe?"

Swiftly he pulled her to him, then rolled her to her back and covered her body with his. Then he fastened his mouth to hers and rose up on his forearms. With urgent ardor his thickly muscled legs slipped between her soft thighs and pushed, coaxing her to open for him.

She responded instantly, and he smiled at the sweet feel of his bared manhood now resting against her. Adjusting his lower body, he nudged her legs to spread farther for him, then he slipped himself between her folds.

She sighed at the feel of his soft strokes. And when he felt she was ready, he guided himself to her opening.

"*Are you all right?*" he asked softly.

"Yes, Eric. All I want is to be as close to you as possible."

It was enough for Wolfe. In one possessive thrust he pushed into her, breaking through the thin barrier high inside in one swift movement.

For a moment he saw the surprise cross Miranda's face and felt the tension in her body, but she quickly relaxed again and slipped back to the pleasure of feeling him fill her.

" '*Tis a miracle,*" whispered Wolfe as he moved in a gentle rhythm and felt Miranda wordlessly respond.

She laughed as the sensations filled her, and he gloried in his ability to give her pleasure over and over again. And then it was his turn.

"I love you," she whispered in his ear. The tickle of breath and the declaration sent him over the edge. In a frenzied pace Wolfe thrust into her. She rode the wave with joy, shouting with pleasure once more as he plunged one last time and shuddered with his own release, collapsing down a moment later.

Miranda held him in her arms as he sailed the waves of overwhelming sensations. When he finally drifted back, she was stroking and kissing his black hair.

"It's soft and silky," she whispered, her voice incredulous. "It's not like straw anymore."

Wolfe wasn't sure what she was speaking of, and for the moment he didn't care. He raised his head and planted a kiss on her lips.

"What's that for?" asked Miranda teasingly.

"What? Can't a man kiss the woman he loves?"

Miranda smiled. "So you *do* love me."

"Aye, girl. I thought you knew that."

"Sure, I did," she said after a moment. "But it's nice to hear anyway."

"Then hear it again, dearest. I, Eric Wolfe, late captain of the clipper Windward, *love you with all my soul."*

Miranda closed her eyes and Wolfe moved a hand to her cheek. With the rough pad of his thumb he caught a tiny glistening tear.

"Salt," he said with joy. *"You taste of salt."*

"Like the sea?"

"Nay, my love. Much sweeter."

With those words, thunder rumbled softly in the distance, but Wolfe barely heard it. His attention was quite occupied with the woman below him, and the sudden stirring in his loins.

"Wolfe?"

"Aye, love?"

"Are you still inside me?"

"Aye."

"And are you—?"

"Aye, love, without question."

As Miranda smiled, Wolfe began to move his thick length within her again, but this time very slowly. The languid movements put a moan of pleasure on Miranda's lips and a dreamy glaze over her eyes.

Wolfe smiled with proud pleasure, deciding to take his good time with her on this next voyage, and, if he were lucky, give her something to dream about for years to come—years, he knew, that would be spent without him.

"Close your eyes now, Miranda," he whispered. *"And enjoy the feel of the ride."*

"Oh, sir. If that's an order, I'm ready to obey."

"Good," said Wolfe with a chuckle. *"Then consider it so."*

"Aye, aye, sir."

Chapter
Twenty-three

Drip.

Drop.

Drip-drop-drip.

In the hazy gray of early morning, the light splashes of drizzle tapped a rhythm on Wolfe's forehead.

"Enter," he barked, thinking the tap was a knock upon his cabin door. When the tapping failed to cease, he rolled over and made dull contact with something.

Abruptly, his eyes opened.

And then his lips curled.

How could a man ask for more than this? Waking up to the curve of a creamy breast and the memory of making love all night?

"Miranda," he whispered.

Next to him, Miranda stirred and yawned but failed to open her eyes, and Wolfe considered the devilish ways he might wake her.

With a determined hand he pushed the crumpled edge of the blanket down to her waist, exposing her breasts to the temperate sea breeze as well as his heated blue gaze.

"Mmm," she murmured, eyes still closed.

He moved his thumb and forefinger to the tip of her breast and languidly began plucking the newly exposed nipples, pale pink buds he watched swiftly tighten at his touch.

The thought of his touch sent a vague flash of regret through him as Wolfe realized his sense of it was back to what it had been before last night—dull and lifeless.

The sunrise had blotted out the miraculous moon and with it their private portal of celestial light. Now Wolfe was back to being no more than a materialized version of his ghostly state.

Yet, she is with me now—for a little longer Wolfe reminded himself as he heard her sweet sounds of pleasure. *And I possess substance enough to please her once more.*

Miranda's eyes remained shut and Wolfe only hoped that his caresses would come as a sweet extension of her blissful dreams.

As he continued to play with her breasts, he pressed his strong body flush to her side, then he moved his hand lower, grazing his fingers along her skin until he reached her waist.

Wolfe pushed the blanket farther down her body, exposing her belly and then the soft triangle of auburn hair at the apex of her thighs. With soft kisses to her neck and ear, he dipped his hand lower, tangling his callused fingers in her.

She writhed at his caress, her eyes still closed, but her breath quickened. Then she arched into his large hand, pressing urgently for more.

And he gave her what she wanted. With two fingers he pushed through her damp folds and into her slickened passage. Then he began to stroke her.

"Oh . . . oh . . . oh . . ."

The sounds were music to him as he judged the right moment to send her over the edge.

When he did, she called out his name, and her arms reached out for him. Her body violently shuddered, and she clung to his strong neck like the trunk of a sturdy mast in a hearty gale.

Finally, when her tremors calmed and her breathing slowed, Miranda's eyes opened.

"Good morning," said Wolfe with a smile.

"Yes," said Miranda with a contented arch of her back. "It is."

"Was I part of your dreams, love?"

"Until I felt you inside me," said Miranda, her fingers drifting to trace circles on his broad chest. "Then I knew you were real."

"But you kept your eyes shut."

"The better to feel you, Big Bad Wolf."

Wolfe chuckled and kissed her nose; that's when a splash of water dropped on his ear.

"What in blazes?"

Consumed with pleasuring Miranda, Wolfe had been too distracted to bother taking in the drizzling conditions around the little sailboat where they'd spent the night making love.

Now he and Miranda turned their gazes to the sky to find that clouds had gathered thickly above them.

"They're moving so fast," said Miranda, alarmed.

"No," said Wolfe sharply. *"It is we who are moving."*

Wolfe snapped to a sitting position and surveyed their position.

"Water," gasped Miranda, sitting up beside him. "There's nothing but water, Wolfe! We've drifted out to sea!"

"Aye. The moorings must have loosened and the tide pulled us right out."

"Oh, my God."

"Don't become upset now. You're with a seasoned sailor."

"In a jury-rigged sloop built for short runs." She glanced up to the sky. "And with a storm coming on."

Wolfe knew she was right, but he needed a calm crew—even if that crew was only one hand.

"Get dressed quickly, love."

Within minutes they were both dressed and stowing the loose articles—cushions and blanket and sleeping bag.

"Where's your life jacket?" asked Wolfe.

Miranda swallowed uneasily as the wind began to pick up and the waves began to rock the small craft. "Drifted overboard."

"In the last storm?"

"Yes."

The one in which she almost drowned, Wolfe realized silently. He felt panic rise within him as he considered how much he loved Miranda—how much he wanted her to keep on living, to discover her destiny and find happiness.

I have to get her through this alive, he vowed to himself. Closing his eyes, he called the *Windward*, but he knew he couldn't count on them being close by, or even leaving their duties to answer his summons.

Steeling his worries, he turned his critical eye to the sky. The clouds were moving faster and darkening with every passing minute. Wolfe gauged their height and shape as the rain began to fall harder.

" 'Tis a squall."

"Then the worst will be over quickly."

"Nay. The rain's come before the wind."

Miranda looked askance.

" 'When the wind before the rain, Let your topsails draw again/ When the rain before the wind, Topsail sheets and halyards mind.' "

"Let's run for land, then."

"No. Reef the sail," ordered Wolfe. *"We'll ride it out."*

"Why just hang on, when we can use the wind!"

" 'Tis foolish. We've lost our bearings with the shore. Reef it. Now."

"No."

Wolfe may have become accustomed to Miranda's contrary stubbornness, but he was *not* accustomed to his seamanship being questioned before a storm. Anger rose within him as he turned on her and lashed out with fury.

"If you wish to survive, girl, do not question my orders!"

"She's my craft, Wolfe!" Miranda shot back with equal fury.

"Miranda, do you see these waves? They weigh more than sixty pounds per cubic foot. A large breaking wave'll heave more than twenty thousand pounds of water at a boat going thirty knots."

"We won't be going that fast."

"You must put your efforts toward hanging on and dodging the worst waves. Sailing into them is too perilous even without the patchwork rigging you've got now."

"But I know my craft, and the *Sea Sprite*'s a stable, heavy-heel vessel," said Miranda, boldly stepping up to him. "She can take the weather without capsizing, and I'd say heading for the Sound is a better alternative than being dragged farther out to sea!"

Wolfe didn't agree. There were too many variables, from poor visibility to shoals and traffic, but he stopped his tongue before it lashed her again. It was Miranda's fierce determination that stalled him. She showed not one ounce of fear, nor doubt; and in a sudden realization Wolfe understood that Miranda was no less than a confident skipper making a firm assessment of her own craft. And it was a craft she had every faith in—not unlike his *Windward* that black day he'd driven it, dismasted, 'round the Horn.

He gazed down at her bright eyes and rain-slicked cheeks, and understood at that moment that they were much more alike than he'd ever realized.

He understood, too, that this was a face he adored on a spirit he loved. And perhaps it was this, above all else, that commanded him now.

"Eric," asserted Miranda, "do you understand what I'm saying?"

Wolfe reached out his hand and let his thumb gently brush a raindrop from her cheek. Miranda blinked, obviously surprised by the sudden gentle caress after so fiery a display of his temper.

"Eric?"

"Aye, Miranda. I know you want me to see you as the captain of the Sea Sprite.*"*

"And? Do you?"

"Aye. I do. But I also think that two captains are two too many for sailing out storms in small craft."

Despite the thunder in the distance, Miranda's lips curled with a small smile. "Then maybe we should work together. As mates?"

Wolfe's eyebrow rose. *"I've never before called a female by that particular designation."*

"Don't you think it's about time?"

"Aye," admitted Wolfe, gazing into her eyes. *"Perhaps it is."*

"So what shall we do?"

"Well . . ." Wolfe surveyed the horizon. *"I'd say land's likely southwest. How far is a guess by any stretch. So if you've really the nerve—and stomach—for harnessing the squall's winds to advantage, then we'd better prepare."*

"Aye," said Miranda with a broad smile of triumph.

"Just be sure you understand the risk, Miranda. If we get close to land, we may be thrown up onto a lee shore. Remember, the power of man stops at the shore. The sea is fickle, and you cannot control the direction of the wind."

"Maybe not," said Miranda, turning her determined gaze toward the oncoming storm, "but I sure can try to ride it."

"There's a sailor," said Wolfe with a nod. *"Now, let's get to work. You've already got a trysail jury-rig, so let's secure the boom with a lash, else we'll be whacked into the drink for sure."*

"Aye, mate, right away!"

Chapter
Twenty-four

"If you see the shore, sing out!" called Wolfe over the din of wind and rain and booming thunder.

"Aye!"

Miranda gripped the tiller with determined might. The heart of the squall had hit them ten minutes before, and Miranda sat steady at the helm, working the tiller in tandem with Wolfe's commands. He'd insisted the stern was the smartest station for her in the rough water, for he'd had much more practice than her in working rigging on pitching decks—like about a century and half more, so how could she argue?

"How's her balance feel!" called Miranda.

"Good! I had Jack and Angus carry your trysail as close to the mast as they could get her. It's helpin' us now!"

"Don't forget, she's got a heavy-heel hull too! I told you she'd hold up!"

"Hang me, Miranda, you're the most headstrong female I've ever encountered!"

"Thank you!"

"You're welcome!"

As the rain lashed them and the wind kicked up, Miranda felt the prow begin to ride a high gray wave.

"Hold on!" cried Wolfe as a moment later they fell over its crest and smashed down.

"Yowza!" she cried, wiping the salt spray from her eyes.

"Watch her balance now!" cried Wolfe. *"Here comes another!"*

Miranda had one eye on the foredeck, keeping her balanced by the sight of the horizon as Wolfe had advised her. As the wave came toward them, she treated it like a surfer, searching for the best place to cross.

It was working. The *Sea Sprite* was heeling and they were making steady progress.

"Wahoo! We're doing it, Eric!"

"Aye, love! Watch the helm now!"

The ride was wild as the thunder rolled over them and the flash of lightning sent a brilliant jagged yellow streak through the air. The wind and the rain and the foam and the spray were a thrilling mix for Miranda's blood. Her heart pounded with the challenge, and she found fear and joy mingling inside her was an intoxicating blend.

She'd never felt more alive.

"This is why!" she called to him.

"What?"

"Why you love it. Why you never left it!"

Wolfe's blue gaze found hers in the mayhem and a look of strange recognition passed between them. Recognition and acknowledgment.

"My God . . ." rasped Miranda, feeling the shift of something deep inside her. "I've *known* you before! I've known you before!" she shouted in shock.

Wolfe's grip on the halyard slackened and, as they crested another wave and crashed down, he nearly lost his footing.

"Eric, be careful!"

Wolfe caught himself but looked shaken. And Miranda

suspected it was not from the jolt of the wave.

She stole glances at him as she worked the tiller. His focus seemed set on his work, but his glance back told her that he was troubled by her revelation. Wolfe had *recognized* her, too, she was certain of it!

She wanted nothing more than to ask him, to find out who exactly she'd been in his life. But the sea would allow them not even a moment's peace. And then, within minutes, Miranda saw a thin brown line.

"The shore! I see it!"

"Don't head in!" cried Wolfe at once. *"Steer her parallel."*

"Why? We made it this far!"

" 'Tis too dangerous. The wind may shift and we'll be scuttled. Sail the course parallel, Miranda. Do as I say."

"Aye—" she began to shout, and then stopped. "My God, Eric! What the heck is that!"

Miranda stared in horror at the black hulking vessel she saw approaching on the horizon.

"Blasted wretches! I thought we scared them back to hell!"

"Eric? What is it?"

"A devil's ship, Miranda. The same that brought those damned souls to terrorize us last night."

"Then, what's it doing next to that old trawler? Hey, that's Old Ron Runyon's boat!"

"Who?"

"They're my friends, Eric!"

The words were barely out of Miranda's mouth, when she saw a sight that left her blood cold. Black, shapeless forms jumped down from the deck of the dark vessel to the trawler. The waves were tossing and the rain lashing, and the trawler was fighting to make progress.

"What are they doing, Eric?!"

"Trying to scuttle her, Miranda."

"No! We can't let them! Ron and Tina might be aboard!"

Miranda immediately pulled on the tiller, and angled the boat toward shore.

"Miranda, stop! 'Tis too dangerous! Let me try to call the Windward *again."*

"Call them! But I'm not waiting. We have to help them too."

Wolfe was silent a moment. He looked out to sea, closed his eyes, and again called his ghostly crew. Then he turned on Miranda, his eyes sharp as blue crystal. *"Watch your waves, then!"* he barked. *"And watch the wind. If the direction changes, we'll be pounded to the shore."*

"I'll be careful," assured Miranda.

"Then take us to her."

They swung in swiftly. The stuttering of the trawler's engine grew louder as they closed in.

"They've stalled her engines," said Wolfe.

Miranda shuddered as she realized the trawler was in terrible trouble. The tide was pulling her toward the rocky shoreline as the waves battered her to and fro like a child's bath toy.

"Ron! Tina!" screamed Miranda as they closed the distance.

A moment later she saw Tina's round face peering over the rail. "Miranda! Look, Granddad, look! It's Miranda! We were coming to find you, when the storm hit!"

A formless shape loomed close behind Tina. Miranda barely made out the dark ghost's hideous face. It seemed to be laughing.

"Get off the trawler!" warned Miranda. "It's going to sink!"

"Miranda, you're nuts! You should be the one coming on board! Sail closer!"

Wolfe leaned toward her. *"They can't see me, nor the devil's deckhands. You'll have to convince them to jump to the* Sea Sprite."

"Tina! Get your grandfather and jump down to my deck!"

"No! Take the line and climb aboard the trawler! He'll get the engine started any second! We've reported our position! Don't worry!"

It was at that moment the dark ghosts decided to turn their attentions to the *Sea Sprite*.

"We meet again, Wolfe!" cried one of the dark ghosts.

And then two of the formless nightmares were jumping down to the *Sea Sprite*'s deck. Frantically, they jumped and moved until the little boat capsized.

Miranda screamed as she splashed into the cold salt-water, arms flailing. Then all sound stopped as she felt the heavy waves close over her head.

Wolfe cursed when he felt his solid form enter the water. Beside him the dark ghost of Leach Muldavey had launched an attack.

Kicking and punching, he managed to drive him off, then swam a circle, looking frantically for Miranda.

Diving down, he searched the water with no luck. Then he dove down again and swam with all his might. He saw her, finally, her clothes and shoes dragging her down, no life jacket to buoy her.

Wolfe pushed hard to reach her, then hooked an arm around her and dragged her to the surface.

"Breathe, love! Breathe!" he commanded. *"Ah, God, help me!"*

Wolfe felt her life slipping away from him. Her eyes were shut, her skin unnaturally pale. He cast about frantically, trying to find help. But all he saw was the devil's ship departing for the open sea, and the trawler being pulled by the surf straight for the rocks, the *Sea Sprite* close behind in its wake.

"Miranda!" called a voice across the waves. *"Where are you? Answer me!"*

Wolfe looked in the direction of the voice to find a dark-haired girl floating beside an old man. Each was in a life jacket. The girl was treading water while the old man seemed to be hanging on to an inner tube with all his limited strength.

"She's here!" cried Wolfe, but they failed to hear him. He kicked his legs to try to get her closer, but it was a

good distance and Miranda's weak form seemed unable
to keep her head above the water.

"Dammit to hell!" cursed Wolfe.

"You two there, in the water!" boomed a male voice.
"Stay calm!"

It was a voice Wolfe didn't recognize. He twisted his
head to find a coast guard cutter floating toward Miranda's
friends. Its captain was shouting through a bullhorn.
"We're coming to get you!"

In the next minute, two strong male divers dressed from
neck to foot in wet suits were jumping into the high surf
and swimming swiftly toward the girl and the old man.

"Hold on to my shoulders, miss!" called one of the
men.

Wolfe watched the two men help the girl and her grandfather to the cutter.

"Come back!" Wolfe cried, trying his best to pull Miranda toward the cutter. But a fine mist was rolling in
quickly now, and the coast guard officers could not see
her in the high waves.

Wolfe clenched his jaw in frustration and rage as he
saw the cutter begin to pull away. Out of sheer desperation he shouted with all his soul, but his voice had long
ago died to such mortals, and there was nothing he could
do but watch the bow of the vessel disappear into the mist.

Frantically, Wolfe peered into Miranda's pale face. He
wasn't sure if she was still breathing—and even if she
weren't, what could he do? He had no breath to give her!

"Damn my impotency! And damn my soul!" he cried
to the sky. *"But hear me, heaven! Do not make her pay
for my weakness!"*

If Wolfe's form could have shed tears, he would have,
seeing now the terrible consequences of his actions.
That's when he decided that Riley had been right. He had
been a fool to think any good could have come from loving her.

"Please," he begged heaven. *"Please! You granted
her this second chance on earth. Do not take it from her
now!"*

Wolfe closed his eyes in despair, ready to weep, when he thought he heard something . . . a sound that kept him from giving up hope. It came to him dimly at first, then grew in strength, like a lighthouse beacon through rain and mist.

"Hold on! Hold on!"

"Riley," rasped Wolfe with joy.

"Drive her to port, China Jack, I see them!"

Wolfe opened his eyes to find the glimmering glow of the *Windward* skimming the dark waves with ease. In no time, she swept close to them—as near as the next foamy crest. Wolfe watched the anchor drop and then the foot rope.

Riley was the first man down. *"Take my hand, Wolfe."*

"No! I won't leave Miranda!" Wolfe knew that mortals could not ride a ghost vessel. The *Windward* and ghost ships like her were seaworthy no more to the living—only the dead.

"Wolfe, there's nothing you can do. Look at her. Look up to the sky. The light's coming for her, Wolfe. Heaven's taking its claim back on her soul. Let her go now and come aboard."

Wolfe saw the tunnel of light slowly descending down from the clouds. *"No!"* cried Wolfe in anguished fury. *"Damn you, Riley! I'll not give up! Drop the rope ladder."*

"She can't come aboard! She's not passed over yet!"

"She's not comin' aboard. And she's not passing over. Not if I can help it. Drop the rope, damn you!"

The rope was down an instant later and Wolfe pulled himself out of the water, dragging Miranda close to his body. *"Now take off for that coast guard cutter. She's puttin' in to the nearest harbor."*

"But—"

"Do it, or I'll have your hide for breakfast!"

"Jack, hard about!" shouted Riley at once. *"And find that coast guard cutter. Now!"*

In an instant, Wolfe felt the *Windward* fly over the

foam. He held Miranda with all his strength as they were towed above the chilly waves.

"There she is!" shouted Riley within thirty seconds.

The *Windward* approached the cutter and Wolfe shouted to Riley, *"Tell the helm to watch my position— get me to her stern!"*

"Jack, come up on her port side!" relayed Riley. *"Close in!"*

Wolfe surveyed the cutter's stern. *"There's a low rail!"* he shouted to Riley. *"I can jump to her deck!"*

"You can't make that with her, Wolfe!"

"I can. An officer's coming aft. He'll see her! He'll help her!"

Wolfe tightened the arm holding Miranda and climbed higher on the rope ladder. *"Hold on, love,"* he whispered. *"Hold on."*

And then he jumped.

The hard wood deck came up at him fast and then he felt the jarring impact. He shook his head and looked immediately to Miranda. She was still unconscious.

He bent toward her, his eyes closed as he pressed his lips to her cheek. *"Hang on, my love,"* he whispered, and then he was on his feet.

The officer he'd seen coming aft—where was he?

He looked about but did not see a single mortal. Then he spotted the dark-haired man talking to another officer, a blond one with an honest face and strong build, who was still wearing the wet suit from his dip in the water to save Miranda's friends. Wolfe wasted no more time. He had to get their attention!

Grabbing up a boat hook, Wolfe headed straight for them.

"Holy cow, Mitch, what the heck is that?" cried the dark-haired officer.

The officer in the wet suit, the blonde named Mitch, turned, and Wolfe saw his face drop. Clearly, all the man was seeing was a boat hook waving around in midair.

Wolfe carefully drew the hook back toward Miranda. Like a charm, the two young men followed. When they got to the deck, Wolfe dropped the hook next to her.

"My God! Where the heck did *she* come from!" shouted the dark-haired young man.

"Who cares! Get the medic. Now!" cried Mitch. "And make sure he brings his gear!"

Wolfe watched with frightened paralysis as the medic worked on Miranda. Above, he watched the fateful tunnel of light descend farther from the sky. Below, he saw the brilliant glow rising out of her body, her spirit beginning to separate.

She'll be taken by heaven, he realized.

And Wolfe knew he might never see her again. Heaven had allowed her the chance to come back to earth once; this would not easily be granted to her again.

Self-rage filled Wolfe's soul. Whatever the spirit of Jenny Smithton had come to accomplish, she'd not had the chance to discover it—and it was all because of him!

Wolfe had thwarted her chance for happiness once on earth; he could not let it happen again! He would not!

"*My love!*" he cried from the depths of his soul. "*You've got to fight for what you want. Where's that grit I saw on the water? Fight, damn you! It's in you, girl!*"

The glowing shape of her spirit hesitated, its face peering straight at Wolfe. With trepidation he watched the tunnel of light draw closer to the cutter.

Wolfe clenched his fists. "*Ride it out, love!*" he tried in one last desperate try. "*Prove to me that you're a sailor!*"

In the next moment the formless glow above Miranda Burke's body began to lay back into its physical form. Within seconds the eyelids fluttered.

"I've got a pulse," said the medic next to her.

"Look, she's moving—"

Miranda was doing more than that outside of an instant. She was actually fighting the man giving her resuscitation, pushing the bag from her mouth. Then she began violently coughing up seawater and gulping down air.

Wolfe backed away, a tremor of relief and love shaking his spirit. He looked up to heaven, nearly weeping at the sight of the tunnel of light receding back to its home.

"*She lives,*" he whispered. "*She lives.*"

"My God, Granddad, look! It's Miranda. . . ."

Wolfe turned to see Miranda's friend, the dark-haired girl named Tina step out on the aft deck with her granddad. They both quickly moved toward Miranda and the small group of officers.

"Is she going to be all right?" asked Tina, tensely clutching the blanket at her shoulders.

"She should be," Mitch told her.

"She's my friend."

The young officer placed a strong arm around Tina. "I'm sorry. But try not to worry. She's in good hands now."

It was then that Wolfe noticed the old man was looking at him. *Straight* at him.

"Don't I know you from somewhere?" asked the old man, adjusting the blanket around his shoulders.

"Granddad? Who are you talking to?" asked Tina.

"That one, there. The sea cap'n," said the old man, pointing to the rail.

Other faces looked, but clearly saw nothing.

Wolfe shifted. "*You see me, old man?*" he asked softly.

"Aye . . . wait now . . . I know you, I'm sure of it—"

"Granddad—"

"Aye!" exclaimed the old man, his eyes bright with recognition. "You was the one! Back in '38! You was the ghost cap'n who saved my schooner!"

"Granddad," repeated Tina in an embarrassed tone. "There's *no one* standing there. Who are you talking to?"

"*Wolfe! Grab the rope and come aboard!*" Riley called down from the deck of the *Windward*.

Wolfe's gaze instantly found Miranda's face.

Not without her, he wanted to answer, but he knew it was impossible now.

Miranda's skin was pale, her body shivering as the medic placed a blanket around her soaking wet form, then helped her to her feet. Wolfe knew what she needed now was the kind of physical care that he could not give her— care for her mortal body.

With an unbearable feeling of loss, Wolfe cast one last look upon Miranda's face. *"I will always love you, little mermaid,"* he whispered on the sea air. Then he turned toward the *Windward* and reached for her rope.

"Where're ya headed?" asked the old man on the aft deck.

"Back where I belong," answered Wolfe, steeling himself to the desolate emptiness that would likely follow him for all eternity. *"Back to the sea."*

Chapter Twenty-Five

MEMORIAL HOSPITAL
GROTON, CONNECTICUT

"As I told you over the phone, Mr. and Mrs. Burke, she's delirious."

"Meaning?"

"She's speaking of things that make no sense, Mr. Burke, and have no basis in reality. It's an elaborate delusion. . . .

Through the thick gray mist Miranda heard the people clearly, though her eyes saw nothing more than shadowy images. Her mind was a haze now. Memories of faces and rooms, people and places, raced through it with confusing speed.

"The accident—"

"No. An accident in and of itself is not enough of an explanation. I believe its root cause is something else."

"What do you mean? Like what?"

"She was missing, Mr. Burke. I fear it's likely something traumatic happened to her—other than her near drowning. From our mental examinations of her thus far, I believe she'll need long-term treatment."

"But she can go home with us—"

"That's out of the question. Mr. Burke. She'll need to be hospitalized."

"She's already hospitalized, Doctor. Or are we not standing in a hospital room?"

"Teddy dear," interrupted a female voice, "the doctor means . . . Doctor, don't you mean another kind of—"

"A *mental* hospital. Mrs. Burke. Miranda will have to be watched and evaluated. We've got her tranquilized now, but you should be prepared to understand that her condition may need long-term medication, possibly for the rest of her life."

"You see, Mother, it's what I thought."

"Josh is about to get his graduate degree in psychiatry."

"Ah, very good. Well, you might want to keep a close eye on your sister, Josh."

"She's not my sister. We're not related."

"Oh, well, in any case, you have a personal interest."

"Yes, Doctor, he does. Don't you, Josh?"

"Yes, Mother, of course."

"And I agree with the doctor, Josh. You should keep a close eye on Miranda—and her case."

"I want to know more about this so-called delusion—"

"Look, Teddy, her eyes are fluttering."

"Miranda? Miranda, can you hear me? Dr. Wilcox is here with you. Miranda . . . ?"

Miranda listened to the voices. She recognized them, but they meant little to her spirit. There was only one voice and one image that meant anything to her now . . . only one to whom she wanted to respond. . . .

"Eric?" she whispered, then repeated in a louder voice. "Eric . . . take me back . . . please . . . don't leave me . . . Eric . . . Eric!"

"Who in the devil is Eric?"

"Calm down, Mr. Burke. This is part of her delusion.

In her more lucid moments, she's told us that Eric is a dead sea captain from the mid-1800s, and that she's been with him for the last two weeks. She says he saved her from drowning twice.''

"What!"

"She believes he was haunting a house where she had taken up residence."

"Where is this house?"

"It's in my notes . . . let's see . . . she claims to have been living in Blue Nights Cottage, on Crescent Cove outside of Stonington."

"Very good, Doctor. I'll have my private detectives check it over. And what else does she say?"

"She says that she fell in love with this Eric, and that he's sure to be waiting for her back there."

"Love, you say?"

"Yes, sir."

"Good God, you don't think she's—"

"Mr. Burke?"

"Just a moment. Joan and Josh, would you step outside?"

"No need, Teddy. We're part of the family."

"Mmm. Very well, then, Doctor, do you know if she's still a virgin?"

"I do not."

"Well, I'd like an examination done. And a pregnancy test."

"But how can you be certain she was . . . intact before she ran away."

"My private detective checked her doctor's reports. She'd just had a checkup the week before she left."

"I see."

"Look, Doctor, don't you think this Eric delusion is a cover for some sort of illicit boyfriend? Perhaps that's the reason she ran off in the first place."

"No, Mr. Burke."

"Well, then, what do you—"

"An elaborate delusion such as the one your niece has created that repeats even under medication is often constructed as a way of coping with trauma It could be that what she experienced was . . . well, was something so unpleasant that she coped by blocking it and creating another memory. Something more unpleasant than simply running away with a boyfriend.''

"Rape?"

"Yes, that's likely. Possibly in the very house she's claimed to have been in with this fictional ghost captain. She may have even been held there for many days, against her will. I've been waiting for her to stabilize before I've pressed her memories—or had a more . . . ah . . . *invasive* physical examination done.''

"Oh, Teddy, how unsavory.''

"Horrible stuff. Horrible stuff. Pitiful ruin of a lovely young woman. One wonders how she could speak of love for such a person.''

"Quite explainable. Mr. Burke. As we know from many case studies, hostages sometimes begin to identify, even befriend, their captors. It's a survival mechanism—though the Helsinki syndrome usually takes much more time to develop. This is an interesting case in that respect, a good case study, to be sure.''

"Well, Doctor, whatever can be done, please do it. Cost is not a factor.''

"Yes, Mr. Burke, of course.''

"Oh, Teddy, it's just awful. One wonders if she'll ever recover enough to live a normal life. Josh, you'll stick close to her now, won't you?''

"Of course, Mother. As the doctor points out, she'll make an interesting case study.''

"Well, I'm due at a meeting. Doctor, do keep us informed of where you decide to, ah . . . admit her.''

"Yes, Mr. Burke. Consider it done. Oh, Mrs. Burke, there's a young woman and her grandfather who've asked to see Miranda. We turned them away until her immediate family had the chance to see her, but would you like to allow them a visit?''

"Who exactly are they?''

"Let me see my notes . . . ah, names are Tina Runyon

and her grandfather, Ronald Bartholomew Runyon. They were fished out of the water by the same coast guard cutter as your niece—"

"I see . . . Josh, do you know these people?"

"Ah . . . yes, I've heard their names. They're rounders, Mother. I believe they operate that shabby little boatyard at the seedy end of town."

"My goodness. Doctor. I doubt Miranda knows these people. Please, I must insist that you restrict Miranda's visitors to her immediate family only."

"Of course, Mrs. Burke. Whatever you wish."

Part Three

Though the seas threaten,
they are merciful . . .

—WILLIAM SHAKESPEARE,
The Tempest, V, i

Chapter
Twenty-six

Miranda's body moved languidly beneath the crisp linen sheets, her white silk nightgown twisting around her legs.

Are you still inside me?

Aye.

And are you—

Aye, without question . . .

Against the soft mattress, Miranda's back arched with contentment. This was an exquisite feeling, one that warmed her blood and flushed her skin.

You taste of salt.

Like the sea?

Nay, my love. Much sweeter . . .

Instantly the scene changed. Miranda's heart began to pound, her pulse race. Back and forth she tossed until finally she felt herself falling . . . falling and falling into the dark depths.

If you see the shore, sing out!
Aye!
The sea was in a jealous rage. It surrounded her, pressed in upon her, began to smother her until everything in her vision vanished.

Don't leave me. Eric! Please! Please, don't go!

A jarring ringing jerked Miranda to a sitting position. With a groggy moan she brushed her short brown hair back off her sweaty forehead, then reached for the cell phone on her night table.

"Hello."

"Miranda?"

"Aunt Joan? What time is it?"

"Nearly nine, dear. Did I wake you?"

"Yes. Where are you?"

"I'm at the club. I've got to shower, then I thought I'd swing back home to pick up you and Josh for a bite of breakfast before we drive down to the shore."

"The shore."

"Yes, the Kennelworth auction."

"Auction?"

"You haven't forgotten! Miranda, is something wrong?" Joan's voice dropped to a theatrically low level, as if she were afraid someone in the tennis club's locker room would overhear how imbalanced her niece was. "You're not having another one of *those* dreams, dear?"

Miranda sighed. "No, no. Just . . . tired this morning."

"Well, next time, get up and come to the club with me like you usually do. Just have a shower, sweetie, you'll feel better. And don't forget your medication."

"No. I won't."

Miranda clicked off the phone and kicked off the covers. She needed a splash of water on her face. As she swung her legs over the edge of the bed and rose to her feet, she cursed. The nightgown around her legs was twisted so tightly, she nearly fell on her face when she tried to step forward.

"Hang me!" she cried, stumbling to keep her balance.

With a deep breath, she closed her eyes. Where had *that* odd curse come from? Her dream, no doubt.

In frustration, she stepped to the large marble bathroom of her aunt and uncle's mock Tudor mansion and ran some water. The chilly splash sluiced the beaded sweat from her forehead but failed to wash away the dream images.

She grabbed a towel and dabbed at her dripping face, reflected in the lighted mirror above the sink. At thirty it was a much different face than that of her youth.

Gone were her wild auburn curls. Her Aunt Joan's hairdresser had cut and straightened the wild mass into a tame, conservative coif, taking the brassy red noise away with a quieting brunette rinse.

Gone, too, was the fiery stubborn fight in her blue-green eyes, replaced now with a glazed resignation. At times Miranda hated her eyes, thinking them withdrawn and lifeless—but her doctor always reassured her that this was the look of maturity. Acceptance and calm was what mattered now.

Trembling slightly, Miranda opened the medicine cabinet and reached for the amber-colored plastic bottle with the typed white label. It was as familiar to her now as her own glazed reflection. She twisted off the cap and took out the prescribed amount of tablets. Then, with a quickly filled glass of water, she downed them.

Closing her eyes, Miranda took a deep breath, then turned and headed back to the bedroom. She glanced at the small calendar on her vanity, and a chill touched her skin.

"May first," she whispered. "That's why . . ."

No matter how hard she worked to dispel the haunting images, the dreams always came back with the first hint of warm summer weather. In one month it would be the ten-year anniversary. Ten years since she'd run away on the *Sea Sprite*. Ten years since she'd seen Blue Nights Cottage.

For many of those ten years, Miranda had resisted Dr. Wilcox's treatments, insisting her memories were real.

But time and the persistence of everyone around her had worn her down. Now she knew she'd simply been young and foolish to have run away.

She also knew it was better for everyone that she try to get better. And, with the help of her daily medications, she was making progress—or, at least, that's what Dr. Wilcox kept telling her.

She just wished she knew why, with so many people around her, trying to help her, she felt so empty. So isolated and unhappy. So alone.

Perhaps Dr. Wilcox had been right. Perhaps it was her deep attachment to her own delusion that kept her from being truly happy.

Miranda fingered the diamond solitaire on her left hand. Perhaps if she moved on with her life, finally allowed Josh to set the date for their wedding, perhaps then the dreams would leave her forever and she'd be happy.

"The sea captain was a delusion," she told her reflection firmly. "Not a memory. Get it through your head!"

She sighed with pure frustration.

"If only I could make the breakthrough."

Over the past ten years, Dr. Wilcox had tried everything to release the blocked memories of Blue Nights Cottage, but he'd failed. Even hypnosis had not worked.

The police and private detectives had been no help. They'd found only her own personal items in the parlor of Blue Nights, nothing to lead them to any sort of psycho or rapist. Everything else in the place had been years old.

The saddest part of all was that her father's notebooks were nowhere to be found. The one piece of evidence that might have helped her prove her own story to herself had left her with the sickest feeling of all—that it *had* all been a delusion.

The thought of what might have really happened to her in that place—all the ugly implications—had often driven Miranda into nightmares.

Good God, her own flash of memory at being handcuffed and her face pushed down on the musty sofa was enough to make her believe the doctor when he posed the possibilities.

Unfortunately, her nightmares of what *might* have happened to her had become more common now than the fanciful dreams of her captain.

Ten years ago, some ex–deputy sheriff on her missing persons case had reported to her uncle's private detectives that he'd followed a lead to the cottage but saw nothing. After hearing this, many people believed that she may even have been taken to other locations—places she obviously couldn't recall.

Feeling a headache coming on, Miranda checked the bedside clock, wondering for a moment if she had time to make a quick call to Dr. Wilcox for reassurance.

Perhaps the pills would take effect and she could work through it alone, she told herself. But then she glanced down at her hands. They were shaking.

"Hang me," she whispered, then reached for the phone and dialed her psychiatrist's portable phone number.

"Dr. Wilcox, it's Miranda Burke. I'm having another bad morning . . . can you help me?"

Chapter Twenty-seven

"It's such a lovely day and pretty blue sky," said Miranda with a small sigh. "It's a shame they erected a tent to cover the chairs."

Miranda's low-heeled pumps stepped through the neatly trimmed grounds of the Kennelworth Estate, her long, flowered dress swirling around her legs. With a hand to her wide-brimmed hat, she tipped back her head and let the afternoon sun warm her cheeks, the sea breeze toss her bangs.

Joan Cunning Burke sighed at Miranda's comment as if it were either tiresome or completely inane. "Josh," she said after taking a sip of champagne. "What do you think of the *lot*."

"It's all right, I suppose." Josh shrugged. "Looks like a bunch of old stuff to me."

Joan laughed. "How accurate. I must say, antiques really aren't my style."

"Oh, Mother, then why did you come?"

"For the Ina scuptures. He's the hottest artist in the

234

New York galleries and that young Kennelworth widow just doesn't know what she's put on the block."

"I *like* the antiques," said Miranda softly.

"What's that, dear? Did you *say* something?"

Miranda studied the ground. "No. Nothing."

"She's had a bad morning," Joan murmured to Josh as if Miranda weren't standing two feet away. "Another dream, I think."

"Has she had her pills?"

"Yes, she told me she took them first thing."

Miranda shifted uncomfortably. She hated it when they treated her like this, as if she were some sort of brain-damaged child that could barely comprehend the English language. But Miranda knew better than to protest. It only made things worse—caused a scene that made other people think she really was some kind of a nut-case.

"That's the one . . ." whispered a female voice nearby.

Miranda glanced back and noticed a group of women were glancing her way and speaking in hushed tones.

She felt her body tense. How she detested the way people sometimes looked at her, and murmured about her—even her own family. The news of her disappearance and mental condition had hit all the papers and major television networks at the time, and people still remembered.

Her connection to the wealthy Theodore Burke, owner of the nationwide Pita Pockets chain, had been played to the hilt; and even though she'd changed her appearance considerably since then, people still gossiped when they heard her name. And, it seemed to Miranda, if some people didn't remember, her aunt made *sure* they did.

The Burkes' entire social circle knew of her lengthy stay in the private mental hospital, the medications, the treatments. It had clearly spooked people into remaining distant.

Especially men.

The thought of their intimate knowledge of her private demons made Miranda feel more exposed than ever. And that made her withdraw even further into herself.

"I don't want to be here," said Miranda quietly, feeling

the familiar panic begin to grip her. "Let's go back home."

"Now, dear, you know what Dr. Wilcox says. Getting out is good for you. Josh, why don't you take care of her?"

Miranda looked to the handsome face of her fiancé, now a practicing psychiatrist. He tossed back a lock of blond bangs and flashed a white, toothy smile. She weakly returned it, trying her best to feel something for him.

Dr. Josh Cunning was always so sweet and attentive. And it was painfully obvious that Josh was the only young man in their social circle who was willing to take on the baggage of a young woman with mental health problems. For that she had to be grateful, even if she didn't feel much else for him.

Maybe gratefulness was enough.

"C'mon, dear," soothed Josh, placing an arm around her shoulders. "Let's find a seat."

Miranda allowed herself to be led from the sunny lawn into the shadows of the tent. The group of about two hundred bidders soon followed and took their seats in the many folding chairs that had been set up to face a low stage with a podium.

"Good afternoon, ladies and gentlemen, and welcome. Let us begin the auction with lot number one . . ."

The bidding ensued, and Miranda stifled a yawn, her gaze drawn to the shoreline beyond the estate's grounds. In the distance, a small sailboat was coasting over the calm blue waters. The sight set off a series of little tremors deep within her.

"And here we have lot number seventeen," announced the auctioneer. "Portrait of a sea captain."

Miranda's eyes flew to the front of the tent.

"There he is, ladies and gentlemen, as authentic a portrait as you'll ever find of one of our local sailing men. A Yankee clipper captain, painted in the mid-1800s by the admired maritime artist J. M. Smithton. Appraised at four thousand. Bidding starts at five hundred."

"That portrait," whispered Miranda.

"It's awful," pronounced Joan at her left.

"Quite awful," agreed Josh at her right.

"What am I bid?" asked the auctioneer.

"One thousand!" called Miranda suddenly, the bid bursting forth from a place she could barely control.

Joan and Josh stared in slack-jawed horror at the woman sitting between them.

"Miranda, what in the *world's* gotten into you?" asked her aunt Joan, clearly appalled.

"Thank you," said the auctioneer. "I'm bid one thousand. A bargain price. Do I hear fifteen hundred."

"Fifteen hundred!" called another voice.

"Thank you. Do I hear—"

"Twenty-five hundred!" called Miranda.

"Miranda! What are you doing!" exclaimed Joan Cunning Burke. "Stop right now."

But the glaze over Miranda's eyes was clearing in the sunny sea air. And she turned their clarity upon her aunt. "No."

"Three thousand!" called another voice.

"Thank you. I'm bid three thousand dollars for this excellent antique painting of a clipper captain—"

"Thirty-five hundred!" called Miranda.

"Miranda, I must *insist* you stop this ridiculous display. What, may I ask, are you going to use as money?"

"My father's trust fund," said Miranda calmly. "I'm thirty now. I can have access to it, can't I?"

Joan sputtered for an answer. It was the very first time she'd ever brought the subject up, and it had clearly taken her aunt off guard. She watched the woman's thin lips purse and her eyes shoot a glaring look to her son.

"Miranda," said Josh soothingly, placing a firm hand on her forearm. "Whyever would you want to waste your money on that old thing?"

"Because I want to."

"Four thousand!" called another bidder.

"Oh, thank heaven!" said Joan, leaning back in her chair with relief. "That's the appraised price, Miranda, so you can simply stop your bidding now. No harm done."

Miranda frowned and glanced once more beyond the shadows of the tent. Her vision held the small white sail, drifting like a mirage on the beautiful water. Drifting farther and farther out to sea. *Like my dream,* realized Miranda. It would soon be beyond her vision.

"Going . . . going . . ."

"Ten thousand dollars!" cried Miranda, leaping to her feet.

"Miranda, are you *crazy*!" blurted out her aunt Joan.

Beneath the tent the small crowd fell to a stunned silence.

"I'm bid . . . ten thousand," announced the auctioneer, a bit surprised himself. "Are there any . . . any other bids?"

The crowd began to murmur.

"Take the bid back," urged Joan, tugging on her arm. "Hurry, before the gavel is banged."

Miranda felt her will falter. Everyone was staring at her, murmuring about her. A flush of embarrassment and shame began to creep along her cheeks as she struggled with her options.

"Going . . ." announced the auctioneer.

Miranda felt her mouth open, felt herself giving in to her aunt's wishes. But then she looked once more into the sharp blue gaze of the sea captain.

You've got to fight, my love. Fight for what you want.

"It's the voice," whispered Miranda. "The voice from my dreams. It's still inside me."

"Take it back," ordered Joan.

". . . going . . ." warned the auctioneer.

But Miranda shook her head. Suddenly, there was no more struggle, no more doubt. The critical stares around her faded away as Miranda saw only the captain's eyes. It was easy then to turn her own bright vision upon her aunt.

"No," she said firmly. "I know what I want."

"Gone! Sold to the lovely young woman in the third row."

"Well, that takes it," said Joan in disgust. "And what *exactly* are you going to do with that thing?"

"*Look* at it," said Miranda pointedly, then reached for her purse.

Chapter
Twenty-eight

Glimmering blue eyes. Shining darkly. Like an ink-stained sea. Miranda stared into them later that day in the intimacy of her bedroom.

They were alluring and frightening at the same time, sitting in the rugged, square-jawed face of the unsmiling sea captain who seemed so familiar to her.

Miranda stepped closer to the painting she'd hung on her wall. The form was as sturdy as the jaw—powerful, strong, and held with erect confidence. Arms folded across a brawny chest, hip slightly, almost insolently, propped.

The expression was a curious mix of authority and intimacy. A man who clearly had something rather intense on his mind. Miranda felt her skin shiver with a little thrill. It almost felt as if the man in the portrait were seeing her—and, as strange as it seemed, *desiring* her.

"It's as if he wants to kiss me," she whispered, a private smile touching her lips.

Her slender fingers reached out to trace the line of his jaw and a tingling seemed to touch her—or the memory of a tingling.

"Who were you, Captain?" she asked. "And why are you haunting my dreams?"

"Miranda?" A light knock followed the male voice. "May I come in?"

"Yes, Josh! The door's open."

"I'm taking you out to dinner."

Miranda watched Josh step into her bedroom. Sunny blond hair, dashing smile, casually elegant tan blazer and chocolate pants. The familiar face of Josh Cunning had been in her bedroom many times, but for some odd reason Miranda suddenly felt uneasy. As if he didn't belong—and the captain did.

"I don't know, Josh. That's nice of you, but I'd rather not."

"What?" asked Josh, perplexed. He was obviously unaccustomed to anything but quick compliance from Miranda. "Come out, Miranda. The doctor says it's good for you."

"Blast it! Why's everybody always quoting what Dr. Wilcox says? Why don't you listen to what *I'm* saying!"

Josh's eyes widened in surprise at the outburst. Miranda herself couldn't explain it. She was usually so docile and agreeable. But ever since her trip to the seaside, something beneath her skin was beginning to peck at her, as though there were a chick inside her that was sick to death of being trapped in its shell.

"Aren't you feeling well?" asked Josh softly. "Have you taken your evening medication yet?"

"I'm sorry I raised my voice. Please, just give me my privacy for tonight."

Miranda waited for Josh to turn and go, but he didn't. Instead, he glanced from her face to the portrait on the wall behind her.

"Is *that* thing the cause of all this upset?"

Miranda felt her heart begin to race. "Please don't jump to conclusions. I'm fine."

"No. You're not. Look at you. Your face is flushed and your breathing irregular. Miranda, it's unwise to keep this portrait in here." Josh stepped past her and reached for the carved wooden frame. "I'm going to take it down right now."

"No!" shrieked Miranda, lunging for Josh's arms. With a forceful tug she pulled him away from the painting. "Don't touch it!"

Josh stumbled back, stunned for a moment, then a look of disgust shadowed his sunny face. "Look at you, Miranda, you're clearly regressing. And it's that painting that's doing the harm. Don't you want to get better?"

"I—I want the painting. I want it left here."

"Well, what does your *doctor* want?" snapped Josh, clearly annoyed. "Or haven't you mentioned it to him yet?"

"I . . . will."

"You do that. Or I will."

"Just get out of here, Josh."

"Fine by me. *After* I watch you take your medicine."

"Stop acting like my doctor. You may have a psychiatric practice of your own now, but I'm not your patient."

"Miranda, do you want to go back to that hospital?"

Miranda felt her blood chill in her veins. "No," she rasped.

Josh folded his arms in triumph. "Then *take* your medicine."

With clenched fists, Miranda nodded slightly, but she didn't move. Josh strode impatiently to the bathroom. "Come on."

Reluctantly, Miranda followed. She watched him retrieve the plastic amber bottle of tablets. He shook out two, poured a glass of water, and presented both to her. With trembling hands she took them, and swallowed.

"That's a good girl. Now I'll leave you . . . but promise me you'll talk to the doctor tomorrow about that portrait. I'm sure he'll agree with me—that it should come down."

Miranda glared angrily at Josh. "Why can't you all just leave me alone!"

"Because we want what's best for you."

"Do you?"

"Of course." Josh leaned in to plant a kiss on her forehead, but Miranda pulled away.

"Just go."

"All right, then. Be angry. But remember, I want you to marry me. Soon. And I won't have another man's portrait hanging in our bedroom."

"Threats won't work, Josh. I want to keep the captain."

"I'll see you tomorrow, Miranda. *After* your medicine has calmed you down and you've talked to Dr. Wilcox. He'll convince you to get rid of that awful portrait."

"Go already!"

Miranda sighed when the door finally shut. She wished she had some kind of lock to ensure her privacy, but she was told that she could not have one.

How she wanted just to be left alone.

Alone with her captain.

She could feel the medication seeping into her body now, taking the anger and fight from her mind. But in her last little dying flame of personal will, she dragged a heavy chair in front of her door.

"That'll keep them out," she murmured to the captain on her wall. "At least until morning."

"Stop moving."

"Hang me, girl, I've been sitting here forever."

"Summon your patience."

"I have no use for patience."

"That's because patience is a virtue and you much prefer vice."

"Don't speak of such things."

"Oh, why not, Eric. You know it's true."

"I know of no such thing."

"Well, you're easy to paint, at least. I'll give you that."

"Full-color sort, am I?"

"No. God gave you good lines and angles on your face."

"I see. Nothing to do with me."

"Well, I suppose you are easy on a girl's eyes."

*"Mmm. Better be careful. Flirting with the likes of me
may lead to vice."*

*"From what I've heard. Eric, a girl can't be too careful
around you. I know what your men call you."*

"Blast . . ."

"Eric? What's wrong?"

*" 'Tis not right. That you should have learned that
name. 'Twas never meant for a lady's ears, least of all
yours."*

"I know you too well. Sea Wolf."

*"Don't, Jenny. Don't call me by that name. Not here,
in your own parlor."*

"Eric, you think you know me. But you do not."

*"Indeed I do know you, Miss Smithton. I've known you
all my life."*

"I think you do not. I certainly know you better."

"Ha! Prove it."

*"All right . . . I know what you've been thinking all af-
ternoon, sitting for me."*

"What?"

*"You're thinking you'd rather be on deck, annoying
some poor second mate about the slowness of the seamen
on the lines."*

"Mmm."

"I'm right, aren't I?"

*"See to your painting, girl, or I'm likely to end up with
three eyes and a pig's snout."*

"Now, there's an idea. Could be an improvement."

The slam of a car door on the street outside awakened
Miranda from her fitful dream. She turned on her pillow
and opened her eyes.

"My God!" The sea captain was standing over her bed.
Miranda swiftly sat up, and then just as swiftly slumped
back.

"It's just the painting," she realized, shaking her head
at the sea captain's penetrating stare. Her dream had been
so vivid, so realistic, that for a moment she was certain

the raven-haired seaman was actually in this very room, posing just for her.

With a strange sigh that was part relief, part disappointment, Miranda lowered her gaze to the small alarm clock at her bedside.

"One-forty," she whispered, then caught sight of the book on her nightstand, the one she'd been reading before she'd drifted off—*Connecticut Maritime Artists*.

"It has to be the book," she murmured. After all, she'd purchased it today specifically for its chapter on J. M. Smithton.

It was the only explanation for her vivid dream, in which she took on the visage of a lovely young woman with blond curls and pretty blue eyes, sitting at an easel with paintbrush in hand, teasing the captain with every stroke.

Still, thought Miranda, there was something so intimate about the whole scene, so sweet and familiar, she could not help feeling that it had some kind of special meaning for her.

Outside her uncle's mansion, steps sounded on the walkway. Voices drifted up through Miranda's second floor window, and one of them sounded like Josh's.

"Shhhh . . . don't . . . wake . . ."

With eyes wide open, Miranda sat up and swung her legs off the bed. A glass of water would calm her, she decided, and maybe her sleeping pills.

The trip to the bathroom and back took under two minutes, but her anxieties kept her tossing and turning for hours after.

Miranda knew there was something buried deep inside her. Something like lost memories—and, yet, something more than that. Something that she had to dig out soon or risk going crazy again.

"Maybe I should finally do something about it myself," murmured Miranda, half asleep, "before I end up back in the hospital."

Was the captain nodding in agreement? Miranda peered at the painting. She didn't know what he was thinking, but she knew what *she* thought: this terrible torture would not stop until she finally found the courage to take that trip.

The trip that was long overdue.

Downstairs, in the large sunken living room of the Burkes' expansive home, Joan Cunning Burke watched her son's imported Italian loafers shift uncomfortably on the thick pile of the Persian rug.

"Answer me, Josh, what would Miranda say if she saw you with this woman?"

"Please, Mother, don't start. Miranda practically threw me out of her room tonight, and every man's entitled to a little recreation—"

A high-pitched giggle came from the collegiate-looking blonde standing next to Josh, and Joan rolled her eyes in disgust.

"Quiet down, young woman," snapped Joan before turning back to her son. "Josh, you've been drinking, and she's clearly inebriated. Such reckless behavior is outrageous."

"Oh, please—"

"And I've just about had it with your extravagant lifestyle. Teddy's tired of my asking him to pay your bills. He's just put me on a budget as it is. He may even start charging you rent."

"Let him. He can keep accounts. His niece will pay up once we're married. Her trust fund will cover my lifestyle quite nicely."

"Oh, is that so? And has Miranda agreed to set the date?"

"No, but she will."

The blonde next to Josh giggled, her weight shifting a bit. Josh moved to prop her up. "Joshy, where's your bedroom already?"

"This is outrageous," Joan said in disgust. "What would Miranda if she saw you?"

"Don't make me laugh. Miranda's so malleable, she's eating right out of my hand. I could tell her this girl's one of my patients in need of private counseling, and she'd believe me.''

"How can you be so cold?''

Josh leveled his gaze. "I had a good teacher.''

"To hell with you. Even if you are my son. I was wrong to have encouraged your relationship with her. I've grown fond of Miranda, and I don't want to see her hurt.''

"Take it easy, Mother. It's a fair trade. I mean, no other man would ever marry that pathetic creature. Don't you think I deserve some compensation for my willingness to be a live-in companion?''

"Miranda is getting better, Josh. She may want more from you—''

"She's hanging by a thread as it is. You should have seen her a few hours ago, hysterical over that silly portrait she bought. God, it's pitiful watching her sink.''

"Get out of here, Josh. And take that piece of espresso-bar trash with you.''

"Well, la-dee-da-da—'' giggled Josh's date.

"C'mon,'' said Josh, "Let's go back to your apartment—''

"Can't,'' said the girl. "Sssss bein' fumigated for buggies!''

"Fumigated? That's inconvenient. You see, Mother, if we just quietly slip upstairs—''

"Josh, you're trying my patience! Take her to a hotel or a bar or a brothel—wherever! I don't care. Anywhere but this house!''

"C'mon, honey, guess it's the Marriott tonight.''

"Oooooo, I like room ssservice—''

Chapter
Twenty-nine

"Blue Nights Cottage?" The gas station attendant scratched his crew cut and squinted into the afternoon sun. "Don't know if I've heard of it."

"It's in Crescent Cove."

"Aw, yeah. That old house. Five miles down north on route one, then take Puxton Lane toward the water. Unmarked turnoff to the left is private. It's a pretty old dirt road, but it'll get you there."

"Thanks," said Miranda as she handed him the twenty for the fillup. "Keep the change."

"Thank you, ma'am. Y'know, they say that house is haunted."

She gave the attendant a weak smile. "Do they? Well, I guess I'll be seeing that for myself."

Miranda pulled the silver BMW out of the tiny gas station and headed for Blue Nights. She'd spent days calling dozens of Realtors, then slipped away from her uncle's mansion that morning without telling a soul.

All of her patient tracking had paid off. She'd finally

found the present owner of the old cottage. The name she'd been given stunned her, but she placed the call to him nonetheless. If she was lucky, he'd already be there.

As she neared the dirt turnoff, tremors of memories streaked through her. For a moment she wondered if this was so wise, taking this trip by herself. She'd been told by Dr. Wilcox that returning to Blue Nights might do her great harm. But ever since she saw the portrait of her captain, Miranda could not stop herself.

After turning onto the private drive, she followed the bumpy road until she reached the water. She pulled the car to a stop behind an old blue pickup truck and stepped out.

"Miranda? Miranda Burke?"

A lovely young woman with long, black hair and large brown eyes walked swiftly toward her. She was dressed simply in blue jeans and a white blouse, and her lively spirit shone brightly in her broad, happy smile.

"Tina? Tina Runyon?"

"Well, actually it's Tina Peters now."

Miranda met her old friend, stepping into her outstretched arms with an ease that warmed her heart.

"God, Tina, I'm so happy to see you!"

"You too, Red!"

Miranda laughed—the sound felt like a rusty hinge on a long-closed door. She touched her short brunette hair. "I'm afraid you'll have to find another nickname."

"No, never. You'll always be Red to me."

"How have you been?"

"Married. Happy. Pregnant. Two kids and one on the way."

"Oh, my God! Congratulations!"

"Thanks."

"And who is Mr. Peters? Not the lead singer for Live Wire, I hope."

"God no! You might remember him, actually. He's a coast guard officer by the name of Mitch Peters. One of those divers who fished me and Granddad out of the drink all those years ago."

"Oh, Tina, I'm so happy for you."

"Mitch and I run the boatyard now. Y'know, we bought the *Sea Sprite* from your uncle when you were in . . . ah, you know, the hospital."

"No, I didn't know. No one told me. I'd assumed the *Sea Sprite* was lost for good, smashed on the rocks that day."

"Naw, she's a solid little thing. Been through a lot, but we fixed her right up. We rent her out now for day sails. You're welcome to take her out anytime you want. No charge, of course."

"Thanks, but I don't sail anymore. I don't think I even remember how."

"Tina!" called an older male voice from inside the house. "Bring your friend to the house!"

"Yes, Granddad!"

Old Ron Runyon slowly made his way out to Blue Nights' porch, and Miranda and Tina walked to meet him. The old man's legs were even more crippled than Miranda remembered, and he was now using a three-pronged cane to move slowly around, but he still sported a handsome gray beard and his bright eyes had plenty of spark left in them.

"Miranda Burke," began Old Ron, "do you mean to tell me that after all these years you're thinkin' of *buyin'* this old place?"

"Yes, I think so. My trust fund is under my control now and . . . well . . . it's something I feel I need to do."

"Grandfather inherited it himself about a year ago," explained Tina. "It's odd how things work out."

"Came down to me through the Wolfe branch," said Old Ron. "Ya want to take a look inside? Needs an awful lot of repair work. Been about four years now since anyone's tried to improve the place."

Miranda nodded, and they moved toward the back porch door. Her lungs burned as she stepped into the dark daylight of the parlor. She was holding her breath, she realized, waiting for something terrible to hit her, some horrible breakthrough memory, some ugly revelation.

But there was nothing.

Miranda only smelled must and dust, and felt the cobwebs of a very old home.

"Needs lots of repair work, as I say," repeated old
Ron. "But the structure's sound."

As Tina and her grandfather drifted into the kitchen,
Miranda hung back a moment. She closed her eyes and
tried to feel something, some trace of him . . . some sign
of him . . . *anything*.

But there was nothing.

"Eric?" she finally whispered into the air.

Dust particles spun from her breath. There was no other
movement, no other sound in the still deadness.

But then she heard something. A voice. It came to her
not from this place, but from a place inside her. *From the
first time I saw Blue Nights, I felt that I belonged here.
That it wanted me here, needed me here.*

That voice had been her own.

"Miranda Burke, are ya comin'?" called Old Ron.

Miranda opened her eyes with renewed hope. Maybe
the ghost of her captain was no longer in this house, but
the ghost of *herself* surely was. And the renewed feeling
that she belonged at Blue Nights was enough of a sign
for Miranda.

"Yes," she called to Ron, "I'm on my way."

"You can't be serious. I mean, you don't *really* want
to buy it, do you?" asked Tina on the back porch an hour
later.

"Pretty remote place for a young woman to be takin'
up residence, don't ya think?" agreed Old Ron.

Miranda considered the words of her old friends, but
her senses took in the rippling blue waters of the sunny
cove and the fresh salt of the sea breeze, and she knew
the answer.

"I do want to buy it," said Miranda firmly. "I feel I
need to live here—for a while at least. It's something
inside me, something that needs to find out . . . I don't

know what. Maybe I just need to prove some things to myself.''

Miranda felt a flush on her cheeks as she looked into the perplexed faces of her two old friends. "I suppose you think I'm acting a little irrational here.''

"No,'' said Tina. Then after a short pause she admitted, "Well, maybe just a little. I suppose it has something to do with what happened ten years ago?''

"Yes. I've been having these dreams that—'' abruptly Miranda stopped herself. "I'm sorry. I don't expect you to understand.''

"Worlds full of strange and wonderful things,'' said Old Ron with a wink. "But here's a bit of free advice: Don't expect anyone to understand your dreams but you. Most people can barely understand their own.''

Miranda smiled, then leaned in and kissed Old Ron's cheek.

"What's that for?''

"It's just long overdue,'' said Miranda, then she turned with confidence to look again at the house. "Now, let's get down to business. Can you recommend a good construction firm? I'll want to move in by the end of May.''

Chapter
Thirty

"Farewell, Wolfe, see you in a month!"

Eric Wolfe waved to his crew from the shallow waters of his shoreline and watched the glowing shape of the *Windward* set sail again.

The sea captain's mood had been relatively good until he turned to look at his beloved home. One look at Blue Nights soured him quickly—because it was more than obvious that the mortals were back.

Life energy radiated from his home like a beacon, and there were significant physical changes to the place since the last time he'd taken his leave.

Fresh blue paint brightened the repaired exterior. New glass sparkled in place of the old broken windows, shutters were rehung, and roof shingles replaced.

"Blasted living," he cursed as he waded to shore. With every step, the heavy weight of his materialized form

253

melted away, but not the heavy chore ahead of him.

"These people are dug in," he complained. *"Haunting them out'll be a real effort."*

Wolfe stepped onto the back porch; the boards beneath him were now in fine shape. The rotting planks had been replaced, and the repairwork looked flawless, blending perfectly into the original design.

He hated to admit it, but whoever the hell had dared to move into his beloved home had at least made the effort to treat it right.

Still, it was *his* home.

And the mortals were trespassers.

Wolfe saw no reason to wait. He barreled through the closed back door and straight into the cottage. The interior was clearly improved, he saw at once, but not nearly finished.

Ladders, scaffolds, drop cloths, and buckets were everywhere. Wolfe hauled off and kicked a pile of cans, deciding the racket was loud enough to wake the dead, let alone any trespassing mortals.

"Come forward, you lazy landlubbers!" he cried, his ire rising with every step.

Wolfe circled the half-restored first floor in search of these mortals, but there was no sign. So he headed for the staircase.

"Likely in bed," he surmised. *"Just as well. Mortals are all the more spooked when they're woken in the middle of the night."*

Wolfe checked the three smaller bedrooms but found them cold and empty. So he approached the newly varnished master bedroom door, which radiated with the warmth of life.

"Got you now," he murmured with ghostly glee. Then he stepped through the thick dark wood.

A woman with short brown hair was asleep in his old four-poster. The heavy carved wood had clearly been sanded, polished, and revarnished, the mattress and bedclothes replaced. The piece looked as good as the day he'd bought it in the port of New Orleans.

"No matter," he told himself. *"The lady must go at once."*

He vowed to never again make the mistake of getting any closer to mortals than saving their lives on the sea or—when it was required—haunting them straight *out* of his home.

"Get up, madam!" he cried, knocking over a chair and kicking a large, unopened box. *"Get up and get out of my home!"*

The woman stirred and turned over but failed to waken.

He tried again. Striding to the fireplace, he took up a poker and rapped it loudly against the bedpost, right by her head.

"Madam, get up!" he cried. *"Get out, if you please!"*

The lady moaned, but still she did not waken. Wolfe threw down the piece of metal in clanking disgust.

What in hell was the matter with her? Had she taken some sort of sleeping potion?

He bent closer to look into her face, then suddenly stilled.

The moonlight was splashing in from the half-raised window, shining enough light for him to make out the features of her face.

"My God. It can't be."

Wolfe stepped back in shock, his form partially passing through the fallen chair behind him. He felt the tingles in his legs but ignored them, staring instead at the face of the woman now sleeping in his old bed.

" 'Tis my Miranda. And she's in my bed."

It was his dream come true.

And his nightmare.

Wolfe slowly receded from her, tremors of emotion overtaking his spirit.

"What are you doing here?!" he demanded as he paced the length of the bedroom in agitation. It had been a decade since she'd nearly drowned at his hands. Yet, in all that time, she had never returned.

Wolfe had assumed long ago that she'd forgotten him— that she'd chalked him up to some youthful fancy and decided, quite rightly, to move on with her mortal life.

"*Why?*" he commanded of her sleeping form. "*Why have you returned now?*"

Wolfe had to assume she was married. Either that or involved with some mortal man.

"*You must be,*" he murmured, bending close to her again. "*Look at you, you're beautiful.*"

Wolfe reached out, wanting nothing more than to touch her soft-looking cream-colored cheek, but his long, translucent fingers merely passed through her skin. He felt the slight tingling and wondered again why she would not waken—why she had yet to sense his presence.

He surveyed the outline of her form beneath the bed-clothes. Unable to resist, he focused his power and began to move the blanket and sheet back, slowly pulling them down to reveal her figure.

The first thing he saw after her sweet neck and delicate shoulders was the scooping neckline of her short, satiny nightdress, the color of moonlight.

Beneath that he could see that her physical form had matured quite magnificently. The slender, athletic young woman he remembered was still there, but her curves had filled. Her legs and arms were softer and rounder now, her hips more pronounced, and her breasts were fuller than he remembered.

Wolfe's dark blue eyes caressed the creamy skin of her long, bared legs, then traveled upward to the flare of her hip and the soft hills of her breasts, rising and falling beneath the thin white satin of her short gown.

"*Oh, my Miranda, what I'd do to you now if I could.*"

Wolfe felt the stirrings deep inside him, feelings that had been dormant for a decade, feelings that reminded him too well that he'd once been a virile mortal man.

But he was that no longer.

And he'd seen what devastation was waiting when he'd try to pretend he was more than what he was.

"*God, this is too much!*" he cried in agony. "*Why do you torture me!*"

In a raging despair, Wolfe turned from the bed and

strode away, passing through the wooden door and down the staircase, kicking out at cans and ladders and furniture without regard for the clattering noise and scattering mess he left in his wake.

He barreled to the shoreline, wading into the shallows, ready to call back the *Windward,* ready to leave Blue Nights forever and never return.

But his movements stilled.

Slowly he turned and ascended the hill again. At the porch he collapsed into his old rocking chair, now polished and varnished and repaired. He dropped his head into his hands and closed his eyes.

"I cannot stay with you," he murmured miserably. *"And I cannot leave you."*

For once, in all his life and afterlife, this decisive, fearless captain of the sea had finally reached a point where he'd never been before.

"I'm lost," he confessed in misery.

Then, as he'd done in all his years as a captain, he looked to the one place that could give him guidance. Rising to his feet, he stepped off the porch and turned his eyes to the stars.

"Heaven," he whispered with more humility than he'd ever before revealed. *"If you give me a clue how to steer this ship, I promise you, I'll obey."*

Then his gaze turned to the window of the master bedroom, where Miranda now slept.

"I love her, you see," he rasped. *"God help me, I love her still."*

So what course was there but one?

The woman he loved was warming his bed. It was that simple. How could any man in heaven or on earth ever try to resist that?

Chapter
Thirty-one

The next morning Wolfe opened his eyes in his own four-poster, lying next to Miranda. He turned and propped himself to better observe her sleeping form.

"Miranda?" he murmured gently.

She moaned softly.

"Wake up, dearest . . ." he whispered close to her ear.

Abruptly, her arm flung out. It passed rudely through his chest, sending bright shocking tingles up and down his form.

"Miranda!" he shouted in surprise.

Her eyelids fluttered and finally opened. Then she turned her head and looked straight at him.

At last, thought Wolfe in relief.

"Good morning, my love," he murmured softly.

Then he stared, waiting to see what her response would be to him after all these years. Without ceremony she proceeded to yawn right in his face.

"Hang me, woman! What kind of welcome is that?!"

She did not answer. She merely stretched, then moved

toward him. Wolfe was cheered until she continued to move right *through* him to reach the edge of the bed.

The intimate contact of her spirit moving through his own stunned him completely, leaving him weak and shaken.

"*Miranda . . .*"

But she was unaware. Unaffected.

"*No,*" he rasped in realization. "*Oh, no . . .*"

Yet, the evidence was clear enough. She could no longer see him. No longer hear him. No longer feel him.

He watched her disappear into the bathroom and emerge soon after, showered and clean with nothing more than a fluffy white towel wrapped around her.

Knowing it was an invasion of privacy for her, and an exercise in torture for him didn't stop Wolfe from remaining in the room while she dressed.

He circled her slowly, admiring her naked physical form, her ivory skin even lovelier in the streams of morning sunlight than it had been under last night's brilliant moon.

As he'd observed the night before, her shape was a softer, rounder version of her younger self. His eyes took in the fullness of her breasts, tipped in pink, the soft rise of her belly, the flare of womanly hip and curve of thigh.

Wolfe felt the response through his spirit as he swirled around her, the tension of his mortal memories coiling deep within him. How he wanted to bury himself within her now, feel her life energy surround him again.

But how could he? When she did not even know he existed?

Wolfe contemplated his options as she finished dressing and left the bedroom. *I should leave her,* he told himself. *Leave her to her mortal life.*

Why should he endure the torture of watching her take a lover and a husband, for if she hadn't already, she surely would. Eventually she'd raise a mortal family in this house—the offspring of another man's loins, another man's passion and love—and Wolfe's hell would be complete.

Why wait around for it to happen? he asked himself. Unless he truly *wished* to drive himself into spiritual insanity?

"Because it is my *home!"* he bellowed at her aloof physical form. *"And if anyone should leave, Miranda, you should!"*

Wolfe followed her down the staircase, his ire rising with every step. He saw her perplexed look at the mess he'd made last night. Impatiently, he swirled around her as she took her time cleaning up the scattered cans and righting the overturned ladders.

Finally, she moved into the kitchen, her steps in slow motion compared with the swift bouncing gait she'd once used.

Wolfe pathetically followed her, unable to stop his puppylike trailing of this woman he still loved.

"Riley was right," he murmured in self-disgust, *"Women are plain bad luck."*

Miranda glanced at the wall clock as she lethargically brewed a pot of coffee. The construction crew was due at eight-thirty, so she still had about twenty minutes to herself.

Unfortunately, the ringing of her cell phone put a quick end to that.

"Miranda?"

"Good morning, Josh."

"Have you come to your senses yet, sweetheart?"

"Please, Josh. I don't want to argue anymore about this. Please. Can you try to understand?"

"I'm coming down tonight for dinner. And as a bribe I've decided to bring you that awful portrait you've been whining to me about for weeks."

"You shouldn't have taken it from my bedroom in the first place."

"I told you, Miranda, Dr. Wilcox and I agreed it wasn't good for you."

"I want the portrait, but not if it means arguing with you tonight. Please don't come. We've been through it already, and I don't think I have the strength to fight you. Please—"

"I won't take no for an answer, sweetheart. We're setting our wedding date tonight. Expect me at eight."

Miranda's stomach rolled sickly at the sound of the summary click in her ear. She set down the phone in despair.

"Why won't he listen to me?" she whispered weakly to the air. "Why won't he at least try to understand?"

But then, that was what her life had become, after all, hadn't it? thought Miranda as she poured a cup of coffee and slumped down at the table.

Everyone in her life had become used to steering her vessel, and she was now expected to just sit quietly and not say a word.

Well, that may have been okay when she'd been in the hospital, but she was out now, and trying to make it on her own. It was time she began to think for herself, steer for herself, even if the turns ended up being the wrong ones.

Why couldn't Josh understand that's what she needed right now?

Miranda stared with trepidation at her amber bottle of pills sitting next to the lazy Susan of condiments. She picked up the brown plastic and swirled the white pills around. Listening to the mesmerizing shake, she considered how this entire undertaking with Blue Nights had made her a nervous wreck.

Josh, Dr. Wilcox, and her aunt and uncle had fought her every step of the way on purchasing the run-down cottage, and she'd actually had to hire a lawyer to have her money released for the expensive purchase.

Though Miranda had planned on stopping her medication, she didn't yet believe her nerves could take it. Even now, since Josh's call, her hands were shaking.

With a resigned sigh, Miranda poured out two pills and quickly swallowed them, chasing them with a gulp of coffee.

"That'll help," she assured herself.

Closing her eyes, she sat still and breathed deeply, waiting for the pills to take effect.

"Instant tranquillity," she whispered as the feeling of emotionless calm cast its veil over her agitated nerves once more.

"She's changed," Wolfe realized with unease.

Much more dramatically than her physical appearance, Miranda's spirit had changed. He could see it now in the timid, lethargic way she moved about the house, and the frightened, pleading little voice she'd used on the phone to some idiot named Josh.

"Your eyes, Miranda," he murmured, leaning closer. *"Where's the life in them, love? Where's the fight?"*

Wolfe observed her shaking hands, and the way she took the pills, as if they were her only sustenance.

As the morning wore on, he continued to follow her. He observed how the pills changed her, making her even more subdued, glazing her eyes and draining them even further of their life.

"Dammit . . ." he whispered, appalled. *"Dammit to hell. I'll not part from you like this,"* he swore.

No matter what it took. No matter what pain it caused his own spirit, Wolfe knew his heading now. All the angels of heaven could not have made it any plainer.

He would not leave this woman until she was restored to the fearless spirit she had once been. With determination, Wolfe returned to the kitchen and focused his power, then reached out and grasped the bottle of pills.

"I will not allow her fire to die," he promised heaven as he strode out the back door and toward the shoreline, *"not while I am still allowed awareness on this earth."*

And then he cocked back his arm and threw her tranquillity into the sea.

Chapter
Thirty-two

"Where are they?!"

Miranda's anxieties were overwhelming her as the hour neared eight. The construction crew had gone for the day, and she had everything else ready for Josh's arrival—except one thing.

Her *pills*!

"They've got to be here somewhere," she muttered, rifling through every inch of the kitchen. She was certain she'd left them on the table, but they were nowhere to be found.

She turned to the cabinets and began searching through every one. "Where are they, where are they!"

How could this have happened? Everything else was perfect. The evening was warm and clear, and she'd set up a table on the porch with cheese and bread. The dinner was a simple meat loaf and apple pie. It wasn't exactly elegant, but it was hearty, good food, what she preferred.

Still, she was beginning to worry what Josh would think. He was always taking her to expensive pan-Asian restaurants and trendy French bistros.

"What if he doesn't like it?" she whispered, feeling her nerves begin to unsettle her further.

"Miranda, I'm here! Where are you?"

"No. Oh, no." The sound of Josh's voice had set her hands shaking. Miranda closed her eyes and shoved them into the skirt pockets of her summer dress. Maybe she could calm herself down enough to control the tremors.

"Miranda!"

"In the kitchen!"

"Hello, sweetheart," said Josh with a toothy smile. "I brought you a little present."

"Wine, how nice."

Miranda was ready to reach for the bottle of merlot but held herself back. "Why don't you open it, Josh. The corkscrew's on the table."

"Yes, of course."

Miranda turned from him and hid her trembling hands as she opened a cabinet. With as much will as she could muster, she steadied her shakes and reached for the first two glasses she saw, then placed them quickly on the table and returned her hands to her pockets.

"How are you feeling, sweetie?" Josh asked as he struggled with the wine cork.

"All right. No, better than that," she answered. "I mean, I like it out here."

Josh popped the cork, then looked at the mismatched glasses she'd placed on the table—one was a tall water glass, the other a ruby-colored tumbler. He raised a disapproving eyebrow. "Don't you have any *crystal*, Miranda?"

"No," she said weakly. "Not yet."

"Even cheap wineglasses would be preferable to those."

"I'm sorry. Haven't had a chance to . . ." Her soft voice trailed off as an embarrassed flush came to her cheeks.

Josh sighed in that same censorious way of his hyper-critical mother. "Then I *suppose* these will have to do."

The tone of the remark annoyed Miranda. Abruptly, she

felt something spark inside her, a tiny flame.

"Yes, Josh," she found herself snapping out. "They *will* have to do, because I just moved in."

Josh's eyes widened a bit at her change of tone. He looked at her with a closer eye. "Miranda? Have you taken your medicine today?"

"Yes," she said uncomfortably.

"*Both* doses?"

Miranda turned from him. "I've got to get dinner," she said. "It's ready."

"Don't try avoidance, Miranda. Not with me."

Miranda felt another flare of anger flame up inside her. She did her best to control it. Oh, why couldn't she have found her pills! This was exactly the kind of unexpected emotional response that the pills usually helped her control!

Unnerved, she fumbled quickly for the oven mitts and jerked open the hot door. Her hands had not stopped shaking, but she attempted to reach for the steaming loaf pan as best she could. She almost made it to the table, until she felt an abrupt jarring.

"What the—"

It felt to Miranda as if some invisible hand had actually *pushed* the loaf pan! Her grip slipped and the hot container crashed and clattered to the floor, the meat sliding out in one greasy lump, right over the pristine white leather of Josh's docksiders.

"Jesus Christ, Miranda, you're such a klutz!"

"I'm sorry, Josh. I'm sorry!"

"You ought to be! I just bought these shoes."

"You did?" Miranda took a closer look at his shoes, and her brow furrowed. "But those are rubber-soled docksiders."

"So?" snapped Josh, grabbing up a pile of napkins from the table to wipe at the leather.

"Those are *boat* shoes, Josh. And you don't even like the water."

"It's for *fashion*, Miranda. You know, *image*. Christ . . ." he replied with an impatient roll of his eyes.

Miranda stared at Josh, who was still frantically attempting to save his shoes from grease stains. It suddenly seemed so ridiculous to her—all she could think of was how grungy her sneakers always got when she went to work on cleaning and polishing the *Sea Sprite* with her late father.

She'd never cared about the stains. And neither had her father—because fashion was never the point for them.

Image was never what mattered.

Substance was.

Miranda tried her best to picture Josh on her little sailboat. But she could not. Instead, another image came to her mind.

A tall, broad-shouldered man in a black cable-knit sweater was standing at *Sea Sprite*'s halyard, smiling and laughing and giving her the most substantial support she'd ever experienced.

Giving it, she realized, in the height of the worst squall she'd ever sailed through.

I still remember it, she realized. Even after all the therapy and medicines and treatments, she *still* remembered the wind and the rain and the mist and the sea. . . .

"Remember, Miranda," the ghost whispered next to her ear. *"Remember our day on the water . . . how we agreed to ride out the squall . . ."*

The ghost watched Miranda's shifting sea-green eyes and knew that her mind was trying to reach out.

"Part of you can still hear me, Miranda, I'm certain of it. Part of you still knows how to reach out for what you want. . . ."

Miranda blinked and turned her head.

Had someone *whispered* to her?

She saw no one, but something was happening. Deep inside her mind she could hear the voices of a decade before, shouting over the waves.

Suddenly she was back there, riding out the squall, test-

...ng her own courage, her own will, against the pitch of the raging sea. . . .

"Wahoo! We're doing it, Eric!"

"Aye! Watch the helm, now, love!"

"How's her balance feel?"

"Good!"

"I told you she'd hold up!"

"Hang me, Miranda, you're the most headstrong girl I've ever encountered!"

"Thank you, Eric!"

"You're welcome!"

"Oh, Eric, this is why!"

"What?"

"Why you love it. Why you never left it! It makes you feel alive!"

Miranda blinked again, and she was back in the kitchen of Blue Nights. Josh was trying to speak with her. His mouth was moving and moving, but she failed to hear a word. His voice no longer had any meaning for her, she realized.

No wonder she couldn't hear him.

"Miranda! For God's sake, are you losing your mind again?"

Miranda stared into Josh's blue eyes. They were terribly pale eyes, she noticed.

Paler than the sea.

Paler than the sky.

Paler than her memories of the captain's gaze.

Paler, in fact, than anything she cared about.

"Go home, Josh."

"What?"

"We're through talking."

Miranda turned from him and strode from the room.

"Wait a minute! Where in hell are you going?"

"To your car's trunk. You brought it, didn't you?"

"Yes, but I wasn't going to give you that portrait unless you agreed to set a wedding date."

"Well, I'm not agreeing, and I still want it. After all, it is my property." Miranda marched up to his shiny red

Corvette, then snapped out her hand, palm up. "Give me
your trunk key."

"No."

"Give me your trunk key, Josh," she said sweetly, "or
I'll smash your precious Corvette's windshield with a
builder's two-by-four."

"Bless my soul!" shouted Wolfe with pure joy. *"Now,
that's the girl I remember!"*

With glee, Wolfe circled the couple as Josh angrily dug
out his keys and slapped them into Miranda's outstretched
palm.

She quickly opened the trunk and retrieved a flat object
wrapped in thick brown paper.

"Miranda," snapped Josh, "you know what Dr. Wilcox said. He agreed with me about that ridiculously awful
painting. That's why he had me take it away from you."

"It's not awful. And it's not ridiculous," said Miranda,
tearing carefully at the paper until the image was revealed.

When Wolfe saw what lay beneath the brown paper,
his spirit stilled in stunned paralysis. *"Bless my soul,"*
the ghost whispered. *" 'Tis Jenny's painting."*

"There he is," barked Josh angrily. "Your precious
captain. I suppose you've decided he's the one who
haunted this house. The one you fell in love with."

"I never said that!"

"You don't have to. It's obvious. Why else would you
want to put it in your bedroom."

"And what business is it of yours how I choose to
decorate my bedroom?"

"It's my business if I'm going to share it."

"Josh, for heaven's sake, don't you get it yet? You're
not!"

"Of course I am. Once we're married—"

"We're not going to get married, Josh. Why can't you
ever *hear* what I'm saying to you?"

"Miranda, we *are* getting married. I've stuck it out
with you for ten years."

"Listen to yourself. You've *stuck* it out—like it was a

chore. But I don't want to be anyone's chore. I don't care if I'm alone for the rest of my life. I want love, Josh. Real love. The kind that puts blankets on you at night, and sings to you in the morning, and shouts its support through storms.

"I know it can exist. I believe it can, in my heart. It's what I *want*. What I wish, what I dream. And you're simply not capable of it . . . at least, not with me."

Wolfe listened to Miranda's words with shock and amazement. *"After all these years, she still believes in my love . . ."* he whispered to the sea air, his own love for her growing even more than he thought possible.

"Miranda," answered Josh, exasperated. "I love you—"

"Please, Josh, don't. Not now. It's such a lie. I don't know what you feel for me, but it's not love. You've never even kissed me on the lips!"

Wolfe watched Josh hesitate a moment, then step close to her. The captain's spirit thrummed with tension as he watched Josh awkwardly press his thin lips to Miranda's own.

"It's too late, Josh," she said softly, removing her solitaire from her left hand. "We both know it would never have worked out."

"That's not true, Miranda," asserted Josh, pushing back the ring. "Don't make any hasty decisions."

"It's not hasty. I've thought about it a lot." Miranda slipped the ring into his side pocket. "So this is goodbye."

"No, Miranda. I won't let you go. I know you haven't had your medicine. I know this isn't the *real* you."

"Josh, I don't think you'd know the real me if I came up behind you and bit you on the—"

"Miranda! This is ludicrous. You need your medicine. It's obvious you're regressing, and that painting started it all. You've become infatuated with this dream image of a sea captain you've conjured up in your mind. And that painting just reinforces it."

"Better to love the image of a man with substance than

a man who's substance is nothing but image."

"You're jabbering nonsense, Miranda."

"It makes perfect sense to me."

"Fine, then what in hell are you saying?"

"I'm saying that this so-called imaginary captain of mine has more substance for me than you!"

"You really have lost your mind again."

"Good night, Josh," said Miranda, picking up the painting and turning on her heel. "And good-bye."

"I'll be back," warned Josh. "With Dr. Wilcox."

"Better bring your own wineglasses, then," called Miranda without looking back.

Wolfe laughed like hell at that one as he watched Josh slip into his Corvette's bucket seat and start the engine. Then Wolfe watched the man hesitate, pull the parking brake, and fling the door open.

Clearly Josh Cunning had decided to have one more go at Miranda. But Wolfe would have none of this.

Levitating a nearby builder's two-by-four, the angry ghost stepped up to the wide-eyed Josh and poked him threateningly in the rib cage. *"Hit the road, you scurvy scum."*

"Good God!" cried Josh. "Miranda! Miranda! Look at this!"

The ghost poked him again, then focused his power on the Corvette and released the parking brake.

The crunch of the Corvette's wheels on gravel turned Josh's head. "What in hell!" he shrieked, seeing his Corvette begin to roll away.

"Ha-ha! Looks like you lost your anchor, ya blockhead landlubber!" cried Wolfe as he watched Josh take off after his sports car.

And this time, when the smirking man slipped into the bucket seat, he swiftly drove away.

Chapter
Thirty-three

Hammer in hand, Miranda stepped down off the chair in front of her master bedroom's fireplace.

"*His* bedroom's fireplace," she whispered with quiet pleasure. Gazing up at the painting she'd just hung, she felt her skin shiver with a tiny thrill.

The rugged, square-jawed face of the clipper captain seemed so real to her. Like the sea at night, his dark blue eyes appeared both captivating and intimidating. Their living intensity seemed to pierce through the very canvas.

Miranda sighed at the man's brilliant confidence. Arms folded across a brawny chest, hip brazenly propped, he embodied a combination of supremacy and seduction.

"But whom are you trying to seduce?" she whispered. "Me, or the woman who painted your portrait?"

"*Both.*"

The hammer she held clattered to the floor as Miranda stumbled backward. "Who said that?" she murmured, quickly glancing about.

But the air was completely still.

The room completely empty.

Miranda's gaze returned to the portrait. The captain was as entrancing as ever, but something about him seemed terribly dangerous too. The slight upturn at the edge of his unsmiling mouth made her feel as though he were smirking at her —or playing with her.

With unease she dragged the chair she'd been using back to its corner. Then she moved to the master bath. The day had been a taxing one. Her medicine was still nowhere to be found, and she needed some rest.

It was time to get ready for bed.

Wolfe watched with fascination as Miranda went through her nighttime routine. Brushing her teeth and hair, washing her face, moisturizing her skin.

He leaned against the fireplace mantel with masculine pleasure as she slipped out of her flowered summer dress and carefully hung it in her standing closet—what had once been *his* standing closet. The intimacy of sharing it with her now sent a surprisingly powerful sense of satisfaction through his being.

Wolfe watched her move to an antique chest of drawers and pull out the short, satiny gown he'd seen her wear the night before. With a slow smile he watched her unfasten her bra and step out of her panties, then shiver the pearl-colored satin over her bare shoulders, like the sea slipping on the moon's light for the evening.

"Lovely," he couldn't help but whisper.

She stilled.

He surveyed her tense movements, her glance about the room. Had she heard him?

Wolfe was tempted to speak again but held his voice. He had something else in mind tonight. So he continued to watch her.

She seemed uneasy as she stepped back to the bathroom. Wolfe followed, wondering what she was up to.

Her hands seemed to be shaking as she opened the cabinet above the sink. Wolfe tensed when he saw the bottle of pills—*sleeping* pills, he read on the label.

"Don't, Miranda," he whispered at her ear. *"Not to-night. Find the courage to keep your head clear."*

Wolfe watched Miranda's hands still. But she did not put the bottle back. Instead, she shook two sleeping pills into her hand and ran a glass of water.

How Wolfe wanted to knock the pills loose. Prevent this artificial veil from clouding her mind like her other medication.

But he did nothing.

Wolfe knew from his many years on the sea that sailors either found the courage or left the ocean. There was no amount of commands that would put the will in a sailor's blood—and no amount of orders that would take the fear from his heart.

In the end, the sea found the truth in each sailor, as each sailor found his own truth upon the sea.

"Your head is clear enough now, Miranda," whispered Wolfe. *" 'Tis your decision this time."*

Miranda was about to pop the pills into her mouth. But at the last moment she looked into the mirror. Leaning toward the glass, she paused to examine her blue-green eyes.

With a sigh, she looked down at the hand holding the pills. It was still shaking. Yet, she did not lift it to her lips. Instead, she turned it over and let the pills drop into the sink.

Wolfe felt the relief flow through him as Miranda turned off the light and headed for her bed—what had been *his* bed, he reminded himself with pleasure.

"It's time at last, my love," he murmured. *"Time for dreams to begin."*

"I'm not a real man, Miranda."

"You feel real enough tonight, Eric . . . real enough to fill me."

Miranda's erotic images began to play back from al-most the moment she shut her eyelids. The dream of lying in the sea captain's arms was so vivid, she could almost sense his touch.

"Does that feel good, my love?"

"Yes, Eric . . . don't stop . . . please . . ."

"Close your eyes, then, and enjoy the feel of the ride. . . ."

"Aye, Captain . . ."

Miranda's body began twisting and turning beneath the blanket. Her back arched with the tremors of sense memory shuddering through her.

It was a warm June night, unseasonably warm, and her sleeping body grew impatient with the coverings. In a few kicks they were off her legs.

"My love, I'm here. Can you feel me?"

Miranda's body quieted at the last words she'd heard.

They weren't from her dreams. They'd been spoken inside her awakened mind. She listened intently to the night. For a long time she heard nothing but the mesmerizing lapping of the sea surf outside her window. And then the surf seemed to whisper . . .

"Feel me, little mermaid."

With eyes shut, Miranda could swear she felt a feathery touch caress her ankles. She jerked a moment, wondering if she'd actually felt the touch or it had been part of her dream.

When the touch came again, she forced herself to keep still. Slowly, it made its ticklish way up her shins and over her knees, then farther still, climbing the heated skin of her bare thighs.

Miranda's breath caught as the silky touch moved intimately between her parted legs. Her back arched with the thrilling pleasure.

Was this truly happening? she wondered again. Or was she dreaming?

Miranda gathered the courage to reach her hand down. She bumped a soft, silky object and let her fingers close around it. Her eyes opened and she sat up. In her hand was a long, white sea gull feather.

She gasped, and her gaze swiftly searched the silvery bedroom, illuminated by the risen moon.

"Captain?" she whispered, her eyes finding the shad-

⸱wy portrait above the cold fireplace. "Is it you?"

She didn't dare hope. And yet she did.

"Miranda . . ."

"Captain?"

"Aye, little mermaid. 'Tis me, Wolfe. Have no fear."

But she did have fear. It had been ten long years since she'd last spoken to her dream captain. And most of those years, she'd been made to believe that he was nothing more than a figment of her imagination.

Was he that? Or was he truly real?

Miranda searched the bed beside her for some sign of him. But she saw nothing. No one. She searched the shadows of the room, but the room was empty.

"My God . . ." she whispered in trepidation. "What if I'm really cracking up?"

"You're not, Miranda. Come with me now."

"Come where? I can't even see you. How am I supposed to follow you?"

"Follow my voice, love."

And so, Miranda did. She swung her legs off the high bed and let her bare feet touch the smooth floorboards.

"Come, dearest."

The voice took her out of the master bedroom, down the heavy staircase, and out the back door. She followed across the porch and into the soft grass, then down the hillside to the rock and sand of Blue Nights' beach.

"Follow me, Miranda."

The rhythmic lapping of the salty seawater beat a cadence on the smooth stones around her. She stepped carefully past them and onto the soft, wet sand.

"Eric?"

"Aye, love. I'm here."

Miranda swallowed uneasily and continued to follow the voice. She stepped farther into the wet sand until she reached the lapping waters, warm against her ankles.

"Come, my love, don't stop now."

But Miranda wanted to stop. The water was dark as the night sky and she was unsure what lay ahead in it.

Maybe there'd been a time in her life when black water

did not frighten her, but that time was long ago. She knew now that the unknown held more than just exciting possibilities. It also held pain and heartache.

And that was enough to make her hesitate.

"Miranda, don't be afraid."

"But I am," she rasped. "What if you're not real? What if you're my crazy subconscious, some insane suicidal impulse that's luring me to self-drowning."

A loud laugh came from the shallow water.

"What's so funny!"

"You."

"Well, I don't think this is funny."

" 'Tis beyond funny. 'Tis comical."

Miranda's brow furrowed in annoyance. She stepped out farther to find the ghost's voice. "It's *not* comical! It's a very rational, sane evaluation of a bizarre situation!"

"Exactly my point, dearest."

"What point!"

"How on earth might you be suicidally insane if you are looking rationally at your own actions?"

Miranda stopped and stared into the darkness. She looked down at the seawater, which was now halfway up her shins. The voice had lured her into the shallows.

"You're a very tricky ghost, you know that?"

"You used to say I was clever. But no more clever than you."

Miranda smiled weakly. "I *did* say that to you, didn't I?" she whispered. "It wasn't just some crazed dream. . . ."

"Nay, Miranda. And neither is this."

"But . . . why can't I see you, then?"

"You can hear me, can you not?"

"Yes, though it feels as though your voice is more in my head than in the air. It's odd—"

" 'Twill be a long way back to your true self, my love. Your spirit's been veiled."

"I don't understand."

"The girl you once were had forged a connection to the living spirit inside of her."

"What do you mean? Living spirit?"

" 'Tis the living spirit that sees and hears and feels beyond the earthly coil. 'Tis what calls every mortal to his life's voyage."

"Every mortal?"

"Aye, Miranda. But not everyone heeds this call. 'Tis unnerving for you mortals to sign on for such a voyage. Like a green sailor, you must find the nerve and will to endure the perils and challenge, the unknown and unpredictable."

Miranda sighed. "My head is swimming, Captain. I don't think I understand what you're saying."

"But you can at least hear *what I'm saying. You can hear my voice?"*

"Yes."

"Let us try another step, then."

"Wh-what step?"

Miranda felt herself trembling when the voice fell silent for a moment. And then she felt a tender touch at her cheek, as if a man's callused thumb were wiping away a tear. The gentle touch moved over skin, tracing down the outline of her face and jaw. Fingerpads joined in at her neck, trailing over her shoulder and down her arm.

"Eric?" she whispered. "Is that you touching me?"

"Aye, love."

What felt like large, strong hands grasped her waist. They moved up the length of her back, sending tingling sensations through her entire being. When they reached her shoulders, they began a slow, sensuous massage that relaxed every particle of her and released a low moan of pleasure from her lips.

"Tip your head upward, dearest."

Miranda obeyed without thinking and immediately felt the sweetest brushing of her lips.

"Oh, Eric . . ."

Closing her eyes, Miranda reached her hands out to the place she assumed he would be standing, but she could

grasp hold of nothing but air. Her fingers curled in disappointment and dropped back to her sides.

"Do not give up, little mermaid," he murmured into
her ear. *"The Miranda I once knew would never give up."*

Miranda swallowed and tried again. This time she let
her mind reach back—back to a time when she was
young, when she had no fear of the unknown, back to a
time when she could actually *see* the captain.

With effort she reached for her memory of the day she
first saw him, the moment he stepped out of the shadows
of Blue Nights: *"Okay!"* she'd boldly called into the
dark corners of the parlor. *"I'm coming over there!"*
Then she'd willfully forced her legs to swing down off the
sofa. . . .

Slowly, Miranda opened her eyes. It was the present
now, and she was standing in the shallows of Crescent
Cove. She heard the lapping waves, felt the moving surf
swirling at her feet, and she stepped forward, just like that
young woman a decade earlier.

She stepped forward into the darkness, into the unknown. The fear was there, but she pushed it down, refusing to let it block her other feelings. Instead of the fear,
she made herself connect with the memory of her own
will, and courage, and faith.

And, most of all, she made herself connect with the
love.

"Miranda?"

The voice came to her now without its veil. Finally,
she heard it as she once had, not in her head, but in the
air, mingled with the voice of the rhythmic sea.

"Miranda, do you see me?"

Miranda looked toward the sound of his voice, and
slowly he began to appear to her—the imperious silhouette of a broad-shouldered man standing in a halo of
moonlight.

Chapter
Thirty-four

Miranda blinked.

The image of the man was still there. With shaking limbs she cautiously moved toward it, afraid for a moment that her slightest step would make the miraculous vision disappear.

As she neared it, the features became clearer—the square jaw and chiseled cheeks, the raven hair and piercing eyes, their color as alive and alluring, as enduring and eternal, as the blue of the deep.

"Eric?"

"Aye?"

"It *is* you."

"Aye, little mermaid."

"Did I make you appear?"

"No, I was always there, my love. You just needed to believe in me again."

"Oh, Eric."

Miranda stretched out her hands, this time with pure love. And this time her reach connected.

His chest felt like iron beneath the thick cable-knit sweater, and she traced the width to the other side to feel the strength in his broad back. The years of labor were there, the hauling and heaving, the self-made captain who pulled crews of men through the storms of hell by sheer force of will.

Her fingers moved to his sturdy jaw. She traced the outline of his lips and chin, his cheeks and eyes, and finally let her hands move to the nape of his neck—a mast of a neck, strong and sturdy and ready for the play of her fingertips.

Slowly, she pulled his head down toward her own. And when the tickle of her breath touched the top of his lip, he moved his arms around her.

Miranda gasped at the unexpected force of his possessive tug, which splayed her soft form against his hard length. She felt his large hand move to the back of her head. With gentleness he cradled it as he moved his lips toward hers.

There was nothing lacking in the kiss. It was warm and soft and damp and sweet. It was the kiss of pure love, a gesture that resuscitated her soul.

"You feel just like . . ."

"Aye, love?"

"Like a living man, Eric."

The ghost smiled weakly. *"As you did so many years ago, my love, it seems you have breathed new life into me—for the moment."*

"Then, Eric, let's not lose the moment."

Wolfe's blue eyes burned brightly with her words. And he gazed at her now with a look far different from the one she remembered from a decade earlier.

At once, she understood. The Sea Wolf no longer saw a young virgin before him—what he saw was a mature woman. A woman who was more than ready to experience the full power of his passion.

Miranda returned his burning gaze with equal heat. At his little nod, she allowed a small smile of anticipation.

Wolfe stepped back. In one swift movement he removed his sweater. The turtleneck came next. Miranda remembered the old-fashioned undergarment, and her hands reached to help him unfasten the buttons.

Wolfe smiled down at her as he parted the material and dragged it from his broad chest and muscled arms. She itched to feel the hard planes again, the swirls of dark hair.

Wolfe closed his eyes, allowing her to remember through touch, and then his hands palmed her breasts, sliding along the satiny moon-colored material. He bent his head, taking her mouth roughly as he fondled her aroused nipples.

Miranda wanted more of him. He gave her his tongue and she pressed her mouth into him as her hands traced a path over the hard ridges of his abdomen.

"You feel real to me," Miranda whispered from memory as she moved her hand lower still to find the hard outline beneath Wolfe's heavy pants. "Real enough to fill me."

A raw sound of need vibrated from deep in Wolfe's throat, and he reached for the hem of her short nightgown, pulling it up and over her head. Then he flung it to the shore and stepped back.

As the warm sea breeze caressed her naked curves, Miranda tensed.

"*What's wrong, my love?*" asked Wolfe.

"I'm so . . . exposed. . . ."

Wolfe smiled. "*'Tis no need for shame. Look at you, Miranda. You are beautiful, and I wish to enjoy you.*"

She tried to relax. Instead of her unease, she concentrated on Eric's face, the love she felt for him, the love she saw burning in his eyes.

"Seen enough?" she teased.

"*Never. Never for all eternity will I see enough of you, my dear.*"

Miranda smiled as Wolfe stepped up to her, taking her small wrist in his large hand and pulling her closer. Then his callused fingers reached for her waist. His touch was rough against her soft skin, yet tender in its caresses.

Wolfe bent his head, his raven hair falling to his forehead as his mouth closed over the tip of one breast. Miranda closed her eyes and sighed as he lathed his tongue over one and then the other, swirling then sucking until she thought every molecule inside her had melded with the rushing surf.

"Eric," she whispered on a gasp, "I need more . . ."

"*Aye.*" His hands reached for his belt buckle, and in another few seconds he was naked before her, closing the distance again.

Miranda reached to stroke him, but he stilled her hand.

"*Allow me the helm tonight, dearest. I fear a loss of control is more than likely,*" he murmured with a smile and kiss to the top of her head.

"But I want to feel you . . ."

Wolfe laughed, fitted his hands to her bottom, and pulled her tightly against him. The length of his arousal pressed hard against her.

"Feel *me, then.*"

Miranda's eyebrows rose. "You just can't stop being clever, can you?"

"*Hang me, woman, you've got what you want. Why complain?*"

"Why indeed?"

Miranda reached up with renewed desire and pulled Eric's lips to her own. The kiss was raw and hungry, and she pushed her tongue hard into him, unashamed now to expose her own long-veiled desires.

As their lips parted, Wolfe murmured her name, then his large hand grasped the soft flesh beneath her thigh. With swift strength he lifted her leg.

Miranda didn't hesitate. She curled her arms around Wolfe's strong neck and pulled herself up, making it easier for him to guide himself through the tangle of auburn curls to find the softness beneath.

He poised at her opening and smiled devilishly, toying a bit with the sensitive bud at the apex of her damp folds.

Miranda gasped, not expecting that mere skillful foreplay could unleash such a violent tempest within her. Her body shuddered as she clung to him.

"Hang on to the rail, little mermaid," he advised with a roguish tone. *"Don't be falling overboard now."*

"You're . . . simply . . . determined . . . to surprise me . . . aren't you?" challenged Miranda through labored breaths.

"Aye, but you'll let me do as I please."

"And what . . . makes you . . . so sure?"

"Because," he growled in her ear, *"I'm real enough to fill you."*

Miranda laughed as her own words came back to haunt her. But she barely caught her breath before his hardness was thrusting upward, through her soft folds, and finally into her.

With eyes closed, Miranda moaned her pleasure at the feel of Wolfe's exquisite length traveling through her, higher and higher, into her tight passage. With one aggressive stroke he had buried himself completely.

She felt him pulsing inside her and she moved her own muscles to hold him.

"Aye, my love, aye," murmured Wolfe. *" 'Tis heaven."*

"Yes."

Slowly, he moved, bringing them both to a swift and powerful climax. When he cried out, Miranda lifted her face to find the deep blue of his eyes.

For a moment she thought she'd lost herself inside them, and then she realized the truth.

She was not lost.

She was found.

Chapter
Thirty-Æve

"*You sleep like an angel.*"

Miranda heard the captain's low voice beside her. "Mmm," she murmured with eyes closed, "a snoring angel."

At Wolfe's throaty chuckle, Miranda lifted her lids, then stretched her naked form with lazy contentment. Turning toward his voice, she smiled at the sight of his long, muscular body propped on an elbow next to her.

"Eric, have you been there all night?"

"*Aye,*" he said, gazing down at her. "*I followed you up near dawn.*"

"Hey, you're . . . you're . . ."

"*Sans clothing, my dear?*"

"Yes! How can you—"

"*My ghostly clothing sits on the floor, next to your mortal nightdress. It seems since you've . . . uh . . . worked your magic on me, I am much more sensitive to heat and cold.*"

"I see. But are you still—" Miranda reached out her

hand and watched her fingers pass through his chest.

"That tickles, you know."

"You're still—"

"Of course I'm still without substance, Miranda. We're on land. Some things cannot be changed."

"I see."

"Disappointed?"

"Are you kidding? For the last decade I thought you were a figment of my insanity. I couldn't be happier to find you're simply a figment of my libido."

"Watch it, my dear, I still have the power to brain you."

Miranda shifted. "I'm more interested in your power to alleviate itch. I've got sand on my bottom."

"Mmm. Shall I help?"

Miranda's eyes narrowed. "How?"

"Turn over."

"Eric—"

"Turn."

Miranda was skeptical, but she did, summarily presenting him with her bare bottom. In the next moment, she felt the ticklish brushing of terry cloth against her skin.

"Eric! What are you doing!"

"Hand towel, my love, from the bath."

"You can manipulate objects, can't you?"

"Aye. I'm surprised you've forgotten."

"I did."

"Well, suffice it to say I can find ways to pleasure you here in our bed as well as in the shallows."

"Mmm. I can't wait to see how."

"You'll have to. The sun's up and the day's begun. And I have something for you."

"What?"

"Sit up, my dear, and you'll see."

Miranda did sit up, and when she saw what Eric had brought her, she cried out with joy.

"The notebooks! My father's notebooks!"

The ten bound leather volumes were spread out at the

foot of the large four-poster. Miranda pulled her robe from the chair beside the bed and tied it around her, then she picked up each one to feel their weight.

"*Sea Stories.*" She read out the script at the beginning of one. "*Sea Songs and Chanteys.*" She read out another.

"*I hid them for you, love.*"

"When?"

"*The day after the storm. I went back to Blue Nights to find some unsavory-looking suits sniffing around the parlor, and I didn't want your notebooks in their hands.*"

"Thank you, Wolfe." Miranda picked up another volume and leafed through it, smiling when she saw how her father's handwriting left off and her own took it up, doing its best to fill up the blank pages he'd left behind.

"My guardians lied to me about the *Sea Sprite,* you know, told me she was scuttled. It's just as likely they'd have lied to me about these too."

"*Well, they're in your hands now, little mermaid.*"

"And that's where they'll stay. In fact, I can keep working on them, and maybe get them published. Yes! That's what I'll do. It'll be a book on the stories and songs of the sea, and you can help me finish writing it!"

Wolfe shrugged. "*'Tis easy to spout off my sea stories, love. I'll help you with anything you like.*"

"Good!" said Miranda, bounding from the bed with one of the notebooks and striding to the fireplace. She gazed up to the portrait of Wolfe above the mantel. "And I'll use this wonderful painting of a fearless sea captain for the book's cover!"

"*Mmm.*"

"What? Don't you like your portrait? I think it's magnificent."

"*It's rendered skillfully. Aye.*"

"Then what's the matter?" Miranda stepped up to the signature. "J. M. Smithton was a noted local artist, you know. In fact, I have one of the books in which she's featured."

"*Miranda, don't—*"

"No, I've got it right here." Miranda stepped into a

spare bedroom, dug into a box and pulled out her book
Connecticut Maritime Artists.

"Let's see," murmured Miranda, walking back into the
master bedroom and leafing through the pages of the
heavy title. "Here she is . . . J. M. Smithton, aka Jenny
Smithton, born 1822, died 18—"

"Forty-nine."

"Oh," said Miranda, looking up when Wolfe spoke.
"She was young when she died, wasn't she? Twenty-
seven."

"Aye. 'Twas a shame."

Miranda studied Wolfe's troubled brow. "You knew
her, of course."

"Aye. She painted my portrait, did she not?"

Miranda frowned at Eric's chilly tone. "What's the
matter, Eric? What's wrong?"

"Drop the subject, my love. 'Twas long ago."

"A bad memory?" pried Miranda.

"Let's just call it the past."

In the woods beyond Blue Nights, the warmth of the
day was dispersed by a dense layer of emerald leaves.
And the cool of the shade became even more chilled as
a shadowy figure moved beneath the living canvas. When
he neared the old cottage, he stopped and stared.

"Ahoy, Sea Wolf, I'm back," muttered the dark ghost,
his vision trained on the restored porch. It now looked
just as it had the night Eric Wolfe delivered him his death
blow.

The ghost of Leach Muldavey whispered a vile, hate-
filled curse, then receded into the shade of the trees,
knowing he'd have to be patient.

When he'd heard of the mortal girl's return to Wolfe's
cottage, he had to see the evidence for himself. And he
did. The physical improvements to the place were as obvious as the intense heat radiating from the master bedroom window.

"Enjoy that heat, cousin," warned Leach, *"for I'll
soon see it burn you good."*

Like ten years before, Leach planned to strike out at Eric by harming the girl. And Leach knew his best chance was using a mortal descendant.

"Only this time I'll be findin' a much smarter mortal than that lamebrain deputy sheriff. . . ."

This time Leach would use a mortal who was far brighter . . . and, if he was lucky, much more ruthless. But it would take time, planning, and a nasty delight with the cruelest little details. The exact skills he'd employed in his mortal days as a murdering thief.

"To hell with you, cousin, and your little mortal bitch as well. I'll have my revenge yet."

Chapter
Thirty-six

"*Remember, Miranda, adjusting your helm only compensates for the imbalance. It does not fix it.*"

"Right."

"*So when you feel the tug, pull back on the tiller, and do not forget—*"

"I know, I know, I pull in the opposite direction I want the boat to go."

"*Aye, that's right.*"

"Now, let's let her sails fill and run with the wind."

Miranda nodded and watched the flexing muscles of Eric's shoulders as he worked the *Sea Sprite*'s rigging. It was a breezy June morning, two weeks since he'd come back to her, and the sea was still yawning, its lazy waves bluer than the sky.

The week before, Miranda had happily purchased the *Sea Sprite* back from Runyon's Boatyard. She'd also bought some auburn rinse to return her hair to its brassy old color and some shorts and T-shirts for her materialized ghost to wear on the water. Her gaze couldn't help but stray now to his bare legs and arms, the cut of muscle the swirl of raven hair. She sighed with love at every particle of him.

To Miranda it felt as though she were living out her dearest dreams. In the mornings Eric gave her sailing lessons, and in the evenings they made love in the shallows or on the bobbing deck of her old beloved boat.

In between, they laughed and talked and enjoyed each other's teasing as Miranda worked to restore Blue Nights' interior to a livable home.

Most of the heavy construction work was done now. It was down to wallpapering and painting and decorating—things Miranda found satisfaction in doing with her own two hands.

"*Are you feeling more confident, love?*" asked Wolfe as he moved to the boat's stern and took the seat beside her.

"Yes, Eric."

"*You're doing very well. Do you feel your memory coming back? You were once quite good at handling her.*"

"Thanks. I think I'll be good again. The hardest part is judging the wind."

"*Aye. 'Tis the skill to master. Just remember there are two types of wind, the true wind and the apparent wind.*"

"Tell me again."

"*The true wind is what a sailor feels when standing on a pier. But when the boat sails, the feel of the true wind changes. What you feel now, Miranda, is the* apparent *wind. It is the apparent wind that you must be aware of as you set your course.*"

As she listened to Wolfe, Miranda's brow furrowed.

"*Love? Are you confused. Would you like me to explain the difference again?*"

"No, Eric."

"*Then, what's the matter? Where's that lovely smile I've enjoyed all morning?*"

"It's still there," she said softly, leaning over to nip his neck. "Just sitting under a bit of anxiety."

Wolfe responded with a loving caress of her cheek. *"What anxiety, Miranda? Tell me."*

"Apparent wind, Eric. Where's it taking us?"

Wolfe sighed, clearly understanding that she was not referring to the *Sea Spirite.*

"As I've said before, Miranda, 'tis up to you to set your course. On this subject, you sit firmly at the helm, not I."

"I know. You've told me that before . . . and I've been giving it a lot of thought."

"Aye. And what have you decided?"

"I've decided that I want to make it work between you and me."

"Are you sure, Miranda? Are you sure you wish to make a home . . . make a life with the ghost of a man? One who goes off to sea ten months of the year?"

Miranda laughed softly.

"Something amusing here, my dear? I fail to see it."

"You would have lived like that with any woman had you lived beyond thirty. And don't try to deny it."

Wolfe's sharp blue gaze glanced away, telling Miranda she'd guessed correctly.

"Don't feel bad, Captain. It's obvious you prefer the sea to anything and everything else."

"Not everything," he said softly.

"No?"

"Not you."

In the distance, Miranda thought she heard a soft rumbling, as if the sea were angered by Wolfe's bold admission. A rough wave heeled the hull suddenly, and she had to jerk back hard to hold the helm under her control.

When she turned her gaze on Wolfe again, she found his jaw tight and his imperious posture stiffer than usual. She wondered if this was hard for him—to admit he preferred her to the sea.

"Eric, do you really mean what you said?"

"Aye, Miranda." He sighed. *"If I had only known . . ."*

"Known? Known what?"

Wolfe gazed at the horizon and then glanced back,

meeting her eyes. *"I never would have . . . I . . ."*

Miranda was amazed. Wolfe had never seemed so awkward, so reluctant to tell her something.

"I'm sorry," he finally said, his shoulders sagging.

"For what?"

"You know," said Eric cryptically. *"It's in you."*

Miranda shook her head. "I don't know, Eric. What are you *talking* about?"

Wolfe stared into her eyes for a long time, as if he were willing her to remember something. But, for the life of her, Miranda could not make the connection he seemed to need her to make.

Gently, Wolfe moved his large hand to cover her own on the tiller.

"Take us in," he said softly. *"The air is growing heavy, and I fear a storm is coming."*

"Oh, no. Not them. Not now."

"Who, my dear?"

As Miranda angled the sailboat next to Blue Nights' restored wooden dock, she instantly recognized the black sedan pulling up to the cottage.

"It's Josh—"

"Not that idiot."

"And my aunt Joan," added Miranda, seeing the figures emerge from the sedan. When a third figure emerged, Miranda's stomach muscles clenched. "Oh, no."

"What now?"

"They've brought Dr. Wilcox."

"Who is—"

"My psychiatrist."

Miranda saw the perplexed look on Eric's face. "He's someone who helps people who are—" She paused, hating to say it.

"Sick?"

"Yes, but not sick in the body. Sick in the . . . head."

"Hang me."

"I'll have to go see what they want." Miranda dropped anchor, tied off the boat, then moved to reef her sail.

"Let me do—"

"No, they're looking down here already, and I don't want them wondering how the *Sea Sprite* suddenly came equipped with self-furling sails."

"Aye, Miranda. You do it, then."

Wolfe tensely stood by with crossed arms as Miranda worked the lines with patience. When the sail was tightly tied, she rechecked the anchorage. "God," she whispered, glancing up to shore, "how will I do this? My hands are already shaking."

"Keep your guard and anger up. And stoke that stubborn will of yours."

"It's not easy, Eric."

"Then let me take care of them. A few floating two-by-fours and I'll have them runnin' for their car inside of a minute."

"No! For heaven's sake, Eric, don't make matters worse. Just make yourself scarce for a little while and I'll handle it."

"I'll not leave you to face those vipers alone."

"Eric, they're not—"

"It's no use, woman. You'll just be wasting breath."

Miranda exhaled in frustration. "Then at least stay quiet."

"I'll not promise a thing."

"Miranda!"

"Blast her anyway!" cursed Miranda. "Her bellow's just as annoying as it was when I was young."

"Ha-hu!"

"And don't you aggravate me either!"

"Now you're angry. Good! You're ready for 'em."

Miranda shook her head as she stepped onto the dock, and Josh, Joan, and Dr. Wilcox were upon her from the moment she stepped off.

"Well, Miranda, how are you!" exclaimed Joan.

Miranda's aunt was smartly styled as usual, with every dyed blond hair harmoniously curved into place, her makeup perfect, her understated wardrobe of tailored beige slacks and white blouse without so much as a crease.

But there was something about her voice. It was strained, Miranda realized as Josh stepped and applied an unwanted peck to her cheek.

"My darling. I've missed you so much."

"Hello, Josh."

"Good afternoon, Miranda," said the tall, middle-aged man with the penetrating brown eyes and thinning sand-colored hair.

Dr. Wilcox was the hardest of the three to greet. Miranda felt guilty at having abandoned his treatment of her without so much as a farewell.

"Doctor," she said, a nervous tremble beneath her voice, "how are you?"

"More to the point, Miranda: How are you? It's been quite a while since your last session."

"Only a few weeks," said Miranda quietly.

"That's quite a long time for someone who needed to speak with me almost every day."

"Yes, it is, Miranda," agreed Josh at once. "We, that is, Mother and I, were worried. So we spoke to Dr. Wilcox and invited him down for a visit."

"Tell them to shove the hell off!"

Miranda jumped at the sound of Wolfe's voice suddenly blaring in her head.

"Miranda, are you all right?" asked Dr. Wilcox. "You look a bit unnerved."

"I'm fine," said Miranda quickly.

"You don't *look* fine," her aunt pointed out. "In fact, you look terrible. Don't you think so, Josh?"

"What do you know, you old crone?"

A giggle escaped Miranda's lips and all three of her guests stared at her in silence. She swallowed and did her best to banish the smile from her face.

"Shall we go up to the house?" she asked, starting the walk up the hill.

"Miranda, I'm warning you," pronounced Wolfe. *"I'll not have that twit boyfriend of yours in my home."*

"Stop it, Wolfe," whispered Miranda.

"Stop what, dear?" asked Joan.

"Nothing. Forget it."

"Do you see what we mean, Doctor?" Miranda's aunt whispered, a few paces behind.

Miranda's muscles tensed with anxiety.

"Shhh, Mother," came the comment from Josh.

"I swear to heaven I'll blow the man down."

"Be quiet!" whispered Miranda.

"What's the matter, Miranda?" asked Dr. Wilcox.

"Ah . . . I thought it would be quieter if we stayed on the porch, you know, with the workmen inside and all. I'll just get some iced lemonade."

"And a drop of vermouth in mine, dear, will you?" called Joan as she took a seat on one of the porch chairs.

"Sure, Aunt Joan," Miranda answered, opening the screen door, "if I have it."

"I'll help you, Miranda," Josh offered.

"Miranda, I'm warning you--"

"No, Josh!" cried Miranda, terrified at what Wolfe might do if Josh entered his home. "Stay on the porch! Uhm . . . you should . . uh . . . enjoy the view while you're here!"

"Miranda, what in the world is the matter?" demanded Josh.

"It's all right," said the doctor soothingly as he stepped toward the door. "How about if I help you. I'd like a few words with you in private anyway."

"Now, what's this dim-witted quack want?"

Miranda stiffly nodded to the doctor. "If you like," she said weakly, then moved inside.

"Your aunt and fiancé are worried about you," the doctor began as soon as they reached the kitchen.

"Josh is no longer my fiancé."

"He says you haven't been yourself since you purchased that sea captain's portrait. And now, purchasing Blue Nights . . ." The doctor's voice trailed off.

"Yes, what about it?" asked Miranda.

"Have you had any flashbacks, any breakthroughs?"

"Tell the quack I'll give him a breakthrough—"

"Stop it, Wolfe!"

"Miranda? To whom are you speaking?"

Miranda exhaled. "He's here, Doctor."

"Who's here?"

"The sea captain," said Miranda, then she turned her gaze to what would look to the doctor like empty air. "Eric, can you please come out, so Dr. Wilcox won't think I'm raving mad?"

"Nay, Miranda, the quack can't see or hear me."

"I know he can't see or hear you. So make him. Just show yourself, materialize, or substance-ize, or whatever it is that ghosts do."

"Miranda, I thought you understood. 'Tis not in my power to be seen by mortals who are veiled."

"Not in your power!"

"Miranda," broke in Dr. Wilcox, looking alarmed, "calm down."

"You might have made that clear before I started speaking openly to you! Now he'll think I'm certifiable!"

"Miranda, perhaps you should—"

"What difference does it make. Tell 'em all to shove off!"

"Oh, pipe down!"

"Miranda?"

"Not you, Doctor. Oh, blast it!"

"Ha-ha! Now you're steaming! I like a woman with a good honest temper. Shows the passion she's capable of—"

"Eric, you're trying my patience!"

"Miranda," interrupted the doctor with alarm. "I'm going to step outside a moment."

"Go on and get out, you scurvy cracker!"

The doctor turned and strode quickly toward the back door, and Miranda glared at Wolfe, who suddenly turned sheepish.

"What did I do? You wanted them gone, didn't you?"

"I give up!" exclaimed Miranda, throwing up her hands. "Just wait here!"

Turning on her heel, she walked quickly toward the back door.

"... And I believe we should be careful about how to confront her delusion," said the doctor softly to Josh and Joan.

"Dr. Wilcox," Miranda interrupted, stepping onto the porch, "don't jump to any conclusions."

"Miranda!" Josh exclaimed as he leaped to his feet with a completely false cheer.

"Oh, knock off the condescension, will you," snapped Miranda before turning to her psychiatrist. "Listen to me, Doctor, I don't want you to get the wrong idea. I've actually been doing very well. I've gone off my medication and I—"

"You've *what*!" exclaimed Joan.

"I'm *off* the pills," reiterated Miranda.

"Do you need a new prescription?" asked the doctor.

"No, and I'm never going to need another one. I'm never going on those things again. And I'm off the sleeping pills as well—"

"You see, Doctor," Josh interrupted. "She's clearly in need of supervisory care, and, as I said, I would be happy to see that she's brought back to her uncle's home in Hartford and—"

"I'm *not* going back to Hartford!" exclaimed Miranda, outraged. "I'm not going anywhere. Blue Nights Cottage is my home—as it was always meant to be."

Three sets of eyes glanced uncomfortably at one another and then turned back on Miranda.

"What do you mean?" asked the doctor carefully. "That it was always *meant* to be?"

"I just meant that . . . I meant that I've always belonged here, that I've always had a right to be here. I . . . I love it here."

"You mean that you love *him*," said Josh, egging her on. "That you feel you were always meant to be with *him*?"

"Yes," she admitted, the fire of fight in her eyes. "I love him."

"*Who* does she love?" whispered Joan.

"The sea captain," said Josh, finally exchanging his saccharine grin for an open sneer. "The *ghost* she thinks haunts this house."

"Dr. Cunning, please," said Dr. Wilcox sternly, turning to scold Josh for his overt rancor. "You're not helping."

"It doesn't matter, Dr. Wilcox," confessed Miranda with a sigh. "It's true. I *am* in love with Eric. My ghost."

"Oh, my God," muttered Joan. "Josh was right. You are still crazy."

"Mrs. Burke, please!" exclaimed the doctor. The he turned to his patient.

"Miranda, I'd like you to come back with us," he said as if he were speaking to a spooked animal.

"No," said Miranda firmly. "I told you already. I'm home."

"*Tell, 'em, woman. Tell, 'em to—*"

"I will, Eric," said Miranda calmly. "As my ghost was about to suggest, would you all now please just *shove* off?"

Joan, Josh, and the doctor all stared at Miranda with slackened jaws as a ghostly chuckle rolled through Miranda's head.

"Come on, Eric, let's take a walk along the beach," said Miranda with a wave.

And then her three guests watched the former mental patient chat amiably with the air as she strolled away.

Chapter
Thirty-seven

"My God, what do we do now?" asked Joan Cunning Burke, visibly shaken. One trembling hand reached out for the porch's wooden railing.

"We'll have to bring her back to the hospital, I'm afraid," admitted Dr. Wilcox, gazing sadly after his pretty patient.

Dr. Josh Cunning forced his lips to remain in a straight line. He could barely contain his self-satisfied glee. "You see, Dr. Wilcox?" he needled his fellow psychiatrist.

"Yes, Dr. Cunning," admitted Dr. Wilcox. "I'm afraid you were right."

"When?" asked Joan. "When will she have to be—"

"I'll have to have the papers drawn up. It will take a day or two. Then we'll bring an ambulance. She may resist."

"She *will* resist," assured Josh. "Count on it."

The intense chill within Josh's soul was almost icy now, and his own need to see Miranda dragged away, kicking and screaming, filled his spirit with an inordinate amount of almost uncontrollable satisfaction.

It wasn't total, however. Deep inside Josh a surge of decency made him hesitate. Sympathy for Miranda stirred within him, along with a sincere wish to help her. It was this part of Josh that harbored distress at the unsavory idea of seeing her committed to a mental hospital once more.

But another part seemed to be taking fast control of his mind. It was the chilly part of Josh that reminded him of his mounting debts. The cold part that had him concentrating on the intense delight of knowing his money troubles would soon be over.

Miranda would be drugged again and back in confined care, realized Josh. Then he'd have to find some way to solidify his position with her. But how?

Listen to me, Josh. Think only of yourself and what you deserve. After all, ya stuck it out for ten years now, didn't ya? That alone deserves a payoff, don't it? And I've got some ideas on how to persuade the bitch . . .

Josh shivered at the raw thoughts entering his mind. But he did not shrug them off. Here was a way to make sure Miranda agreed to their marriage. After she was back in confined care, he'd pay her a series of private little midnight visits until he made certain she was carrying his child—that alone would be enough to force her agreement to the marriage.

It'll all be so easy. Ye've got the access to drugs, don't ya? Inject 'em into her sleeping veins and there'll be no chance for resistance, only giddy, dizzy yielding.

Josh could see the idea was a good one. If she were carrying their child, she'd certainly agree to marriage. And then, of course, if she were diagnosed as incapable of handling her own affairs, her trust fund would fall under his control.

Aye, that's right, Josh. And it will all begin very soon . . . very soon.

"I suppose we should take precautions," said Dr. Wilcox with reluctance. "I'll bring sedatives."

"And a straitjacket," said Josh quickly, perhaps a little

so quickly. He forced his next words to come out more slowly, more in keeping with the image of a concerned fiancé. "As a last resort, of course, Dr. Wilcox."

"Of course."

Wolfe was restless for the remainder of the day. The rain began in earnest at noon and increased its speed and force by evening.

"Shall I light a fire in the bedroom?" asked Wolfe after dinner, knowing there would be no trip to the shallows or the boat deck tonight.

"Yes, that's a good idea," said Miranda, clearing up her dishes. "I'll just make a pot of tea and be right there."

Wolfe nodded, moving swiftly up the staircase. The master bedroom's curtains were snapping fitfully, billowing like a trysail in a squall. Wolfe went to the open window and let his gaze take in the black violence of the stormy sea.

"Damn your rage, you jealous siren. Blow all you want, but I'll not come to you tonight—for I'm on leave!"

The wind howled at Wolfe's brazen outrage and he cursed back once more for good measure before focusing his power and slamming the window shut.

He wheeled and turned his attention immediately to starting the fire. Once the blaze began, he stepped back. The portrait above the mantel caught his eye, and he narrowed his gaze at his own arrogant face.

Wolfe tried to recall those days when Jenny had painted him. What dress had she worn? What words had she said?

He could not recall.

The foolish youth that he was had dismissed her as a silly, romantic girl.

"Look at you, Eric Wolfe," he barked at his old image. *"You were such a fool back then. Aye, fool, I say! There you were in all your glory, proud as a peacock with your wealth earned on the sea—and all that time you were blind to the rarest gem of all, sitting right there in front of you!"*

Beyond that she was sweet and pretty with blond curls

and button-blue eyes, he had barely committed Jenny's face to memory—even though she'd carried his own likeness in a locket around her neck all her life. The same locket she'd asked to be buried in.

"Aw, Jenny . . . if only I had known your true spirit," he whispered to the portrait. *"If only I'd had a hint what was hidden under those prim little dresses, that genteel manner, that poor, fragile form . . . if only I had seen beneath all that and known you held the spirit of Miranda."*

The sudden rattling behind Wolfe sent a frisson of alarm through him. He turned abruptly to find his dearest love standing in the doorway, her teapot and cup shaking like the storm's wind.

Wofle's eyes met hers.

"Who was she, Eric? Or, rather, who was I?"

Chapter
Thirty-eight

"*Hang me, Miranda. You should not have heard me!*"

"*But I did hear you!*"

Miranda strode into the room and slapped the teapot and cup onto the dresser top, then turned to confront Wolfe. "Eric—"

"*Miranda, please do not ask this of me—*"

"I have a right to know. Who was she? Who was I?"

"*Stop this!*" cried Eric as he paced the room, Miranda's tense form right on his heels. "*'Twas your own spirit that chose to deny you the knowledge! I cannot betray its better judgment! 'Twas my damned weakness that's blundered . . . again!*"

"Eric, you didn't blunder. I do remember things . . . I had dreams of Blue Nights, and you, even before I first met you—"

Wolfe stopped so abruptly that Miranda passed partially into him. Both quickly shook themselves clear of the stunning tingling that resulted, then Eric responded.

"*You've not shared this with me.*"

"And I dreamed of living in the past, of having yellow hair and small hands. I dreamed of painting you—"

"Hang me, Miranda."

"I thought they were just fanciful dreams, but clearly there's more. Eric, why do you think I was drawn to that portrait? And the house. Don't you see, it's not just you— it's me too. It's *my* destiny that's mixed up in all this. I need more clarity, don't you see? I want to make sense of it all. But I only know enough now to know that I want answers. Answers that I see *you* can give me."

"But—"

"Please, Eric. Please . . . I know you love me."

"Yes, of course, with all my soul."

"Then help me to understand. I'm not asking you to find my way for me, I can do that, I just need you to stand by on the rigging . . . okay? Hold the halyard for me."

"Aye. All right. What do you wish to know?"

This time it was Miranda's turn to pace. "Well," she began, crossing her arms. "I've always felt that I had a right to be here at Blue Nights, that I somehow belonged to her, and she to me. Why do I feel that way, Eric?"

"Because you were betrothed to be my wife—when you were Jenny."

Miranda closed her eyes, trying to connect with the memories deep in her living spirit. "Since we were small children."

"Aye."

"And then something happened?"

"My parents died. First my mother, of fever. And then Father, at sea. The family money was split far too many ways, and I went to sea myself to make my fortune."

"Why didn't you marry me, Eric?"

"Because when you were Jenny, I did not know your spirit. I saw you very little, and when I did, you were part and parcel of a sitting room; of parlors and sewing and household business. It was not my world, and I was not at ease in it."

"But there was more to it than that, wasn't there?"

"Aye," said Wolfe slowly.

Miranda opened her eyes. She could see he was struggling, but she needed to know. "Please, Wolfe, tell me
everything. Don't you think it's a little late to worry about
hurting Jenny's feelings?"

"Hang me, Miranda, you're a tough one."

"Thank you, keep that in mind."

*"Aye. The thing of it is, you—Jenny, that is, was weak-
ened by fever at twelve and she seemed so fragile and
delicate to me, not a woman who could handle the man
I'd become."*

Wolfe began to move about the room in agitation. *"I
had no idea you painted more than my own blasted face!
I had no idea you had a passion for the sea as you did,
that you painted five rooms full of seascapes and ships!"*

"When did you—"

*"When you died, I discovered it all. That you'd kept
my picture in a locket about your neck—a locket I never
saw you without. You asked to be buried in it."*

"I must have loved you very much."

*"You would not marry another. For your own good, I
tried to release you from our engagement a half dozen
times, but you would have none of it—or any of the other
suitors who came 'round. You simply said over and over
that you would wait. You wished to wait until I was ready
to leave the sea . . ."*

"Stubborn girl, hunh?"

Wolfe met Miranda's eyes, nodding with the grim acknowledgment. *"Would that I had seen your strength of
spirit at the time."*

"So I was waiting until you were ready to leave the
sea. But you were never ready, were you, Eric?"

*"No. You must understand. I was no longer at home
on land. And yet I knew that I wanted a wife and a family
in my home someday. I was selfish, and harbored in my
mind the cozy notion that when I was ready I would make
you mistress of Blue Nights. And so I continued to visit
you and write you and engage your hopes and dreams
and affections."*

"Why didn't you just marry me and leave me for your

voyages? There are enough seamen who've done much.''

"At that age, I could not yet trust myself to be faithful for months at a time, and I did have some honor, Miranda. I knew I could not live with myself if I'd vowed chastity to you before God and then betrayed that vow in a port of call. I was weak and foolish and stupid and blind.''

Wolfe sadly sat himself upon the bed.

"I assure you I've paid for it,'' he continued, "I've paid a thousand and one ways as ever a man has paid for a tragic lack of faith. Every time I return to this barren, desolate, empty home of mine, a home that should have been filled with my descendants—and yours, my love—I pay dearly.''

Miranda watched Wolfe bury his head in his hands, and she felt her heart lurch. How could she stand seeing this powerful, fearless man racked with such heartwrenching sorrow.

"Oh, Eric, don't do this to yourself . . .''

" 'Tis not what I am doing, Miranda. 'Tis what I have done.''

Miranda moved to him, wanting nothing more than to reach her arms around and comfort him. But she knew it would only cause him more pain to be reminded of his state.

So she simply sat down beside him.

"What happened to me? Was it the fever again?''

"No. 'Twas your heart. Your physical form was weakened by your childhood fever. Your heart gave out at twenty-seven. When I heard you were failing, I asked what I could do, if there was a medicine, a physician, anything I could bring back to you on my clipper.''

"And what did I say?''

"You asked for a mystical thing. You thought it would help preserve your life.''

"A mystical thing? What?''

" 'Twas an urn—a cat-shaped container still fashioned by the peoples of North Africa. Your father was a scholar

d you'd read about it in one of his French science jour-
als. The urn, if fashioned correctly, 'twas believed to
preserve the life of the dying.''

"An urn? How odd. And you retrieved one for me?"

"I retrieved three. 'Twas on that terrible voyage to
North Africa that the seeds were sewn for my own death.''

Miranda began to recall bits of a conversation. It had
been with Wolfe's first mate. "Your mate told me of your
death. You were shot by thieves, weren't you? And one
was your cousin."

"Aye. Leach Muldavey. He and his scurvy crew thought
the urns had priceless value, so they came to take them.
They managed to grab two, but in a drunken rage I hung
on to the last—as if I were hanging on to the last part of
you. I killed my own cousin with the very urn to his head
after he put the bullet in me.''

"Leach Muldavey," murmured Miranda, recalling Riley's story.

"Aye. He follows me still. Every decade or so, he rears
his vengeful head off that devil's ship he serves to vex
me.''

"What happened after I died? Were you sorry then . . .
that we never married?"

"Aye, Jenny, aye. When I heard of your death, I could
not believe I lost you. It was then I realized what you
meant to me. That you were my harbor for the future. And
in the six weeks of drunken raging after your death—and
before my own—I'd convinced myself that I had truly
been the cause of your heart giving out.''

"You believed you'd broken my heart? Literally?"

"Aye.''

Miranda considered his question. She closed her eyes
and searched her soul, looking for an honest answer.
"You didn't, Eric."

"I—''

"No. I believed that you would have loved me," said
Miranda softly. "If given time."

"Aw, Jenny! If only I'd known we'd have so little time.
I would have left the sea.''

"We have time now."

Eric shook his head. *"Miranda, 'tis impossible. As self-ish as I wish to be again . . . how can I ask you give up the possibility of a life with a real man in exchange for one with a mere ghost of one? 'Twould be my mistake with Jenny all over again."*

"You're not asking me to do a thing, Wolfe. You never did. Just like Jenny, *I'm* the one who's making the decision to wait for your return from the sea."

" 'Tis no matter what you think you've decided. I cannot allow it. I can see now it was a mistake to do more than renew the fire to your spirit. When the Windward *comes, I shall be on it. And I shall not return."*

"Oh, *yes,* you shall!"

"I'll not argue."

"You damn well better. Because I'm not going anywhere. And, come to think of it, why should you if you don't wish to any longer? When the *Windward* comes, just tell them to shove off."

Eric shook his head in despair. *"Have you forgotten, Miranda, upon my death the sea took me for eternity to serve her. Otherwise, I'll weaken to a state unfit for any living spirit."*

Miranda's brow furrowed. "But you've changed your mind, haven't you? I mean, you're ready to leave her, to make a life with me."

"Miranda! I'm a ghost! What kind of 'life' can we have!"

"Eric, what if together we could find a way to change things?"

"Change things? Change what? What are you saying?"

"What if we found a way to get you another chance?"

Beyond the shaking cottage windows, the sea howled in a voice that almost sounded human. A chill traveled up Miranda's spine as she realized the implications of what she proposed.

"You're suggesting we push at the boundaries again, aren't you?" he whispered. *"The boundaries of heaven?*

e last time we tried that, you almost drowned.''

"I don't care. The angels gave my spirit a second chance to find its dream, didn't they? Why not you too?"

"You have more faith than me, my dear."

"But not more love, my darling," she pointed out. "I can see that now. And maybe, with enough love, anything is possible."

Chapter
Thirty-nine

The visit to the library took hours. The pacing of the shoreline, hours more.

"Miranda, you'll drive yourself into fits." Wolfe approached her with concern in his eyes. *"Will you talk to me now?"*

"I just need time to think."

"You've been thinking, girl. The sun is setting."

"There's got to be a connection. Something in the past. The cat was the symbol of eternal life to the Egyptians, and that urn you described is mentioned in some writings thought to be part of the Egyptian Book of the Dead. Jenny was right in her research. People of North Africa still believe such an urn will preserve the life of the dying."

"Aye, and what of it?"

"I don't know. I've been trying to connect in my mind with what Jenny knew, but I can't. So I'm trying to puzzle out some answers. There's got to be a key in the way you died. Your cousin shot you, then you struck him. And, as result, you're both in some kind of tangled dance in the afterlife, that much is clear.'' Miranda looked at Wolfe. ''Tell me again, Eric.''

''*Must I—*''

''Yes, there's something missing. What happened after you were shot *exactly*? Tell me the smallest details.''

Wolfe sighed. He closed his eyes. ''*I staggered off the porch as Muldavey's murdering gang fled.*''

''Do it now.''

''What!''

''Reenact it for me, Eric. Please.''

Wolfe's fists clenched in frustration, and he grumbled as he climbed the incline to his porch, but he did as she asked. Miranda followed him as he described staggering down the slope that led to the cove's shoreline.

''Then what?''

Wolfe closed his eyes once more. ''*I staggered into the dark mist, hoping it would hide me from Muldavey's thugs.*''

''Did it?''

''*Aye, but it didn't matter. They had no courage and fled as soon as their leader was struck down.*''

''Then what happened?''

''*I . . . I fumbled for something. My pocket watch, that was it.*''

''Why?''

''*There was a reason. Something about midnight. Aye, Jenny asked that I remember her at midnight on New Year's Eve by placing a lock of my hair in the cat urn with her own lock of hair, then flinging the urn into the sea.*

''*She'd folded the lock of her hair into her last letter to me and wrote that the turn of the New Year was the symbol of new life and new beginnings, just as the sea was. 'Twas something about binding us together in spirit.*''

''Hmmm, I see it did.''

''*At the time, I sincerely wished to complete her last request of me, though, in truth, I regarded it as nothing more than one of her silly romantic notions."*

"Guess you were wrong."

"Evidently."

"And then what?"

"I could see that I was losing blood. I felt the darkness overwhelm me, and I collapsed, despairing that I would die before completing her last wish."

"And did you?"

Wolfe closed his eyes. *"I recall placing a lock of my hair in the urn with hers. I held it close against my chest, and before the surf took me, I remember the container growing warmer as I grew weaker—"*

"Are you telling me you were clutching that urn to you as you died?"

"Aye."

Miranda bit her lip and stared at the last reddish light of the twilight horizon. "You had the urn and the urn is said to preserve the life of the dying. Eric, could it be possible that the sea took you before you truly died—that your life was somehow *preserved*? Could it be the urn had the power to open up a door to a kind of a pocket for you to be preserved, a twilight existence somewhere between life and afterlife?"

"Sounds daft."

"Does it? Then why have you haunted Blue Nights two months of the year for the last hundred and fifty years? Do the other ghosts return to their old homes?"

Wolfe was silent a long time. *"No,"* he admitted. *"I am the only spirit who is granted time at my old home."*

"Eric, don't you see? Blue Nights is part of the key to our second chance. It was to be our home together. It was my lifelong wish to join you here as your bride. And it's the place that brought us together ten years ago. Some force of the universe—heaven or the angels or *something*—knows this place is our destiny and granted us the chance to meet here again. We just need to find out how to release you from this pocket you may be living in."

"Miranda, this is all rather far-fetched, even for a ghost to believe."

"You have to believe, Eric. I do."

"But, Miranda, what's the use? What's the answer?"

"I don't know." Miranda's shoulders dropped, and she took a deep breath of sea air.

"We must stop this now."

"No. Did you do anything more? I mean, after you placed the lock of hair in the urn?"

"No."

"Are you sure?" she asked weakly.

"Miranda, this is too painful for you, please do not press this. I am not a living man. I am dead and gone. You must accept. It is useless to fight. . . ."

Miranda stared at Eric. "That's not what you told me ten years ago when I was lying on that coast guard cutter deck."

Wolfe looked away.

"Please *try*," urged Miranda softly. "Don't give up now."

At Wolfe's slight nod, she swallowed and tried again. "Was there anything more that happened, Eric. Anything?"

Wolfe closed his eyes. *"I said the last rites over my own body. I did my best to recall the words that I'd read over dozens of other men's bodies before we'd buried them at sea."*

"Recite them now," insisted Miranda.

"But—" Wolfe was about to argue, but after looking into Miranda's eyes, he relinquished his objections and began. *". . . Deliver me, dear Lord, not into the bitter sorrow of eternal death, but commit my body to the deep, and grant me resurrection of the body when the sea shall give up her dead."*

"The sea shall give up her dead . . ." murmured Miranda.

"Aye."

"Those rites committed your body to the sea."

"Aye, and that's when I felt the wash of water rush toward me and saw the glow upon the waves. 'Twas the first ghost ship on which I served."

Wolfe sighed heavily, closing his eyes. *"Ah, Jenny, only I'd committed my body to you instead of the sea.*

Miranda swallowed down the emotions overwhelming her as she gazed at Wolfe. How she needed this man. How she loved him. *I can't give up,* thought Miranda, *and I won't give him up. Not again.*

Restlessly, she turned and began to pace the rocky sand. "I'm the reincarnation of Jenny Smithton," she murmured to herself. "One hundred and fifty years ago I was engaged to Captain Eric Wolfe. It was my right to become the mistress of Blue Nights, and to marry the man I loved."

Miranda knew the answer was here. She *almost* had it. She stopped at the shoreline, closed her eyes, and tried with all her heart to connect with the memories of Jenny inside her.

"I waited and waited and I waited all my life to become Eric Wolfe's bride, waited for him to leave the sea, but instead of a wedding, I had a funeral. And because I loved him so much, the angels of heaven granted me a second chance to come back and win him back from . . ."

Miranda's voice trailed off as her eyes took in the rushing surf at her feet.

"My God," she whispered.

"Miranda?" asked Wolfe, stepping up beside her.

"I understand now, Eric. It's the *sea.* The sea is what's held you all these years. The sea is what's come between us."

"Aye, but—"

"Don't you understand? In your last breath you committed yourself not to me but to your mistress, the sea—as you had all your life. So to break the sea's hold, you must make a new commitment, Eric, a new vow. You must give up your mistress for a proper wife."

"A wife?"

"We must marry."

"Marry? Hang me, Miranda, how can you wed a ghost?!"

"Oh, Eric, wedding you will be easy. It's the 'how'

part that's going to be a heck of hard one to answer. I mean, who's going to perform a ceremony with an invisible groom?''

"*Heaven help us.*"

"Oh, it will, Eric. I *know* it will."

Chapter Forty

"And where is the groom?"

"Um, he's right here actually."

Miranda smiled sweetly at the justice of the peace. She'd called him the night before and arranged for him to stop by Blue Nights the first thing in the morning. She now stood before him in the parlor with a white sundress and sandals, her hair twisted prettily off her neck with baby's breath peeking daintily out of the brassy auburn strands.

"Where?" The heavyset fortyish man's eyes darted to the staircase in confusion. He took out a handkerchief to wipe his damp brow.

"*Here*. You can go ahead and start."

"My good woman, I can't start without the groom. Now, where is he? Upstairs getting ready?"

"Uh." All night, Miranda and Wolfe had debated *what* exactly to tell the justice when he arrived. She'd been doing her best to stall because she did *not* agree with Wolfe's solution.

"Just tell him the truth, Miranda," blared Wolfe's voice in her head. *"Tell him I'm a ghost."*

"No!"

"Oh," said the heavyset justice irritably. "Well, I haven't got all day, miss. Is he on his way over?"

"Tell the pudgy bureaucrat the truth!"

"No!"

"Miss, really. Is something wrong? Is he—"

"He's *here*, your honor, it's just that you can't . . . ah . . . see him."

The justice raised a caterpillar-thick eyebrow. "I can't. And why is that? Is he hiding? Does he have an outstanding warrant?"

"No, you see, he's a . . . a . . ."

"Tell the man now, or I swear I'll fling a piece of furnishing at him."

"He's a ghost."

The justice stared sternly at Miranda. "I am not amused."

"But he is. He's right here beside me now."

"My good woman, if your fiancé has stood you up, I'm quite sorry. But I will not be a party to your odd expression of hostility toward the male of the species. Good day."

"But, I don't care that he's a ghost! I still want to marry him!"

Miranda heard Wolfe curse as the pudgy man strode angrily to his blue sedan, started it up, and drove away.

"Wonderful," said Miranda with a fling of her arms.

"Don't blame me," said Wolfe, pacing the porch.

"Don't blame you! It was *your* idea to tell him!"

"Because you could come up with no better solution!"

"I knew I was right not to tell him. But you pestered me into it!"

"He needed an answer or he would have left."

"Ah, wake up! He's left anyway!"

"Hang me from the yardarm, then!"

"Oh, blast," said Miranda, slumping against the porch rail. "What do we do now? I mean, who on earth would

be willing to marry us when there's no mortal but m
who can *see* you?''

Miranda saw Wolfe suddenly stop his pacing.

''Eric? That's true isn't it? I'm the only mortal who
can see you, right?''

A smile broke over Wolfe's face. Sun in winter.

''No,'' he said with certainty. *''There is another.''*

''Dearly beloved,'' Old Ron Runyon read aloud from
The Book of Common Prayer. ''We have come together
in the presence of God to witness and bless the joining
together of this woman and this . . . ah . . . this, ah . . .''

Miranda's brow furrowed. She did her best to keep her
balance on the small polished deck of the *Sea Sprite* while
Old Ron, who'd assumed command as captain, began the
ceremony.

''Say *man,*'' whispered Miranda to Ron. ''Just follow
the words in the book.''

''Well, okay,'' said Old Ron. ''That okay with you,
there?'' he asked the ghost. ''Or maybe I should just say
. . . er . . . *sailor.*''

''Say whatever you like,'' said Wolfe, shifting uneasily
as he held Miranda's hand. *''Just get on with it, if you
don't mind.''*

''Don't be impatient, Eric,'' Miranda scolded.

*''Hang me, woman, I've waited a century and a half
to marry you. I believe I've been patient enough!''*

Old Ron cleared his throat and began again. ''We have
come together to join this woman and this . . . er . . . *sailor*
in holy matrimony . . .''

Miranda sighed and glanced at the sky uneasily. When
they'd walked out to the boat dock, the air seemed crisp
and dry, but now it smelled damp. Gray clouds were
quickly moving over the horizon, sweeping in from the
open sea.

''The union of husband and wife in heart, mind,
and . . . uh . . .'' Old Ron scratched his head.

''Just say it,'' snapped Wolfe, his blue eyes sparking.

''. . . body,'' continued Ron, ''is intended by God for

their mutual joy; for the help and comfort given one another in prosperity and adversity; and, when it is God's
will, for the procreation of children—''

Miranda felt Wolfe's hand squeeze hers. She smiled up
at the handsome image of his face, and, for the first time
that day, felt less nervous about this bizarre step into an
unknown future with this ghost of a man.

Still . . . far off on the horizon she could hear an angry
rumbling, as if the sea were once again threatening her
jealous rage.

''Therefore, marriage is not to be entered into unadvis-
edly or lightly, but reverently, deliberately, and in accor-
dance with the purposes for which it was instituted by
God.''

''*Amen*,'' whispered Wolfe.

Old Ron smiled his approval. ''Into this holy union,
Miranda Burke and . . .'' Ron pursed his lips. ''Honey,
what was the ghost's name again?''

''Eric Wolfe,'' stated Miranda clearly.

''Miranda Burke and *Eric Wolfe*,'' continued Old Ron,
''now come to be joined. If any man can show just cause
why they may not be married, speak now, or else forever
hold your peace.''

Thunder rumbled louder, and a large wave jostled the
Sea Sprite. Miranda shifted to regain her balance on deck
and glanced toward the nearby dock. A perplexed Tina
Peters and her husband, Mitch, were looking on as wit-
nesses—to what, it was clear they weren't sure. To their
eyes it would surely appear as if Miranda were marrying
a block of empty space. Miranda smiled and nodded at
them. They smiled back, their expressions highly confused.

Miranda sighed. They were good people to agree to
such a bizarre favor for a friend—especially when that
friend appeared to be having a relapse into nutsville, and
taking their senile old relative with her.

Lightning crackled over the cove, and Miranda shuddered as a drizzle began to mist the air around them.
Wolfe's form was tense beside her as he glanced at the

horizon. She saw him close his eyes tightly, then open them again.

"Wolfe?" she whispered, sensing his unease. "What is it?"

"Storm's heading in fast," murmured Wolfe dismissively.

But Miranda suspected Wolfe was worried about more than a little weather. She turned to look where he'd been gazing, and inhaled sharply. Barreling toward their cove was a looming black form, a ship from hell. A prickle of dread touched the back of Miranda's neck as she recalled their encounter with that devil ship a decade ago—and how it nearly cost her life.

"Better hurry it along," said Wolfe quickly to Ron, squeezing Miranda's hand again, this time for reassurance.

"Miranda," continued Ron, "will you have this man to be your husband—"

"I will," said Miranda quickly.

"Not yet, missy," said Old Ron. "Got to finish the whole passage. Now, let's see, where was I—"

Miranda turned to Wolfe. "Do you see it?" she whispered.

"Aye."

"What do we do?"

"Nothing, love. I've done all I can."

"What?"

"I've summoned the Windward."

"Miranda, will you have this man—uh, that is, *sailor*—to be your husband, to live together in the covenant of marriage? Will you love him, comfort him, honor and keep him, in sickness and in health, and forsaking all others be faithful to him as long as you both shall . . . ah . . ."

"Just say *it,"* urged Wolfe impatiently.

"As long as you both shall *live,"* finished Ron.

"I will," said Miranda boldly.

"What's going on here!" cried a familiar voice.

Miranda, Wolfe, and Ron turned to find two men striding onto the dock—Josh Cunning and Dr. Wilcox.

"Blast it!" cursed Wolfe. *"What in hell are* those *idiots doing here?"*

A glance up the hill answered Wolfe's question. Miranda saw the ambulance from her old hospital parked next to Blue Nights. Two men in white coats stood next to it.

"They're here for me," whispered Miranda, the warmth draining from her face as she overheard Josh call out to Tina and Mitch.

"You two! What is Miranda Burke doing out there dressed like a bride?"

Miranda swallowed sickly at Mitch Peters's easy reply. "She says she's marrying a ghost."

"Christ! She's gone off the deep end!" cried Josh. "Dr. Wilcox, call down your orderlies—"

Wolfe turned to Ron. *"Hurry it up now. Finish the ceremony."*

"Okay," said Ron. "Eric, will you have this woman to be your wife, to live together in the covenant of marriage? Will you love her, comfort her, honor and keep her, in sickness and in health, and, forsaking all others be faithful to her as long as you both shall . . . ah—"

"Live!" finished Wolfe quickly. *"With all my soul, I will!"*

The devil's ship was almost upon them, and Miranda could now hear a voice calling down terrible curses.

"Damn your soul, Sea Wolf!" cried Leach Muldavey. *"Damn your soul! You cannot marry a mortal!"*

Wolfe's hand squeezed Miranda's. *" 'Tis the dark spirit of my wretched cousin."*

"What does he want, Wolfe? Why is he so angry?"

"I fear he knows we're mucking with whatever happened the night of our deaths," guessed Wolfe. *"Whatever door we're trying to close here may alter his own existence as well, since he died by a blow from that urn."*

"I knew it," murmured Miranda. "I knew that was why you've been linked through time. It wasn't simple vengeance, it was the *urn!*"

"Damn you, Sea Wolf, stop this, I say!" screeched Muldavey again.

"I won't let him harm you, Miranda. I swear it," assured Wolfe.

"I'm not so worried about the ghosts anymore," said Miranda, spying the men in white coats striding down the hill from the house's drive. "I think I've got more substantial problems at the moment."

"Pronounce us married!" commanded Wolfe of Ron.

"Rings first," stated Ron.

"Rings?!" exclaimed Wolfe. *"I haven't got—"*

"I do," said Miranda softly as she reached into the pocket of her long, white sundress. She brought out the gold bands, a bit scratched up but polished to a shimmer nonetheless. "My father's and mother's," she told Wolfe.

He smiled down at her. *"Aye, that's fine."*

Wolfe concentrated his power and took the smaller ring.

"Repeat after me," said Ron.

"I know it, sir," said Wolfe, and he turned to Miranda. *"In the name of God, I, Eric Wolfe, take you, Miranda Burke/Jenny Smithton, to be my wife, to have and to hold, from this day forward, for better or for worse, for richer, for poorer, in sickness and in health, to love and to cherish until we are parted by death. This is my solemn vow."*

Miranda's spirit surged with joy at his tenderly spoken promise. With tears in her eyes she watched Wolfe's living spirit place the ring on her left hand.

Thunder sounded and a wave slammed the *Sea Sprite.* Wolfe caught hold of Miranda as she swayed on the heels of her sandals.

"My turn," she said softly, then repeated the vow. She took her father's ring and held it up. With care she slipped it on his materialized finger, and a jagged flash of lightning tore at the sky above them.

"Let's see, where are we—" murmured Ron as he looked back to the little red book in his hands. "Now that Miranda and Eric have given themselves to each other by solemn vows, I pronounce that they are husband and wife. Those who God has joined together let no one put asunder."

"Amen," said Wolfe through the loudest and angriest boom of thunder yet. The wind whipped hard around them as Wolfe turned to his new bride, her white dress billowing like a loose sail. *"Now, kiss me, my love."*

"Pull the boat in!" commanded a voice from the dock.

It was Josh, standing with the two orderlies on the wooden plank. At the next moment, the burly men in white jackets began hauling on the rope.

The *Sea Sprite*'s hull was yanked backward, and Miranda stumbled. Before she could even tip up her head for Wolfe's kiss, she felt herself falling over the side. The rough surf rose quickly, and before she knew it, she was swallowed by the angry sea.

The water was chilly as it closed over her head, but she fought hard against its salty claim, pulling herself against its current to break the surface. The waves were cresting high as she flailed about. Frantically, she searched for her new husband.

"Eric!" she cried. "Eric, where are you?"

"Here, love! Here!"

Wolfe had jumped in right after her. "Are you mortal again?" she asked quickly as he swam toward her.

"I don't know—"

Miranda twisted back toward the dock. She called to her friends. "Tina, Mitch! Do you see him now?" she asked. "Do you see the sea captain in the water?"

Tina and Mitch looked at each other with deep concern. Then they looked back to Miranda and simultaneously shook their heads no.

"They can't see you, Eric!"

The devil's ship was bearing down on them now and pulling to a halt only a few yards away. The dark forms descended the rope ladder like black lightning.

"Stop, you son of a bitch!" screeched the first dark ghost off the ladder. He moved toward them with a small gang of dark shapes behind.

"To hell with you, Muldavey!" Wolfe cursed. Then he turned quickly back to Miranda. *"Kiss me,"* he urged. *"That's what'll seal our vows. Kiss me now."*

Miranda opened her arms to him, then gasped as she felt herself being jerked backward. A thick arm had surrounded her torso and was forcibly pulling her away from Wolfe.

"Drag her back to shore!" yelled Josh from the dock to the burly orderly who'd jumped into the water after her.

Miranda pulled against the orderly's strong grip, trying with all her might to reach Wolfe. But the dark, ghostly shapes from the devil's ship had descended on her sea captain, and now he, too, was struggling to break free.

"Pull him to shore!" commanded Leach of his fellow damned spirits. *"Make him watch as his little mortal is dragged away, kickin' and screamin'. You'll like that, won't ya, Sea Wolf? And here's the best part of all— there's no chance of rescue from that smiling rapist over there who I'm proud to call me direct descendant!"*

"Miranda!" cried Wolfe, desperately fighting to break free. *"Miranda get away! Run away!"*

"Eric! Eric!"

"Heaven!" cried Wolfe to the thundering sky. *"Help us! Please!"*

Miranda closed her eyes and prayed those same words. "Please give us this chance," she added. "This one last chance."

But her only answer was a booming sound of thunder.

And then another.

And another.

Miranda opened her eyes as she realized that the repeating booms were not the squall's thunder at all.

They were the sound of ghostly cannon fire!

"It's the *Windward*!" exclaimed Miranda. "Eric, it's your ghost ship!"

"Avast your seizure of our good captain!" cried Riley from beneath the tattered sails of the barnacle-covered clipper now swiftly flying over the waves toward Blue Nights. *"Fire once more, Mr. Bonner! Into her broadside, if you please!"*

The boom sounded through the cove, and Miranda exhaled in relief as the dark shapes holding Wolfe now fled in terror for the black hull of their besieged devil's ship.

Only one dark form remained behind. Leach Muldavey. He swam to the shore, where he began to rage, shaking his fists and cursing the fleeing cowards that were his damned shipmates.

The moment Wolfe was free, he tore through the shallows to reach Miranda. She was still being dragged to shore by the burly orderly whom she continued to fight.

"Eric!" she cried as he closed in on her.

"Kiss me, wife," he whispered, taking her head in her hands and moving his mouth over hers.

She did. Offering her lips and closing her eyes, she felt the brush of her new husband's kiss, knowing it was the final seal of their new vow, their sincere promise to each other—a promise before heaven and earth, before man and God.

Miranda opened her eyes, expecting to see her new husband before her in flesh and blood at last.

But there was no new husband.

In fact, there was no one at all.

No man

No ghost.

"Eric?" called Miranda, still struggling against the orderly's grip. "Eric?"

Her voice grew louder as the panic set in.

"Eric!"

Suddenly, a terrible shriek echoed through the cove and Miranda looked toward the sound. It came from the part of the shore where Leach Muldavey had been raging.

A death-black cloud was now rising from the parted earth. Its long, fingerlike tentacles reaching out to pull the screeching ghost into its awful maw.

The scream continued as Leach's form vanished, the terror-filled sound echoing up from the fathomless depths as the dark ghost was pulled downward. Miranda blanched in horror as she realized that she was watching the end that came to a damned spirit's existence.

Then a sickening chill took hold of her.

If Wolfe's marriage to her had somehow ended the 150-year spell of the urn, then what had happened to Wolfe?

Miranda searched frantically for any sign of her ghostly husband, but she saw only the rising waves of the sea. The *Windward* was turning to chase the devil's ship back to the open ocean, and she saw no sign of Wolfe aboard.

Thunder crashed and jagged lightning tore at the sky as rain began to lash down in full force.

"Come on!" cried Josh Cunning from the shore. "Bring her in already!"

Miranda felt the orderly's grip on her torso tighten. He grunted something to her about giving up already, and pulled harder.

What's the use, thought Miranda as her strained muscles slackened. Without Wolfe she didn't care anymore. What did it matter if she spent the rest of her life looking at four white walls and bars on her windows. Nothing mattered now—not without the man she'd loved for 150 years, the man she'd left heaven to find again.

"Good-bye, my love," she whispered to the sky, realizing that their marriage must have not only broken the hold of the sea but also closed the strange, mystical door that the urn had opened on his and Leach Muldavey's twilight existence. Without the sea's hold, Leach was now claimed by hell, and her wonderful, courageous, and caring sea captain was surely claimed by heaven at last.

Like a wet rag doll, Miranda allowed herself to be dragged through the rocky shallows. She stumbled as the orderly pulled her to her feet.

"I don't want to hurt you," he said with surprising politeness. "Can you make it on your own?"

"What is taking you so long!" complained Josh loudly. "It's pouring down rain, will you just *drag* her up here to shore already!"

"Hey, let her go!" cried a familiar female voice.

Tina Runyon Peters and her husband, Mitch, were rushing up with worry on their faces.

"Yeah!" agreed Mitch. "Let her go."

The orderly did, and Miranda blinked and stumbled farther up to shore. But before she could reach her friends, Josh grabbed her wrist roughly and yanked.

"Come on. Fun and games are over now, Miranda. The welcome wagon awaits," sneered Josh.

"What gives you the right to do this?" demanded Tina, stepping up to confront Josh.

"She's gone delusional again," Josh snapped. "And her doctor is committing her."

"And who the hell are *you*?" demanded Mitch.

"That's Josh Cunning," said Tina to her husband. "He's the one I told you about. Remember? In my Granddad's boatyard office, he's the one who tried to—"

"Oh, yeah. I remember the story," said Mitch. The former coast guard officer turned toward Josh with a dangerous fire in his eyes. "I know who you are now."

Miranda gasped as Mitch's big fist cocked back and let loose. A terrible crack sounded, and Josh Cunning was sent reeling.

"Mitch!" cried Tina. "What are you doing!"

"That's for assaulting my wife!" cried Mitch.

Miranda's eyes widened, and the orderly behind her chuckled softly. "Guess the bastard had it coming," he muttered.

"Good heavens!" shrieked Dr. Wilcox, rushing toward the group. "What's going on?"

"C-c-call the p-police!" stammered Josh, holding his bleeding mouth. "This animal is at-attacking me!"

"Oh, *please*!" exclaimed Tina.

"Forget the police," said Dr. Wilcox. "We don't want to involve the police. We don't want complications. Now, let's all just calm down." The tall, middle-aged man with the kind brown eyes turned to his patient.

"It's time to go now, Miranda," he said soothingly. "You understand what's happening, don't you?"

"Yes."

"And you'll go quietly now, won't you?"

"Yes."

"No, Miranda," said Tina. "Don't let them—"

"What does it matter?" said Miranda weakly, feeling

the spirit inside her die along with her hopes and dreams for the future.

She turned toward the shore and was about to take her first step toward the ambulance, when she suddenly stilled.

"Did you hear that?" asked Miranda.

"What?" asked Tina.

"That voice."

"Ahoy . . . ahoy there!" cried the voice from far down the shoreline. "Ahoy . . . I'm coming . . . ahoy!"

"I hear it," said Tina softly. "It's a man's voice."

The group turned to the sound of the call to find a man stumbling out of the sea. Miranda's jaw slackened as she saw the raven-haired man was wearing old-fashioned-looking clothes—thick woolen slacks and a black cable-knit sweater.

"It's that man," murmured an alarmed Josh Cunning, still holding his bleeding mouth. "That man in the portrait."

"You see him?" asked Miranda, incredulous. She turned to the group. "Do you all see the captain?"

They nodded in stunned silence, and Miranda exhaled in profound relief.

"They can finally see him," she whispered. "They can see my ghost."

Chapter
Forty-one

"That's no ghost," said Mitch. "That's a living man."

"Yes, he is!" murmured Miranda as she turned to run toward him. "He is!"

"Stop her!" cried Josh to the orderly, but Mitch stepped forward with a forceful glare, and the orderly took significant note of the consequences awaiting him.

"Sorry, Doc," said the orderly, backing away. "I don't get paid nearly enough for thrashings. *You* stop her."

Miranda heard the commotion behind her but didn't care; she had only one care in the world now, and that was to feel her new husband's arms around her. The sea had given up her dead, she realized as she reached Wolfe, given him up to the living woman whom he had finally chosen instead.

"Sea Wolf," she called. "Have you come home to me for good?"

"Aye, my lovely wife," he said. "For good and forever."

Miranda wrapped her arms around Wolfe's thick, damp

329

neck and she felt his strong arms envelop her. The kiss
was on fire with his living heat, more vibrant and more
passionate than any she'd ever felt before. Her lips parted
to accept the tip of his warm tongue, and her own danced
with his as she pressed tightly against his wet sweater,
glorying in the feel of his rising and falling chest, and the
muted tapping of his beating heart.

Wolfe moaned with satisfaction as he deepened the
kiss. And when they finally came up for air, they were
both gasping giddily.

The slate-gray sky had lightened. The storm clouds
were dispersing, and the sun rays were breaking through
with a heaven-sent warmth. Through the prism of the
misty rain, a pale rainbow arched across the cove.

"Are you all right?" Miranda asked Wolfe, touching
his cheek.

"Fine, for someone who's just returned from the
dead."

Miranda smiled. "I suppose you'll want to captain the
Sea Sprite now."

"No," he said softly, holding her close. "But in about
another decade or so, I think I'll want my daughter to
have that honor."

"Not bad, Sea Wolf," Miranda said with a laugh.
"You get lots of points for that one."

"Miranda!" cried Tina, rushing toward them. "Is this
him? Is this your sea captain?"

Miranda nodded.

"I'm pleased to meet you face-to-face," said Wolfe
politely. "You don't mind if I don't let go of my wife,
do you? It's been a while since I've been able to hold
her."

Tina laughed. "Sure, it's fine by me. I suppose you
know Mitch?"

"Hello," said Mitch, looking a bit perplexed.

"We meet again," said Wolfe with a wink. "And this
time I don't have to levitate a boat hook to get your attention."

"Miranda!" called Dr. Wilcox, striding up to them

with Josh Cunning in tow. "What's the meaning of this? Who is this man?"

"He's my ghost, Dr. Wilcox. My sea captain. I told you he was real."

"But he *can't* be. It's not *possible*."

" 'Tis not only possible, 'tis actual," stated Wolfe calmly. "Am I not the man in the portrait?"

"He does *look* like the man," admitted Josh. "Perhaps the portrait's a forgery."

" 'Tis Jenny Smithton's best work," said Wolfe with irritation. " 'Twas painted over a century and a half ago."

"I disagree," said Josh. "In fact, I think—"

"I don't give a damn what you think," said Wolfe tersely. "Because *I* think 'tis past time you removed your scurvy selves from my property."

"*Your* property—"

"That's right," agreed Miranda. "Blue Nights was always Eric's."

"Pardon my error, love. We're wedded now, so Blue Nights is actually *ours*." The sea captain's tender gaze then turned from his beloved wife and flared to a fierce glare. "So get the hell off *our* property. *Now*."

The two modern men stepped backward at the iron ferocity of the nineteenth-century clipper captain's stern order.

"Perhaps we *sh-should* go," stammered Dr. Wilcox.

"For now," said Josh.

"*Forever*, ya smarmy morons. Miranda is my wife, do you hear?" Wolfe said as he gently took her ringed hand and held it up with his own. "And I'll not have you quacks pronouncing her anything less than a sane and passionate woman, ready for a life of love and happiness with a man who loves her with all his soul. And, now, all his *body* as well."

"Well, that's it, then, Dr. Cunning," pronounced Dr. Wilcox, throwing up his hands. "Her husband's going to fight this commitment, no matter what her relatives say, and I've about had it with this case anyway."

"But—"

"That's it. I'm gone."

Josh sputtered but could do nothing more than trail Dr. Wilcox and his white-jacketed orderly back up the hill to their vehicles.

Miranda released a sigh of relief when she finally saw them pull away from Blue Nights. It was then she noticed that Old Ron Runyon was finally taking the hard trip down the rocky slope with his three-pronged cane.

"Pleased to meet you in the *flesh*," he said as he hobbled up to the group on his arthritis-crippled legs.

Wolfe smiled. "Thanks for marrying us, Captain Runyon."

"I'm not much of a cap'n anymore. But I'm glad ya *do* remember I was one after all these years."

"Aye, sir."

"It was back in '38 I met the captain here," Ron told Miranda, Tina, and Mitch. "My schooner nearly crashed against Blackrock Shoal. But his ghost crew saved my ship and my men, and I'll never forget it." Old Ron turned his gaze back on Wolfe's face. "I been waitin' a long time to return *you* a favor."

"Glad I could help."

Ron cast a warm glance at the newly married couple. "Me too, Cap'n Wolfe. Me too."

Chapter Forty-two

"Stay inside me," whispered Miranda.

"Aye," agreed Wolfe after partially collapsing onto her. "An easy order to obey."

Miranda snuggled against the soft mattress of Blue Nights' four-poster and wrapped her arms around her husband.

"It's nice to make love on a mattress, isn't it?" asked Miranda as her slender fingers gently stroked the strong muscles of his broad back.

"Mmm. Softer than the *Sea Sprite*'s deck, for sure." Wolfe growled with satisfaction as he nestled into her. When he found a tender spot between her shoulder and neck, he began to nuzzle and nibble her warm flesh.

"How do I taste?"

"Sweet," murmured Wolfe.

"Sweeter than the sea?"

"Most assuredly."

Miranda laughed. Their lovemaking had gone on for nearly four days straight since their wedding—with time out for romping swims in the cove and fast-food deliveries. She'd discovered quite a bit about her sea captain in the past few days. He had incredible stamina for lovemaking, an innate talent at back massages, and a real affinity for pizza, fried rice, and Coca-Cola.

"We're tempting fate by insulting the sea, you know?" teased Miranda.

"My old mistress will have to make do without me. I have a new wife to attend to now."

"But you'll still sail with me, I hope."

"Mmm, now, that's an idea. Perhaps I will sail again. But a larger craft than the *Sea Sprite*."

"How much larger?"

"Well . . . smaller than the *Windward*. How's that for compromise?"

"I'm game."

"Good, because I'll need a crew."

"One person does not a crew make."

"Perhaps a few hands in the Wolfe family will do the trick."

"*Which* Wolfe family?"

"This one."

Miranda felt Wolfe shift his position over her, moving his weight back onto his forearms. With undying devotion his dark blue eyes gazed down into her face, while deep inside her body, Miranda felt the growing evidence of her husband's renewed passion.

"Shall we get back to the important business of recruiting our hands?" he asked.

"Oh, aye, Captain," she answered languidly as he began moving inside her once more. "Aye."

Hours later, Miranda lay sleepily in Wolfe's arms. The sun was barely peeking over the eastern horizon, casting a beautiful purplish-pink light through the dark room. The soft lapping of the sea's waves outside caressed her ears, and her limbs tingled from hours of Wolfe's lovemaking.

It felt to her like she'd entered paradise.

With great contentment, Miranda stretched and yawned.

"Sleep, woman," grumbled Wolfe, his eyes still closed. " 'Tis barely dawn." Then, with a possessive arm wrapped around her, he pulled Miranda's form tightly against him.

Miranda giggled at the feel of her naked flesh against the wiry hairs of Wolfe's masculine form. "You tickle," she whispered.

"Belay the chatter, wife. Get some shut-eye."

"Eric?"

"Mmm?"

"Did I tell you about Muldavey?"

Wolfe opened one eye. "What about him? He's gone with the devil's ship, hasn't he?"

"No."

Wolfe opened the other eye. "What is it? Are you concerned he's lurking about? Ready to cause trouble again?"

"Oh, no. I know he won't be causing trouble ever again."

"And why's that?"

"Because I saw him swallowed."

"Swallowed?"

"It was a terrible thing. I wasn't going to talk about it, but I was just lying here thinking how I feel like I've entered paradise, and I realized that Leach went the other direction."

Wolfe partially sat up. "You saw the hand?"

"Hand?"

"The hand of hell? Aye, 'tis terrifying."

"Yes, it was."

"Then hell's taken him at last. No need to feel bad, my love. The damned souls always go the same direction—and in the same screaming agony. It's terrifying, and a part of you can't help but feel sorry for the poor bastards, but I must be honest, Miranda, I'm relieved that I'll never again have to worry about your safety—at least not where the spirit world is concerned."

"Then it's smooth sailing from now on," said Miranda happily, snuggling back against Wolfe's chest.

She listened to his heartbeat, marveling in the warmth of him, the life in him. And then she realized that he wasn't relaxed against the bedsheets.

"Wolfe?" asked Miranda. "Is something wrong?"

"Aye, wife."

"Well? What is it?" asked Miranda after a few silent minutes.

" 'Tis nothing."

"No, clearly it's something," said Miranda, sitting up enough to look into his face. "Tell me."

Wolfe reached out to stroke her auburn hair. "Silky," he whispered. "Beautiful."

"Wolfe, *tell* me."

" 'Tis the *Windward*. She'll be back to pick me up again."

"What do you mean, to pick you up again? You're mortal now, and you've resigned your sea's service. They can't pick you up again!"

"Aye, they can. If . . ."

"Eric?"

"There's a chance, my love, albeit a small chance, that this miracle of our is short-lived. I pray that heaven allows me to remain mortal."

Miranda sunk down into the sheets, a fist tightening around her heart. "When will we know for sure?" she whispered.

"A few more days. The *Windward*'s due at midnight the last of the month. And she'll be looking for her captain."

"It's the last test, isn't it?"

"Aye, my love. But have faith."

"I will," said Miranda, turning in the soft sheets to caress her warm husband. "I always have."

Chapter
Forty-three

"Miranda, have another glass of wine."

"I can't."

"Your pacing will wear out the porch planks."

"I don't care."

Wolfe chuckled, leaned back in his old, carved rocking chair, and placed an ankle over a jeans-clad knee. The bowl of his pipe glowed red as he inhaled the long-missed aroma of a sweet tobacco.

"How can you be so relaxed?" asked Miranda, wringing her hands and peering out toward the dark sea for the thousandth time in the last hour. "The *Windward* will be here any minute."

Wolfe tipped his head and exhaled a plume of white smoke. He watched it travel north, then dissipate into the night.

"Ah," murmured Wolfe, "how I've missed this."

337

"What?"

"The smell of the night. The damp, heavy salt of the sea air, the taste of a good pipe, the sturdy feel of a solid wooden chair beneath me."

Miranda stopped her pacing and placed her nervous hands into the pockets of her jeans. "I'm sorry I'm so worried," she said softly.

"Come here."

Miranda stepped toward her husband. He rose from his chair and held out his arms. "I love you, Miranda," he whispered, holding her close and stroking her hair. "And of all the charms to my senses, this is the one I cherish most of all."

Dipping his head, Wolfe took her mouth. The warm taste of Miranda was about the only thing Wolfe truly cared about losing now. The mere possibility wrenched a rawness from his kiss. His lips devoured hers, his tongue pushing through to experience as much of her as possible in these last few minutes before midnight.

Miranda moaned into his mouth as he hungrily moved his lips over hers. He felt her soft, womanly limbs melting into his hard length as the tension slowly seeped from her body—while within his own, a sweet, familiar tension was coiling for release.

"*Ahoy!*"

With sheer force of will, Wolfe broke off their kiss, breathless with renewed need for her. "Ah, Miranda," he said, softly cupping her cheek. "We will soon pick up where we left off. I promise you."

"I love you, Eric," she whispered.

"*Ahoy!*" came the voice again.

"'Tis time now. I hear them coming."

Miranda inhaled sharply as she turned in Wolfe's arms and looked out across the sea. The dim glow on the horizon grew stronger as it approached the cove's entrance.

"Have faith, my dear," whispered Wolfe.

"*Captain Wolfe!*" called the *Windward*'s first mate as the huge ghost clipper swept silently toward the shoreline of Blue Nights.

Wolfe set down his pipe and took Miranda by the hand. "Come."

They tensely walked down the slope to the beach and stepped up to the *Windward*'s first mate, who was swiftly descending the portside rope ladder.

"Ahoy, Mr. Riley," said Wolfe. "How's her sailing?"

"Fine, Captain, fine."

"We chased that devil's ship all the way to hell, I think!" cried China Jack as he descended after Riley.

"Aye!" agreed Tommy Noll.

"Where's Angus?" asked Wolfe as Mr. Riley, China Jack, and Tommy Noll waded up the shallows to the beach.

"Bonner is with the new mate," said Riley.

"New mate?" asked Wolfe.

"Aye," said China Jack. *" 'Twas an old salt gone fishin' this mornin' in a dinghy and had a stroke upon the water."*

"He's a good man," said Mr. Riley. *"Officer material, I should think."*

A surprised Wolfe looked at Miranda with hope, then turned back to his crew. "So, you're four good mates aboard now, eh? Four without me?"

"Aye," said Mr. Riley. *"Which is good for us, since you're obviously unfit in your present state."*

Wolfe allowed a small smile of relief. "You've known? So my new mortal form is no surprise to you?"

"No surprise," said Riley. *"The new mate told us."*

"But who is this new—" Miranda began, when she was interrupted by a vaguely familiar voice.

"Ahoy, there, newlyweds!"

Miranda's jaw slackened to see a young man descending the rope ladder. It was Old Ron Runyon! Only he wasn't *old* anymore, not his voice, or his image. His spirit radiated with the brilliant energy of a man in his prime. Gone was his cane and crippling arthritis, and in its place was a strong-limbed young seaman.

"How d'ya like the new me?" asked Ron, jumping down from the rope ladder and splashing into the shal-

lows, his muscled arms flexing high in a Mr. Universe
pose.

"You're quite handsome," confessed Miranda.

"An able-bodied seaman, to be sure," agreed Wolfe.

"More than an ordinary seaman, I should think," said
Mr. Riley as Ron approached them. *"Runyon's got captain's experience."*

"But not in a clipper like this," admitted Ron. *"My
schooner was less than half the size of this sweet ship."*

Wolfe scratched his chin. "I dare say, then, Mr. Riley,
that you're in a position to assume command."

"Think so?"

"Aye. You've had a century and a half to learn from
me, haven't you? And Mr. Runyon here should make a
fine first mate."

"I'd be honored," admitted Ron.

Angus Bonner drifted in to join the group. *"Ahoy, Captain Wolfe."*

"Retired Captain Wolfe now, Angus. There stands your
new captain."

"Ah, very good," said Angus. *"Pleased to call you
Captain, Riley."*

*"The Sea Wolf looks good as a modern mortal, don't
he?"* piped up young Tommy Noll. *"Blue jeans and all."*

China Jack grunted his approval.

Bonner scratched his head. *"Guess you'll be wantin'
to start a family to finally fill up that big empty house of
yours?"*

"Aye," said Wolfe, pulling Miranda close against him.
"We've been working hard on that happy business,
haven't we, wife?"

"Eric!"

Wolfe smiled at the pretty pink blush blooming across
Miranda's cheeks. "Don't be embarrassed, Miranda. You
stand beside a man who loves his wife and is not afeared
to share it."

"Now, that's a recipe for a good strong marriage,"
remarked Ron Runyon.

"Agreed," said Riley. *"So, I suggest we all shove off*

now and leave these happy mortals to their . . . uh . . . happy business.''

"Farewell, crew," said Wolfe with only the slightest tinge of regret. "Think of me in those last moments of peaceful sunsets when that rare green flash brightens the skies."

"Aye, sir," they agreed in unison. Then one by one each nodded his salute and moved for the rope ladder.

Riley was the last to go. He turned back and smiled at his beloved captain. *"Farewell, sir, I know this is what you've been wanting."*

"Aye, it is."

"Then I shall pray for your happiness." He nodded with respect to Miranda. *"Both of you."*

"Thank you, Mr. Riley," said Miranda, touched.

"Shall we ever meet again, do you suppose?" asked Riley before turning to go.

Wolfe smiled. "I think perhaps we shall. Come back for me in fifty years or so, Captain Riley, when my home is full of children and grandchildren. And when I'm good and ready to leave the earth again, I'll be bringing an able hand along with me." Wolfe shifted his gaze to the woman beside him. "What do you say, my love?"

Miranda smiled at Riley and then looked into her husband's blue eyes, as blue as the fathomless depths beyond all shorelines. "Captain Wolfe, I'd be honored to follow you back to the sea."

"Good, my dear. 'Tis only fitting for two who love to sail as we do."

"Yes," agreed Miranda. "Farewell, *Windward*!" she called when they finally shoved off, and together the newlyweds waved as the bright glow of the ghost clipper slowly diminished on the far horizon.

Then Captain Eric Wolfe turned toward Blue Nights Cottage, his new bride on his arm, ready, at long last, for life to begin anew.

Epilogue

LIBRARY OF CONGRESS CATALOGUING-IN-PUBLICATION
DATA

Title: Ships of Wood and Men of Iron
Publication Date: January 1, 2004
Authors: Milton Burke, Miranda Burke-Wolfe, Captain
Eric Wolfe
Subject: Nautical History
Summary: A lively study on the folklore of the sea with
special sections on never-before-published sea chan-
teys, the legends of ghost ships, factual accounts of
Yankee clipper sailings, and a keenly realized portrait
of one nineteenth-century sailing captain and what
made him tick.
Award Notes: Newton Prize for Nonfiction, Bunyon Prize
for Nautical History, and the Favorite Book Award of
the North Atlantic Seaman's Association.
Dedication: "To our beloved daughter, Jenny, and to all
those souls who bravely sail the eternal sea."

Our revels now are ended. These our actors,
As I foretold you, were all spirits and
Are melted into air . . .
We are such stuff
As dreams are made of, and our little life
Is rounded with a sleep.

—WILLIAM SHAKESPEARE,
The Tempest, IV, i